Season Of The Harvest

By
Michael R. Hicks

Published by Michael R. Hicks
www.authormichaelhicks.com

*For those who perished in 9/11,
and the loved ones they left behind.*

And for Dona: we miss you.

Foreword

Genetically modified organisms, or GMOs.

Just sitting there on the page, the term sounds exotic, doesn't it? Like something out of a science fiction story. You may have heard about them, or you may not. But one thing's for certain: unless you eat only organic food, you've probably put a genetically modified organism in your mouth and eaten it. Many times. Corn. Soy. Rice. Wheat. And others.

There are companies here in the United States and in other nations that have modified the genetic material of many of our most basic food crops to be fundamentally different from their "natural" siblings. Strains of these crops have been engineered to be resistant to certain herbicides, or to repel insect pests. To need less water. To grow faster, or larger. Human engineering has improved on the work of Nature, tailoring these vital plants to our needs. It's a multi-billion dollar industry that controls an ever-larger share of the world's food supply, for the benefit of people everywhere.

And we know that GMOs are safe for us, for our children. For the animals we depend on for our protein. We know this because the companies that produce these wonder crops say so. The government agencies responsible for the safety of our food supplies say so. Therefore, it surely must be true.

Genetically modified organisms. *You are what you eat...*

Acknowledgments

As with any book, the author is only the tip of the iceberg in taking a huge pile of words and transforming them into something both readable and (I hope!) worth reading.

First I have to thank my editors, Mindy and Stephanie, who spent a great deal of their time wading through the original manuscript while trying not to laugh too hard, and with nothing more awaiting them in compensation than some chocolate, an autographed copy of the book, and a t-shirt. You're both gems and when I strike it rich someday, I'll make it up to you.

Next up is my Dad. While my parents have always been supportive of my writing (they even claim to have liked some of it), Dad provided some real sanity checks on some of the more technical parts of the book from his background in pathology and microbiology.

I'd also like to credit "Groundskeeper Pete" for the amazing information he contributed from his web site on the Cold War-era Titan I base that I used as the setting for certain key scenes in the book. Check out www.chromehooves.net – it's some truly amazing stuff.

Then there are my "beta readers," Susan, Geoff, Starfire, and fellow author Margaret Anne Lake, who helped put the final touches on the book. Thank you so much for your time and support – you're the best!

Finally, but never last or least, is Jan, my wife. Thank you for all your support and your love. Without you, I would have no dreams.

Prologue

Sheldon Crane ran for his life. Panting from exhaustion and the agony of the deep stab wound in his side, he darted into the deep shadows of an alcove in the underground service tunnel. Holding his pistol in unsteady hands, he peered around the corner, past the condensation-covered pipes, looking back in the direction from which he'd come.

Nothing. All he could hear was the deep hum of the electric service box that filled most of the alcove, punctuated by the *drip-drip-drip* of water from a small leak in one of the water pipes a few yards down the tunnel. Only a third of the ceiling-mounted fluorescent lights were lit, a cost-saving measure by the university that left long stretches of paralyzing darkness between the islands of greenish-tinged light. He could smell wet concrete and the tang of ozone, along with a faint trace of lubricating oil. And over it all was the scent of blood. In the pools of light stretching back down the tunnel, all the way back to the intersection where he had turned into this part of the underground labyrinth, he could see the glint of blood on the floor, a trail his pursuer could easily follow.

He knew that no one could save him: he had come here tonight precisely because he expected the building to be empty. It had been. Almost. But there was no one to hear his shouts for help, and he had dropped his cell phone during the unexpected confrontation in the lab upstairs.

He was totally on his own.

Satisfied that his pursuer was not right on his heels, he slid deeper into the alcove, into the dark recess between the warm metal of the electric service box and the cold concrete wall. He gently probed the wound in his side, gasping as his fingertips brushed against the blood-wet, swollen flesh just above his left hip. It was a long moment before he was sure he wouldn't scream from the pain. It wasn't merely a stab wound. He had been stabbed and cut before. That had been incredibly painful. This, however, was far worse. His insides were on fire, the pain having spread quickly from his belly to upper chest. And the pain was accompanied by paralysis. He had lost control of his abdominal muscles, and the sensation was spreading. There was a sudden gush of warmth down his legs as his bladder suddenly let go, and he groaned in agony as his internal organs began to burn.

Poison, he knew.

He leaned over, fighting against the light-headedness that threatened to bear him mercifully into unconsciousness.

"No," he panted to himself. "*No.*" He knew he didn't have much time left. He had to act.

Wiping the blood from his left hand on his shirt, cleaning it as best he could, he reached under his right arm and withdrew both of the extra magazines he carried for his weapon, a 10mm Glock 22 that was standard issue for FBI special agents. He ejected the empty magazine from the gun, cursing himself as his shaking hands lost their grip and it clattered to the floor.

It won't matter soon, he thought giddily as he slumped against the wall, sliding down the rough concrete to the floor as his upper thighs succumbed to the spreading paralysis, then began to burn.

Desperately racing against the poison in his system, he withdrew a small plastic bag from a pocket inside his jacket and set it carefully next to him. He patted it with his fingertips several times to reassure himself that he knew exactly where it was in the dark. His fingers felt the shapes of a dozen lumps inside the bag: kernels of corn.

Then he picked up one of the spare magazines and shucked out all the bullets with his thumb into a pocket in his jacket so he wouldn't lose them. Setting down the now-empty magazine, he picked up the tiny bag and carefully opened the seal, praying he wouldn't accidentally send the precious lumps flying into the darkness. For the first time that night, Fate favored him, and the bag opened easily.

Picking up the empty magazine from his lap, he tapped a few of the kernels onto the magazine's follower, the piece of metal that the bottom bullet rested on. He managed to squeeze a bullet into the magazine on top of the corn kernels. Once that was done, he slid the other bullets into place, then clumsily slammed the magazine into the weapon and chambered a round.

He took the bag and its remaining tiny, precious cargo and resealed it. Then he stuffed it into his mouth. The knowledge of the nature of the corn made him want to gag, but he managed to force it down, swallowing the bag. Crane suspected his body would be searched thoroughly, inside and out, for what he had stolen, and his mind shied away from how that search would probably be conducted. His only hope now was that his pursuer would be content to find the bag, and not think to check Crane's weapon. He prayed that his body and the priceless contents of his gun's magazine would be found by the right people. It was a terrible long-shot, but he was out of options.

His nose was suddenly assaulted by the smell of Death coming for him, a nauseating mix of pungent ammonia laced with the reek of burning hemp.

Barely able to lift his arms, his torso nearly paralyzed and aflame with agonizing pain, Crane brought up his pistol just as his pursuer whirled around the corner. He fired at the hideous abomination that was revealed in the flashes from the muzzle of his gun, and managed to get off three shots before the weapon was batted from his faltering grip. He screamed in terror as his pursuer closed in, blocking out the light.

The screams didn't stop for a long time.

One

Jack Dawson stood in his supervisor's office and stared out the window, his bright gray eyes watching the rain fall from the brooding summer sky over Washington, D.C. The wind was blowing just hard enough for the rain to strike the glass, leaving behind wet streaks that ran down the panes like tears. The face he saw reflected there was cast in shadow by the overhead fluorescent lights. The square jaw and high cheekbones gave him a predatory look, while his full lips promised a smile, but were drawn downward now into a frown. The deeply tanned skin, framed by lush black hair that was neatly combed back and held with just the right amount of styling gel, looked sickly and pale in the glass, as if it belonged on the face of a ghost. He knew that it was the same face he saw every morning. But it was different now. An important part of his world had been killed, murdered, the night before.

He watched the people on the street a few floors below, hustling through the downpour with their umbrellas fluttering as they poured out of the surrounding buildings, heading home for the evening. Cars clogged Pennsylvania Avenue, with the taxis darting to the curb to pick up fares, causing other drivers to jam on their brakes, the bright red tail lights flickering on and off down the street like a sputtering neon sign. It was Friday, and everyone was eager to get home to their loved ones, or go out to dinner, or head to the local bar. Anywhere that would let them escape the rat race for the weekend.

He didn't have to see this building's entrance to know that very few of the people who worked here would be heading home on time tonight. The address was 935 Pennsylvania Avenue Northwest. It was the J. Edgar Hoover Building, headquarters of the Federal Bureau of Investigation, the FBI. Other than the teams of special agents who had departed an hour earlier for Lincoln, Nebraska, many of the Bureau's personnel here at headquarters wouldn't leave until sometime tomorrow. Some would be sleeping in their offices and cubicles after exhaustion finally overtook them, and wouldn't go home for more than a few hours over the next several days.

A special agent had been brutally murdered, and with the addition of another name to the list of the FBI's Service Martyrs, every resource the Bureau could bring to bear was being focused on bringing his killer to justice. Special agents from headquarters and field offices around the country were headed to Nebraska, along with an army of analysts and support staff that was already sifting through electronic data looking for leads.

Everyone had a part in the investigation, it seemed, except for Dawson. In his hand, he held a plain manila folder that included the information that had been forwarded by the Lincoln field office. It was a preliminary report sent in by the Special Agent in Charge (SAC), summarizing the few known facts of the case. In terse prose, the SAC's report described the crime scene, the victim, and what had been done by the local authorities before the SAC's office had been alerted. And there were photos. Lots of photos. If a picture was worth a thousand words, then the ones Dawson held in his shaking hands spoke volumes about the agony suffered by the victim before he died. Because it was clear from the rictus of agony and terror frozen on Sheldon Crane's face that he had still been alive when–

"I'm sorry, Jack," came a gruff voice from behind him, interrupting Dawson's morbid train of thought as Ray Clement, Assistant Director of the Criminal Investigative Division, came in and closed the door. It was his office, and he had ordered Dawson to wait there until he had a chance to speak with him.

Ray Clement was a bear of a man with a personality to match. A star football player from the University of Alabama's Crimson Tide, Clement had actually turned down a chance to go pro, and had instead joined the FBI as a special agent. That had been his dream since the age of ten, as he had once told Jack, and the proudest moment of his life had been when he'd earned his badge. Jack knew that a lot of people might have thought Clement was crazy. "I loved football," Clement would say, "and I still do. But I played it because I enjoyed it. I never planned to do it for a living."

Over the years, Clement had worked his way up through the Bureau. He was savvy enough to survive the internal politics, smart and tough enough to excel in the field, and conformed to the system because he believed in it. He could be a real bastard when someone did something stupid, but otherwise worked tirelessly to support his people so they could do their jobs. He wasn't a boss that any of his special agents would say they loved, but under his tenure, the Criminal Investigative Division, or CID, had successfully closed more cases than under any other assistant director in the previous fifteen years. People could say what they wanted, but Clement got results.

When he had first taken over the division, Clement had taken the time to talk to each and every one of his special agents. He had been up front about why: he wanted to know at least a little bit, more than just the names, about the men and women who risked their lives every day for the American Taxpayer. They were special agents, he'd said, but they were also special human beings.

Jack had dreaded the interview. Whereas Clement could have been the FBI's poster child, Jack didn't quite fit the mold. He was like a nail head sticking up from the perfectly polished surface of a hardwood floor, not enough to snag on anything, just enough to notice. Outwardly, he was no different than most of his peers. He dressed the same as most special agents, eschewing a suit for more practical and casual attire for all but the most formal occasions. His well-muscled six foot, one inch tall body was far more comfortable in jeans and a pullover shirt, with a light jacket to conceal his primary weapon, a standard service-issue Glock 22. While he had no problems voicing his opinions, which had sometimes led to respectful but intense discussions with his superiors, he had never been a discipline problem. He was highly competent in the field, and was a whiz at data analysis. At first glance, he seemed like what he should be: an outstanding special agent who worked hard and had great career prospects.

But under the shiny veneer ran a deep vein of dark emptiness. Jack smiled, but it never seemed to reach his eyes, and he rarely laughed. He was not cold-hearted, for he had often displayed uncommon compassion toward others, especially the victims, and their families, of the crimes he was sent to investigate. But he had no social life to speak of, no significant other in his life, and there were very few people who understood the extent of the pain that lay at Jack's core.

That pain had its roots in events that took place seven years earlier, when Jack was serving in the Army in Afghanistan. His patrol had been ambushed by the Taliban and had taken heavy casualties before reinforcements arrived. Jack had been badly wounded, having taken two rounds from an AK-47 in the chest, along with shrapnel from a grenade. The latter had left its mark on his otherwise handsome face, a jagged scar marring his left cheek. That had been rough, but he was young, only twenty-six, and strong, and would make a full recovery from his wounds.

What had torn him apart was what happened back in the States. While he lay unconscious in the SSG Heath N. Craig Joint Theater Hospital in Bagram, his wife Emily was kidnapped while leaving a shopping mall not far from their home outside Fort Drum, New York. Emily had her own home business, and they had no children, so no one immediately noticed that she'd gone missing. Four days passed before a persistent Red Cross worker who had been trying to get in touch with Emily about Jack's injuries contacted the provost marshal at Fort Drum. Two military policemen went to the house, and when they found it empty, they contacted the local police.

The police located her car that same day: the mall's security center had ordered it towed away after it had sat in the parking lot overnight, reporting it to the police as abandoned. The next day, the fifth since she had disappeared, police investigators found footage on one of the mall security cameras that vividly showed what had happened to her. A man stepped around the back of a nondescript van as she had walked by, laden with shopping bags. With a casual glance around to see if there were any witnesses, he turned as she passed and jabbed her in the back with a stun gun. Scooping her up in one smooth motion, he dumped her into the van through the already open side door, and then collected up the bags that had fallen to the ground. He didn't rush, didn't hurry as he threw the bags into the van. Then he climbed into the back and slammed the door closed. After a few minutes the van backed out of the space and drove away.

It had all happened in broad daylight.

Because it was clearly a kidnapping and so much time had passed since the crime had been committed, the local authorities contacted the FBI.

That was when Jack learned of his wife's disappearance. Immobilized in the hospital bed, still in a great deal of pain, he was paid a visit by his grim-faced commander and a civilian woman who introduced herself as an FBI special agent. His commander told him what had happened, and over the next three hours the FBI agent gathered every detail that Jack could remember about his wife's activities, associations, family and friends. Everything about her life that he could think of that might help track down her kidnapper. It had been the three most agonizing hours of his life. The special agent had assured him that everything was being done to find his wife and bring her back safely. Jack prayed that they would find her alive, but in his heart he knew she was gone.

His intuition proved brutally prophetic. Her body was found a week later, buried under bags of trash in a dumpster behind a strip mall in Cleveland, Ohio. She had been repeatedly raped and beaten before she'd finally been strangled to death. The FBI and law enforcement authorities in Ohio did everything they could to find her killer, but he had covered his tracks well and was never found.

When Jack was well enough to travel, the Army arranged for him to be flown home, where one of his first duties had been to formally identify Emily's battered, broken body. He had seen his share of horrors in Afghanistan, and some might think it would have made the trauma of viewing her body somewhat easier. It hadn't. Thankfully, the family lawyer, an old friend of his parents, who themselves had died in a car wreck a year before Jack had gone to Afghanistan, had made all the necessary arrangements for her burial. Jack's simply had to endure the agony of laying her to rest.

After the funeral, Jack had found himself at a loss. His time in the Army was nearly up, and he was tempted to simply lapse into an emotional coma to shut off the pain and the nightmares of Emily's tortured face.

But a cold flame of rage burned in his core at what had happened to her, and the bastard who had done it. He found himself sitting in the kitchen one morning, holding the business card of the female special agent who had interviewed him in Bagram. As if his body was acting of its own accord, he found himself picking up the phone and dialing the woman's number. The conversation that followed was the first step on the path that eventually led him to become a special agent in the FBI.

She had tried to dissuade him, warning him that he wasn't going to find answers, or vengeance, to Emily's death. In truth, while the thought of finding her killer was more than appealing, he realized from the beginning that avenging Emily wasn't what was pulling him toward the Bureau: it was the thought that he might be able to help prevent what had happened to her from happening to others.

When he got to the FBI Academy, one of his fellow agents was Sheldon Crane. Sheldon had an irrepressible sense of humor, and immediately glued himself to Jack. At first, Jack had resented the unwanted attention, but Sheldon had gradually worn through Jack's emotional armor, eventually becoming the Yin to Jack's Yang. Sheldon was a self-proclaimed computer genius, recruited to work in the Bureau's Cyber Division, while Jack's skills in intelligence analysis and experience in combat made him a good candidate for the Criminal Investigative Division.

Jack had done well in CID, but remained an outsider, something of a mystery to his fellow agents. Most of his supervisors knew his background and were content to let it be, but when Clement took over and began his interviews, Jack had heard that he could be very pointed in his questions. Jack didn't want to be interrogated again about his experience in Afghanistan or Emily's murder. He didn't want anyone's sympathy. He just wanted to move on.

Clement had completely surprised him. He didn't talk or want to know about anything related to Jack's past or his work. Instead, he asked questions about Jack as a person outside of the Bureau, what he liked to do in his free time, his personal likes and dislikes. At first, Jack had been extremely uncomfortable, but after a while he found himself opening up. Clement talked to him for a full hour and a half. When they were through, Jack actually found himself laughing at one of Clement's notoriously bad jokes.

After that, while Jack couldn't quite call Clement a friend, he had certainly become a confidant and someone he felt he could really talk to when the need arose.

Now was certainly one of those times.

Clement walked across the office toward Jack, but stopped when his eyes fell on the folder Jack clutched in one hand. Sighing, he said, "Dammit, don't you know any better than to grab files off my desk, Special Agent Dawson?"

"Yes, sir," Dawson told him. "I took it from your secretary's desk."

"Lord," Clement muttered as he moved up to Dawson. Putting a hand on the younger man's shoulder, he said again, "I'm sorry, Jack. I'd hoped to have a chance to talk to you before you saw anything in that file." With a gentle squeeze of his massive hand, he let go, then sat down behind his desk. "Sit."

Reluctantly, still clutching the folder containing the professional analysis of Sheldon Crane's last moments alive, Jack did as he was told, dropping into one of the chairs arrayed around a small conference table before turning to face his boss.

"Why aren't you letting me go out with the teams to Lincoln?" he asked before Clement could say anything else.

"Do you really have to ask that?" his boss said pointedly. "Look at yourself, Jack. You're an emotional wreck. I'm not going to endanger an investigation by having someone who isn't operating at full capacity on the case." He raised a hand as Jack began to protest. "Don't start arguing," he said. "Look, Jack, I've lost close friends, too. I know how much it can tear you up inside. But you're not going to do Sheldon any favors now by screwing things up in the field because you're emotionally involved. I promise you, *we will not rest* until we've found his killer."

"My God, Ray," Jack said hoarsely, looking again at the folder in his hand, "they didn't just kill him. They fucking tore him apart!"

He forced himself to open the folder again. The top photo was a shot that showed Sheldon's entire body at the scene. It looked like someone had performed an autopsy on him. A deep cut had been made in his torso from throat to groin. The ribs had been cracked open to expose the heart and lungs, and the organs from his abdomen had been pulled out and dissected, the grisly contents dumped onto the floor. Then something had been used to carve open his skull just above the line of his eyebrows, and the brain had been removed and set aside. Another shot that he dared not look at again showed what was done inside the skull: his killer had torn his nasal cavities open.

Another photo showed Sheldon's clothing. He had been stripped from head to toe, and his clothes had been systematically torn apart, with every seam ripped open. In the background, on the floor next to the wall, was his gun.

Jack had seen death enough times and in enough awful ways that it no longer made him want to gag. But he had never, even in the hateful fighting in Afghanistan, seen such measured brutality as this.

The last photo he had looked at had been a close-up of Sheldon's face and his terrified expression. "He was still alive when they started...cutting him up."

"I know," Clement said, his own voice breaking. "I know he was."

"What was he doing out there?" Jack asked, sliding the photos back into the folder with numb fingers. "This couldn't have just been some random attack. What the hell was he working on that could have driven someone to do this to him?"

Pursing his lips, Clement looked down at his desk, his face a study in consideration. "This is classified, Jack," he said finally, looking up and fixing Jack with a hard stare, "as in Top Secret. The kind of information you have to read after you sign your life away and go into a little room with thick walls and special locks on the door. Even the SAC in Lincoln doesn't know the real reason Sheldon was there, and the *only* reason I'm telling you is because you held high-level clearances in the Army and you can appreciate how sensitive this is and keep your mouth shut about it."

Jack nodded. He had been an intelligence officer in the Army, and knew exactly what Clement was talking about. He also appreciated the fact that Clement could lose his job for what he was about to say. That was the level of trust that had built up between them.

Satisfied that Jack had gotten the message, Clement told him, "Sheldon was investigating a series of cyber attacks against several research laboratories doing work on genetically modified organisms, mainly food crops like corn. The FDA was also hacked: someone took a keen interest in what the Center for Food Safety and Applied Nutrition was doing along the same lines. And before you say, 'So what's the big super-secret deal,' there was also a series of attacks against computers, both at home and work, used by specific individuals across the government, including senior officials in the Department of Defense and the military services. Sheldon was convinced the perpetrators were from a group known as the Earth Defense Society, and that they're somewhere here in the U.S. He's been out in the field for the last three weeks, tracking down leads." He frowned. "Apparently he found something in Lincoln."

"What the hell are they after?" Jack asked, perplexed. It seemed an odd potpourri of targets for hackers to be going after. He could understand someone going after one group of targets or another, but what common thread could run through such a mixed bag, from labs working on how to improve crops to the military?

"That's the sixty-four thousand dollar question, isn't it?" Clement said. "So, now you know what Sheldon was doing. Just keep your mouth shut about it and pretend this conversation never happened."

Standing up and coming around his desk, Clement continued as Jack rose from his chair, "I want you to take some leave. Get out of here for a few days until you've pulled yourself together. Then come back in and we can talk. And I promise you, I'll keep you informed of what we find."

"Yes, sir," was all Jack said as he shook Clement's hand. He turned and walked out of the office, closing the door quietly behind him.

As Jack left, Clement saw that he still had the copy of Sheldon's case file in his hand. With a satisfied nod, he returned to his desk and checked his phone, which was blinking urgently. It hadn't been ringing because he had ordered his secretary to hold all of his calls. Quickly scanning the recent caller list on the phone's display, he saw that the director had called him. Twice.

He grimaced, then pulled out the two smart phones that he carried. He used one of them for everyday personal communication. That one the Bureau knew about. He had turned it off before talking to Dawson to avoid any interruptions, and now he turned it back on.

The other smart phone, the one he flipped open now, was used for an entirely different purpose, and something of which his bosses at the Bureau would not approve. Calling up the web application, he quickly logged into an anonymizer service and sent a brief, innocuous-sounding email to a particular address. Then he activated an application that would wipe the phone's memory and reset it to the factory default, effectively erasing any evidence of how he had used it.

Putting it back in his pocket, he picked up his desk phone and called the director.

Two

Jack didn't remember the drive to his small two-bedroom home in Alexandria. He sat at the kitchen table, drinking a beer in a vain attempt to help numb the gnawing agony inside him. He looked around the kitchen, then out into what he could see of the living room through a cutout in the wall that sported a breakfast bar. One of Sheldon's many girlfriends had insisted on helping Jack decorate the house, and she had actually come up with ideas that appealed to him. The furniture was masculine, mainly dark leather and sturdy dark wood, with some of his own paintings on the walls. Sheldon had made a big deal out of Jack's painting, and had insisted on taking several that he liked to be framed for his girlfriend to hang up in strategic locations throughout the house.

Painting was Jack's main passion outside of work. He didn't consider himself any good at it, but everyone who visited the house had embarrassed him by gushing over the work. He outwardly dismissed the compliments as people just being polite, but a part of him, deep down, enjoyed the praise. Most of the paintings were still lifes, ranging from an apple sitting on a table, lit by the glow of a setting sun through the window, to his memory's view of some of the rugged hills of Afghanistan. They couldn't be called cheery or dark, nor did they follow a particular theme. But each one seemed to evoke an emotional response in those who saw them. Jack painted because he found it inwardly satisfying, and it had been good therapy after Emily's death. That others might enjoy looking at his work had never really occurred to him.

Tonight, his easel sat in the corner of the living room with a bare canvas. That was how he felt inside as he listened to the rain drum against the roof in the darkness. Bare. Empty.

With a sigh, he took another swig of beer and set the bottle down on the table before flipping open the folder containing the initial field report on Sheldon's murder.

Next to the folder was the digital photo frame that Sheldon had bought for him a month ago, and Jack sadly watched the images fade in and out as they had day and night since Sheldon had given it to him. It was an outrageous gadget that Jack never would have bought for himself, but it was the perfect gift from a gadget nut like Sheldon. The frame not only had a tiny storage card that could hold thousands of photos, but even had Wi-Fi wireless networking, and Sheldon had insisted on hooking it up to Jack's home network so Sheldon could remotely upload his latest ridiculous photos for Jack to enjoy. He was a true character, the perfect complement to Jack's role of straight man, and Jack desperately missed him.

Unable to look at the photos anymore, he turned off the frame and carefully set it down on a shelf next to the table. There would be a time for grieving and remembrance, but not now. Not yet.

With a heavy sigh, he opened up his laptop and logged into the FBI Intelligence Information Reports Dissemination System (FIDS) to check on any updates on the case. It didn't take him long to determine that the special agents in Lincoln hadn't found anything that leaped out at him as being terribly significant. The forensics team was still hard at work gathering physical evidence, and the small army of special agents was interviewing anyone and everyone who could have had access to the Lincoln Research University building, a special genetics research facility, where Sheldon had been found. So far, no leads had turned up. No one who'd been interviewed remembered ever having seen Sheldon Crane.

Fine, he thought, frustrated, *let's see what we can figure out on our own.* Jack didn't consider himself brilliant, but he had a knack for looking at a pile of seemingly unrelated or contradictory information about a case and coming up with a story of what happened. It was all about making associations between the different elements and seeing the underlying patterns. In a way, it was akin to painting, and the "pictures" that he came up with were usually spot on.

Unfortunately, he had very little to work with so far, but that was real life: you never had all the answers you wanted, especially right off the bat. So he started with what he had.

He normally used paper for his initial brainstorming, idly doodling on the page as his mind processed information, later typing things up on the computer. Pulling a sheet of paper from a small stack, he took a pencil and began to write.

Murder scene: Lincoln Research University genetic research labs; maintenance tunnel. Lincoln Research University. He'd never heard of it. A quick search on the web told him that "LRU" had opened its doors only two years before. He had assumed that it was an extension of the

University of Nebraska at Lincoln, but it wasn't. Digging deeper, he found that LRU was a graduate institution that had been largely funded by a grant from New Horizons, a huge agribusiness whose main focus was on producing insect- and herbicide-resistant commercial crops like corn. Technically, some might argue that it was a graduate college focusing on a single discipline and not a university, but for Jack's purposes the difference was meaningless.

LRU's web site touted its genetics research labs as the most advanced in the world, and a key asset in developing the next generation of genetically modified, or GM, products in the New Horizons line. If nothing else, the school had certainly attracted a breathtaking array of talent, based on the lofty-sounding bios for the faculty and the incredibly steep entry requirements for student applicants. While it was billed as a learning institution, it was clear that anyone short of a genius would have a tough time getting their foot in the door, which seemed to have driven potential applicants into a frenzy of competition. If the web site could be believed, LRU accepted only one percent of the applicants who met the admission requirements. Having earned a *summa cum laude* in your bachelor's program meant nothing at LRU.

The dean was Rachel Kempf, Ph.D. The photo on her bio page showed a formidable-looking middle-aged woman with an expression that would have been at home on a drill sergeant's ID card. Toward the bottom of her long list of impressive accomplishments was a mention that she was also on the board of directors at New Horizons.

No big surprise there, Jack thought as he scribbled more notes on his first sheet of scratch paper. He paused a moment and looked over what he'd written, surprised at how much he'd come up with and how few doodles there were. Most of it was probably academic (*Bad pun, Jack*, he scolded himself), but it was generally better to have too much data than too little.

But whatever had drawn Sheldon to LRU didn't fit with the cyber attacks against other genetics research labs that Clement had told him about. Checking FIDS again, he couldn't find any incident reports of malicious attacks against computers of LRU's facilities or staff. So, Sheldon had probably gone there for some other reason.

Jack's chain of thought was interrupted by a plaintive mewling noise. Looking down, he saw a pair of brilliant green eyes staring up at him from a black, furry face. It was Alexander, his cat. Alexander's long hair had a tuxedo pattern, glossy black except for his belly, chin and paws, which were pure white. His long whiskers were also white, and stood out nearly five inches on each side of his muzzle.

"Don't tell me you're hungry," Jack said, darting a glance at the stainless steel bowl on the floor near the refrigerator. He didn't remember feeding Alexander, but there was still food in the bowl, so he must have. Sighing, Jack leaned back and moved his arms aside, and twenty pounds of sinewy Siberian forest cat leaped nimbly into his lap. Sitting up so he could supervise Jack's work, Alexander began to purr, the surprisingly loud and deep rumbling filling the kitchen over the sound of the rain.

As he stroked the big cat's soft coat, Jack began to relax. He thought about how uncanny Alexander was: he could be a royal pain in the ass when he felt like getting into trouble, which seemed to be most of the time. But when Jack felt down, Alexander always knew that his human needed some therapy.

Damn cat, Jack thought, a small smile coming to his face despite his melancholy mood. *Who needs Valium?*

Pushing his frustration aside, he focused more closely on the details of the crime scene. According to the field reports, Sheldon had been found in one of the service tunnels running under the lab complex. The on-site team had found a trail of blood, believed to be Sheldon's, leading upstairs to one of the second floor labs.

The entrance to the lab where the blood trail terminated was through a heavy steel fire door set into the concrete-core walls. The door was controlled by a lock that required both a coded access card and five-digit entry key to open. It would have taken a small explosive to blow the lock, but there was no sign of forced entry. So Sheldon, or his assailant, must have had at least one card, and had known the code. Unfortunately, the digital access logs for the door had conveniently been erased, as had the previous twenty-four hours of recordings from the building's security cameras, four of which were in this particular lab.

Someone had gone to a great deal of trouble to conceal what had happened there, and it almost certainly had to be someone on the inside. Who else would have that sort of access to the university's security systems?

From the digital images that had been forwarded over FIDS from the investigating agents and forensics technicians in Lincoln, Jack could see that a life or death struggle had taken place in the lab. In fact, it looked like a bomb had gone off in the middle of the large room, with what was no doubt incredibly expensive scientific equipment knocked over or flung from the heavy metal benches lining the room. Several laptops and workstations had been smashed, as if someone had rolled right over the top of them. Along one wall, a bank of huge stainless steel freezers stood open, their contents – hundreds of small containers of corn kernels and other biological samples, the report said – strewn across the floor. On the floor near the door that led out to the main hallway were traces of blood.

Most significant, Jack thought as he read through the attached document, glancing periodically back at the images, were the cartridge cases that had been found scattered over the floor by the door. Fifteen of them had been recovered, all from .40 caliber rounds that were probably fired from Sheldon's Glock 22 pistol. The forensics team had found two slugs, probably .40 caliber, lodged in the walls and a third in the ceiling, but there was no trace of the other twelve. The immediate conclusion, pending confirmation from the forensics and ballistics experts, was that Sheldon had hit whatever he had been shooting at.

But the only blood found at the scene seemed to be his, Jack thought. A DNA analysis would be run to make sure, but initial on-site testing matched Sheldon's blood type.

Jack sat back, a chill running down his spine, his hand momentarily frozen in mid-stroke on Alexander's back. Sheldon had never been in the military or seen combat, but he'd been involved in two shootouts in his career, and had been as calm and cool as one could expect in such a situation. He wouldn't have panicked, even if he'd been surprised by an assailant. He wasn't nearly as good a shot as Jack, but he was no slouch, either. At the distances that must have been involved in the lab, a couple dozen feet at most, given the layout of the equipment and the various lab tables, Jack knew that Sheldon would have hit his target with most of his shots.

But Jack couldn't get around the one major gap in his theory: there didn't appear to be any trace of blood from anyone but Sheldon. Jack was well aware that body armor could certainly stop .40 caliber rounds at close range, but it was a long stretch for him to believe that Sheldon's opponent had absorbed twelve bullets without leaving a single drop of blood behind. How likely could it be that not a single bullet had hit a part of Sheldon's opponent's body that wasn't protected by armor, which typically only covered the chest and back: an arm or a leg, or the head. Even if a bullet didn't take down the target, it would have left traces of blood behind.

Yet, there was nothing.

The shootout appeared to have happened amidst a physical struggle across the lab that had also left traces of Sheldon's blood and various fibers on the sharp edges of several pieces of equipment. There was remarkably little in the way of other evidence aside from fabric fibers that the forensics team had tentatively identified as being from the standard lab clothing worn by the people who worked there. It was a controlled environment where anyone entering was required to wear sterilized scrubs, caps, masks and gloves, just as if they were in an operating room. The only fingerprints or other questionable physical evidence found so far had been from Sheldon.

The same was true of the small electrical equipment alcove where the body had been discovered early that morning by a maintenance worker. Three more bullet casings, believed to be from Sheldon's gun, had been found, but there were no bullets lodged in the walls, no traces of ricochets. And the range this time, even if his target had been across from the alcove along the tunnel wall, would have been point blank: he could hardly have missed.

What the hell happened, Sheldon? Jack asked himself. It's like you were shooting at a goddamn phantom that could absorb bullets.

Alexander, annoyed that Jack had stopped petting him, began licking Jack's hand, trying to get his attention focused on more important matters like feline ego maintenance. Jack absently began petting him again, but his mind was twelve hundred miles away, trying to visualize Sheldon's encounter at the LRU lab.

Staring at a blank spot on the wall and clearing his thoughts, he tried to visualize the lab in his mind. It was a technique for associative analysis that he had developed while he was in Afghanistan. Sometimes you could go analytically from A to B in an orderly, logical way, given the data you had on hand. Other times you couldn't, and Jack had found that his subconscious could often help him "see" things that his conscious mind missed. It didn't always work, and then he had to resort to more traditional analysis. But when it did work, it worked damn well. His commander in Afghanistan had thought Jack was full of shit the first time he had done it while planning for an operation to take down some suspected Taliban targets. That attitude changed after Jack's analysis and "staring at the wall bullshit" led him to believe that his unit was being baited into an ambush. The commander was unconvinced, but he was a prudent man: he prepared for both contingencies. It was indeed a trap, but when the jaws sprung, the American troops were ready, and wound up taking down nearly twice as many Taliban fighters as they had expected to find, at a cost of only two of their own soldiers lightly wounded. After that, Jack's commander gave him all the time he wanted to sit and stare at the wall.

Now, sitting in his kitchen, the LRU lab as he'd seen in the photos slowly came into focus and the movie in his mind began to play.

Using a badge and key access code that he'd gotten from someone who works at LRU, Sheldon enters the lab. His LRU contact has access to the security systems and has shut them off to cover Sheldon's illegal entry. Sheldon's a cyber expert, investigating network attacks against facilities like this. He looks around and sees what he's come for: the computers. They have data that he wants, but he can't access or hack these systems remotely, or he would not have taken the risk coming here: they're isolated from the rest of the university's intranet. Physically secured in this lab.

He takes out the USB flash drive containing hacking programs that he lovingly refers to as his "toolbox" and gets to work, breaking into the computers. He has to do this because his inside contact at LRU who gave him physical access to the lab does not have access to the computers, or doesn't have the knowledge to get at the data.

Time passes, and Sheldon finds something. The data he came here for now points him in a new direction. He looks up at the big stainless steel freezers along the wall. There. Quickly covering his tracks in the computers, erasing all signs that he had accessed them, he gets up and goes to a particular freezer. The data on the computers is maintained by some of the most gifted scientists in the world, working for one of the world's most powerful corporations. Everything maintained here is orderly and precise. The data has told him exactly where to look for the prize, the true reason he has come here.

Taking a set of mitts to protect his skin from the extreme cold, he opens the freezer and slides out one of the many shelves, each of which holds dozens of tiny sample containers. He sets the tray on a nearby lab table and carefully picks up a particular container. It looks exactly the same as the others, and the writing on the label indicates it is in sequence with the others on the tray. But something about this one is different. The computer data told him so.

He could simply take the sample container, but that would be too suspicious. Instead, he takes another container, perhaps a small bag that he has brought with him, and extracts some of the contents from the sample container he has taken from the freezer. Corn kernels. He carefully puts the corn into a pocket.

The meticulous scientists who work here would know exactly what was in each sample container; this would be logged in the computer. They would know quickly that something was missing from this container, for this item was the main focus for the research here. Sheldon considers substituting samples from another container, but abandons the idea: the scientists will know soon enough. Too soon. He needs to conceal his theft for as long as possible.

He looks at the sample tray and the dozens of containers it holds, all of which look exactly alike except for the small labels. Coming to a decision, he upends the tray, dumping the containers onto the floor.

Moving quickly, he does the same to the remaining trays in this freezer, then moves on to the others. Soon the white linoleum tile is covered with plastic containers, and Sheldon kicks and scatters them across the lab as he moves from freezer to freezer. It will take the scientists who work here weeks to undo this simple act of vandalism and discover what was taken. Or so he hopes.

This is when things go wrong. Whether drawn by the noise, the security monitoring system being shut off, or perhaps just by chance, someone enters the lab. Sheldon goes through the motions of informing the newcomer – or newcomers – that he is an FBI special agent, showing his badge and trying to bluff his way out. But the newcomer knows that Sheldon is on his own: he has no warrant, no authorization. No backup. He is alone.

They struggle. Sheldon opens fire, and keeps shooting as they careen across the lab, further spreading the mess on the floor, knocking equipment from the benches, smashing things to pieces. He empties his weapon's magazine, firing at his assailant.

Then...something happens. Something that allows Sheldon to break away. But he does not escape cleanly: at the last moment, just as Sheldon can reach the door and freedom, his assailant somehow injures him, the wound serious enough to leave a clear trail of blood as Sheldon escapes the lab.

He heads downstairs to the maintenance tunnel; perhaps this is how he entered the otherwise secure building, or perhaps he knows he is cut off from the other exits. His injury is more severe than he thought, and he is bleeding badly. He would have called someone, would have called Jack, for help, but could not. Perhaps there was no signal, or he had lost his cell phone during the struggle. He is all alone now.

Exhausted, scared, and slowly bleeding out, Sheldon holes up in the dark alcove. He reloads his empty weapon, knowing that his pursuer or pursuers will find him; the trail of blood will see to that. He knows they will find what he has taken, the precious, mysterious sample from the lab. Having come this far, he would not simply give it up, allow them to find it easily. Sheldon is smart: swallowing the stolen material would be the logical thing to do, the obvious thing. He must find another way.

He takes some precious time to hide some of the kernels...somewhere, in a place that his pursuers will not think to look. The rest, he swallows: he will let his enemy find what they expect to find, drawing attention away from the other hidden cache.

Having done what he can, he waits, waits for his assailant to come as more blood drains from his body.

When his enemy arrives, Sheldon fights to the last, firing three more rounds before he is overcome. After that, there is only agony as his enemy cuts into his flesh and cracks his bones apart, a sea of pain until darkness finally falls...

Jack blinked his eyes, clearing the last horrible image from his mind just before the tears came. Tears of loss, tears of rage for his murdered friend.

Alexander, still purring, rubbed his big head against Jack. Jack gathered the big cat up in his arms and held him close, burying his face in Alexander's soft fur as he wept.

After the tears stopped, he looked down again at the photographs and spread them out so he could see the one that clearly showed Sheldon's butchered body. Beside that he put the photo showing the meticulously torn clothing.

It makes sense now, he thought grimly. He hadn't been far from the mark when he had thought Sheldon's wounds looked like someone had performed an autopsy on him. But *autopsy* wasn't quite the right word: his friend had been vivisected, cut to pieces while still alive, and not simply as an act of cruelty. His murderer had been looking for something.

"Jesus, Sheldon," Jack rasped as warm tears continued to trickle down his cheeks. "What could have been so important that they'd rip you apart to get it back?"

But the real question now was where had Sheldon hidden the rest of the sample he had stolen, if Jack's analytic insights were right?

Sensing that Jack no longer needed his feline therapy services, Alexander uncoiled and hopped down to the floor to investigate his food bowl as Jack pulled out his smart phone. The step he was about to take would likely land him in extremely hot water with Clement, but Jack couldn't stay away, couldn't sit on the sidelines. Not on this one.

He was going to call the SAC in Lincoln, but wasn't sure of his prospects for getting additional information. Jack had worked with Special Agent Carl Richards on a case two years ago, and knew him as an incredibly competent agent who was an equally monumental asshole. Sighing, he punched in the number for Richards that he'd pulled up from the FBI contact database.

The phone rang twice before a clipped nasal voice answered, "Special Agent Richards." In the background, Jack could hear a dull roar of people talking.

"This is Special Agent Jack Dawson," Jack said.

"What the hell do you want, Dawson?" Richards snapped. "You're not on this case and I don't have any time to waste on idle conversation."

Jack bit back a sharp reply. *Stay cool*, he told himself. "Listen, Richards, I think I know why Crane was there and what he was looking for."

"That's classified, Dawson," Richards growled. "I wasn't given access to that information, and I know you weren't, either."

"I don't know the details of what he was investigating," Jack said, "but I don't think he was there as part of his assigned investigation. He didn't have a warrant to conduct a search, did he?"

"No, he didn't," Richards grudgingly admitted. Then, after a pause, he said, "Dawson, when was the last time you saw or spoke to Crane?"

Jack hadn't really thought about that. He and Sheldon were close, but it wasn't like they were in contact every day. Their schedules were hectic and work took them off to different places around the country, sometimes for weeks at a time. It wasn't unusual for them to go a week or more without even exchanging emails. Now that he thought about it, it had been a fairly long time since he'd heard from his friend. Not so long that it was terribly unusual, but longer than normal. "Three weeks ago," Jack said. He remembered that Sheldon had held a party before leaving town and, as always, insisted that Jack come.

"That would track," Richards told him. "Dawson, Crane started working undercover three weeks ago. He was filing updates until last week, when he just dropped off the face of the planet. We've been trying to track him down since then."

Jack sat back, stunned. What could have caused Sheldon to break contact with the Bureau? Had he gone rogue? "What did he find before he...bugged out?" Jack asked.

"It's all classified, dammit!" Richards cursed. Then, sighing, he said, "But I've read the reporting he sent in, and most of it was pretty limp. If there's a tie-in to what he was doing after he dropped out of sight, I don't see it." There was a sudden increase in the volume of the voices in the background, and Richards said, "Listen, Dawson, I've got special agents interrogating half the population of Lincoln. If you've got something for me, spill it. Otherwise, stop wasting my time."

"All right," Jack said, fortifying himself for Richards' reaction to what Jack was about to tell him. "Here's what I think went down..." He briefly described what he thought had happened, based on the information from the file he'd taken from Clement and the subsequent reporting on FIDS from the field teams in Lincoln.

When Jack finished, there was a long pause on the far end of the line, and all he could hear was the hubbub in the background. He thought for a moment that Richards had given up on his tale and had just forgotten to hit the end call button on his phone.

Finally, Richards spoke. "Shit."

"And here I thought you were going to either hang up on me, or tell me that was the most ridiculous thing you'd ever heard," Jack said drily.

"The only thing I wish right now, Dawson," Richards told him, "was that Clement hadn't been such a sentimental idiot and had sent you out here instead of sending you home to cry over Crane buying the farm. We'd figured out some of what you've come up with, but your story makes sense, just like it did on the Bronsky case. You're sharp, Dawson."

Jack nearly fell out of his chair. Richards never complimented anybody on anything. But he wasn't a fool: Jack had helped him solve the Bronsky case, a multiple murder spree that had spanned four states and had completely stumped the investigators. Richards hadn't bought in to how Jack had done his part in putting the pieces of the puzzle together, but to him it didn't matter: all Richards wanted was to sort out what happened and nail bad guys. For him, the only thing that mattered was results. With Jack's help, Joseph Bronsky and his brother Cain were finally stopped, killed in a shootout after refusing to surrender.

"Can I make a suggestion or two?" Jack asked him, deciding to try and press his advantage.

"I'm listening."

"First, pull any hard drives or other data storage devices for any of the computers in the lab and get them to forensics to see if they can recover anything from them. I'll bet at least one of them was a standalone machine, not connected to any networks."

"That's going to be a bit difficult," Richards said slowly.

"Why?" Jack asked.

"Somebody already beat us to it. You must have seen in the photos that those machines were smashed to bits. The hard drives were literally ripped out of every single one of them. Didn't bother with screwdrivers. You sure your buddy Crane didn't yank them out?"

"No," Jack told him, silently cursing that bit of bad luck. "That wasn't his style. If he had tampered with hardware, it would've been subtle, precise. Most of what he did was with software. Unless his assailant took it, you should find a USB flash drive...somewhere."

"We'll look again, but so far we didn't find one, either in the lab or on his body or clothing."

"The next thing is an accomplice," Jack said. "He had help getting into the lab, and I'll bet it was the same person who erased the security camera recordings and data logs."

"We had that figured out," Richards said, his voice tinged with annoyance as if to say, *We're not complete idiots, you know*. "And we actually have a likely suspect: Ellen Bienkowski. We've found all of the university's security people who had the necessary access, except her. She wasn't scheduled to go on leave, but she hasn't returned any calls and her house is empty. We're trying to track her down."

Frowning, Jack told him, "The other thing to find is the samples Sheldon must have taken. I'm convinced that was really what he'd come for. Hacking into the computers was just a means to an end."

"But why the hell would he want to steal some stupid corn or whatever?" Richards asked, exasperated. "Industrial espionage?"

"Could be," Jack admitted. "New Horizons is pulling in nearly six billion dollars a year in profits, and I'm sure whatever they were working on in that lab would probably be worth a fortune to a competitor. But I can't see Sheldon as a player in something like that. And the MO of his murder seems a tad extreme if he was double-dealing."

"Don't be naïve, Dawson," Richards said flatly. "People have sold out their country for peanuts, and almost everybody has a price, if someone makes the right offer. You know that nobody joins the Bureau to get rich on our government salaries. As for the MO, I'll grant that it's definitely out of the ordinary, more like a ritual killing than something that even a pissed off mafia hit man would come up with."

Jack suppressed his anger at Richards' remark about almost everyone having a price. *Sheldon would never have sold out*, he told himself. *No way.* "It doesn't matter," he told Richards. "I don't know why he wanted the corn samples, only that he did. They have to be there somewhere."

"Yeah, right," Richards said sourly, and Jack could picture him standing in the lab, looking around at the sea of sample containers spread across the floor, each and every one of which could potentially be evidence. "Well, there are plenty here, that's for sure." Sighing, he added, "We'll look. But the forensics guys went over every inch of the service tunnel where we found Crane and there was nothing. We're still going over the lab, but–"

"No," Jack interrupted. "He wouldn't have had time to hide it in the lab. If I'm right, he would've hidden them in the service tunnel, or maybe somewhere along the way from the lab. But I'm betting on them being near where his body was found."

"Okay, we'll look again, but I'm not holding out much hope."

"Is there anything else you've found that hasn't been reported yet?" Jack asked him, hoping for some additional clues.

"We found his cell phone, smashed in the lab. That's being written up now. What was left of it was under one of the pieces of lab equipment that was knocked over during the fight that went on in here.

We also found a stun baton with Crane's fingerprints on it. Is that something he normally carried?"

Jack shook his head as he answered. "No. He only carried his regular service weapon and a Glock 27 in a leg holster for backup. He never carried a stun gun or a Taser that I know of."

Richards was silent, and Jack got the feeling there was something else. "What is it?" he asked. "What else did you find?"

"The coroner found it a little while ago before they took Crane's body away for the autopsy," Richards said quietly, and Jack knew they were both thinking the same thing: the coroner's work had already been done for him. "There was a piece of paper, rolled up and shoved down Crane's throat."

"What did it say?" Jack asked, wondering at this last insult that his friend had suffered.

"It's a banner for something called the 'Earth Defense Society.' Ever heard of it?"

"No," Jack told him, shaking his head, "but it sounds like some sort of eco-preservation group or something. Any idea who they are?"

"Not yet," Richards said grimly. "But I intend to find out, because I don't need your fancy intuition to tell me that they're probably the ones who killed your buddy Crane."

Three

After Jack hung up with Richards, he did a search for "Earth Defense Society" on the web and came up with over eight hundred hits. The first one, amazingly enough, appeared to be a very professionally maintained web site for an organization that bore the name. Jack felt a chill run down his spine when he saw the logo on the site's header: it was the same as on the paper found in Sheldon's throat. Richards had just emailed him a photo of it. The other hits appeared to be links from other sites back to this one, and he got a sinking feeling as he took a quick scan through. Almost all of them were about UFOs or alien abductions and the like.

As he began to read the EDS "about" page, he felt his face flush with anger. "You've got to be fucking kidding me," he cursed, shaking his head in disbelief.

The Earth Defense Society is dedicated to defending the Earth and all its life forms from a long-term program undertaken by a non-human intelligence to transform the planet's biosphere into one capable of supporting their form of life. This enemy has secretly occupied key positions in the government, military, and industries, such as pharmacology and genetics research. We – all of us, humans and every other creature on our planet – are in danger of becoming nothing more than a food source for these invaders..."

Jack turned away from the words on the screen in disgust. Either someone had played an incredibly bad joke with the paper that had been stuffed down Sheldon's throat, or the Earth Defense Society, the EDS, had at least one homicidal lunatic with the balls or stupidity to murder an FBI special agent.

What made him angry was that he wanted Sheldon to have suffered and died for something important. The thought that some lunatic who believed in garbage like Area 51 might have killed him for nothing more than some bizarre delusion turned Jack's stomach.

Gritting his teeth, he forced himself to read the rest of what the site had to say, mostly elaborating on the ridiculous "aliens are here to eat us" theme. Over the next three hours, he read every page on the site, taking notes as he went. He didn't write down anything having to do with the alien invasion trash, only the tidbits he thought might be important to obtain a warrant to go after this "society." He knew that Richards would have a dozen people doing the same thing right now, but that didn't matter: this was something Jack had to do, and it was always possible he'd find a tidbit that they might have missed.

The big prize was Naomi D. Perrault, Ph.D., M.D., who seemed to be the leading contributor to the site. There weren't any pictures of her, but there was plenty of impressive-sounding biographic information, presumably to help legitimize her ridiculous claims. What really caught his eye was that she was a former senior researcher at New Horizons, who claimed to have jumped ship after she discovered that little green men were guiding the development of genetically engineered crops at New Horizons for their own nefarious purposes.

Yeah, right, he thought coldly. Men from Mars are the last thing you should be worrying about now, lady.

Since there weren't any photos of her on the EDS site, he went digging around on the New Horizons site, hoping there would still be something left from when she'd been working for the company. He found a small bio that said nothing that was different from the EDS site, and a slew of papers she had written that were so technical he had no idea what they said. But there were no photos.

Moving on to FIDS and several state and federal databases, he found something truly disturbing: every document that matched her name had a photo of an obese African American male. Whoever she was, someone had gone to extraordinary lengths to mask her electronic past.

His cell phone rang.

"Dawson," he said.

"I hope you've been spending your crying time wisely, Dawson," he heard Richards say.

"What the hell is that supposed to mean?" Jack said, shocked that Richards had bothered to call him.

"The EDS site," Richards answered. "Don't tell me you haven't been pawing through every ridiculous word of it."

"Yeah," Jack said. "Sorry. I'm not trying to muck around in your turf, but I couldn't help looking. Now, I'm almost sorry I did."

"Don't be. The whole EDS thing smells like one big murdering rat," Richards said, barely restrained anger evident in his voice. "And since you did me a good turn, I figured I'd return the favor, although if you ever breathe a word of any of this to Clement, I'll kick your ass."

"Thanks, Richards," Jack said, meaning it. "I appreciate it."

"Forget the mushy sentiments," Richards told him brusquely, returning to the matter at hand. "I've had an entire team turning that web site upside down and inside out, and tracing down every individual and other site that's associated with it. The individuals they list on the contributor page appear to be real people, but all of their critical records have either been tampered with or deleted. Social security, military documents, driver's licenses, bank records, credit cards. Everything. The guys from the Cyber Division that I've talked to about this weren't happy at all: whoever did this was good. Really good. And I'm getting really tired of seeing the same fat black guy that they used to replace every goddamn photo of these people." Jack grunted his agreement, wondering why they'd chosen that particular photo. "He actually turned out to be a lead," Richards went on. "We ran an image match and found him. The only problem is that he died three months ago of a heart attack, right after he was tossed into Joliet prison. Go figure."

"What was he in for?"

"Arson," Richards told him. "Our late friend Gary S. Woolsey got caught torching a lab called Outland Genetics in Chicago nine months ago. He managed to burn the facility to the ground, killing the CEO and four employees."

"Jesus," Jack said, stunned. "And let me guess: Outland Genetics was somehow involved in genetically engineered crops."

"Bingo," Richards said. "And get this. According to the trial records, his attorney was loony enough to put Woolsey on the stand, and under cross examination by the prosecution he broke down. He confessed to the whole damn thing, apologizing for killing the employees, who were, as he put it, 'at least fellow humans.' He claimed the CEO was a goddamn alien. After that, his counsel tried to plead an insanity defense."

"The jury didn't swallow that trash, I take it."

"No," Richards said. "Neither did the judge. It was a quick trial, and Woolsey got five consecutive life sentences, with no parole. Not that he got to enjoy much of Joliet's hospitality before he kicked off." He paused. "The weird thing was that he had no priors, not even a parking ticket. He just came out of the blue and murdered five people."

"What was his background?"

"Would you believe that he used to work for New Horizons?" Richards told him.

"No shit?" Jack said, furiously scribbling notes. "Was he a geneticist?"

"No," Richards said. "We got his bio from the legal people at New Horizons, who are happily bending over backwards for us on this. It turns out that Woolsey was an IT guy, a network engineer type. He was the head honcho of their wide area network infrastructure linking up the company's labs across the country. And – get this – he was also the guy who led the IT installation at Lincoln Research University."

Jack sat there, watching as the pencil in his right hand, as if it were moving of its own accord, made a dotted line on his notepad from Woolsey's name to Sheldon's, then made a big question mark in the middle. "Can we get a list of the facilities that he may have worked on?" *What are the odds that they're the same facilities that had been hacked, and that Sheldon had been investigating?* he asked himself.

"I don't know," Richards said, "but we'll ask."

"So what happened to him?" Jack asked.

"They fired his ass a year ago," Richards replied. "Get this: when he wasn't installing networks for the company, he was robbing them blind. If he needed five routers, he'd bill the company for ten and sell the rest on the side."

"That seems a little obvious for somebody who was smart enough to be a network engineer," Jack told him.

"Even bright people do stupid things," Richards replied. "In any case, he got caught in a routine internal audit and was terminated for cause."

"A year ago," Jack mused. "Right about the same time that our good friend Dr. Perrault left the company."

"It wasn't 'right about the same time,'" Richards told him. "It was the very same week. New Horizons said that Perrault walked out after being accused of trying to steal proprietary technology by her boss."

"And who was that?" Jack asked.

"Dr. Rachel Kempf," Richards told him. "She's–"

"–the scary-looking dean at LRU," Jack finished for him. "So, Perrault joined the staff at LRU when it opened its doors?"

"Right. She was one of their star attractions." Jack heard him rustling some paper notes in the background. "Let's see: she got her doctorate from Harvard's Biological and Biomedical Sciences program at the ridiculously young age of eighteen, won just about every prize you can win in the field of genetics, then went on to get her M.D. before being picked up by New Horizons as a senior researcher. She spent the next nine years playing a key role in developing the company's genetically engineered commercial crops, and was hand-picked by Kempf over a ton of other well-known researchers for a first-string position on the new LRU faculty lineup.

"Then a year ago, just when Woolsey pulls his little arson stunt, good Dr. Perrault is caught stealing company secrets and they kick her out on the curb," Richards finished.

Jack frowned. "I don't get it," Jack told him. "She was one of the stars of the show, and then she suddenly decides to risk it all by trying to steal from the company? Something's not adding up here. How much was she making?"

"According to New Horizons, at the tender age of twenty-eight, just before she walked out, Dr. Perrault was pulling down an annual salary of one and a half million, plus bonuses and options. So figure a gross income of nearly three mil a year." He chuckled, but there was no humor in the sound. "Sort of makes you wish that you'd been born a genius, doesn't it?"

"But if she was making that much, what was the motive for stealing something?" Jack asked.

Richards sighed in resignation, as if Jack were a complete idiot. "Greed, Dawson. You could give the moon to some people and they'd still try to steal the stars if they could reach them."

"Did New Horizons know what happened to her after she left?"

"They told me that she just disappeared," Richards said. "Poof. They hired an army of private investigators to find her, but she was just gone. Ironically, one of Perrault's neighbors called the cops because she hadn't seen Perrault for days, and the good doctor always told her when she was going on vacation."

"Did the PIs find anything?" Jack asked.

"Not a goddamn thing to follow up on," Richards told him bluntly. "All that was missing for certain was Perrault's laptop, which she took with her everywhere, and her cat. The only other oddity that popped up was that there wasn't a single photograph of her in the house. None of the neighbors saw her after the day she left the LRU campus. Her car was still in the garage, and there weren't any obvious signs that she'd packed in a hurry to flee. She also didn't have a security service, so there weren't any records of when she might have entered the house that day. And after she left, there was no trail from her credit cards, ATMs, phone, or her known computer accounts. No hits on her passport or airline ticketing. Nothing. She just dropped off the grid. And she has no known surviving family: she was an only child and her parents died in a car wreck when she was in college. We're still trying to find any friends or extended family, but so far the only thing we've got is the EDS web site."

"She had tons of money," Jack mused, "so it wouldn't have been impossible for her to disappear, and there are ways she could maintain a presence on the web – assuming what's on the EDS site is really from her – and not be easily traced. But if she did a disappearing act, she must have prepared it in advance: that's not the sort of thing you could manage at the drop of a hat. It also seems a little extreme for the trouble she was in with the company. It's not like she'd committed murder, after all. At least, not then," he added darkly.

"I wouldn't be so sure," Richards told him. "One of the New Horizons reps told me that the technology involved in the theft she was accused of was potentially worth billions. They weren't just going to let her walk away with it. Hang on," he said suddenly. In the background, he barked some orders at someone as if he or she were a complete idiot. Then he came back on.

"Stupid idiot people," Richards growled. "We're still trying to track down Kempf. She's on vacation in Italy, and we've got the Legal Attaché in Rome yammering at the Italians to scour the countryside for her. Apparently she refuses to take a cell phone when she travels, and the only other way to contact her is to leave a message with her travel agent, who gets a call from her once every few days to check if she's gotten any messages. Idiot. And speaking of traveling, are you up for a drive?"

Glancing at his watch, Jack grimaced. It was just after midnight. He'd been awake since five a.m. and felt completely exhausted. "Sure," he lied.

"Good. Because if you manage not to kill yourself in a car wreck on the way to Quantico, maybe you can sweet-talk your lab analyst friend down there into letting you look at what we're sending back. There's certainly plenty of blood for her to sample before the rest of the forensics and ballistics people can touch anything. The plane should be arriving at Washington National in two hours. Even if you take a nice little nap and a shower, you shouldn't have any trouble beating the team couriering the evidence down to the lab."

Jack's "lab analyst friend" was Jerri Tanaka, Ph.D., who worked in the FBI's DNA Analysis Unit that specialized in characterizing nuclear DNA from blood or other body fluids. The unit was part of the state of the art FBI Laboratory facility located at Marine Corps Base Quantico in Quantico, Virginia, about a forty minute drive from Jack's home.

Jack had met Jerri while he was at the FBI Academy, which was in the same compound as the lab. They'd developed a friendship while he'd been in training that had become more serious after he graduated and received his badge. They'd had a brief love affair, but Jack had found that he simply wasn't ready for another relationship yet. Jerri had been very understanding, and they had remained friends after breaking off the romantic part of their relationship. She had never been as close to him as Sheldon, but she and Jack had stayed in touch and made sure to visit one another when she happened to be at headquarters, or when he went down to Quantico. It was one small bit of good fortune in a terrible situation, because Jerri would almost certainly be one of the first to have her latex-gloved hands on whatever the plane was bringing back from Lincoln.

"That's another one I owe you, Richards," Jack told him. "Just think of the damage this must be doing to your reputation."

"Yeah, right," Richards told him. "Don't worry: I'm sure my standing as the Bureau's number one asshole is still locked in, Dawson, although I'll put it at risk one more time before you can kiss my ass goodbye. One of my people just showed me something interesting. It turns out that the old lady who lived next to Perrault had a recent photo of her that she was willing to fork over. One nice thing about hardcopy prints: they can't be deleted from a database. Too bad the old lady had no idea where Perrault ran off to. Check your email."

With that, he hung up.

Jack shook his head, idly wondering at what must have happened in Richards' life for him to turn out so surly. Then he hit the check mail button on his laptop, and was rewarded with a happy beep that announced incoming new mail. It was from one of the special agents in Lincoln, and the subject line read "Dr. Naomi Perrault."

Opening it up, Jack felt his breath catch in his throat. It showed what must have been Perrault's neighbor, a kindly-looking woman in her seventies wearing an outrageous floral print dress, arm-in-arm with a much younger woman, Perrault, who was holding a clearly displeased white cat. Perrault was beautiful, with lush brunette hair tied back in a ponytail that fell over her left shoulder like a silken waterfall. Her flawless skin was light, but not pale, and clearly was only exposed to the damaging rays of the sun with great care. She was smiling shyly, her full lips parted to reveal perfect teeth. A body-hugging sleeveless white top showed off her bust and cleavage in a tastefully pleasant way, and revealed shoulders and arms that were trim and toned from regular exercise.

But what captivated him were Perrault's eyes, which echoed the smile formed by her lips with perhaps just a hint of innocent mischief: one was a deep, almond brown, while the other was a bright azure blue. He had never seen anyone with eyes like that before, and he had a hard time tearing his gaze away from them.

"Talk about deadly beauty," Jack muttered, his brain conflicted between the exotic-looking woman in the visual image before him and the near-certainty that she had somehow been involved in Sheldon's murder. "Shit."

Four

With the image of Perrault's face still haunting his thoughts, Jack checked his weapons, strapped them on, and donned a light rain jacket. After sliding his phone and badge into the inside pockets, he went to the door to the garage, not looking forward to the drive that lay ahead of him.

He heard a sudden pattering on the wood floor behind him, and turned to see Alexander trotting after him, chirruping in the way that Siberian cats often did. He held his favorite stuffed toy mouse, its tail and ears long since chewed off, in his mouth: Jack had taught him to play fetch, and he hadn't gotten any play time today.

Crazy cat, Jack thought, kneeling down to scratch Alexander in his favorite spot right above his tail, eliciting a deep purr. *You should've been born a dog.* "Sorry, boy," he said, "no fetch today, and no walks, either." He kept Alexander as an inside cat, but would take him out morning and evening for a walk, putting a chest harness and leash on him. Alexander accepted the indignity with amazingly good humor, but Jack suspected that was only because several of the neighbors always seemed to be out and about, conveniently laden with cat treats. "Try to stay out of trouble, okay?"

Alexander's green eyes promised no such thing, and Jack just sighed in resignation as he gave him one final pat on the head before heading into the garage, locking the door behind him.

After sliding into the seat of his battered but well-maintained Land Rover Defender, he pulled the door shut as the garage door opener hummed, raising the roll-up door to reveal the dark downpour in the rear-view mirror.

I should call Jerri, he thought, sensing the phone's weight in his jacket, and let her know that I'm coming down. Hell, I should call Clement and tell him what I've been up to. I hate sneaking around behind his back.

After a moment's reflection, he discarded the idea. Clement would crush Jack's testicles in a garlic press for sticking his nose into the case without authorization, and Richards would take the squashed remains and deep fry them for getting him into trouble with Clement. *Okay, just call Jerri, then.*

He was reaching into his jacket for the phone when it chimed, alerting him to new voice mail. Pulling it out, he saw that there was a message from Jerri. She must have tried to call him during his last conversation with Richards. He hit the play button.

"Jack, this is Jerri," she said before biting back a sob. Jack knew that she was like a precision machine at work in the lab, flawless and unflappable. But she was also a woman of extraordinary emotional depth, and was extremely sensitive to the feelings of others, especially Jack. "The watch center called me in, but wouldn't say why. I just found out now after getting to the lab. God, I'm so sorry, Jack. I'm so sorry. You know we'll do everything we can here for Sheldon." She paused for a moment, trying to stifle more sobs. "Call me. Let me know that you're okay. I..."

I love you, Jack knew she wanted to say, and his gut twisted with guilt. He knew she had loved him, and still did. Jerri was a wonderful woman, and he knew that had his own past been different, they would probably have been very happy together. But the past was what it was, and he couldn't change it, any more than he could change the emptiness he still felt in his heart that she simply hadn't been able to fill.

"Just call me when you can," she finished in a weak voice before hanging up.

He knew he should call her back, but this was too important: he didn't want to tip her off that he planned to come down to the lab or she'd tell him not to. If she'd wanted him there, she would have invited him when she called. He knew that she would be doing the right thing, the professional thing, by not letting him get involved. He hoped that if he just showed up down there, she'd at least let him observe. She might be angry with him, but Jack doubted she would turn him away. He felt like he was using her, taking advantage of their relationship, and it twisted the knife of guilt a bit deeper.

"Fuck it," he cursed, starting up the Defender and backing out into the rain, the garage door rolling closed behind him.

Winding his way out of his neighborhood, he got onto the Capital Beltway, heading west toward I-95. He had to keep his speed down because of the rain, and was thankful that there wasn't too much traffic at this wretched time of night. He'd had enough tragedy for one day, and didn't need any idiots on the beltway to make it worse. His

Defender, which he'd bought after Emily's death, had already weathered two accidents on the beltway. The tough SUV had come through with little more than a few dings and scratches, while the other cars had ended up as lumps of misshapen metal. Fortunately, no one had been seriously injured, but the accidents had put to rest any guilt Jack had felt at spending so much on a vehicle.

He was halfway to the ramp for I-95 South when he saw the exit for Van Dorn Street, and it suddenly struck him that Sheldon's condo was only a mile and a half away. He and Sheldon had long ago exchanged keys (and, in Sheldon's case, the code for his condo's security system) so they could check on each other's places when business trips took them off somewhere. Sheldon usually told Jack not to bother checking his place, since if anything went seriously wrong the condo management would take care of it. Jack hadn't been there since before Sheldon had left on his most recent assignment.

Jack vacillated over whether he should go there. The Bureau had probably already sent a team to look for leads in Sheldon's murder, or would be as soon as they could get a search warrant. It probably wouldn't be a good idea for Jack to drop by while his fellow agents were going through the place.

On the other hand, he did have a legitimate reason to be there: he was the executor of Sheldon's will, and was going to have to face that unpleasant duty sooner or later. But that would be a thin excuse to Clement if other agents found him wandering around Sheldon's place. Jack could hardly claim he didn't know Sheldon's condo would be searched, but he doubted Clement would bust his ass over it.

His indecision almost made him miss the exit, and he had to stomp on the brakes and swerve to make it. Still going too fast, he had to wrestle the Defender through the tight loop that took him back over the beltway to the intersection with Van Dorn.

"Okay," he breathed, his system pumped full of adrenaline from nearly rolling over in the turn, "I'm awake now."

From there, he drove north the short distance to Sheldon's condo, and pulled into an empty parking space near where Sheldon usually parked. Jack took a quick look around, but couldn't see his friend's car. Sheldon generally left it here when he went on trips out of town.

More importantly, there weren't any FBI or police vehicles here. Yet.

Darting through the rain, he entered the lobby area that was empty except for a bored-looking young woman behind the counter. He waved to her as he walked across the lobby, but she didn't bother looking up.

Jack moved on to the elevators, punching the "up" button. One of the elevators opened immediately, and Jack got in and pushed the button for the tenth floor. Once there, he headed down the hallway to Sheldon's place.

He felt a chill as he turned the key in the lock and opened the door: the security system remained silent. It should have been beeping urgently, warning him that he only had thirty seconds to enter the code before the alert center and the front desk were notified of a possible break-in. Sheldon always set it, even if he was just running out for a few minutes. Jack had once joked that he thought Sheldon was paranoid. However, after his friend had finished explaining how much some of the computer equipment he had in his back room was worth, Jack never joked about it again.

The condo had an entryway vestibule that blocked the view to most of the darkened living room area. Jack felt stark naked as he stood in the doorway, silhouetted by the light from the hallway. The hair on the back of his neck suddenly stood on end and he felt gooseflesh break out on his arms.

Something's not right.

He quickly stepped through the door, out of the light, and eased the door closed, careful not to let it latch in case he needed to make a fast exit. Then he drew his Glock and flipped off the safety. Crouching down in one corner of the vestibule, his gun aimed into the living room, he let his eyes adjust to the darkness while he listened intently for the sound of any potential threats.

The first thing he noticed was the smell, a strange jumble of odors in the apartment. It was coming from the kitchen, which was immediately to his left. It was as if someone had taken the kitchen's contents and mixed them together on the kitchen floor.

There was something else, too, very faint among the other scents, but still distinguishable, that he couldn't quite place. It was like nothing he'd ever smelled before, an unpleasant cross between ammonia and burning hemp that would have been nauseating had it been any stronger.

He waited a full minute, listening intently as he fought to keep his own breathing as quiet as possible. All he could hear was the faint noise of cars going by on the street beyond the parking lot, ten floors below. There was no sound from the adjoining condos, or from the units above and below: everyone in this part of the building seemed to be asleep.

Staying low, he reached around the wall to the right, feeling for the light switch in the living room while his eyes and weapon remained fixed on the living room area. His finger tensed on the trigger as he flipped on the lights and saw what lay before him.

"Holy shit," he breathed. The living room looked like a tornado had ripped through it. Every piece of furniture had been upended and torn apart, the stuffing from the chairs and sofa mounded in white, fluffy piles.

As he continued to scan the room over the sights of his gun for any threats, he further considered the scene. This is a fully-occupied condo building, he thought. Whoever did this couldn't have made a lot of noise, or someone would've called building security or the cops.

After a moment, he had the chilling realization that the living room furniture bore more than a passing resemblance to Sheldon's body at the murder scene. The sofa and chairs hadn't merely been torn apart: they had been very methodically dissected. The fabric had been ripped or cut along the seams and folded beside the bone-like frames, and the stuffing was piled carefully, with no loose fibers scattered about. It was all neat and orderly. Precisely cut to pieces. *Just like Sheldon*, he thought grimly.

Changing position in the vestibule, he aimed the gun toward the hallway that led to the kitchen, bathroom, and the two bedrooms. He noticed that all the vent registers had been unscrewed from the walls and set aside, exposing the ducts. Whoever had searched this place had been thorough, indeed.

From what he could see with only the living room lights on, the kitchen was just as much of a mess as the living room. The contents of every single container from the refrigerator, freezer, and cabinets had been emptied onto the floor. The empty boxes, jars, and cans were stacked neatly along one wall.

Jack moved quickly from the cover of the vestibule to the hallway. He quickly checked the lavatory, again noting how everything that could be opened had been carefully searched and discarded. Then he moved farther down the hall to the two bedrooms. The master bedroom, where Sheldon slept, looked just like the living room: a shambles. The master bathroom was the same.

Stepping quietly to the end of the hall, Jack poked the muzzle of his gun into the darkened second bedroom, where Sheldon had all of his computer and audio equipment. He flipped on the light.

Like the other rooms, everything had been meticulously searched. The computer cases, all seven of them, had been torn or hacked open and the hard drives ripped out. The two laptops Sheldon used for his audio work, one for composing, the other for mixing, were cracked open like crabs, the drives pried from the cases.

The thing that most disturbed him was the strange ammonia-burning hemp smell: it was the strongest in here, far stronger than it had been in the kitchen.

"What the hell were they looking for?" he wondered aloud. Satisfied that the apartment was clear, he still held onto the Glock. Just in case.

He took one last look around the computer room before moving back down the hallway toward the kitchen, turning the lights off behind. He wasn't concerned about leaving fingerprints, because his prints and fibers were already all over the condo from the many times he'd been here. He just hoped that he hadn't destroyed any possible evidence of the intruder or intruders in the course of his search.

Jack found himself standing in the kitchen, careful to stay well away from the mound of dumped-out food beside the central island. He didn't want to leave any smoking-gun evidence that he had been here before the cops or other Bureau agents.

Looking at the top of the island, he saw that its surface was smeared with a mishmash of food. Jack realized that the intruders must have dumped out every container onto the island's big cutting board, sifted through the contents, and then swept it all off onto the floor before setting the container carefully against the wall. It was bizarre. And the containers hadn't been opened as the manufacturers had intended: cans, boxes, and plastic bottles looked like they'd been gnawed open, while glass jars and beer bottles were all broken off at the top, as if whoever had opened them had either bitten down on the glass, or perhaps had been so strong that the container simply shattered. Glancing at the mound of food, he could see glittering glass fragments and crushed lids poking out of the runny debris.

Kneeling down, he looked carefully at the pile of food surrounding the island like a moat. *No footprints*, he thought, shocked. The intruders must have been standing right next to the island while they tore

Sheldon's kitchen to bits, dumping all the food on the floor, but there wasn't a single footprint in the entire ankle-deep mess to show where they'd been standing. There also weren't any prints or smears of food on the floor leading away into other parts of the house or to the front door, which was the only exit. It was as if the intruders had been levitating while they'd made this mess.

"That's not possible," he whispered.

The counters that formed a U shape around the island held all of the dishes, bowls, glasses, and other kitchen paraphernalia that had been in the cabinets. In stark contrast to the mess around the island, the items on the counter had all been stacked neatly, no doubt after having been removed and inspected for whatever the intruders hoped to find here. A rack for Sheldon's copper-bottomed pans and pots hung over the island, but Jack knew it couldn't support a man's weight. He had helped Sheldon put it up, and while it was sturdy, it wasn't *that* sturdy. There was no way someone could cling to it to stay clear of the mess before somehow springing into the living room to reach the front door to leave. There were no prints evident on the island, although that could only be verified with a thorough examination by a forensic team.

The only thing Jack saw that he was sure was new was a set of deep grooves near one edge of the cutting board, as if someone had driven some sort of wave-shaped blade into the wood. It gave him the creeps, but he didn't know why.

The fresh condition of the perishable food dumped on the kitchen floor told him that the condo had been ransacked recently. He knelt down and with the back of his hand touched the mangled remains of a frozen roast that had been hacked apart. It was no longer frozen, but was still quite cold.

They were here only a few hours ago, he thought, a chill running up his spine as he snatched his hand away and stood up. Had he gotten it in his mind to drive over here earlier, perhaps after leaving the Hoover Building that evening, things might have been interesting to the point of being deadly.

He moved back into the living room, his mind again returning to the question of *why*. It was about information, he felt certain, something that Sheldon had found before he died. The computers were the obvious thing to start with, and the intruders had simply torn out the hard drives, just like the ones at the LRU lab in Nebraska.

But the search of the furniture, the food, even the toilet cleaning supplies told him that they were also looking for something else, something that wasn't in the computers. They'd spent a considerable amount of time here and taken a lot of risk to dig through everything, so they had some expectation that it, whatever "it" was, would be here.

It must have been small, he thought, *or they wouldn't have bothered searching through the smaller jars and containers.* He couldn't think of what it might be, unless it was some sort of small data storage device, like the thumb drive that Sheldon used for his hacker tools. Presumably his killers found that, because he never went anywhere without it, and Richards had said it hadn't been found in the search at LRU.

Frowning, Jack recalled that Sheldon had never mentioned a secret or special place, a wall safe, perhaps, where he might hide something here. He didn't even have a safe deposit box, and Jack felt confident that if he did have one he would have told Jack, and probably given him a key. That was the level of trust the two men had shared.

But why didn't he tell you what he'd gotten into? Jack asked himself.

Frustrated, Jack knew he had to get down to Quantico, but found himself in a conundrum. He had to report this and get a crime scene crew in here, but he didn't want to be delayed in getting down to the lab or drop himself into hot water by being here in the first place. He knew he must have been recorded by the security cameras in the lobby, even if the woman at the front desk hadn't gotten a good look at him, so he couldn't just pretend not to have been here. If he called headquarters, there was a better than even chance that Clement would find out in about five minutes and pin him to the wall for getting involved after he'd been told to butt out. He also couldn't just call the local cops to delay the information getting to the Bureau. Clement would kick his ass even harder for that. Calling the Washington Field Office would normally have been the best choice: located on 4th Street Northwest, it had jurisdiction for the greater D.C. area, its territory extending south and west into Virginia. Unfortunately, even that would probably land him in front of Clement's desk. It would just take about ten minutes longer.

He only had one remaining alternative.

"Shit," he muttered as he pulled out his phone and dialed.

After two rings he heard, "Special Agent Richards. This is getting pretty tiresome, Dawson."

He's got me in his address book now, Jack thought with a grim smile. "I've got something for you, but I need you to keep Clement off my back until I'm done at the lab."

"You're not there yet?" Richards snapped.

"No..." Jack hesitated. "I stopped at Sheldon's condo on the way."

"You dumb fuck!" Richards exploded. "You know better than that!"

"Listen," Jack said quickly, cutting him off from what he knew would be a well-deserved tongue-lashing, but now wasn't the time, "the place has been methodically torn to pieces. I've never seen anything like this. They pulled Crane's hard drives just like they did at the LRU labs, but I don't think they found what they were really looking for. And I'm pretty sure the condo was ransacked in the last few hours."

"Goddammit, Dawson," Richards growled, and Jack could imagine his bald head flushed red with barely suppressed anger, "you just contaminated the crime scene, you idiot."

"Bullshit," Jack told him. "This place is already loaded with physical evidence from me: I've been here quite a few times, remember?" He shook his head as he looked around at the gutted living room, recalling the vision of the mess in the kitchen without any hand- or footprints anywhere. "No, aside from the mess itself, I don't think the forensics guys are going to find much of anything here. This is really weird, Richards. This job was tackled by a ghost."

"Same here," Richards told him, his voice taking on a tone more of resigned frustration than anger. "I hope your lab girlfriend has more luck, because our forensics team here hasn't come up with anything at all other than bits and pieces of Crane. If we had to make a case based on nothing but the physical evidence we've got here, we'd have to say that he gutted himself."

Jack cringed at the words, and was shocked to hear Richards apologize.

"Sorry, Dawson. That was a shitty thing to say, even for me."

"Don't worry about it," Jack told him. "But listen, I need you to cover for me. We've got to get a team over here right away, but I want to get down to the lab before Clement wrings my neck."

Richards sighed. "Jesus, Dawson, you're pulling an awfully big tiger by the tail," he said. "All right. Give me the address there so I don't have to look it up." Jack told him. "I'll come up with some bullshit story to cover your ass for now, but you're going to have to pay the piper on this one eventually. So will I, I'm sure. You owe me, big time."

"How about a lifetime supply of Rogaine?" Jack asked as he backed out of the condo and carefully closed the door, making sure it latched and locked before he headed down the hall.

"Real funny, Dawson," Richards grunted. "Fuck you and the horse you rode in on." Then the line went dead.

Five

Back in his Defender, Jack made his way from Sheldon's condo to I-95 and headed south toward Quantico. The trip passed in the rhythmic blur and scrape of the windshield wipers as he tried to focus on what had happened since he'd found out about Sheldon's death. He was letting his mind spin again, just as he had at home, trying to figure out what the intruders at the condo had been looking for, but his brain refused to cooperate.

He got off on Exit 148 toward Marine Corps Base Quantico, then turned right onto Russell Road. From there, it was one and a half miles to the base entrance. After showing his badge to the Marines on duty, Jack drove two miles through the pitch-black woods of the base to the entrance of the FBI compound where the Academy and the lab were located. He checked through another guard post before he turned left on J. Edgar Hoover Road, then circled around the lab complex and entered the parking garage. He pulled into one of the open spaces on the ground floor and turned off the Defender's engine.

Sitting there for just a moment, listening to the *tink...tink...tink* sound as the engine cooled, he suffered another twinge of guilt at not having called Jerri, and knew that she would probably not be at all happy that he'd turned up here. But she would forgive him for it.

A bit late to worry about it now, he chided himself as he got out of the car and jogged through the rain along the curving concrete path to the front entrance. In the daytime, it was an impressive multi-storied structure of stone and glass, with nine large vent pipes in clusters of three rising from the roof. While Jack had never been partial to modern architectural design, the lab's architects had made a functional design that was also fairly attractive.

Right now, in the dark and pouring rain, lit by periodic flashes of lightning in the distance, he had the sudden impression of Frankenstein's castle on the fateful night when the madman's monster was brought to life.

Making his way through the main entrance, showing his badge to the building's security officers, he headed straight for Jerri's lab. He had barely pushed the door open when she was in his arms.

"Jesus, Jack," she said after kissing him on the cheek, then drawing him back into a tight embrace. The top of her head came to just above his shoulder. Her hair was jet black and long, flowing down her back nearly to her waist. She had almond-shaped eyes that were as beautiful as they were expressive, and the complexion typical of someone of Japanese ancestry. "Why didn't you call me?" she asked softly.

"Because I wanted to be here when they brought in the evidence, and..." The words caught in his throat and he felt his eyes begin to tear up again.

"And you thought I wouldn't let you come down," Jerri finished for him, standing back enough to meet his gaze. "You should know me better than that."

Jack, at a loss for words, only nodded as he fought to keep himself together.

"Listen," she told him, cupping his face in her hands, "don't do the macho idiot thing on me, okay?"

"Okay," he breathed. "I promise. No more macho crap."

She smiled, then stood up on her tiptoes and kissed him lightly on the lips. "Good," she told him. "Now, let's—"

"Jerri!" someone said urgently, poking his head in the door from the hallway, "It's here!"

"Okay," she told him, giving Jack a reassuring squeeze before she turned to the man in the hallway. "We're ready. Let's get rolling."

A small army of technicians went through everything that was in the boxes sent from the Lincoln team, sorting out what needed to go where. The FBI Laboratory was made up of nearly twenty units that focused on various aspects of crime scene and related analysis, including Jerri's unit, DNA Analysis Unit-1, which specialized in nuclear DNA analysis. Many of the samples retrieved by the on-scene forensics team had traces of blood on them, and Jerri's unit had to analyze the blood before the other units could do their work.

She quickly organized her staff to take samples from the clothing and other items that had been sent, and set up the necessary tests for samples that had been swabbed from the walls and other areas around the murder scene and the LRU lab by the forensics team in Lincoln.

The last cardboard evidence box to be opened, and the one she decided to handle herself, was the one containing Sheldon's weapon and two extra magazines. Weapons were normally unloaded before they

were transported for analysis, but in the case of weapons that had blood
or other evidential residue that might be at risk if the weapon were
handled to unload it, the weapon was put on safe before it was bagged,
tagged, and boxed, with a warning on the box indicating it was loaded.
Sheldon's weapon and the magazines had certainly fit the criteria: they
were all spattered with blood.

Wearing latex gloves and a face mask, Jerri first removed the two
magazines from the box. She took several swabs of the blood on each
one, with Jack carefully bagging and cataloging everything.

"Okay," she said after she'd swabbed the exterior of the first
magazine, "go ahead and unload it, and I'll take a couple of samples
from the bullets, just for grins. We won't test those right away, but I
don't want to leave anything to chance on this. Swabs are cheap."

After Jack unloaded the bullets from the first magazine, Jerri took
three swabs of bullets that looked like they had some traces of blood on
the casings from where blood had seeped inside the magazine. Then
she swabbed the outside of the magazine.

They repeated the process for the second magazine, with Jerri
taking swabs from three spots on the metal, then handing them to Jack
to file.

He had just sealed the second magazine into an evidence bag and
was marking it when he heard a low voice behind him.

"He shouldn't be here."

Turning around, Jack found a man wearing lab gear, staring at him
as if he were a particularly offensive insect.

"He's here on my authority," Jerri grated, standing up from her lab
stool. "Jack," she said with cool formality, "meet Dr. Martin Kilburn.
He was sent over from CODIS to give us a hand." The CODIS Unit
was where the Combined DNA Index System, or CODIS, was
managed. The results from the DNA tests from Jerri's team would be
entered into the massive CODIS database for storage and cross-
indexing. "He seems to forget who's in charge here." She stared up at
Kilburn, her normally warm eyes ice cold.

Kilburn ignored her, and continued to stare at Jack.

"Hey, doc," Jack said, nodding. Shaking hands was out of the
question with everyone wearing latex gloves and handling evidence,
but Jack wouldn't have been inclined to shake Kilburn's hand anyway.
His rude behavior and disrespect toward Jerri had already seriously
pissed him off. "Don't you have some work of your own to do?"

"He shouldn't be here," Kilburn repeated, finally glancing at Jerri. "He's emotionally involved and he's not assigned to this unit."

"Neither are you," Jerri snapped. "Now get back to what you were sent down here to do or get the hell out."

Kilburn stared at Jack for a moment more, then turned and stalked out of the lab.

"Jesus," Jack whispered, "what a creep."

"He's only been here a few months," Jerri told him, shaking her head in disgust. "Don't feel bad about the way he treated you. He's like that with everybody. Not surprisingly, nobody likes him, but the CODIS people say he's a whiz over there with the DNA database. I'll take their word for it."

"Where the hell did they dig him up?"

"I think he was working as a researcher for an agri-business before coming here," Jerri said. "New Horizons, I think."

Jack felt like someone had rammed a frozen steel rod down his spine. "New Horizons, huh?" he said quietly. *Now there's a coincidence*, he thought. "The university lab where Sheldon was killed was set up by New Horizons," he told her. "And we think he may have been investigating computer intrusions against their other labs."

She sat back on her stool, eyes wide in surprise. "No kidding? Any idea as to who's doing it?"

"Yes," Jack grated, the image of Naomi Perrault flashing into his mind, unbidden. "It looks like a group that's screening itself behind UFO garbage on the web, if you believe that. The Earth Defense Society, EDS. The team in Lincoln found one of their flyers crammed down Sheldon's throat. We don't know yet, but it looks like they're engaged in some sort of industrial espionage, possibly stealing genetic technology from New Horizons. Apparently they decided to move up the criminal ladder by killing an FBI agent."

They both looked up as Kilburn reentered the lab. He threw Jack a smug smile before returning to his table and getting back to work, looking for anomalous fibers in Sheldon's torn-apart clothing.

"Asshole," Jerri muttered as she nudged Jack. "Let's get back to it."

Not trusting himself to say anything more about the good Dr. Kilburn, Jack reached into the cardboard evidence box and withdrew the bag containing Sheldon's Glock 22. His backup weapon, the Glock 27, was also in the box, in a separate bag, but wasn't a priority right now: the field team in Lincoln had determined that there wasn't any blood or other suspicious residue on it, and it hadn't been fired. After being inspected carefully in the field, it had been unloaded and packed into the evidence box.

The Glock 22, however, had definitely been fired. Sheldon had emptied one magazine, the one Jack and Jerri had just finished sampling, of its fifteen rounds, and had fired at least three more just before he was killed, based on the number of brass casings that had been found by the body. The weapon had blood spattered all over it.

And there was something else.

"Unidentified residue on gun muzzle," Jerri murmured as she read the note that had been stuck on the outside of the box containing the weapon.

"I wonder why they didn't have that in the report?" Jack said.

Jerri glanced at him, a wry smile on her lips. "You read all the field reporting?"

"Well...yeah," Jack confessed. "It was all in FIDS." He shrugged. "Listen, Clement sent me home because he thought I was an emotional basket case, which maybe was true. But what was I going to do? Just sit and watch the boob tube?"

"Well," she told him, "this *was* reported. It was in a follow-up they added just before they shipped it out. You were probably on the road by then. One of the more senior techs in Lincoln took a second look at the gun and found something odd around the muzzle that didn't appear to be blood."

"Right," Jack said. "Okay, let's get this done."

He carefully removed the weapon from the stiff cardboard box and laid it on the table under the lights. Jerri focused a high definition video camera on the weapon, looking at the magnified image on a flat panel display. She tapped a few buttons on the touch-sensitive screen to enhance the resolution and add some color filters to help make the residue stand out more.

"Yeah," she murmured, pointing to a very faint speckling of an amber-colored liquid right around the gun's muzzle. It was very faint, and she was surprised the Lincoln team had found it. "See, right here, there's definitely something, and it's not blood. If I had to guess, I'd say it's back-spatter from a bullet impact at extremely close range."

"We're talking inches, Jerri," Jack said grimly, trying to imagine who, or what, would have gotten so close to a man who was still firing a gun.

"At most," she agreed, zooming in even further.

"And why is it just around the muzzle?" he wondered. "Why wouldn't there have been other traces left at the scene?"

"I don't know, Jack," she said, shaking her head as she wondered the same thing. "I can't imagine what it is."

"One way to find out," Jack told her, handing her a set of swabs.

She took several samples, then told Jack as he cataloged them, "Set those aside for me, please. I want to take a look at those as soon as I've finished sampling the outside of the weapon. I'm pretty sure the rest of this is going to turn out to be Sheldon's blood, but whatever this is on the muzzle is definitely something else." Then she began to methodically take swabs of blood from the weapon to finish up the job.

"Okay," she said, finally handing him the last of five bloody swabs, now stained a dark maroon. "I think we're done with his weapon. Go ahead and unload it and get it boxed up." She picked up the swabs of the unidentified substance they'd taken from the gun and told Jack, "I'm going to get these set up for analysis. I'll be back."

Jack watched her head off toward the lab next door where the DNA analysis equipment was, her feet beating a rapid tattoo across the hard floor. He caught Kilburn looking at him again. The man smiled slyly before turning back to his work.

"Pissant," Jack muttered as he turned back to his own task. Making sure the Glock's safety was engaged, he released the magazine, then pulled the slide back to eject the round in the chamber before putting the weapon in a fresh evidence box that he'd already labeled.

Then he changed his gloves, not wanting to accidentally contaminate the magazine that had been in the weapon before he examined it. Aside from a trace of blood on the bottom, which Jerri had already sampled, the magazine's exterior appeared to be clean. The rear of the magazine had holes that showed how many rounds remained. Counting the glint of the bullet primers showing in the holes, Jack saw that the magazine, which had a capacity of fifteen rounds, held only twelve now. While ballistics would need to confirm it, Jack felt certain that the three .40 caliber brass cartridges the Lincoln team had found around Sheldon's body were from this magazine.

Looking more closely, Jack saw something odd. In the hole for round thirteen, which should have simply been dark and empty, he saw...something. He couldn't tell what it was, even through the zoomed-in view on the video display.

"What the hell," he muttered. He began to thumb the rounds out of the magazine, since he had to unload it anyway, carefully putting each bullet into a bag that he'd already marked for the purpose.

He was just about to take out the last round when his cell phone rang. He felt his stomach suddenly curl into a tight, acidic ball, because the ringtone was that of a dog barking, and the only numbers he'd assigned that particular ringtone were the ones that Clement used.

"Shit," he cursed, quickly setting down the magazine. Forgetting to remove the latex gloves, he grabbed the phone from his pocket and hit the answer button. "Special Agent Dawson," he answered, trying to muster as much dignity as he could. Out of the corner of his eye, he saw Kilburn set down his samples before strutting in Jack's direction.

"I'm going to call your house phone in exactly sixty minutes," Clement said quietly. "If you don't pick up the phone and give me your word of honor that you won't stick your nose any further into Sheldon's case, I'll expect to see you at eight a.m. sharp to turn in your gun and your badge. Do you understand what I just said, Special Agent Dawson?"

"Yes, sir," Jack said, feeling like a turd for disappointing Clement. He wanted to try and explain himself, but now definitely wasn't the time. He stared daggers at Kilburn, who stood right next to him now with a gloating expression on his face. "I understand. I'll talk to you in an–"

Clement hung up before Jack could finish.

"You son-of-a-bitch," Jack growled as he turned to confront Kilburn.

The DNA specialist suddenly seemed to realize that being so close to an enraged man who outweighed him by a good twenty pounds, had experience in close combat, and was also armed probably wasn't a good thing. Shuffling backward a few steps, he pointed at Jack. "You're not properly trained in this line of work!" he said in righteous indignation. "You–"

"*What the hell is going on?*" Jerri said from behind him, a fierce glare in her eyes.

"Your buddy here ratted me out to Clement," Jack said, clenching his gloved hands. He knew he would be canned if he did it, but the urge to throttle Kilburn was nearly overpowering. "I've got to go."

"We'll see about that!" Jerri nearly shouted, drawing sudden looks from the other technicians working in the lab. Then she started in on Kilburn, using a vocabulary that Jack never would have guessed at.

"Jerri," he tried to interject, "forget it..."

She didn't hear him, or pretended not to as she continued to ream Kilburn. The man, gesticulating wildly, sputtered in protest, and the two of them made an incredible scene that brought the work in the lab to a complete halt as everyone watched in silent amazement.

With a heavy sigh, Jack turned back to the magazine lying on the table, deciding that he had enough time to finish unloading it before getting back on the road toward home. He carefully thumbed out the last bullet and watched, dumbstruck, as four golden kernels of corn popped out into his gloved hand.

Shit, he thought as his eyes went wide with realization, and his mind suddenly spun back to his mental image of Sheldon's last moments. *This is what he'd been after in the lab, what he'd taken.* Even the last shots he fired at whoever killed him had probably been another distraction: who would think of looking for something hidden in a weapon that had just been fired? Instead, his killer figured that Sheldon had swallowed the corn, and had carved him up to find it.

Jack then had a sudden flash of insight, one that was based not on rational, considered thought, but on instinct alone. *Kilburn*, he thought. Jack was somehow sure that Kilburn's presence here in the lab wasn't an accident. Kilburn coming from New Horizons to work for CODIS, then just happening to be tapped to help with the evidence from Sheldon's murder, seemed like too much of a coincidence.

Despite the promise Jack was going to make to Clement to butt out of the case to save his job, he had to at least call Richards in Lincoln and give him a heads-up that Kilburn might be in league with the EDS. There was no way that Jack was going to let Kilburn see what had been hidden in the magazine of Sheldon's weapon, because he felt sure in his gut that was why Kilburn was here: to find anything that Sheldon's killer – or killers – had missed.

That clinched it. Jack knew that he would be fired, and could possibly face a prison sentence, for what he was about to do, but he saw no alternative. Concealing his hand from Kilburn behind his body, he dropped the bullet he had been holding into the evidence bag while still holding onto the kernels. Then he peeled off the glove, trapping the kernels as the glove snapped inside-out. He took off the glove from his left hand and threw it away, while surreptitiously sliding the glove containing the corn into one of the outside pockets of his jacket.

"Listen, Jerri," he said, gently taking her by the shoulder and turning her away from her confrontation with the still-blustering Kilburn, "I've got to go."

"I'm so sorry, Jack," she said hoarsely, blinking back tears of anger, her entire body shaking with rage. "Promise me you'll call me?"

"I will," he told her, meaning it. He had to talk to her about the corn, although he wasn't sure how he was going to do it without making an even bigger mess of his own situation. "I promise."

"Good." Then, turning to Kilburn, she said in an ice-cold voice, "And please escort Dr. Kilburn out of my lab, if you'd be so kind. His services are no longer needed here."

"With pleasure," Jack said with a feral smile, gesturing toward the door. "Doctor, shall we?"

There was a moment, a brief flash in time, when Jack saw a look of deep suspicion pass across Kilburn's face like a fleeting shadow.

Then it was gone. With a final sneer, Kilburn turned on his heel and stalked out, slamming open the heavy door to the lab.

After giving Jerri's hand a gentle squeeze, Jack followed him out. By the time he got to the door, Kilburn was already out of sight, having turned down one of the other corridors.

Jack made his way back out of the building, running through the continuing downpour to the parking garage. Wrenching the door shut on the Defender after he got in, he slammed his hands on the steering wheel.

"*Fuck!*" he shouted, venting an emotional brew of anger, frustration, and fear. Glancing at his watch, he saw that he had to get going if he was to meet Clement's deadline. He started up the car and backed out of the space, then roared out into the rain.

***

After Jack left, Jerri went around the lab, seeing how the others were coming with their own evidence samples, and explaining the cause of the scene she had made earlier with Kilburn.

Once that was done, she went back over to the DNA analysis lab to look more closely at the anomalous residue from the muzzle of

Sheldon's weapon. When she had brought the swabs over earlier, she had asked one of the lab techs to take a swab and prepare a wet mount slide for Jerri to check before she went ahead with any further testing.

Now, after the emotional confrontation with Kilburn, it was a relief to sit quietly behind a microscope and let her body and mind cool off. At least a little.

Cheryl, the lab's senior tech, had prepared the slide as Jerri had requested, and had mounted it on one of the microscopes arrayed along the wall of the lab.

"Beats the heck out of me what that is," Cheryl said, shaking her head.

Jerri glanced at her, frowning. Cheryl was a competent biologist who had worked in the lab for a dozen years and had seen just about anything that one could look at through a microscope. That she had no clue what was on the slide came as a surprise.

As Jerri bent down to look through the stereo eyepiece, she caught a glimpse of what was on the slide and involuntarily recoiled. "Jesus," she whispered, looking with wide eyes at Cheryl.

"That was my first reaction, too," she said quietly.

Jerri checked the magnification, which was set at 20X. Had this been a blood sample, the field of view would have been filled with hundreds of roundish red blood cells, some completely opaque, some largely transparent except for the outline of the cell membrane, along with the other cells that called the bloodstream home.

But this was...different. The cells in the sample varied wildly in size and shape. The only common traits appeared to be a spherical cellular nucleus that was barely discernible at a magnification of 40X, and a uniform, sickly amber coloration.

"What the hell," she breathed. Flipping on the video output from the microscope, she sat back and looked at the image on the seventeen inch high definition display. "Do you see that?" she asked Cheryl, pointing to what appeared to be a fuzzy cast, almost a blur, over the strange cells. "What's causing that?"

"I don't know," Cheryl said slowly. "The slide's clean. Whatever that is, it's in the sample."

Frowning, Jerri bumped up the magnification to 100X, then 400X. The blurriness seemed to be resolving into a pattern of lines that didn't become completely clear until she pushed it up to the maximum magnification of 1000X.

"My God," Cheryl breathed. "Look at that!"

The amorphous cells were joined together by a complicated web of tiny strands, like the haphazard web of a Black Widow spider, without the sense of order and pattern found in the webs of most other spiders. Even more shocking was that some cells had partially-extended stubs, as if the cells had been in the act of extending or retracting the strands when the sample had been taken.

They didn't notice Dr. Kilburn, staring through the door he had cracked open. His eyes were fixed on the strange cells on the display. After a moment, he silently closed the door.

***

Kilburn walked down the hall to his cubicle in the CODIS unit, ignoring the other lab workers he passed along the way. Next to his desk, there was a file cabinet in which he kept notes and other information that he used as part of his daily work. Glancing around to make sure there was no one who could see what he was doing, Kilburn unlocked the cabinet and opened the bottom drawer. Pulling it all the way out, he reached behind the last set of folders and withdrew a bulky manila envelope. On the outside was written in sloppy script, "A.P. Hawking – Dissertation Draft." Kilburn had brought the envelope in with him one day, right through security, and even left it on his desk in plain view for a while. It wasn't a secret that he periodically mentored graduate students in their DNA studies, although no one could believe a student would willingly pick Kilburn as a mentor. To everyone who happened to see it, it was just another dissertation someone had sent him to review.

He closed and locked the file cabinet. Tucking the package under his arm, he made his way back down the hall to the DNA analysis unit's lab.

But instead of going through the door that would have taken him back into the lab where he and Tanaka had had their confrontation over Dawson, he stopped in front of an electrical closet that was between that lab and the adjoining one where Tanaka had seen...*it*, where she had gotten a glimpse of The Secret.

Glancing up and down the corridor to make sure he was alone, Kilburn slipped on a set of latex gloves, then took a large ring of keys from his pocket. Choosing the key he wanted, he opened the door to the electrical closet. Stepping inside, he quietly closed the door behind him.

The term "closet" was a misnomer, as it was actually a small room, festooned with electrical cables and junction boxes, which jutted into both of the adjoining labs.

Kilburn tore open the envelope and extracted the contents: four M112 demolition charges, bound together, with four embedded primers linked to a detonator with a countdown timer, and an unregistered cell phone. The package held five pounds of C-4 explosive, enough to kill everyone in the adjoining labs and gut most of this floor of the building. He set the timer for ten minutes before stuffing the bomb behind one of the electrical junction boxes.

The door suddenly flew open behind him, and he turned to find Jerri Tanaka standing there.

"What the hell are you doing in here? And how did you get a key?" she demanded, stepping just inside the doorway. "I was just leaving the lab down the hall when I saw you close the door. Don't tell me you're an electrician, too," she added sarcastically.

"No," he said, shaking his head and dropping the phone into his lab coat pocket. "I'm not an electrician. But I do know how to fix things."

Jerri didn't have a chance to respond before he lunged across the three feet separating them, jabbing his right hand, flattened like a knife, into her throat. She gasped for air through her crushed larynx and sagged toward the floor. Kilburn grabbed her by the hair and dragged her into the closet. After a quick look outside, relieved that no one else was in the hallway, he closed the door.

"You have no idea how much I've loathed working with you people," he told her. "But you've made my job a little easier by coming here."

Removing the bomb from its hiding place, he grabbed one of her hands and forced her fingers onto the metal casing of the detonator. Jerri struggled, but it was no use: her body was burning up what oxygen her blood stream had left, her chest heaving in vain to draw breath. And he was strong, much stronger than he looked. "It's a long shot, but with a little luck the investigators might be able to take partial prints from the debris. If not, there's always mitochondrial DNA analysis from any tiny bits that will be left of you here, where you planted the bomb." He grinned at her. "Too bad it went off before you made your getaway. Sloppy, Dr. Tanaka. Very sloppy. I also took the liberty of tucking some information about the Earth Defense Society into your files." Her eyes widened. "Yes, you recognize them from what Dawson told you, I see. I overheard him telling you. The network data center should survive the blast when the bomb goes off, and I'm sure the investigators will find the incriminating documents. If not on their own, I'll help them along, as I plan to survive this.

"And don't worry about your friend Dawson," he told her as he pulled out the cell phone. "We'll take care of him, too." He sent a text message to a twin of the phone he held, another that was unregistered and untraceable. The message said *Jack Dawson knows something.* Then he set the phone on the floor and smashed it with his heel.

Unable to speak, unable to breathe, Jerri could only shake her head, *No.*

He smiled. "The ironic thing is that I'll be able to truthfully tell the investigators that I saw you come in here right before the bomb went off." She stared at the detonator as he put it back in place, then she struggled to reach it. "No, I don't think you'll be doing any last-minute heroics," he told her. "Goodbye, doctor." Then he reached down, took her head in both hands and twisted it savagely, snapping her neck.

With a last look at Jerri, whose lifeless eyes stared up at the ceiling, Kilburn stood up and left the electrical closet. He closed the door behind him, acting as if he had authorization to be there. He wasn't worried about anyone seeing him now, as everyone in the nearby labs would be dead in a few minutes.

As it turned out, no one happened to be in the hallway to appreciate his acting performance or witness his exit from the electrical closet. He returned to his cubicle in the CODIS unit at the end of the hall, where he sat quietly for the next few minutes until the bomb exploded.

Six

Jack had just made it through the door when the phone rang, but it wasn't the house phone, which is what he was expecting: it was his cell phone. He glanced at the caller ID, sure that it would be Clement, but saw with some surprise that it was Richards, out in Nebraska.

"Dammit," Jack muttered, hitting the answer button. "Dawson here," he said. "Make it fast, Richards. I'm expecting a call from Clement…"

"Didn't you hear?" Richards interrupted him.

Jack stopped in his tracks at the tone of the other man's voice. "Hear what?" he asked.

"A bomb went off in the lab at Quantico," Richards told him, "a little less than an hour ago. We're wrapping things up here and heading back to Virginia right now, along with half the field agents from the rest of the goddamn country."

Stunned, Jack simply stood there, staring at his reflection in the sliding glass door to the patio. He felt completely numb, as if every nerve ending in his body had suddenly died.

"Dawson, are you there?"

"Yeah," Jack whispered. "Jesus. It must have gone off right after I left." He shook his head, trying to focus his mind. "Do you know how bad the damage was?"

"Really bad," Richards said. "The entire wing, the floor where the DNA labs were, is just gone, like a giant took a fucking bite out of the building. The CODIS unit was mangled, but a couple people survived." He paused. "Nobody from either of the DNA analysis labs made it, Dawson. I'm sorry."

"Jerri…" Jack fumbled with a chair at the kitchen table, practically falling into it. *First Sheldon, now Jerri*, he thought, horrified. *What the fuck is going on?*

"Listen," Richards went on. "When Clement called me to recall our teams, he told me to pass on to you to stay the hell put and not get involved. He said he was supposed to call you, but he's taking the lead as SAC on this himself, and he's got more urgent things to take care of right now than babysitting your ass. You got that?"

"Yeah," Jack told him, biting back the anguish that suddenly threatened to overwhelm him. "Yeah, I got it."

"And Jack," Richards said, which got Jack's attention because Richards never called other agents by their first names, "you're probably going to get grilled over this. You know that, right?"

"Why?" Jack asked angrily. "Am I a suspect?"

"If you were in my shoes, what would you think?" Richards said evenly. "It's the timing, Jack, and the fact that you weren't supposed to be there. Everybody's going to be extra paranoid right now, and anything that stands out is going to draw attention like bees to honey."

"And flies to shit," Jack muttered. "Yeah, I'd do the same."

Richards paused before saying, "I've gotta go, Dawson. Stay put and don't do anything stupid for a change."

"Thanks, Richards," Jack said before hanging up and setting the phone down on the table.

He looked down as Alexander brushed up against his leg and made a mournful meow, begging for attention. Jack reached down and picked him up. Alexander curled up in his lap, and Jack absently stroked him as he thought about what Richards had said. *Jerri and the others were dead. The only survivors from that part of the floor were from the CODIS unit.*

A surge of anger welled up from his core as he imagined Kilburn, battered but alive, staggering out of the smoldering wreckage while Jerri's broken body lay somewhere in the debris.

His mind automatically began churning over possibilities about what happened at the lab. But it was useless, like an engine running in neutral and going nowhere because he knew absolutely nothing. He decided that he was going to follow Richards' advice and not get involved in this one. He wasn't even going to log into FIDS. He was afraid of what he might find there.

Jack didn't know how much time had passed before a chiming ringtone sounded. At first, he thought it was his laptop, but it was closed, in standby. When he finally looked at his phone, he saw that it was an Internet chat program that Sheldon had insisted on loading onto it. It was the same program they had used to stay in touch with one another on the computer, but Jack had never used it on the phone: he hated trying to type on the tiny touch keyboard.

Frowning, he pulled the phone closer, and felt his stomach turn to ice at what he saw:

feeb_master is requesting a chat. Accept? Y/N

feeb_master was Sheldon's user ID on the chat service. "Feeb" was a slang term for an FBI agent, and like everything else with Sheldon, his user name was humorously irreverent but not excessively obnoxious. "Master," of course, referred to his not-so-humble belief that he was the top dog in the Cyber Division in terms of computer smarts, if not in-house political savvy.

What chilled Jack to the bone was that he knew Sheldon would never, ever have compromised any of his on-line information: he changed his passwords constantly, and they weren't anything that someone was going to guess or even break with a password cracker unless they had a powerful computer and a lot of time on their hands. Beyond the braggadocio, Sheldon was – had been – a pro at what he did. So whoever was trying to call Jack now had either been given the information willingly before Sheldon was killed, which seemed damned unlikely, or had forced it out of him with torture or drugs.

An image of Naomi Perrault again sprang to mind, her blue and brown eyes looking out at him over a pretty smile as she stood, figuratively or literally, over Sheldon's mutilated body.

The phone chimed again, and Jack's hands were shaking as he reached for it. He wanted to hit the *N* key and terminate the connection, but he had to know. He *had* to.

He hit the *Y* key, accepting the chat request, and a second later the application's interface popped up on the phone's screen. Then whoever was on the far end, using Sheldon's pirated account, began to type:

feeb_master: they r cmng 4 u, jack. soon.
feeb_master: we r sndng help but may not arrv in time.

Jack bit back a curse as he typed a response, which was the question he wanted answered more than anything, because he felt sure it was the key to the entire puzzle of Sheldon's death, and now Jerri's.

jack_dawson7: who are you?
feeb_master: u have a cat.

"What?" Jack exclaimed at the nonsensical response. He glanced from the phone to Alexander, who still sat in his lap, purring, his intense green eyes fixed on the phone in Jack's hand as if he could read the words there.

Before Jack could type anything else, he saw this:

feeb_master: they hate cats. watch alexander. trust his instincts. trust ur own. have ur shotgun rdy. glock wont work.

Had he been typing at his computer keyboard, he would have been hammering at the keys. On the phone, he was nearly crying in frustration as he struggled with the tiny touchpad, finally repeating his question, "shouting" it to whoever was on the other end:

jack_dawson7: WHO THE FUCK ARE YOU???

There was a pause, and then he got his answer:

feeb_master: naomi perrault. b careful jack.

Then the connection was broken. Jack tried to reconnect using the address book in the chat application, but the icon showing Sheldon's on-line status was grayed out. Dead. Just like Sheldon.

"Goddammit," Jack cried, slamming his fist down on the table, wanting to throw the phone against the wall and smash it to bits. Startled, Alexander leaped out of Jack's lap, and he turned to stare accusingly at Jack before lying down on the floor like a living Sphinx, watching his human closely.

Jack didn't know what to do. With Sheldon and Jerri gone, there was no one he could turn to now. Even Richards, as surprisingly helpful as he had been, couldn't help him, because Jack was going to be near the top of the list of potential suspects, and Richards very well might be the one who'd be knocking on Jack's door. Or knocking it down.

Have your shotgun ready, Perrault – if that's truly who it had been – had said in the pidgin English often used in on-line conversations. *The Glock won't work.* Had she just assumed that he had a shotgun, or was it something else she and her EDS friends had squeezed out of Sheldon? What she had said about the Glock was chilling: Sheldon's certainly hadn't done him any good. And what was that ridiculous nonsense about watching Alexander and trusting his instincts?

"If that was her," he said to himself, looking at Alexander, "then she's even crazier than I thought." On the other hand, she also said she was sending "help." Maybe having his shotgun ready to greet them might not be such a bad idea.

Determined to do something and not just sit on his ass, Jack took off his still-wet jacket and draped it over one of the kitchen chairs. Then he got up, went into his bedroom and opened the closet. He grabbed his shotgun from the gun rack and quickly checked to make sure it was loaded. A rarity in America, it was a Russian-made semi-automatic Saiga-12. Jack had always hated pump-action shotguns, and had special ordered his Saiga-12 after returning from Afghanistan. It held a seven-round box magazine, loaded with flechette rounds. It was an autoloader, and didn't need to be pumped: you just kept pulling the trigger until the magazine was empty. He had gotten it as an insurance policy if he ever needed something heavier than his handguns, but had never really expected to use it.

He grabbed an extra magazine, and then went back to the kitchen. Putting the gun in an easy-to-reach spot under the counter that looked out into the living room and the front doorway, he clipped the extra magazine to a holder on the weapon's folding stock.

Just as he was sitting back down at the table, about to break his promise to himself that he wasn't going to check any reports that were being passed along through FIDS, there was a heavy knock on his door.

"Shit," he breathed, startled. "Why doesn't anybody ever use the damn doorbell?"

In typical fashion, Alexander trotted to the door, always eager to greet any guests. Jack first took a careful look at the porch through the living room window, his hand on his holstered Glock. There were three people on his doorstep, getting soaked in the rain. All of them wore dark jackets with "FBI" stenciled on them. Despite his worries about whatever hot water he might be in, he breathed a sigh of relief. At least they were his people. He relaxed, taking his hand off the Glock.

Moving to the door, he took a quick look through the peephole, shooed Alexander out of the way, and opened the door.

"Special Agent Dawson," a stern-looking woman in her early thirties said formally, "I'm Special Agent Lynnette Sansone, with

Special Agents Boardman and Castro from Internal Affairs. May we come in?"

"Sure," Dawson said, before ushering them into the small foyer, "let's get you out of this stinking rain."

The three agents came in, but they declined Dawson's offer to take their drenched jackets. Once in the foyer, they simply stood there, Boardman and Castro looking around the living room with keen professional interest, while Sansone's dark blue eyes never left Jack. The two male agents could have moonlighted as professional wrestlers, and Jack wondered if Internal Affairs only recruited the biggest and most intimidating special agents they could find. Sansone would have been attractive, if it weren't for her reptilian focus on Jack and her ice-cold formality.

Jack gestured toward the living room furniture and said, "Care to sit down?" He figured that if the sofa and chairs had survived Alexander, they probably wouldn't be bothered by a little water from his colleagues' wet jackets.

After an uncomfortable moment when the three agents glanced at one another in indecision, Sansone finally said, "Certainly. Thank you." Once they settled onto the sofa and chairs she went on, "Dawson, you know about the explosion at the lab at Quantico tonight, correct?"

"Yes," Jack told her grimly. "Special Agent Richards, the SAC out in Nebraska investigating Special Agent Crane's death, called and told me just a short while ago. And yes," he went on, wanting to just get it off his chest and out in the open, "I was down there without authorization. Dr. Jerri Tanaka and I are..." He paused, taking a deep breath before going on, "...*were* good friends, and I wanted to help her in the lab. I wanted to do anything I could to help with Sheldon Crane's case."

"I appreciate your openness," Sansone said, as Boardman flipped open a notepad and started taking notes, "which will make our job a lot easier and hopefully will minimize the potential unpleasantness for you." She looked at him intensely, and Jack felt distinctly uncomfortable, as if he were being visually dissected. "While the forensics work has barely begun, we know roughly where the bomb detonated. We think it was in an electrical closet adjoining the two DNA lab areas."

"Yeah," Jack told her, "I know the one you mean. It was clearly marked, maybe a dozen feet from the door to Dr. Tanaka's lab."

Sansone nodded. "We also have an eyewitness who saw Dr. Tanaka go into that closet roughly five minutes before the blast," she told him, her eyes still fixed on him. "Do you have any idea why she would have gone in there?"

"No," Jack shook his head as he tried to come to grips with what Sansone was telling him. "No, I can't think of any reason why she would go in there. Are you saying that—"

"Did you know that she also had several large sums of money transferred into offshore accounts by three members of the Earth Defense Society?"

"*What?*" Jack asked, feeling like Sansone had first kicked him in the groin, followed by an uppercut to his jaw. "That's not possible," he told them, shaking his head. "It's just not possible."

"There's no question about it," Sansone told him. "A data recovery team pulled all of her records and documents. It was a hidden, encrypted file that stood out from the others because it was obviously not intended to be found. The information it contained is very...explicit."

He simply sat there, staring at the three agents for a moment, overcome with shock. He didn't want to believe it, couldn't believe it. *There's no fucking way*, he told himself. "No," he told Sansone firmly, working hard to keep the anger out of his voice. "I had no idea. But why would she keep something like that at work, where anything is subject to search at any time?"

"How often do you think that really happens, Dawson?" Castro asked him testily. "It was probably a lot safer there than in her home, where someone could just snag her computer."

"Dawson," Boardman interjected, "let's go back to what you were saying about Special Agent Crane's death and your helping Dr. Tanaka at the lab. Right now, we have good reason to believe that his death and what happened at the lab, regardless of who committed the crime, are closely linked, and the only common thread we have so far is you. We need to know your account of what happened."

Jack didn't like the sound of that, although Boardman's tone and body language didn't come across to Jack as being accusatory.

"We're particularly interested," Sansone said, leaning forward toward Jack, "in anything odd or unusual that might have been found in the evidence that was sent back from Crane's murder scene in Nebraska. Our working hypothesis right now is that he discovered something that the EDS didn't want us to find, and they were desperate enough to try and destroy the lab to keep us from learning what it was."

"We also suspect that Crane may have had a secret cache of computer data somewhere," Boardman said. "We're sure he didn't...wouldn't have kept it at his home." Jack caught Sansone glancing at the big agent, making an almost imperceptible shake of her head.

I'd bet the last bottle of beer in the world that these fuckers are the ones who trashed his place, he thought with a sudden chill. *Jesus.*

Boardman either didn't see her or ignored her warning, as he demanded, "Did he have any special place he might have stored something unusual? Even something he might have given to you for safekeeping?"

The hair on the back of Jack's neck sprang to attention as internal alarm bells started going off, and he fought for control of his expression as a mental image of the photo frame Sheldon had given him suddenly popped into his mind. "It's got a smart card that can store thousands of pics, bro," Sheldon had told him while demonstrating it. "And I've even got it connected to your home network so I can send you updates on my latest adventures remotely..."

That's where Sheldon hid whatever data he was trying to protect, Jack realized. Suddenly, he wasn't so sure it would be a good idea to tell Sansone and the others everything he had seen and done that night. Thinking about the photo frame and the mysterious corn, still wrapped in the latex glove in his jacket pocket, he forced himself to look down at his hands, rather than glance back toward the kitchen.

"Look, guys," he said, stifling a faked yawn. "Let me just start at the beginning, from when I arrived at the lab until I got back home a while ago. I'm beat, and I don't want to miss any details that might be useful to you."

"I think that's an excellent idea, Jack," Sansone, suddenly all warmth and smiles, said. She was giving him the creeps, but he forced a tired smile.

"First," he said, "do you mind if I get some coffee? I've been running on adrenaline for hours, and I need a serious caffeine injection." He glanced around at the others. "Would any of you like some?"

"No thank you," Sansone answered for all of them. "But please feel free."

As Jack stood up, Castro, who was sitting closest to him, quickly got to his feet and said, "Dawson, would you mind handing over your weapons first? You can keep your badge, but we were told to collect the guns until the investigation is over." He shrugged apologetically. "No offense, but that's what we were told to do."

Yeah, right, Jack thought, hesitating as he looked from Castro to Sansone, then to Boardman. He could tell that all three were suddenly extremely tense.

Knowing that his shotgun was just around the corner in the kitchen, Jack decided to play it cool for now. "Sure," he told Castro, "no problem." Moving slowly, he unholstered his Glock 22 and held it by the barrel toward Castro, who took it. Then Jack leaned down and unstrapped his backup weapon, a compact Glock 27, from his leg and handed that over. "That's it," he told them, pulling up his other pant leg so they could see there weren't any other weapons. He had already taken off his jacket, and his shirt and pants wouldn't hide anything other than a small knife.

"Thank you, Jack," Sansone said, nodding as Castro pocketed the weapons and all three agents visibly relaxed. "Now, why don't you get your coffee, then we can get to work."

"Sure thing," Jack said casually as he turned and walked into the kitchen. Fortunately, he was blocked from their view by the short wall on the side of the breakfast bar as he entered the kitchen and spotted Alexander.

Jack came to an abrupt halt, his spine tingling as Naomi Perrault's words echoed in his brain: *They hate cats. Watch Alexander. Trust his instincts.* Jack hadn't thought about it earlier, but the big cat always mingled with guests, begging for attention and a good scratch behind the ears or under the chin. But he had disappeared after Jack had shooed him away from the door before opening it to let in Sansone and the others, and he hadn't returned.

Now, Alexander was standing under the kitchen table, his back arched and the hair of his long black coat sticking out, making him look twice his already impressive size. Jack could see the gleam of his extended claws, and Alexander was quivering with what Jack assumed to be fear. The cat's eyes darted once to meet Jack's shocked gaze before again fixing on the entrance to the kitchen and the suspicious guests in the living room beyond. His ears were laid back, and Jack could hear a low growl that he had never heard Alexander make before.

It was a sound that Jack would have expected from a vicious dog, and a big one at that. He was surprised that he hadn't heard the cat all the way out in the living room.

"Is there a problem?" Sansone's smooth voice called from behind him, and Jack snapped his head around to see her leaning over the counter, peering in at him through the opening from the living room. Boardman and Castro were behind her, and had their hands poised to draw their weapons.

"No," Jack said calmly as he moved toward the far end of the counter where the shotgun was propped against the bottom cabinets. "No problem." He decided to see if Perrault's information was legit. "I was just wondering about my cat," he told her, glancing away from the table and toward the pantry, trying to lead her with his gaze, but away from where Alexander really was.

Sansone's eyes opened wide as she fell for it, looking at the pantry on the far side of the kitchen. "What cat?" she hissed, missing the dark feline form in the shadows under the kitchen table. Out of the corner of his eye, Jack saw Boardman and Castro reach under their jackets for their weapons, compact 9-millimeter Uzi submachine guns.

Shit, was all he had time to think before everything went to hell.

With a feral snarl of rage and fear, Alexander bolted from under the table and leaped straight at Sansone's face, his claws spread wide and his mouth opened to expose his canines. Caught completely by surprise, she tumbled backward into the living room, making an inhuman screech that turned Jack's blood to ice as she went down under Alexander's slashing claws and snapping teeth.

Taking advantage of the distraction, Jack dove the last few feet to where his shotgun was hidden just as Boardman and Castro opened fire, peppering the kitchen with bullets from their Uzis.

"Jesus!" Jack cried as he caught several wood splinters in his shoulder from a near miss before he grabbed the Saiga-12 and rolled to his knees, using the refrigerator for cover. Even partially deafened by the chatter of the Uzis, he could hear Alexander's ferocious snarls and Sansone's screeching out in the living room. *Fucking cat*, he almost sobbed. *Don't get your hairy ass killed!*

Castro suddenly poked his head around the corner from the living room, and the house was filled with the booming roar of the 12-gauge shotgun as Jack pulled the trigger. His first shot missed, the nineteen flechettes in the shotgun round tearing a fist-sized hole in the far wall. Castro, cringing, pulled back out of sight.

Hiding behind drywall's not going to save you, fucker, Jack thought viciously as he fired again, right through the wall where he knew Castro was standing. The agent's body was sent flying, half a dozen flechettes having penetrated his right shoulder, neck, and head. Having learned the painful lesson in Afghanistan that you kept shooting until you were absolutely sure your target was dead, Jack fired again, the shotgun's flechettes tearing Castro's head apart.

One down, he thought grimly. *Two to go.*

Jack brought the Saiga to his shoulder before quickly peering over the counter and catching sight of Boardman. The big man was pointing his weapon down at the floor, trying to take aim at the writhing mass of fur, claws, and teeth that was Alexander, still latched onto Sansone's face. A detached part of Jack's mind was surprised: there should have been blood everywhere from the mauling the cat must have been giving the woman, but there was none. None at all.

Boardman saw Jack and brought up his Uzi, pulling the trigger before he was on-target and sending a stream of bullets plowing into the wall on the living room side of the counter. Jack pulled the Saiga's trigger, and Boardman was flung backward, the Uzi spinning out of his grip as he somersaulted over the couch.

So, they are wearing body armor, Jack thought absently as Boardman struggled to his knees, gasping, before Jack finished him off with a second round, the flechettes penetrating the weakened chest armor. Boardman slammed against the front wall of the living room before falling over on his side, dead.

Jack ran quickly into the living room, swapping the half-empty magazine for the fresh one as he went. Alexander fled past him, back into the kitchen, finally having had enough of Sansone. He was limping badly, but otherwise seemed unharmed. Jack brought up the shotgun as he turned the corner into the living room, and was stunned to see Sansone standing right in front of him, her blue eyes blazing with unbridled rage. He was shocked to see that there wasn't a scratch on her, which was simply impossible. He knew from painful experience – mostly accidental on Alexander's part – that the cat's claws, not to mention his teeth, were long and incredibly sharp. Sansone's face should have been little more than a bloody, lacerated rag.

With her standing less than three feet away, his shotgun leveled at her abdomen, Jack fired. Sansone bent double, as if a massive hammer had hit her in the stomach and sent her flying. She tumbled over one of the armchairs and rolled to a stop against the hearth of the fireplace.

Keeping the gun trained on her, Jack was moving in closer when she began to slowly sit up.

No goddamn way, he thought. He could tell from the patch of skin under her blouse, visible now beneath the shredded FBI jacket, that she wasn't wearing body armor. And there was still no blood, no sign of injury.

With the weapon's muzzle aimed dead center between her breasts, he fired again. The impact slammed her body back against the stone hearth.

She slumped forward and lay still.

Jack stood there, shaking from the adrenaline rush, feeling like he was going to vomit. *You'll have time for that later*, he told himself. Keeping the Saiga pointed at Sansone's body, he slowly moved forward, then reached out with a foot to kick her over and get a better look.

He yelped in surprise as she grabbed his ankle with both hands and levered him backward. Firing by reflex, nearly blowing his own foot off, he missed hitting her in the face by inches and instead blasted a chunk of stone out of the fireplace.

Jack screamed as her grip on his ankle tightened so much that he was afraid the bones would snap. Then he found himself flying across the living room. He landed hard on the coffee table, losing the shotgun as his gun hand slammed into the table's edge. He slid to the floor in a cascade of magazines and photo books as Sansone stood up.

This is impossible, his mind gibbered at him as she moved toward him, the skin of her breasts clearly visible through her tattered FBI jacket and blouse. He looked desperately for the shotgun, but it was on the far side of the coffee table, out of reach. *Run, you moron!*

Jack scrabbled backward, then turned and ran for the front door just as the living room picture window imploded, sending shards of glass flying through the room. Jack tripped and went down, banging his head against the wall near the door. Stunned, he rolled over in time to see two dark human shapes somersault through the window and roll to their feet, facing Sansone.

One fired a shotgun, blasting her back against the counter, before the other newcomer leaped on top of her and jabbed a stun baton, the tip flickering like lightning, into her gut.

Even as deaf as he was from the gun battle, Jack could hear Sansone's unearthly screech again, far louder than it had been when Alexander had attacked her. He saw her body go rigid, and the man with the shotgun quickly set it down. Extracting a huge syringe from a plastic box strapped to his leg, he held it over Sansone's chest while the one with the shock baton continued holding it against her skin, the flickering blue light filling the room with its glow. Then, as if on a cue that Jack couldn't see, the man holding the syringe suddenly plunged the three inch long hypodermic needle into her chest and pressed down on the syringe's plunger.

Sansone's screeching abruptly ceased, and her body lay still.

Jack, shaking like a leaf, slid himself back against the wall into a sitting position. The floor around him was slick with blood. His own, from the splinters in his shoulder and glass cuts in his hands. *Jesus,* he thought. *What the hell?*

The front door beside him suddenly opened, and a third intruder entered his home. The black-clad figure, this one clearly a woman from the shape of her body under the tactical combat gear, knelt next to him. Looking at her eyes through the black mask she wore, he saw that one was brown and the other blue.

Naomi Perrault.

He didn't know what to think. Had she been involved in Sheldon's and Jerri's murders, or was she one of the good guys? Or were there any good guys in this mad affair?

"Perrault," he said, "what the hell is—"

In a smooth motion, she brought up a stun baton, the same type as her compatriot had used on Sansone, and jabbed Jack almost gently in the ribs before he could finish. He cried out involuntarily as every muscle in his body went rigid, completely paralyzing him.

"I'm sorry, Jack," he heard her say through the ringing in his ears from the gunfire. She took a syringe from a small pouch attached to her combat webbing, then jabbed it into his arm. He barely felt the sting. "This will put you to sleep for a while. We've got to get you out of here quickly." She gave his shoulder a reassuring squeeze. "We'll talk soon. I promise."

"Wait!" Jack gasped as his vision began to turn gray. "In the kitchen...my jacket...photo..." Jack struggled to make himself understood, and Perrault leaned closer. "Photo...frame. Important..."

She nodded in understanding before shouting something at one of the others. When she turned back to him, he thought about how exotically beautiful her eyes were as he floated away into darkness.

Seven

"Jack, can you hear me?"

Before Jack's eyes fluttered open, the memories of the fight with Sansone and the other two agents came flooding back to him. A surge of adrenaline shot through his veins, sending his heart into overdrive, his lungs gasping for air as he began to panic.

"You're okay," a woman's soft voice, a voice he vaguely remembered hearing before, reassured him, and he felt a warm hand gently squeeze his arm. "You're safe. There's nothing to be afraid of."

Turning his head – that's all he could move – Jack saw Naomi Perrault, looking almost exactly as she had in the photograph Richards had sent him, sitting in a chair beside him. Despite what he knew about her, and her likely involvement in Sheldon's death, the sight of her helped to calm him. He took a deep breath and forced himself to relax.

Behind her were two men. One was a tough-looking Korean who stood in a deceptively relaxed posture, his powerful arms crossed and his dark eyes riveted on Jack. The other was a tall, thin black man with a neatly cropped gray beard that offset the baldness of his head. He looked extremely intelligent and equally displeased as he looked at their captive.

Flexing his hands and feet, Jack found that he was bound to a double-size bed by thick leather straps on his wrists, ankles, and chest. The room was small, maybe ten feet on a side, with the walls painted light beige and the ceiling in a slightly lighter tone. The floor was covered in blue patterned vinyl tile, and a dresser and standalone wardrobe covered in a light wood veneer stood along the wall next to the bed. For a moment, Jack wondered if he was in a hospital, except that there wasn't any medical equipment in the room, and the bed, other than the straps binding him, appeared to be quite ordinary.

There were some oddities about the room, however. The first was the light hanging overhead: it was an incandescent fixture that was unremarkable, except that it was suspended from the ceiling by a sturdy-looking spring mechanism. The second thing took him a moment to figure out, but he finally realized that the rear wall of the room was curving inward, as if he were inside a huge dome. The final thing that leaped out at him was that the floor and walls of the room were edged with what looked like some sort of rubber, at least six inches thick. They looked like gigantic gaskets, separating the individual elements of the structure. He'd never seen anything like it.

"Where am I?" he rasped, noticing for the first time that his throat was painfully dry. "What the hell's going on?"

Before Naomi could say anything, something big, black, and furry leaped up onto the bed, right onto Jack's stomach: Alexander, with his right rear leg wrapped in a bright pink bandage.

"Oof!" Jack exclaimed, the big cat nearly knocking the wind out of him. Despite his predicament, he couldn't help but be relieved: anyone who would have gone to the trouble of saving Alexander, whom he was sure would have been ready to claw the eyes out of anyone who came near after his fight with Sansone, couldn't be all bad. "You stupid cat," Jack said, smiling in spite of everything as Alexander curled up on his chest, already purring. Jack looked up to see Naomi smiling, and he quickly looked away as he felt a surge of warm butterflies in his stomach. *Get a grip, you idiot*, he chastised himself. *Now's not the time for a bout of infatuation.* "Thank you for bringing him," he mumbled. "He saved my life." Looking back at Perrault, he added, "Thanks for your warning. I got my shotgun ready like you said, but I was expecting to use it on you."

"Jack, if you give me your word of honor that you won't cause any trouble, I'll have Tan," she nodded to the bodyguard type behind her, "let you up."

Tan showed no reaction to Naomi's words, but the academic type next to him scowled. "As I told you earlier, Naomi, I don't think that's a good idea," he said angrily.

With a tight smile at Jack, Naomi said, "This is Dr. Gregg Thornton. He's in charge of...this place–"

"Damn right I am," he interjected.

"–and we had a little disagreement over how to deal with your situation. But we both agreed that I would handle this," she finished, turning to glare at Thornton, who glared right back at her.

If this is a good cop-bad cop routine, Jack thought, watching the two of them, *they're either really good, or really bad.* He still wasn't about to give out any trust points, but his instincts were telling him that their argument wasn't just for show.

"You have my word," he told Naomi, but was looking at Thornton, "that I won't try anything. For now. But," he went on, turning to meet Naomi's gaze, "if I find out that any of you were involved in any way with the murder of Sheldon Crane or the explosion at the FBI lab at Quantico, I'll tear your guts out."

"This is insane," Thornton muttered before stalking out of the room, slamming the door shut behind him.

"What's his problem?" Jack asked.

Naomi only shook her head, then said quietly, "Tan, let him up, please." Without a word, Tan removed the restraints, freeing Jack. Then he stood tensely next to Naomi, watching Jack carefully. "Thank you, Tan. You can leave us, now," she said. He paused, uncertain. "It's all right. I'm fine."

With nothing more than a slight downturn of his mouth, Tan turned and quietly padded out of the room, softly closing the door. Jack was sure that he was now standing just outside.

"I know you have a lot of questions," Naomi told him, "and I promise that I'll tell you everything that I can."

"How about we start with something to drink," Jack said, catching sight of a carafe of what he hoped was water and a glass on a nightstand next to the bed. Alexander got off him and curled up on the bed. "I feel like I haven't had anything to drink in a couple days."

"That's not far from the truth," she said as she picked up the carafe and poured Jack some water, then handed him the glass. "You've been sedated for a bit over twenty-four hours," she explained. "I'm sorry again for stunning and sedating you, but we had to move quickly and didn't have time then for twenty questions."

"Where are we?" he asked as he handed the glass back for a refill.

"California," she told him as she gave him more water, "not far from a place called Live Oak, if you know where that is."

"No," Jack told her before he drank the rest of the water, which was finally making a dent in his thirst. He had been to some of California's major cities, but Live Oak didn't ring any bells. "So, did you shanghai me out here on a plane after knocking me out?"

"Basically," she told him, leaning back and crossing her blue jean-clad legs. "You're hard to carry and weigh a ton when you're unconscious, Special Agent Dawson," she told him with a grin. "Did you know that? Especially up the steps of an executive jet. It took the three of us plus the pilot to get you into the plane. Getting you down was easy, though. We just dumped you out on the ground."

Jack snorted, which elicited a reproving look from Alexander, who was still purring loudly next to him. "I've suffered worse," he said.

"I know," she told him quietly, her face softening. "Sheldon told us a lot about you. He thought the world of you, Jack. I'm so sorry about what happened to him. We all are."

Jack looked at her, his face rigid with renewed anger at his friend's death. "So, I take it you had nothing to do with his murder?"

"We didn't kill him, Jack," she said, aghast. "Sheldon was working with us. He had been for weeks." At Jack's clear expression of disbelief, she explained, "He had been tracking down our attempts to hack into the New Horizons lab networks. We have some very bright people, Jack, but he was better. Much better. We knew someone was onto us, but we didn't know who it was." She shook her head. "One of our...sources finally figured it out, and we decided to try and recruit him, you might say, to get him on our side before he went to his superiors with what he knew." She shook her head. "It was a close thing, Jack. Sheldon almost had us, and had he blown the whistle on our operation, it would have been a disaster of biblical proportions."

Seeing Jack's skeptical expression, she went on, "I know it sounds melodramatic to you now, but by the end of the day you'll understand that it's not an overstatement. Not at all."

Alexander put out a paw in her direction, demanding her attention, and she leaned forward and scratched him under the chin. Jack caught a whiff, just a trace, of a lavender scent.

"Of course," she went on, "just like you, Sheldon wasn't willing to believe us at first, but after we showed him certain things..." She shrugged. "After that, he became a true believer in our cause. He turned the tables on New Horizons, and was able to succeed where we had failed. We knew that the key was the lab at Lincoln Research University, but we didn't know exactly where to look. He volunteered to break into the lab," she said, her eyes brimming with tears now. "He knew he was the only one who could find what we were looking for in the computers." She reached out and took Jack's hand. "And thanks to you, he didn't die in vain. We have the corn samples and the other data he found. We have everything we need, now."

"Everything for *what*, Naomi?" Jack said, frustrated. He couldn't imagine what Sheldon could have seen to make him go rogue and throw in his lot with the likes of the Earth Defense Society. But Jack also couldn't deny that he believed what Naomi was telling him. That scared him almost as much as anything else. "And who the hell killed him?" he demanded.

"You'll see soon enough, Jack," she said cryptically, letting go of his hand. "We have the security monitor recordings of the lab. I'll show them...and other things to you soon."

Jack opened his mouth to protest, to tell her that he wanted to know *now*, but she put her fingers to his lips.

"I promised you that I'd tell you everything, Jack," she said, "and I will. I won't lie to you or hold anything back. We need your help, just as much as we needed Sheldon's. Maybe more, now that he's gone." She shook her head. "But there are certain things you need to understand first. I know it's hard to be patient after all that's happened, but you've got to trust me. Please."

"I'm not going to say I trust you," he told her, "because right now I don't trust anybody but this silly cat." Alexander ignored him, his attention focused on Naomi, who was still scratching him under the chin. "But I don't exactly have much choice, do I? If nothing you tell me or show me convinces me to support your little operation and I wanted to leave, you wouldn't let me go, would you?"

"No," she told him quietly. "We couldn't, Jack. There's simply too much at stake."

"Would you just kill me if I didn't cooperate?"

"I wouldn't support it, but there are others who would want to." She paused. "But we've never had to do that, Jack, and I pray we never will. What you'll see here will transform your view of the world, believe me."

Jack said, "Okay, start talking."

"First," she began, "you need to understand that we're at war, Jack. Like most wars, this one is for dominance, for control. The difference is that very few people realize that they're caught up in it, and most of those who do don't understand what it's really about, or who the enemy truly is." She sat back, folding her arms under her breasts, shivering slightly as if she were cold. "Everyone today is focused on the threat of terrorism. Before that, it was Saddam Hussein. And for decades before that we were consumed by worry over the Cold War and nuclear holocaust. The irony is that the corn that Sheldon found in that lab in Nebraska, if it ever gets loose in our biosphere, will be far more devastating to humankind and the Earth as a whole than all the nuclear weapons ever made." Her eyes took on that haunted look again that made Jack's skin crawl. "We'll be wiped out if we aren't able to stop it, Jack. The human race will be exterminated."

"How?" Jack asked, shaking off the willies. "It's just corn, for God's sake. And not much, at that: how are four little kernels of corn going to do us in?"

She shook her head. "These are just some of the prototypes, Jack," she told him. "New Horizons got the rest back when they...killed Sheldon. Even if they hadn't, they would have been able to recreate them. They have the genetic blueprints. Within a year there will be seed to produce corn like that, thousands of tons of it that will be shipped to every corner of the world. And wheat and other crops will be following right behind to help spread the devastation."

Jack shook his head. "I say again, so what? Is it laced with poison? Is it carnivorous, the corn cobs chasing after people to bite their ankles? I'm sorry, Naomi, but I just don't buy this. If what you're saying was true, New Horizons would be shut down in a heartbeat, and the FDA and special agents from the Bureau would be in there, tearing those labs and offices apart and burning every bit of the stuff."

She cocked her head, looking at him as if he had just said something incredibly dim-witted. "In an ideal world, that's exactly what *would* happen, Jack. But our world isn't ideal, is it? Your time in Afghanistan should have shown you that. And even if it hadn't, the ordeal with Sansone should have been a wakeup call." She paused, considering. "There's a good reason that New Horizons hasn't been shut down. Do you have any idea how many senior government and military officials have close ties to that company, either from prior or promised future employment, receiving major campaign contributions, or just good old-fashioned bribes?"

Jack shook his head. He didn't like where this was going.

"We've been able to link twenty-six, Jack," she went on. "That number includes the vice president, the deputy secretary of defense, five senior officers in the military, two supreme court justices, the head of the FDA, the chief of staff for Homeland Security..." She paused, looking pointedly at him. "...and the Director of the FBI."

He felt like the world had suddenly fallen away, spinning off into space as he fell down the proverbial rabbit hole. *Someone in the Bureau handed you over to Sansone and her goons*, he thought bitterly. He hoped it wasn't Richards, and prayed it wasn't Clement. But if the director was caught up in this madness, it could have been anyone.

Then there was Kilburn at the lab: he had come from New Horizons, and Jack would have bet a year's pay that he had played a role in Jerri's death.

"Those are just the big fish, Jack," Naomi continued. "There are a lot more out there, the people who carry out the policies that those senior officials make. All of those people do whatever is necessary for New Horizons to fulfill its agenda."

"Which is?" he asked, not sure now that he wanted to know the answer. He felt like he was under water, his body being squeezed, crushed, his lungs unable to breathe.

"There are two parts to it, Jack," she answered. "The first is to control as much of the world's food supply as possible. The second, as I already told you," she said grimly, "is to kill us."

Eight

Before Jack had a chance to respond, an intercom set into the wall next to where he was sitting chimed.

Naomi stood up and reached across the bed to answer it, her face drawing close to Jack's as she did so. He couldn't help but breathe in her lavender scent, and when his eyes met hers, she held them steadily. It seemed to take a long time for her fingers to press the button.

"Naomi," she said, still holding Jack's gaze.

"You need to come see this," Thornton's voice, even more agitated than it was before, rasped through the grill, destroying the moment. "Right now."

"On my way," she sighed, giving Jack a wry smile. She stood up and told him, "Come on."

"Where to?" he asked, more confused than ever.

"The command center," she answered as she opened the door, which took quite a bit of effort to move. He quickly saw why: it was three-inch thick steel plate, and if he wasn't mistaken, the walls were made of concrete even thicker. "It's upstairs."

As Jack slid forward on the bed to stand up, Alexander gracefully jumped to the floor and trotted out the door.

"Alexander!" Jack called, starting to chase after his feline friend, but Naomi caught his arm.

"He's fine," she told him with a quick smile. "Alexander had a chance to explore a bit while you were sedated. He can go where he likes here. Animals are welcome, and necessary, as it turns out. The others here will watch out for him."

"Oh, jeez," Jack sighed, wondering what mischief the big cat would get into as he stepped out of the room.

He found himself in a hallway that looked like it might have been in a modest hotel, except that it emptied into the yawning mouth of a brightly lit tunnel a dozen feet wide. There were doors along the hallway to rooms similar to his, along with a dining area near the tunnel entrance that could seat twenty or so people.

Where the hell is this? he wondered. He might be in California by rough location, but he'd never seen anything like this place.

As he closed the massive door behind him, he noticed a small name plate next to the door frame. Naomi Perrault. *Christ*, he thought, *I was sleeping in her bed*. That brought a set of images to his mind that he hurriedly shoved aside.

Tan, as Jack had suspected, had been standing next to the door, and he fell into line as Jack followed Naomi to a spiral staircase, trying to focus his attention on his feet rather than on her shapely lower body as she quickly took the steps ahead of him.

He was totally unprepared for what he saw upon reaching the top of the stairs. It was a circular room about seventy feet across that looked like the combat information center, or CIC, of an aircraft carrier he had once been on during his tour in Afghanistan. Computers and flat panel displays were arrayed in clusters that faced in toward a raised dais at the center. The walls curved inward to form a dome, with enclosed fluorescent fixtures hanging from shock mounts around the periphery and a matrix of sound baffles in the center of the ceiling. A dozen men and women were at the various consoles, and all of them were staring at Jack as he followed Naomi toward where Thornton stood at the central console.

He suddenly realized they weren't staring at him, exactly, but behind him. Turning around, he saw that about a quarter of the room had been partitioned off by a wall that held a couple of doors and three floor-to-ceiling projection displays.

On the center display was his most recent official FBI photograph, now being broadcast by a national news network.

"Oh, shit," he muttered as he turned to catch up to Naomi. As he passed the various workstations, he saw that some displayed maps of various parts of the world, while others showed what looked like network diagrams and computer code. Still others had only mundane programs like web browsers and chat programs running.

"Play it," Thornton ordered as Jack took his place next to Naomi, Tan silently standing a few feet behind. A man sat at the circular console at the center that had half a dozen screens and several keyboard consoles. He clicked a control and the paused broadcast began to play.

"In what sources are reporting is a devastating blow to the nation's premier law enforcement agency," the newswoman announced, "the Federal Bureau of Investigation has put one of its own on their 'ten most-wanted fugitives' list." A series of photos of Jack paraded across the screen as the woman went on. "Jack Armand Dawson, a former

Army officer and special agent with the FBI for nearly ten years, is wanted for the murder of two fellow agents and the suspected kidnapping of a third. He is also the leading suspect in the lethal bombing of the FBI Laboratory at Quantico yesterday that left thirty-seven Bureau employees dead and more than fifty injured."

Suspected kidnapping of a third? Jack's mind ground to a halt for a moment as he thought of what that might mean before the scene cut to show a mob of cameras surrounding Ray Clement as he stood on the steps leading to the entrance of the J. Edgar Hoover Building. Jack felt his gut twist in emotional agony as he saw how distraught his boss and mentor was, knowing that there was no way to tell him, or convince him, of the truth of what had happened.

"We have good reason to believe," Clement began, pausing as he visibly fought for control, "that Special Agent Jack Dawson was involved in the murders of Special Agents Manuel Castro and Jacob Boardman, and was also responsible for the disappearance of Special Agent Lynnette Sansone."

Jack looked sharply at Naomi. "What happened to her?" he whispered. "What did you do with her body?"

"Later," she said quietly, her attention riveted to the screen.

"The three agents were sent to Dawson's home to question him about the explosion at the FBI Laboratory," Clement was saying, "where he had been handling, without authorization, evidence related to the murder of another agent, Special Agent Sheldon Crane, just before the bomb exploded." He paused again, rubbing his eyes with one hand. "Dr. Jerri Tanaka, a colleague of his who worked at the laboratory, and with whom he had a close relationship, has been directly implicated in the bombing."

Then Jack's face disappeared, to be replaced with Naomi's. It was the same photo that Richards had sent to Jack, and he could see her tense up as Clement continued with his statement.

"We believe that Jack Dawson is in league with an organization known as the Earth Defense Society," Clement said, "which has been implicated in the death of Special Agent Sheldon Crane three days ago in Lincoln, Nebraska. This is a photograph of Dr. Naomi Perrault, who is believed to be one of the group's leaders. Prior to these events, we have evidence to indicate that the Earth Defense Society, or EDS, has been involved in attacks against government and civilian computer networks for purposes of disruption and possibly industrial espionage."

His expression hardened. "We have added both Jack Dawson and Naomi Perrault to the Bureau's top ten most wanted list, and are looking for any leads on them or other members of the Earth Defense Society. That's all I have."

With that, Clement ignored the storm of questions the reporters hurled at him and walked up the steps, disappearing into the building behind a wall of stone-faced special agents and Capitol Police.

"I think that was more than enough," Jack said when the playback stopped, feeling like he was going to throw up.

"So now we have two of the most wanted people in America, and every one of us is going to have FBI agents breathing down our necks," Thornton growled. "You've compromised our entire mission with this foolishness!"

"This isn't the place for this discussion," Naomi said, her tone carrying a great deal more authority than Jack expected.

Without another word, she took Jack by the arm and headed toward one of the doors in the wall that held the large displays. Thornton, Tan, and a woman Jack hadn't been introduced to yet trailed behind.

Naomi pushed open the door and stormed into a conference room with a large oval table in the center surrounded by a dozen chairs. The wall adjoining the command center outside had two big flat panel displays that were hooked up to a video teleconferencing system, while the sloping outside walls held only the shock-mounted lights.

Thornton slammed the door closed after the other woman had entered. Tan waited outside.

"Naomi," Thornton began, "this is a disaster! It was bad enough with just *them* after us. But that was out of the public eye. Now we'll have every cop and agent in the country gunning for you and *him*..." He looked disgustedly at Jack and shook his head, momentarily speechless.

"We knew this day would come, Gregg," she retorted. "And I told you six months ago that we were running out of time." She looked at Jack. "If it hadn't been this, it would have been something else. The turning point is that they know now that we have real evidence of their plans. Before, they were content to harass us when there was opportunity to do so, but they didn't think we could do what we've done. Now they know we're a real threat, and they *have* to stop us." She looked at Jack, softening her tone. "He's an innocent in this affair, and he doesn't deserve to be blamed by you or anyone else. Sheldon sacrificed himself for us, and I wasn't about to let someone else die on our behalf without even knowing why."

"I hate to break it to you lovebirds," the woman who had come in with Thornton said, her voice laced with sarcasm, "but we've got another problem." She looked at Jack, giving him an appreciative once-over from head to toe with her brown eyes, then stepped forward and thrust out her hand. "I'm Dr. Renee Vintner," she said with a thick New York accent. "Nice to meet you, although it would've been a lot better if you'd have brought some beer along. Gregg never orders enough."

Thornton rolled his eyes, but Jack couldn't help but grin as he shook her hand, amazed at how strong her grip was. She was a short, rotund woman in her early fifties with carelessly cut curly black hair that had barely begun to show any gray. She gave him a tight but heartfelt smile.

"Hi," Jack said, happy for a diversion from the frigid tension in the room between Naomi and Thornton. "Nice to meet you, too."

"So, what's the problem, Renee?" Naomi said.

"I found the files that Sheldon hid in the photo frame's memory," she explained. "That was easy enough. We coordinated the encryption and the pass phrase before he went to Nebraska, just in case we got to it first. I didn't have any problem with that, and got the files we were expecting." She frowned. "There's also a file in there that he encrypted a second time, and I don't have a goddamn clue what the pass phrase might be."

"Can't you just break it?" Thornton asked irritably.

"With enough monkeys, typewriters, and time – sure," Renee snapped. "But Sheldon wasn't a monkey. He lived and breathed this stuff. Whatever pass phrase he used is going to take forever for a password cracking program to resolve, even using every network resource I have. It would save a lot of time, maybe years, if someone happened to know what the pass phrase was." She looked pointedly at Jack.

Shaking his head slowly, Jack told her, "Sheldon never mentioned anything like that to me. He never said anything to me about any of this! Even the photo frame: I had no idea it was important. If it hadn't been a gift from him that he made a big deal over, I probably would've thrown the silly thing out. Why did he do that, anyway? Shouldn't he have just sent the data directly to you guys?"

Vintner shook her head. "He would have if the operation had gone as planned," she told him. "But I think that once he was inside, he must have found something that made him think he'd been compromised. He was smart and had a backup in that little gadget he gave you, but was also an idiot for not telling us about it." She shrugged. "Jack, was there anything else that he made a big deal over?" she asked him. "It would have been a name, or number. Maybe a phrase of some kind. It would've been fairly long, something he wrote down or emailed to you?"

"I don't know," Jack told her, trying to think of anything Sheldon might have told him that could be a clue. "I don't remember him writing anything down for me, and nothing that he said or emailed to me stands out." He shrugged. "I'll try to remember, but if you don't mind my saying so, I'm a bit overwhelmed at the moment." Looking from Renee to Naomi, he asked, "What's so important about all these files?"

"The files we were expecting, that Renee was able to extract," Naomi explained, "were the genetic blueprints to the corn and the other crops in the new, and final, product line that New Horizons is planning to market. Those blueprints are both evidence that we can use to help expose their plans to the public, and that, with a lot of luck, we can use to try and develop a countermeasure. As for what this other file might be, I can't even guess."

"It wasn't part of the plan that we prepared Sheldon to carry out," Thornton said. Much of his anger had drained away, as if he had grown tired of carrying a heavy burden. Now he just looked tired. And frightened. "We planned and carefully rehearsed for every eventuality that any of us could think of to help prepare him to get into the lab at LRU, get what we needed, and then get out as quickly as possible. Obviously, something went very badly wrong." Turning to Renee, he said, "Do what you can." With a quick glance at Jack, he said, "Maybe we'll have some *good* luck for a change."

"Come on, Jack," Naomi said in a disgusted voice, stalking out of the room. "Let's get out of here."

Jack turned to follow after her, ignoring Thornton, but giving Renee an apologetic shrug. His mouth dropped open with surprise when she cocked her head in Naomi's direction and gave him a mischievous wink.

"Be sure you show him *everything*, Naomi," Thornton said tersely.

Outside the briefing room, Tan began to follow after them, but Naomi turned to him and said stiffly, "Thank you, Tan, but that won't be necessary. We're fine."

Tan only nodded and stayed rooted where he was as Naomi and Jack headed for the spiral staircase and made their way down to the lower level.

Naomi headed for the small dining hall, stopping in front of one of the three large coffee makers.

"Would you like some?" she said in a tightly controlled voice as she poured a cup. Jack saw that her hands were shaking.

"Sure," he said. "Thanks."

"If you're hungry, go ahead and grab something to eat," she told him, nodding her head toward a table that held several covered warming trays, plus bread, bagels, and lots of fruit. All of it looked fresh and homemade. He was still trying to come to grips with the situation he had been thrust into, and food was the last thing on his mind. But his stomach grumbled from not having had more than a couple beers before the battle at his house and all the time that had passed since then, and he knew that his body needed some fuel.

"Do you want anything in yours?" she asked as he grabbed a plate and piled on some scrambled eggs, turkey bacon, and a bagel.

"No, thanks," he said. "Just black."

She nodded and brought it over to where he'd taken a seat at one of the tables, then sat down across from him.

"I'm sorry about that," she told him. "Gregg's a good man, and he's been crucial to what we've been able to accomplish. But sometimes we don't exactly see eye to eye on things."

"Yeah, I sort of got that impression," Jack said wryly. "What did he mean about showing me 'everything'?"

"He meant that I should show you the same things that we showed to Sheldon and the others who work here," she said cryptically, "to show you the things that convinced them that the war is real, and that we're not just a bunch of UFO nuts or eco-terrorists."

"Listen," Jack said, "I get the stuff about New Horizons, I think. But I'm still not seeing the angle with the little green men."

"There aren't any little green men," she said darkly. "I can promise you that." Sighing, she shook her head. "The web site thing was my fault. After I was...enlightened, one of my crusades was to try and bring the war to the public's attention. That was something else that Gregg tried to talk me out of, but I wouldn't listen. He was right about it, though: the way I presented it just made us look foolish, and attracted every UFO and alien abduction nut around the world."

"If that's the case," he asked, "why did you leave the site up? Why not just get rid of it?"

"Once something gets out on the net, Jack," she said, "it's almost impossible to take it back or get rid of it. As it turned out, it actually did work in our favor in an unexpected way: it made us look like a bunch of crackpots, and I like to think it helped divert some of the scrutiny away from our operations, at least for a while." She shrugged. "We also got a few great recruits out of it, including Renee. She's got a doctorate from MIT in computer science, but has been a UFO buff since she was a little girl." She took another sip of her coffee. "The only thing truly constructive that we managed to do in cyberspace was to eliminate as many visual clues to the senior EDS staff as we could. That was mostly Renee's doing, although Sheldon helped a lot after he came on board."

"And that's why every photo that should be you or any of the others was replaced with one of Gary Woolsey?" Jack gave her a grin, thinking of the photo of the obese African American man he had seen in every database where Naomi's picture should have been. "Certainly you could've found someone more photogenic."

But Naomi didn't smile. If anything, she suddenly looked on the verge of tears. "It was Renee's idea," she told him softly, looking down into her empty coffee mug. "She and Gary were good friends. It was a sort of tribute to him."

"What happened?" Jack asked. "I know he confessed to burning down the Outland Genetics lab and killing a bunch of people, then died right after he was sent to prison."

"He didn't just die, Jack," Naomi said fiercely. "He was murdered. We don't know exactly what happened, because after Gary was arrested, we couldn't contact him." She looked him square in the eye. "I'll go over the things you need to know about EDS with you later, Jack, but one of the cardinal rules is that if you're compromised, you're on your own. We won't help you, and you can't contact us. We can't risk the operation for anyone."

"You saved me."

She shook her head. "That was different. We had to intervene to see if you'd found anything at the lab, which you did, along with the data Sheldon had hidden in the photo frame, which we didn't even know about. We went to your house that night only for that. Gregg wanted me to either kill you or leave you to your fate to cover our trail, but I refused.

"Anyway," she went on, "we think that Gary found something at the last minute while he was setting up the network at Outland Genetics, that a...New Horizons special VIP, let's call him, would be there, one of the very few that we knew about. Gary must not have even had time to contact us before he took matters into his own hands."

"And wound up burning five people to death," Jack said grimly. He had dealt with horrible people and crimes in the line of duty, and his wife had been killed by one, but he still believed in justice, even if it was imperfectly dealt out. Killing five people without a trial was, to Jack, nothing less than murder.

"What Gary did was an extraordinary act of courage, especially for him," she said. "He was a gentle man who'd never committed a violent act in his life, and I think the thought of what he'd done made him crack on the witness stand during the trial. Those who died in that fire were enemies of humanity, Jack. You don't believe or understand that now, but you will. And soon." She looked away again, gathering her thoughts. "He recognized a unique opportunity and struck a tremendous blow against our enemies, Jack. Then, after he was sent to prison, they killed him."

"The coroner's report said he died of a heart attack," Jack said. "Let's be honest here: he didn't seem to be in the greatest shape, and what he must have gone through in the trial and being sent to prison would have put an incredible strain on him."

She shook her head sadly. "No, Jack. We have records from the prison's computer network showing that Gary had a visitor the day he died, someone from the FBI. You might recognize the name: Lynnette Sansone."

"*What?*" Jack said.

Naomi nodded. "That's right. And an hour after Sansone's visit, Gary was dead."

"So, you're saying that Sansone killed him?" Jack asked, incredulously.

"Yes," Naomi replied. "She could have done so quite easily."

"What, she just slipped him something that made him have a heart attack, without anybody seeing it and the coroner not picking up on it?" He couldn't restrain his skepticism.

Naomi nodded, her face momentarily clouded by the haunted expression Jack had seen on her earlier, during their talk in her room. "Absolutely."

"How can you possibly know that?"

"Because we brought her here from your house, Jack," Naomi told him. "And when I take you to see her, I'll prove it to you."

Nine

"I want to see her right now—" Jack began hotly, standing up from the table.

"No," Naomi said quietly. She held up her hand before Jack could say anything else, and told him, "You'll see her soon enough. I promise. But there are some other things we need to do first."

"Like what?" Jack asked, trying to quell his anger. "Dammit, Naomi, I'm tired of..." He clenched his hands into fists, at a loss to describe his feelings.

"You're tired of feeling helpless," she told him, getting up and coming around to stand beside him, "tired of Fate getting to call all the shots." Jack nodded. It was as good an explanation as anything. She gripped his arm gently, saying, "I know. And that's going to change, I promise you. But there are some practicalities we have to take care of. It looks like you're with us now, whether you want to be or not. You need to know a few things before you can function here. Come on." She nodded toward the tunnel mouth that led away from the command center dome. "Let's take a walk."

As Jack followed her into the beige-painted tunnel, which was made out of ribbed steel and was a dozen feet across, he asked her, "What the heck is this place?" The floor material changed from the utilitarian but attractive tile of the command center dome to non-skid steel flooring that had absolutely no give to it, and that Jack suspected was at least a quarter inch thick. Arrays of pipes and conduits for what he assumed must be power and water covered the tunnel's ceiling and traveled what looked to be around fifty feet to a junction that lay ahead.

"Remember my telling you about humanity's preoccupation with the Cold War?" she asked him as she walked along. He nodded. "Well, this is one of the relics from those bygone days." Gesturing around them, she explained, "This used to be a base for Titan I Intercontinental Ballistic Missiles. There were eighteen bases like this built in the early nineteen-sixties. Each one could launch three Titan I missiles with multi-megaton warheads at the Soviet Union. This one was under the 851st Strategic Missile Squadron, headquartered at Beale Air Force

Base here in California. We're right in the foothills of the Sutter Buttes, believe it or not."

"Jesus," Jack said softly as they approached a junction in the tunnel. "This is huge."

Naomi laughed. "Jack, you haven't seen anything yet," she told him. "But you're right, it *is* huge. The irony is that these bases were only used for a few years. This one was commissioned in 1961, and shut down in 1965."

"Our taxpayer dollars at work," Jack said wryly as they stepped out of the tunnel into the junction. It was another huge cylinder, sixteen feet across. There were more pipes and conduits, plus larger ducts, covering the ceiling.

"This is the main junction," she told him. "It's the center of the complex." Pointing at a diagram that hung on the curving wall, she explained the facility's layout. "The complex is made up of six major sections, all joined by the main tunnel." She gestured toward two openings where the tunnel, twelve feet wide, ran through the junction. "At the south end is the old antenna complex, with two silos that used to house the missile control antennas. Now we use them for…other things that you'll learn about soon."

Jack saw her glance at the mouth of the tunnel that led south to the antenna complex, and he felt a chill at her expression. It was only there for a moment before she turned away, but for that instant a look of barely contained rage was in her eyes.

"How far is that?" Jack asked, looking at the diagram. "I don't have any sense of scale from this."

"That part of the tunnel is almost six hundred feet long," she told him.

"Christ," Jack said. "That's two football fields!"

Naomi smiled. "Now you're getting the idea of how big this place is," she told him. "Okay, so the antenna complex is the only thing on that section of the main tunnel, which runs straight here to the junction. Connecting directly to the junction are the command dome, where we just came from, and the dome that contains the lab and our generators." She pointed to a large blast door, directly across the junction from the command dome entrance. "The portal to the surface also connects to the main junction." She nodded toward a set of massive blast doors that had been painted in a glaring yellow and black striped pattern, "I'll show you the portal sometime later when we have a chance to go topside, but I wanted you to know where it is in case we have to evacuate.

"Following the main tunnel north past the main junction," she went on, "you first come to what used to be the old missile fuel storage terminal, which is basically a huge cylindrical tank. We use it for liquid nitrogen storage now."

"What do you need that for?" Jack asked, looking at the diagram. The tank looked huge. "And how much does this tank hold?"

"The tank holds about forty thousand gallons," she told him. "Like everything else here, it's big. As for what we use it for, it's coolant. You see, what used to be the three missile silos, we've converted to huge deep-freeze storage units." She pointed to three sets of three huge cylinders, silos, which were connected to the main tunnel at the north end. "These used to be the launch complexes. There was a missile silo, a propellant terminal, and an equipment terminal for each one. As I said, we've converted the missile silos into huge freezers. We turned the propellant terminals, which used to store fuel for the missiles, into support systems for the silos. The equipment terminals, we converted into living space, like apartments." She turned to look at him, grinning. "Just don't head off to the silo at the end of the main tunnel without taking everything you need with you, or it'll be a long walk back: it's seven hundred feet from here."

"So what's so big that you need to use missile silos as freezers?" he asked, puzzled.

Naomi smiled. "You'll see," she answered.

Jack sighed, rolling his eyes in frustration.

Pointing on the map to what looked like another junction on the main tunnel, she went on, "The first two silo complexes are connected to the main tunnel by what are called blast locks, which were supposed to help contain the damage from a missile if it exploded. We don't have to worry about that now, but we normally keep them closed for physical security."

"Security against what?" Jack wanted to know.

"You'll see," she answered cryptically.

"Great," Jack muttered as he looked at the diagram. The silos were the end of his virtual tour.

"Wait a second," he told her. "When you mentioned the portal earlier, you said 'when we go topside.' Does that mean we're underground?"

"Yes," she said. "The top of the control center dome is about twenty feet below ground. The tunnels here are almost fifty feet down." She glanced at him. "Remember, these bases were built to withstand nuclear detonations on the scale of megatons." She shrugged. "Everything here is built tough, Jack. The concrete is several feet thick in most places, heavily reinforced with steel."

"Perfect for your little war," Jack said.

"It's not *our* war, Jack," Naomi snapped. "It was thrust on us by an enemy who doesn't know the meaning of diplomacy or negotiation, or even surrender."

"Sorry," he said sheepishly.

Naomi shrugged. "It's okay. I don't expect you to understand. Yet." She pointed to the left as they walked on, where there were two huge vestibules in the junction with small access hatches. "That's our primary fresh water storage," she told him. "Two tanks holding thirty-three thousand gallons each. They're supplied from two deep water wells in the power house."

"Good God," Jack said. "That's enough for a small town!"

"Yes, it is. But that's not the way we found it, believe me." She shook her head. "This place was a disaster area when Gregg bought it. Asbestos, PCBs, lead paint: everything that's been banned as environmentally hazardous in the last thirty years was down here in appalling abundance. It was a fright to clean up."

"How the hell did he find it?"

She laughed. It was a sound that Jack thought he could definitely get used to. "Would you believe he bought it from an on-line auction site? The government sold it to a private owner years ago, and it had changed hands several times. The last owner couldn't get rid of it – no one wanted to deal with the hazardous waste down here – and Gregg picked it up for a song."

Jack's jaw dropped in amazement. "You're kidding, right?" He looked around him as they continued through the junction toward another blast door marked "Main Lab."

"No," she said. "It's absolutely true. I imagine the seller must have fallen to the floor in surprise when Gregg bid on it, and then actually paid!"

"But how did he...I mean what did he say he was going to do with it?" Jack asked, perplexed. "I imagine he didn't pay for it with a check that said 'Earth Defense Society.'"

"No, no," she told him. "He bought it through one of our front companies, a trucking business that needed some property to expand. It's completely legitimate, and helps us get around a lot of logistical problems supporting our operations here." She looked up toward the surface. "We're sitting under about a hundred or so trailers, with semi trucks coming in around the clock to drop some off and pick up others. That's how we get our food, supplies, and equipment brought in without us standing out like a sore thumb to anyone who might be looking for us." She looked at Jack and grinned. "They bring in our people, too."

Jack looked up, trying to imagine tractor trailer rigs moving around somewhere above his head, and said, "I don't hear a thing."

"Like I told you, Jack," she said, "we're buried deep."

Stepping up to the door to the lab, she took hold of the badge that Jack had noticed hanging on a lanyard around her neck. She swiped it across a magnetic reader next to a small keypad, entered a six-digit code, then looked into a retinal scanner. "What's in here is really what this whole thing is about."

With two loud warning beeps, the foot-thick blast door was slowly pushed open by a set of hydraulic rams.

Jack followed her into the lab dome. "Good Lord," he breathed, wondering how this had all been built. "This place is *huge*."

The dome they were in now was one hundred and thirty feet across and more than fifty feet high. Painted white and brightly lit, the lower level where he and Naomi were standing was a maze of medical and scientific equipment, with two dozen people in white lab coats sitting at or moving among the various work stations. The room had a second level over fifteen feet above them, a mezzanine that ringed the dome and extended about twenty feet in toward the center, and was open to the lab area below.

Similar to the command center, roughly a quarter of the lab dome's area to Jack's right was walled off, and he saw a sign over a huge door that read, "Power Room."

"Backup power," Naomi told him, following his gaze. "For us, electricity is life for our operation, everything from the lab equipment to the air filtration units that keep the air breathable. We can't even get to the surface without power to open the blast doors. An outage, even a brief one, would be a disaster. The main power room here supplies our backup power with two eight-hundred kilowatt diesel generators. We really only need one to keep our critical systems up, but we have two for redundancy. This dome used to be the site's power house, and had four gigantic generators that turned out a megawatt each, but we don't need nearly that much electricity." She pointed up to the mezzanine level above the power room, and Jack could see another tunnel mouth beyond the stacks of supplies that took up most of the space on the upper level. "That tunnel houses the fuel for the generators. The original site had two sixty-seven thousand gallon diesel tanks, twelve feet in diameter and eighty feet long, plus a smaller five thousand gallon tank." Jack shook his head in wonder at the scale of things in this underground fortress. "We only use the small one and one of the big ones now; that's enough fuel to provide diesel power for over two months. We converted the space used by the other big tank to an emergency battery array that can keep us in business for a week. But we normally just use local power that we lease from another one of our front companies, a small regional wind turbine farm. That way nobody asks questions about why a trucking company uses so much electricity."

"What about fresh air and exhaust?" Jack asked, knowing that running any sort of internal combustion engine in a confined space like this, huge as it was, would quickly asphyxiate everyone down here.

She pointed toward the tunnel mouth above the power room, and Jack saw a set of large pipes snaking up from where the generators were, disappearing down the tunnel. "The exhaust goes out through the tunnel in the direction of the fuel and battery storage, drawn by a huge fan and blown out an exhaust vent at the surface level," she explained. "Fresh air comes in over there," she pointed to a tunnel on the opposite side of the mezzanine, "through a nuclear-biological-chemical filter. Normally both the intake and exhaust vents are closed by massive blast valves. We only open them when we have to run the generators." She gestured around the mezzanine. "Up there is our main storage area. Pretty much everything that isn't perishable or hazardous is stored up there. Sometimes it's not very convenient, but there's plenty of space."

"Yeah," Jack said, again shaking his head in wonder. "No kidding."

"But this," she told him, leading him into the lab area, "is the heart of what we're doing here. We've got one of the most advanced genetics research labs in the world under this dome. We can do any type of karyotyping, we've got FISH stations–"

"Fish?"

"Fluorescence *in situ* hybridization," she explained. "FISH is one of the ways that we study chromosomes. We can do virtually any type of gene-related analysis here, from DNA sequencing to tailoring DNA and injecting it into cells with a gene gun. "

"I'll take your word for it," he told her as they walked up to the outer periphery of the equipment-laden workstations arranged around the huge lab. He couldn't recognize most of what he saw, but even in his ignorance he could tell that Jerri's lab at the FBI Laboratory in Quantico hadn't been this well-equipped.

Several people waved at Naomi, who waved back while Jack gawked.

"They're working on the corn samples you brought," she told him, nodding toward a cluster of seven people on the far side of the lab, "matching it against the blueprints in the data Sheldon sent you."

"What do you expect to find?" Jack asked as he watched. "You've told me how devastating this stuff could be, but I still don't really understand why."

Naomi looked at him. "How much do you know about genetically modified organisms," she asked him, "especially crops like soybeans or corn?"

Jack shrugged. "Not much, really," he told her. "It's not something I've given any thought to. I never saw any reason to before my world blew apart."

"They're in almost everything, Jack," she told him. "At least here in the U.S. Some countries in Europe and in Asia grow or import them, too, but here it's hard to find crops now that aren't genetically engineered." She shook her head. "Over eighty percent of all the corn, soybeans, and cotton grown here are engineered strains, and almost all of it is controlled, directly or through license arrangements with other conglomerates, by New Horizons. There are also strains of rice and wheat, but they haven't gained a majority share of the market yet, thank God."

Figuring that Jack had seen enough of the lab, she led him back toward the blast door and repeated the same steps to open it as when they'd come in.

"Many of the crops are engineered to be more resistant to insect pests and herbicides, or to have a higher yield," she went on as they stepped back out into the main junction. "The original idea was to create crops that wouldn't need a lot of pesticides or herbicides, and when they did have to be sprayed to kill bugs or weeds, the chemicals wouldn't harm the crops. And some strains were engineered to produce more, so you could get more cotton, for example, per hectare of land."

She sighed as she led Jack through the junction and entered the tunnel that would take them to what used to be the base's three missile silos. Jack couldn't make out the end of it, it was so far away. "It was a good dream, Jack," she said wistfully. "I devoted my life to making that dream come true."

"I take it that things didn't work out like you'd hoped," he said.

"No," she said, shaking her head. "At first it *was* my dream come true: I was a young star on an all-star team, doing some of the most cutting-edge research on the planet and being paid a mint for it. But I had no idea what was really going on, or that I and the others in my field were being used to fulfill an agenda we never could have guessed at." She looked up at him. "The crops have had lots of problems, Jack," she told him. "Have you ever heard of the law of unintended consequences?"

He shook his head.

"It basically says that any intervention in a complex system may or may not have the intended result, but will inevitably create unanticipated and often undesirable outcomes." She sighed. "That's what's happened. DNA is a very complex system in itself, not to mention the biosphere that the plants are in, and the place they occupy in the food chain with respect to livestock and ourselves. It doesn't matter if you believe what people say about the problems, ranging from food allergies to overt toxicity," she told him. "What matters is that the government relies on the companies to provide proof that the crops are safe, without any independent verification."

A sudden realization hit Jack as he remembered what Naomi had told him earlier. "And a lot of the senior people in the government who would be responsible for giving the green light are in New Horizons' pocket," he said.

"Very good, Jack," she told him with a wry smile, but her expression sobered quickly. "So, New Horizons and a couple of other biotech conglomerates now control most of the world's food supply. In many places, farmers can't even buy non-GMO seeds, because they've been wiped out of the local market, or are so expensive the farmers can't afford them. And even if they could, the farmers around them are probably spraying herbicides that will kill the non-GMO crops. Not to mention that the chemicals are also toxic to humans and livestock." She stared down the tunnel. "There have been a lot of unintended consequences, Jack, that all could be written off as more of humanity's hubris, seasoned with corporate greed.

"But the truth is that those companies have positioned themselves to be the perfect vector for the next generation of genetically engineered organisms that will be marketed as the be all and end all for farmers everywhere, resistant to insect pests and to several different types of herbicides, plus a little extra twist."

"And it's the twist that's the big catch," Jack surmised.

"Yes," she said quietly. "This new line is being called *Revolutions*, Jack. And it will do everything that the company claims it will. I should know. I helped create it." She frowned. "They also plan to share the technology with the other conglomerates under liberal licensing agreements. We even know from our sources in government that there are congressmen lined up to support federal subsidies to make these particular crops affordable to the most destitute of foreign countries." She walked along in silence for a moment before saying, "And the twist is this: embedded in this particular line of crops will be a retrovirus capable of modifying the DNA of the host that consumes it."

Jack stopped and stared at her. "So what does that mean?" he asked. "That you eat some of this new corn or whatever, and it'll just start changing your DNA?"

Naomi nodded, and Jack felt a shiver run down his spine at the pain etched on her face. "That's exactly what I mean, Jack," she told him bitterly. "We were never able to do anything quite like this before. Gene therapy is an up and coming medical technology that's enjoyed some success, but it's still in its infancy. Revolutions could have really lived up to its name. And then I learned what it was really for."

Jack watched as she blinked tears from her eyes before going on.

"I was on a small, highly secret project at LRU that was working on this, and we had a tremendous breakthrough," she went on. "We were able to saturate corn cells with what you might call a retrovirus placebo, and were able to engineer a delivery system for it that allowed it to be absorbed into the host during digestion. It would even survive cooking and other types of processing commonly used in the food industry if it wasn't too prolonged or at too high a temperature.

"After the host consumed it, it was carried throughout the body in the bloodstream, and wherever it wound up, the retrovirus particles successfully penetrated the host's cells. The placebo didn't alter any DNA, but it proved what we could do, that the delivery system would work." She wiped her eyes again as she started to walk onward down the tunnel.

Jack barely understood what she was saying and wanted to disbelieve every word of it, but he remained silent.

"Just think, Jack: we could have targeted genetic defects or cancer with tailored retroviral packages delivered through food. We could have done nearly anything, and not through expensive treatment of a single individual: we could have treated entire populations. Humans, livestock, fish – anything. The possibilities were endless. As were the potential horrors.

"The night that the breakthrough was made," she told him, "three of the team members died in a car accident. They'd been out celebrating, and the police report said that the driver, Dr. Jaswant Singh, had been drunk and drove the car off an embankment. I was sick that night and didn't go with them. I never thought that I'd be saved by the flu." She shrugged. "I knew Singh well, and he didn't drink anything but water and tea. The police report was a fabrication, or the autopsy was doctored. With those three dead, only myself and Dr. Kempf were left."

"Kempf?" Jack asked. "LRU's dean?"

"Yes," Naomi said. "She was the university dean more in name than fact; the assistant dean took care of all the day to day business, while she spent most of her time in the lab working on the Revolutions project. I hadn't heard about the deaths of the others when I went to the university lab the next morning. I was still feeling terrible from the flu, but I was so excited that I went in, anyway." She wrapped her arms around herself, and Jack could see goose bumps on her flesh. "I joined her in the lab and she...propositioned me." She stopped and looked up at Jack, and he could see the terror in her eyes, lingering from that day over a year ago. "She told me that the project was about to be taken into its final phase, and the others hadn't been able to accept it. She stood there and told me that she'd killed them, Jack!"

Before he could think, Jack had wrapped his arms around her, drawing her shivering body close. "You don't have to say any more," he whispered into her hair as she wrapped her own arms around his waist, holding him tightly.

Naomi shook her head. "No," she rasped. "You have to know this. You have to understand." Taking a breath, she went on, "She said that I had the talent that she needed, that the others had been useful tools, but nothing more. She said she would make me rich, far richer than I could imagine, working on the final phase of the project. I could have whatever I wanted, Jack. Anything. All I had to do was to keep on being brilliant, working with her, the two of us alone, in secret, developing targeted strains of the retrovirus. She didn't say exactly what they would be for, but I knew it couldn't be good." She shuddered. "I had no idea what to do, Jack. I was trapped in the lab with her. I thought she was insane."

"So what happened?" Jack asked softly.

"I agreed," she whispered. "I told her that it sounded like a wonderful idea and rolled out every avaricious desire I could think of."

"And she believed you?" Jack asked, shocked.

After a brief pause, she said, "Yes."

"Why?"

Naomi pushed herself away and looked up at him. "She believed me because I'd been spoiled and greedy, Jack. By that time I was easily worth twenty million dollars. I knew I was a hot commodity and never made any bones about making the company bleed green for my services, especially after working like a slave to position myself to be on the staff at LRU. Yes, I had dreams about doing some good things. I think we all do. But I expected to be well paid for making those dreams come true, and Kempf was appealing to that part of me, the part she thought was strongest." Naomi shook her head as he opened his mouth to protest. "I'm not saying I was a devil, Jack; maybe more like a spoiled brat. I'd never really had to grow up, even after my parents died. I'd always been self-centered in a lot of ways, even more after they died. But I grew up that morning. Fast.

"I was actually lucky," she continued, "that I'd had the flu. I could feel the blood draining from my face as she spoke, but I was so pale and washed-out that my reaction didn't register with her. Kempf told me that I'd be watched closely to make sure I didn't go back on my word, then she let me go."

"What happened after that?" Jack asked. "I know from what Special Agent Richards, the agent in charge of the LRU investigation, told me, that your house was abandoned: you just disappeared."

She took his arm and guided him along the seemingly endless tunnel, toward what looked like another blast door up ahead. "I never made it home," she told him. "Gregg's people had been watching the lab. They knew what Kempf really was, and knew about the deaths of the other researchers on my team. Gregg knew they had to move quickly if they wanted to get me, to get what I knew, before I could do anything that would get me killed." She gave him a wan smile. "After the other night at your house, you can probably appreciate what they did. I drove home, scared to death and feeling terribly ill. I noticed a car that followed me out of the university parking lot. Kempf's watchdogs. They didn't even make a pretense about it, just got up right behind me and stayed there. Along a stretch of isolated farmland that I drove through to get home, a big SUV suddenly pulled alongside the car trailing me and blasted the car off the road with shotguns and assault rifles. I floored it and just took off." She chuckled. "I own...*owned* a Tesla, an electric sports car that makes a Porsche look like a covered wagon. I left the SUV in the dust. Then my phone rang. It was Gregg, telling me that he knew about the lab and Kempf, and offered to get me out of the fix I was in."

"I'll bet he didn't zap you with a cattle prod and drug you to sleep," Jack grumbled.

"Actually," Naomi told him, "he did, if it makes you feel any better." She sighed. "I miss my stupid car. I hate driving rental minivans when I get to go topside."

Unable to help himself, Jack started laughing, and a moment later, Naomi did, too. It didn't last long, but it felt good.

"It's just lucky for Gregg that he saved Koshka, too," she said, "or I would have zapped *him* with an electric prod."

"Koshka?" Jack asked as they came to another huge door marked Blast Lock #2.

She smiled. "She's my cat."

He suddenly remembered the white long-haired cat in the photograph he'd seen of her.

"She and Alexander have been getting along quite well," Naomi said with a grin.

"Oh, jeez," Jack muttered. "He hasn't been any trouble, has he?"

"No, Jack," she told him with a quick smile. "He's sweet. And as you'll see, cats are more than welcome here."

"So, where are we now?" he asked her. The blast lock formed a wall in the tunnel and had two entrances. One was a massive blast door not unlike the one to the lab and control center domes, although not as big. Next to it was part of a cylinder made of steel that was nearly six inches thick and perhaps three feet across, clearly designed to roll back into the concrete wall of the small junction they'd reached.

"This is Blast Lock Two," she told him as she quickly ran through the same entry routine with her badge, a six-digit combination, and a retinal scanner that were in the wall next to the cylindrical door. "When the site was built, this and another lock like it were designed to partition off the missiles from the rest of the complex. In case of an accident, or if a nuclear blast destroyed one or more of them, the rest of the complex would be safe. Now it's one of our main physical security points, modified a bit. We normally just use this smaller entrance to go to this part of the complex, and only open the main door if we need to move something larger."

The cylinder hummed open, rotating into the wall. But unlike the other doors he'd seen so far, this one opened into a man trap: whoever entered couldn't get to the other side without standing inside it while the door rotated and closed off the main tunnel again.

"Come on," she told him. "It'll be a little tight, but shouldn't be a problem."

Shrugging, Jack entered the cylinder behind her.

Holding up her badge to a camera mounted in the ceiling, she said, "It's Naomi and Jack Dawson. Open up, please."

"Roger, Naomi," a man's gruff voice came from the speaker next to the camera. "Rotating now."

Jack looked over his shoulder as the man trap's door began to rotate closed.

Naomi turned around and pulled him away from the closing door. "The first rule of doors in this place, Jack," she said as she pulled him up against her, "is to never get caught in one."

His breath caught in his throat as he looked at her, so close now that their lips were almost touching. His chest tingled where her breasts pressed against him, and he felt a flush of heat and desire as his body immediately began to react. He halfheartedly tried to back away to keep from embarrassing himself, but her hands, still on his waist, pulled him even closer. For a long moment, he was lost in her blue and brown eyes as she looked at him with a mixture of appraisal and invitation.

Then the door hissed to a stop, the other side standing open now, and the moment was over. Slowly, Naomi let go his waist and turned to step out of the man trap into the tunnel.

Jack, at a loss, stood there for a moment, trying to sort out his feelings and failing miserably.

"Come on, Jack," she said softly. "We've got one more stop for now."

With a sigh and a shake of his head as he gradually regained control of his rebellious body, he moved to walk beside her as she took him down a tunnel that branched off the main one.

"Naomi..." he began, not quite sure what to say.

She held up a hand, stopping him from saying anything else. "I'm sorry," she said. "I shouldn't be a tease. Like I told you, I'm still a spoiled brat at heart." She grinned, but it was tinged with sadness. "Living here, and knowing what I know, knowing what's out there in the world, has given me a different perspective. It's like living under the sword of Damocles, living in fear. Wondering if we can stop what's happening, and hoping we don't get killed in the process. I haven't really had anyone to share anything with for a long time." She chuckled. "I'm also dead tired. You've been knocked out the last twenty-four hours, while I've been awake the whole time, working my ass off in the lab. I guess I'm getting a bit punchy."

"Well, I'm not necessarily complaining," Jack said with a smile. He couldn't help but be attracted to her, but part of him knew it was nothing more than stress and the lack of close female companionship since he ended his relationship with Jerri years before. *Still*, he thought to himself, *you could do a lot worse, brother*. "I just...need to get my head around all this," he told her finally. "I still feel like I'm in some sort of bizarre dream, waiting to wake up."

"The dream's going to get worse before it gets better, Jack," she cautioned him.

"What's that supposed to mean?"

"There's something else I have to show you that you're not going to like," she said. "That's the 'everything' that Gregg meant when we left the command center. But we're going to do that after I get some sleep. I just can't face it now."

"Sansone," Jack said, and Naomi nodded.

They came to a small junction, and Naomi turned right. "To the left is the old propellant terminal," she said, "where they used to store the fuel for one of the missiles." They walked past another tunnel that branched off to the left. "That's the silo, one of our deep freezers. I'll show you what's in there a bit later."

Straight ahead of them was a sign that read "Apartment One," but Jack didn't notice. He had been turning over in his mind the things she'd told him, and realized he was still missing a vital piece of the puzzle. "Naomi, if you helped develop this retrovirus delivery system, you must have known all about it. So why did you send Sheldon in there? What was he really after?"

"The prototype retrovirus that Kempf created after I left," she said grimly. "We learned from one of our insiders that she had finished her work on the prototype seeds that were infused with the first functional retrovirus. Sheldon went in to try and get samples so we could see exactly what the retrovirus was intended to do."

"So you never knew what the retrovirus might really be?" he asked, and she shook her head. "Just playing devil's advocate for a minute, what if it's benign? And what about all the stuff on the EDS web site about the Earth being terraformed by some evil extraterrestrials?"

She frowned. "You don't believe it now, Jack – there's no way that you could, not yet – but we believe it's true. But our only proof up to now has been anecdotal information that we've never been able to back up with anything that would stand up to scrutiny in the scientific community or wouldn't come across as a hoax. What we find in that corn, the retrovirus itself, will be indisputable scientific proof of what New Horizons and its allies have in store for us."

"When will you know?" he asked as they came to the normal-looking metal door for Apartment One, which opened quietly on well-oiled hinges.

"It'll probably take two or three days, working around the clock," she told him as they stepped into a hallway that was about twenty feet long, with an elevator in a vestibule area on the right side. There were three doors along the length of the hallway. "This is one of the three 'apartment buildings' we've got in the complex," she told him. "They used to be the equipment terminals for the three missile silos. Each one is a huge four-story reinforced concrete cylinder, forty feet across. We put in three apartments on each floor. Most aren't occupied right now, but probably will be soon." She headed to the first door on the left and opened it. "This one's yours."

As Jack stepped inside, the lights automatically came on. He saw that the apartment was furnished much like Naomi's room in the command center, but was somewhat larger. It had a nice, if compact, bathroom with a shower, and there was a microwave and small refrigerator in one corner. A large flat-screen television was mounted along the curving outside wall, facing a queen bed and a comfortable-looking arm chair.

"God, I'm tired," Naomi said quietly as she leaned against the door frame, eying the bed as Jack explored the room. "Having my room in the command center usually saves a lot of walking, but these rooms sure are a lot nicer."

In the more even light here in his new home, as opposed to the stark overhead illumination in the tunnels, Jack could clearly see the rings under her eyes. She looked as if she was ready to fall over from exhaustion. "Come here," he told her, reaching for her hand.

"Jack..." she said, uncertain.

He smiled at her sudden coyness after how she'd acted with him in the aptly-named man trap only a few minutes ago. "Lie down," he told her, and she finally took his hand and let him lead her to the bed. "You're whipped, and there's no reason to walk all the way back to the command center. Besides, I got to sleep in your bed, so fair's fair." He pulled the covers back. "And I won't attack you in your sleep. I promise."

"Damn. That's no fun," she muttered with a grin as she sat down on the bed, slipped her shoes off, and then lay back on the clean sheets and pillow. She was so tired that she didn't bother trying to take her clothes off.

Jack was partly relieved, and partly disappointed. "Maybe later," he told her softly as he pulled the covers up around her.

"Now go away so I can sleep," she told him.

"Well, I would if I could," he said, "but I think I'm stuck in here with you. I can't get through any of the doors."

"Uh-uh," she murmured. "Just use the intercom. Ask Renee to let you back through to the command center. You should check on Alexander, too."

"Okay," he said, gently pulling the blanket up around her shoulders and brushing a wisp of hair from her face. "I'll do that."

Naomi didn't say anything more. She was already fast asleep.

Ten

After calling Renee on the intercom, Jack wandered his way back through the tunnels to the command dome. He passed a handful of other people who nodded politely at him, but he also noticed that their eyes almost instinctively glanced at his chest, looking for a badge that he didn't yet have. None of them made any comment, however, and he kept on going.

He felt displaced, totally out of sync with reality, as if he were in a bipolar dream world that alternated between the horror of this secret war that he had fallen into and the totally unexpected pleasure of Naomi's company.

Naomi, he thought. *Talk about an emotional roller-coaster.* First he thought he should hate her for being involved somehow with Sheldon's death. Then she saved his life. *And now...Now, what?* he wondered. Part of him felt like his emotions and pent-up desires were just carrying him along, while the logical part of his brain cried, *Whoa! Slow down, boy!* Maybe Naomi was interested in him, maybe she wasn't.

He couldn't deny his own attraction to her. But he'd barely even met her, and he didn't believe in love (or even infatuation) at first sight. It was like time had been compressed, a relativistic effect of the madness he'd fallen into, making it seem like they'd known each other far longer than they really had.

With a sigh of frustration, he looked up at the security camera outside the blast door to the command center and was rewarded with a loud beeping as it began to cycle open. He made his way upstairs to Renee's station and gratefully sat down in a spare chair that she had wheeled over for him.

"Welcome to Oz, kid," she said, handing him a cup of coffee. "Hope you like it black."

"Thanks," he said, taking a sip of the bitter but excellent tasting brew. He looked around, but Thornton was nowhere to be seen.

Tan, however, was working at one of the other stations, and had positioned himself so he could both work and keep Jack in his peripheral vision at the same time.

"Gregg's off shift," Renee told him, knowing exactly who he was looking for. "Don't mind him, Jack. He really doesn't mean it personally."

"He sure fooled me," Jack told her bluntly.

"He's got the world on his shoulders," she explained. "He and Naomi. Before she came along, Jack, this was all Gregg's show." She gestured at the command center around her. "All this, and a lot more, really, is because of Gregg, his determination and organizational genius. He had a lot of help, of course, but he was one of the first ones to learn the truth of what was happening, and took the lead in organizing a resistance. He lined up the funding, set up the front companies, got this place put together." She shook her head in undisguised wonder. "He did all this in just five years.

"The reason he was upset about you," she went on, "was that he's always handpicked the people who come into EDS, and he hates taking in 'strays,' as he calls them. I thought he and Naomi were going to slug it out over her going after you." She took a swig of coffee from her mug. "Knowing we can trust everyone is vital for one simple and important reason: all of our lives, and humanity's survival, depends on our operation remaining a secret. That's a pretty hefty burden. Sometimes we get stuck with a charity case like you." She smiled. "But I'd say we lucked out on that deal."

Jack held his hands up in mock surrender. "Okay, okay," he told her. "The guy pissed me off, but it's not like I hold a grudge. I just still can't believe all this, Renee. I don't *want* to believe it. I mean..." He paused, looking around the command center, imagining all that lay beyond it, buried deep underground. "I know it's real. I know what happened to Sheldon was real, and everything that's happened since. But I still feel like I'm just imagining it all."

"I know, kid," she said, patting his knee as if he were a child. To some people such a gesture would have come across as patronizing, but from Renee it seemed genuine and reassuring. "It's like being fired down the rabbit hole, strapped to one of the old Titan missiles that used to be here. Alice didn't have anything on us!"

"I just wish Sheldon would have told me," he said quietly. "I know I probably wouldn't have believed him, but I wish he would have, anyway. And how he died...Jesus."

"He was a good man," Renee said. "He talked a lot about you, you know. Especially to Naomi. The two of them got to be pretty close, and his death hit her damn hard."

"Oh," Jack said, suddenly feeling very uncomfortable. "Naomi didn't mention that they were, ah, involved." *That figures*, he thought. *Sheldon, you always did have a way with women.* But it made Jack's situation with Naomi a bit more complicated in his mind.

Her eyebrows shot up in surprise. "Involved?" she asked. "Like boyfriend and girlfriend?"

"Well, yeah," Jack said, confused at her response. He was even more confused when she started laughing. Tan looked up from his console, his face as stony as ever.

"Oh, no, kid," Renee said after she'd regained her composure. "He was gay as the day is long. He and Naomi got to be close, but not like *that.*"

Jack's mouth dropped open. "*What?*"

"I guess he had another little secret that he didn't bother to tell you."

Shaking his head, Jack said, "Come on, that's not possible. He had a ton of girlfriends!"

"Of course he did, Jack," she explained, "but they were friends who happened to be women. He cultivated the appearance that they were lovers, but they weren't. He kept that part of his life well-hidden."

"But why?" Jack asked, knowing instinctively that what she was saying was true, but feeling hurt nonetheless by another secret that his dead friend had kept from him.

"He didn't want to screw up his career, and he also didn't want to risk losing your friendship. Those two things were incredibly important to him, Jack, and he made a lot of personal sacrifices to keep things that way." She leaned forward and took hold of his hand. "He was a good man, Jack. And a good friend."

"Yes, he was," Jack said, a small grin breaking through his glowering expression, "but if he was here right now I'd still kick his ass for not telling me this stuff." He looked down at his coffee for a moment before he asked, "So...what's the story with Naomi?"

"What do you mean?" Renee asked, but Jack could tell from the smile on her face that she knew exactly what he meant, but was intent on torturing him over every scrap of information.

"Come on," he said, amazed at how comfortable he felt talking to this woman, "you know what I mean. She seems to almost...know me, I guess, and she has me a bit off-balance." Renee cocked her head at him. "Okay," Jack admitted, "I feel like I've been knocked on my ass and run over by a semi. Happy now?"

Renee chuckled. "Yeah, that's our Naomi," she told him. Then, more seriously, she went on, "She does know a lot about you, Jack. Sheldon talked about you a lot, about how he wished we could get you on the team, but Gregg didn't see the need for another hired gun." She nodded toward Tan. "We've got a fair number of those, probably some of the best in the world, although personally I think Gregg's wrong: we could always use another good one, or a hundred." She paused. "I think Sheldon sort of hooked her on you. I monitor all in- and outbound computer traffic to make sure nobody's doing anything they shouldn't – it satisfies the gossip in me! – and I saw her doing a lot of personal research on one Jack Dawson."

"She was checking up on me, huh?" Jack wasn't sure how he felt about that. In a way it was flattering, but in another way it seemed a little creepy.

Knowing what he was thinking, Renee shook her head and told him, "She wasn't prying, Jack. I think you were sort of an escape for her. Not in a little girl fantasy way, but as a young, brilliant woman having to live like a hunted animal way. A lot of us, me included, even Gregg, believe it or not, still have homes topside. We work down here in shifts under cover of the local front companies Gregg set up, then go home to mow our lawns and bitch about our neighbors. We can pursue semi-normal lives while we try to save the world. We're still under the radar with New Horizons, and our faces aren't on the most wanted lists. You just joined that august group, Jack, and I know you're having a hard time accepting it, especially having come from the FBI yourself.

"But Naomi's been at the top of the bad guys' hit list since she found out what Kempf was doing at LRU, and they've been hunting her ever since. You have no idea of the risk she took in rescuing you. That's only the fourth time she's been topside since Gregg brought her in a year ago. They would give anything to get her, because she's the only one still alive who was directly involved in the final phase gene research." She frowned. "We have our own eyes and ears in the enemy's camp, plus the digging that I and some of the others do through cyberspace, and we know that there's nothing that the powers-that-be at New Horizons would like more than to kill her, except maybe wiping this place off the map." She looked over toward where Tan was working. "Most of the men here are either totally focused on the job, like your best buddy Tan over there, or only have an interest in getting into her pants. That's one reason why she was really close to Sheldon: he was a nice guy who didn't have any ulterior motives. He was a safety valve for her, one that I think she badly needed after being cooped up down here so long. That's what I think she sees in you, Jack: a good guy who's not going to try and take advantage, if you know what I mean." She looked at him, but this time there wasn't any humor in her expression. "I hope she's not wrong."

Leaning back, Jack tried to imagine how horrible it must have been for Naomi to have been down here, cooped up in this place for a year. Then he realized that his own plight was now the same: the FBI would never stop until they found him. At last, he said, "Like you said earlier, I feel like I'm riding a rocket down the rabbit hole. I owe Naomi my life, and sure, I find her very attractive. But if Sheldon told you, or her, anything, it's that I don't exactly rush into relationships." He shrugged. "She may have to wait a while for a proposal."

Renee laughed, satisfied. "Typical male," she chided. "Never willing to commit. Hey, speaking of typical males, there's Alexander and his new best friend."

Jack looked down to find Alexander and Naomi's cat, Koshka, milling around his chair. While Jack didn't consider himself a cat fancier, he figured that she must be a Turkish Angora, and he had to admit that her white coat and regal appearance were a beautiful complement to his own feline companion. With his leg bandaged up, Alexander couldn't jump up on his lap, and stared up at Jack while giving a plaintive meow. Jack reached down and picked him up, and the big cat instantly curled up in his lap and began to purr. Koshka flicked her tail in disdain, then jumped up on Renee's desk.

"Jesus," Jack whispered as Koshka turned around, preening as Renee petted her, and he got a look at her right flank. There was a terrible scar, only partly concealed by her white fur, that went from above her right shoulder blade, curved down across her ribs, and disappeared under her right hip. "What the hell happened to her?"

"It was a stupid accident," Renee said darkly. "One of our...former prisoners escaped and almost got Naomi. Koshka and some of the other cats attacked and distracted it...him...long enough for Naomi to get

away. But four of the cats and two of our people were killed, and
Koshka almost died. That was really hard for Naomi. She felt terrible
about the people we lost, but that cat is all she has left of her former
life." She turned sober, frightened eyes on Jack. "Like I said, having
more gunslingers is never a bad thing for us. Not in my book, anyway."

"How did 'it' escape?" he asked, setting down his coffee so he
could pet both cats. He'd caught her slip with the pronouns. "And what
the hell was it?"

"I'm not allowed to tell you, Jack," she said apologetically.
"You'll find out soon. I know Naomi said she'd tell you everything, and
she will. But only she and Gregg are authorized to take you the whole
way down that path. Trust me: you don't want to go there any sooner
than you have to. There's no pot of gold at the end of that particular
rainbow."

Out of the corner of his eye, Jack saw Tan suddenly stiffen. He
peered intently at his workstation, then picked up his phone and after a
short pause spoke urgently to whomever was on the other end of the
line.

"We've got incoming," Tan said, hanging up the phone. He hit a
button on his console, and a bright yellow bar flashed across the bottom
of the big screens at the front of the command center, with an audio
warning that went off through the complex saying the same thing:
Portal Access In Progress.

"I'll get Naomi," Jack said as he gently set down Alexander and
then stood up.

Tan shook his head. "She's already on her way." Turning to Renee,
he said, "He needs a badge."

"I've already got it," she said. Digging through a pile of clutter on
her desk, she pulled out a photo badge and handed it to Jack. "Here. I
was going to give you this when we finished our little chat, but you
need it now. You can't get through the portal safely without it."

Jack took the thin plastic badge, which had a lanyard to go around
his neck. It had a magnetic strip on the back, and on the front was a
picture he recognized as one Sheldon had taken of him the year before.
Renee must have taken it from the photo frame Sheldon had given him.

"I thought that was a good one," Renee said. "A lot better than the
one in the database for your driver's license, Jack. Good heavens."

He looked up as he heard Tan's voice over an intercom that must
have echoed through the entire complex. "Security team, to the portal."

"Do you guys always go through this drill when you open up this portal thing?"

"Yes," Tan said brusquely as he held out a Heckler and Koch G36C carbine. It fired the same 5.56mm ammunition as the venerable M-16 assault rifle, but at twenty inches with the stock folded, was far more compact and would be easier to handle in tight quarters like the tunnels. "It helps keep us alive. Here, take this. You know how to use it?"

Jack took the stubby rifle, making sure it was on safe. He'd fired other H&K weapons, and this one operated much the same way. "Yeah, I can probably figure it out," he said, unfolding the stock to its open position. He preferred to aim at whatever, or whomever, he was shooting at, rather than spraying ammunition while firing from the hip.

Tan only grunted before turning away, moving quickly to the stairs to the first level of the command center with one of the compact rifles in one hand.

Turning back to Renee, Jack was surprised to see that she was strapping on a shoulder holster with an automatic pistol.

"I told you, Jack," she said, as she moved over to Tan's console, which Jack saw was a security monitoring station, "we're in a war and we don't screw around with stuff like this. Everyone in the base is given weapons training. We do this for every portal opening, but this one's unusual: it's not one of our scheduled deliveries or changeovers that we normally do at night. It's broad daylight, which means that it's a bit of an emergency. Hurry up. Tan won't wait for you."

Doing as she said, he hurried after Tan, just getting through the command center's blast door as it was cycling closed behind him. *Changeovers that we normally do at night*, Renee had said. *God, I don't even know what time it is*, he thought absently as he ran down the tunnel toward the main junction. He saw a dozen men and women, all heavily armed, standing around the huge blast door to the portal that Naomi had pointed out to him on their tour earlier.

As he came to a stop outside the ring formed by the grim-faced security team around the portal entrance, Jack noticed that there were at least ten cats, including Koshka and Alexander, who had darted out of the command center right behind Jack to join the assembly. After seeing Alexander's reaction to Sansone, he understood why they'd use cats this way as part of their security process. He just didn't know what triggered their violent reaction to someone like Sansone, and he was afraid to find out.

Not sure what else to do, he followed the lead of the security team and pointed his rifle at the portal entrance, wondering what to expect.

"Renee, are we secure topside?" a woman's voice asked from behind them.

He turned to see Naomi striding into the junction. Jack knew that she must have sprinted to get here so fast, but she wasn't even breathing hard. She was also heavily armed, with her own G36C slung over her shoulder and a pump-action shotgun in her hands. She flashed him a quick smile as she made her way to the front of the group.

"Confirmed, Naomi," Renee's voice said from overhead speakers. "Outer personnel door is closed and locked. The revolving blast door is secure. No alarms for airborne contaminants. Topside activity appears to be normal. I show one individual standing outside the junction blast door. Her badge ID matches her facial profile, and the thermal scanner shows a normal body profile."

"Open the door," Naomi ordered tensely, and everyone brought up their weapons.

"Portal door opening," Renee's voice echoed in the junction. Jack heard dull thunks as the huge locking bolts slid back and the double-sided door, controlled by two massive hydraulic rams on each side, began to cycle open. This door, Jack saw, was the full height of the vestibule that connected the portal to the junction, a good eight feet high and as many wide, and fully two feet thick.

As the doors parted, Jack saw a woman who looked to be in her late twenties standing on the far side, staring wide-eyed at the rifles pointed at her and holding her hands high. Behind her, he could see a latticework of girders and metal stairs that circled around the inside of the portal structure, which itself was a huge concrete cylinder that was nearly thirty feet across and rose over seventy feet to the surface. In the center was a massive freight elevator that dwarfed the woman standing before them.

Under the watchful eyes of the humans, the cats wandered forward in their own good time, which in itself caused the security team to relax. Slightly.

Tan slung his rifle and approached her with a device that he held up to her right eye. Jack could see the blue luminescence of a laser that scanned her retina. A green light winked on the back of the device.

"Confirmed," Renee said, relieved.

"Welcome back, Ellen," Naomi said, walking up to the woman and giving her a hug. "We're so glad you made it back safely."

"I'm sorry I took so long," the woman told her shakily.

Naomi turned to Jack. "This is Ellen Bienkowski," she said. "She helped Sheldon get into the lab at LRU."

She's the one Richards was looking for, Jack suddenly remembered. Ellen was on the university's security staff, and had mysteriously disappeared the night of Sheldon's murder.

"Yes," Ellen said in a quivering voice as tears welled up in her eyes, "and I know how he died."

Eleven

"Everything was going according to plan," Ellen was saying. She was sitting at the head of the table in the command center's packed conference room, clutching a cup of hot tea. Everyone around her was tense with anticipation.

Jack sat next to Naomi at the table, across from Ellen. He was shocked when Tan had reached out to take Ellen's hand in a subtle but tender display of affection, and realized that they were probably a little more than friends. Jack's own hands were balled into fists that were pressed hard into his thighs as he waited to hear what had happened to Sheldon.

Thornton couldn't be there in person without risking his cover, for he had several important corporate meetings scheduled for the day. He had insisted that Naomi debrief Ellen as soon as possible, and he would watch the recording of the session when he returned to the base.

"I was able to deactivate and spoof the security systems, and got Sheldon into the lab undetected," Ellen went on. "I was monitoring him to make sure he was okay; I could see him through the lab's security cameras, and had voice contact through his radio link.

"He accessed the standalone machine that we knew was there. That's where he found the location of the prototypes in the freezers and the gene map files, just as we expected." She paused, looking around the room before her eyes settled on Naomi. "But there was another machine there, a laptop that I didn't remember seeing before. I...I told Sheldon not to bother with it, that it wasn't part of the plan, but he insisted on taking a look at it."

Jack nodded to himself. *That was Sheldon*, he thought sadly. He had to mess with every computer and gadget he saw.

"Was he able to get into it?" Naomi asked.

Ellen nodded her head in a quick, jerky move. "Yes," she said. "It took him a while, probably ten minutes. That put him behind schedule, but he was able to break into the file system." She paused. "It was Kempf's personal laptop."

"Holy shit," Jack breathed into a chorus of similar exclamations being made around the room.

"What was on it?" Renee asked after shushing the others.

"He...he wouldn't say," Ellen told them, shaking her head. "I tried to get him to tell me, but all he said after he found out that it was Kempf's machine and had checked through a few files was that he had to concentrate and to leave him alone until he was finished. He acted very strange about it; it was very unlike him."

"Then what happened?" Jack asked. Naomi had told him to let her lead the debrief, but he didn't care. He needed to know.

Ellen shrugged. "After he'd finished downloading the files we were after from the standalone machine, he took his thumb drive and put it into the laptop to retrieve more files." She looked at Naomi. "I was getting worried by then: he'd been in there too long. Then he took Kempf's laptop over to one of the networked machines, pulled out the network cable, and plugged Kempf's laptop into the university network."

"*What?*" Renee gasped, her face a mask of horror. The system administrators would be able to trace whatever he did on the network. "In God's name, why?"

"He wouldn't tell me!" Ellen cried. "I could see what he was doing on the video monitor, even though he wasn't telling me that he was doing it. I told him not to, that he had to finish what he'd come for and get out of there, but he just ignored me." She shook her head. "While the laptop was connected to the network, he went to one of the freezers and got the samples, then started trashing the place."

Jack glanced at Naomi, and she nodded. "That was part of the plan," she told him. "We were hoping to put off New Horizons at least a little while by trying to conceal what we were doing as an act of vandalism. We knew they'd immediately suspect what had happened, but they wouldn't *know* until they'd sorted through the mess and found certain samples missing."

"After that, he took out the hard drives from the standalone machine and smashed them," Ellen continued. "Then he watched whatever the laptop was doing until it must have finished, because he unplugged the network cable and replaced it in the machine he'd taken it from, then went to work taking the laptop apart." She looked up at Naomi with terrified eyes. "He had just finished destroying the hard drive when Kempf came into the lab."

"Wait a minute," Jack said, confused. "I know that Kempf was supposed to be on vacation in Italy. The special agent in charge at

Lincoln told me so. The FBI liaisons in Italy were trying to track her down, because she didn't carry a cell phone and could only be contacted through her travel service."

"It was Kempf," she told him firmly. "I've worked at LRU since it opened, and everyone knows the dean. It was her."

"She's one of *them*, isn't she?" Naomi asked in a subdued voice, and Ellen nodded.

"One of *what?*" Jack asked angrily. "Stop speaking in goddamn riddles!"

Naomi told him, "You'll find out just as soon as we're done here." Then, turning her attention back to Ellen, she said gently, "Go on, Ellen."

"Sheldon tried to bluff his way out, telling her that she was being investigated for a long list of crimes," Ellen told them, "but she wasn't having any of it. She said she wanted what he'd taken, that if he gave it to her she'd...give him a quick, painless death."

"He'd never give in," Jack thought aloud, and Ellen nodded, her eyes filling with tears.

"She came at him," she went on. "He pulled out his weapon and warned her off, but it didn't matter. He shot her, but it hardly slowed her down."

"He didn't remember the stun baton, did he?" Tan asked quietly.

"He did, but only after it was too late. He managed to keep his distance from her, trying to work his way back toward the door. He was almost there when she began to change."

Jack looked at Naomi and saw her close her eyes and bow her head, a pained, horrified expression on her face.

"That's when Sheldon remembered the stun baton," Ellen whispered into the deathly silent room. "I don't think he really, truly believed until then, even after all we showed him here. He got close enough to stun it, but not before it...lanced him." She was sobbing now, shivering with fear, and Tan wrapped an arm around her shoulders, his normally expressionless face now reflecting a look of tender compassion.

She paused for a moment, trying to regain her composure. When she was able, she went on with the tale. "He made it out of the lab, and I was able to follow him to the ground level. I don't know why he didn't try to just leave that way and get back to his car. Instead he went to the basement where the service tunnel entrance is. That's where I lost him." She looked around helplessly. "There aren't any security monitors in the tunnels." With a shuddering breath, she said, "The thing...Kempf followed him after it recovered from the stun. That bought Sheldon a minute or two. After it went into the service tunnel after him, I destroyed all the security recordings and the lab access records to cover Sheldon's entry. Then...then I followed my escape plan to get back here, renting cars with my bogus credit cards until I was picked up by an inbound truck that Gregg sent. I heard on the news while I was on my way back that Sheldon was killed. It...Kempf would have gotten the samples back. And his thumb drive with all the data on it." She turned an anguished gaze on Naomi. "It was all for nothing," she whispered. "For *nothing!*"

"No," Naomi told her, looking at Jack. "It wasn't for nothing. Thanks to Jack, we got it all: samples of the corn and all the data that Sheldon downloaded from those machines."

Ellen said, "But that's—"

In the brief moment before her next words, Jack saw something the others didn't: shocked disbelief. Maybe it was from his time in Afghanistan, or the FBI, or both, but he'd had a lot of experience at picking up on lies and deceit. He knew that she had been about to say: *But that's impossible.* His gut was telling him that Ellen somehow knew that Kempf had retrieved the corn samples and Sheldon's thumb drive. The only way she could know that is if she'd talked to Kempf *after* Sheldon had been killed. He knew he couldn't say anything about it now, but he wanted to know more about Ellen Bienkowski. A lot more.

"—wonderful news!" Ellen blurted. She put on a smile that seemed to put everyone at ease. Jack pasted one on his own face that he knew was just as fake as hers.

"That's what he was doing," Renee muttered, inadvertently diverting attention away from Ellen's act.

"What?" Naomi asked her.

"That's why he connected Kempf's laptop to the network," Renee mused, nodding to herself. "He must have found something on her machine that he didn't expect. Something so important that he didn't feel he could even trust Ellen with knowing about it. The sneaky bastard used Kempf's own laptop to encrypt the gene maps and other information that we expected to find, then super-encrypted the data he found on Kempf's laptop. Then he connected it to the university network so he could get the data to a safe location that even we didn't know about." She looked at Jack. "That fancy little photo frame he gave you."

"So..." Ellen began uncertainly, a sudden flush creeping up her neck to her face, "you got all the data? Everything that Sheldon found?"

Renee nodded. "Everything, if my assumptions about what he was doing are right."

"I think they are," Jack said woodenly. Sheldon didn't tell Ellen what he'd found because it had somehow implicated her, he thought, and he was afraid the data and the corn samples would never get back to us. A chill ran through him at the realization that Sheldon must have known then that he was being set up, and he had gotten the data out the only way he could. Jack knew the others around the table would consider that nothing more than ridiculous speculation, but the theory fit all the facts, and his gut told him he was right. Unable to help himself, he stared at Ellen.

She glanced at him before asking Renee, "And what was in the data from Kempf's laptop?"

"We don't know," Renee said with unbridled frustration. "He never left anyone, even Jack, with a password or pass phrase. I'm trying to crack the password with brute force, but I have no idea how long it is. It could take years."

"We don't have years, Renee," Naomi said. She wasn't scolding, simply stating a fact. "Sheldon sacrificed his life for whatever is in that file, otherwise he probably would have made it out before Kempf cornered him." She shivered. "I had always suspected she was one of them, but was never sure until now. God, I worked right next to her for a year!"

"I'm doing what I can, Naomi," Renee said levelly. "I can't change the laws of mathematics." She looked again at Jack. "The only thing other than luck that'll get us into those files is for someone to come up with Sheldon's pass phrase."

"There's something else you should know," Tan told Ellen, ignoring the others. "We have another prisoner."

Ellen gasped with surprise. Jack, watching her more closely than the others, was certain she'd faked it. *She's good*, he thought, seeing that Tan and the others had missed the subtle pause, as if she'd had to think just a fraction of a second before expressing surprise. Her facial expression was just slightly off, like a photograph that would have been perfect with just a little more exposure. He knew that he could be tainting his observations with what had become an unshakable bias, but he couldn't help it. *She already knew that Sansone was here.* He looked across at Naomi, but could tell from her expression that she had no inkling that anything might be wrong here. Unlike the others, who had known Ellen for some time, Jack had no preconceptions about her, only his impressions now. And so far, they weren't good.

Tan looked at Naomi, then Jack. "We can't discuss anything yet, as Jack has not yet been fully briefed."

"You should do that right away!" Ellen exclaimed, turning to Naomi. "He has to know everything."

Naomi nodded. "I'm going to take care of that right now," she said. "Tan, why don't you and Ellen go get caught up on things. I'm sure she could use some rest." Looking around the room, she asked, "Okay, people, let's get back to work."

As everyone began filing out, Naomi told Jack, "It's time for you to learn what we're really up against."

"I can hardly wait," he told her with grim sarcasm as they headed for the stairs to the command center's first level.

After leaving the command center dome, she led him through the junction and into the tunnel that led to the antenna complex nearly six hundred feet away.

"You ready for a bit of a walk?"

"Sure," he said, a chill running down his spine as they headed into the tunnel's mouth. He felt something brush his leg: Alexander, limping, with Koshka beside him. "I'm not carrying you all that way if your leg craps out on you, you dumb cat," he said.

Alexander ignored him, but stopped and stared down the tunnel. He suddenly laid his ears back, as did Koshka, and that really gave Jack the creeps.

"Come on," Naomi told him, taking Jack's arm. The cats followed along behind.

They walked in silence for a while, the cats padding quietly along behind them, before Jack asked, "So what do you use the antenna silos for now?"

"One is used for storage of our hazardous materials," she replied. "Explosives and other things that we don't want anywhere near the habitation and work areas. Both of the silos are seventy feet deep and thirty feet across, so there's plenty of storage space. It's also an auxiliary entrance of sorts, as it has an elevator where the old antenna platform used to be, so we don't have the safety headaches of taking explosives through the rest of the complex.

"The other antenna silo," she went on, "is where we keep our prisoners."

"Who – what – else do you have besides Sansone?"

"Sansone is the only live one," she said grimly. "We've only had two others, and both are dead."

"One of them is the one that almost killed you and Koshka, I assume," Jack said. Naomi looked at him sharply, and he explained, "Renee slipped a little when I asked how Koshka got the scar on her side. She forgot to use the right pronouns."

Naomi frowned, then nodded. "Yes, that was one of them," she told him. "He was a senior manager at New Horizons that we found out about, around four months after I came here. Tan led the team that captured him and brought him here."

"How did he, or it, get out?"

She frowned. "We don't really know. Someone left one of the safety interlocks off on the enclosure, and somehow the bastard managed to get out. They're incredibly innovative and determined, Jack. They're also utterly merciless. If you don't believe anything else that you're about to see, believe and remember that. We're nothing but insects to them."

Jack suddenly had a hunch. "Was Ellen here when this prisoner got out?"

Naomi stopped and turned toward him, her face reflecting a puzzled expression. "What does that have to do with anything?" she asked him. "Ellen has been with us since the beginning, when Gregg first formed EDS. She's been priceless." She shook her head. "What? Do you think she had something to do with Sheldon's death, or that she let the thing here escape?" She looked at him more closely before angrily saying, "You do, don't you."

"I'll be honest with you, Naomi," he told her evenly, refusing to wilt or retreat under her burning gaze. "I've interviewed a lot of people, people who had reason to cover something up, who had reason to lie. And I'm telling you that Ellen wasn't coming clean with us in that debrief. There's something more that she knows, something that she's holding back."

"So, you think she's lying about the whole thing?" Naomi accused.

"No," Jack told her. "That's the kicker: I think most of what she told us in there was the truth. That's what makes the lie so hard to see."

"I don't want to hear any more, Jack," Naomi said, shaking her head as she turned and continued on down the tunnel.

"Naomi!" he called after her, hurrying to catch up. "Was Ellen here at the base when that thing got out or wasn't she?"

"Yes!" Naomi nearly shouted. "Yes, she was! And so was Gregg. So was Tan and Renee, and a few dozen other people. Are they all traitors, too? You'd probably say I was, except that it tried to kill me, so I guess I have a decent alibi. Jesus." She looked at him with a combination of anger and disappointment that made him feel like pond scum, but it didn't change the truth of what his intuition was telling him.

"Fine," he said, holding up his hands in supplication. "I won't say any more."

"Good," she sighed, slowing down slightly, more so Alexander didn't have to work so hard to keep up with them. "And don't ever let Tan hear you say something like that," she told him quietly, "or he'll kill you."

"Right," Jack said quietly, thinking, Well, there goes our budding little relationship.

They continued on down the tunnel in silence. They paused about halfway through, when Jack looked down to check on Alexander's progress and noticed that he'd stopped a few feet back, obviously in pain from his injured leg. With a sigh, Jack picked him up and carried him over his shoulder. Normally the big cat purred any time Jack put a finger on him, but not this time. Alexander kept his head swiveled forward, his gaze riveted on the distant end of the tunnel, his ears laid back. Koshka stayed close by Naomi's side.

Jack was surprised to see three cats making their way back along the tunnel toward the junction. But they weren't moving with the devil-may-care attitude typical of many cats: they were silently slinking along in the shadows under the conduits running along one side of the tunnel. Their tails held low, they frequently stopped to cast a look behind them as if they were afraid of being pursued. They spared no more than a quick glance at Jack and Naomi as they hurried toward the main junction.

"I'm sorry," Naomi said suddenly, not long after passing by the trio of retreating cats.

"For what?"

"For being angry with you. I think you're wrong, Jack, totally wrong, about Ellen. But you're new here and don't know the people, what they've done or been through." She offered him a tentative smile. "It just made me so angry that I spoke without thinking. I don't usually get upset so easily."

"It's okay," Jack said, shifting Alexander's weight to his other shoulder. "I have that effect on people sometimes. I'm used to it."

"Well, it's also hard for me to stay angry at a man who's not too macho to carry his poor, wounded cat."

Jack snorted. "Two-legged servant," he muttered.

That was when Alexander began to growl.

"Christ," Jack said. "What is it with him?"

"It's the prisoner," Naomi said, and Jack saw that she had wrapped her arms around herself. She was afraid to come down here, he realized. "We don't know exactly what causes it, but cats are unusually sensitive to *them*. It's not smell, because the enclosure is hermetically sealed, and if it was a scent-based reaction, certain dog breeds should be even more sensitive to them than the cats, but they're not. So we rely on cats as part of our security system here, and in the homes of those who live topside." She looked at Alexander, seeing how his pupils were dilated wide open in a fear/fight response. "You were lucky, Jack," she said. "If you hadn't had Alexander to give you some concrete proof that something was wrong with Sansone, you never would have believed anything I said before it was too late, no matter what I told you as a warning. They would've killed you before we could've intervened."

"Yeah," Jack said, trying to force a smile through the increasing apprehension that gripped him the closer they came to the door that was now visible ahead of them. "And I'm sure the little beast will never let me forget it."

He saw then that there were at least a dozen cats clustered around the door in various aggressive poses. All of them were growling or hissing.

"Shit!" Jack cried as Alexander's claws suddenly poked into his skin, and he set the cat down to join the others.

"Even before we brought Sansone in," Naomi told him as they stopped to watch the cats' strange behavior, "when we only had the corpses of the other two, frozen in there, the cats would still do this."

She gave Jack a frightened look. "We're not really sure the things are dead," she admitted. Turning back to the cats, she said, "They'll come down here, all the way down the tunnel, and do this until they get so hungry they feel compelled to leave. And then they run back to the junction as if they're being hunted, just like the three cats we passed on the way here. They'll stay away for a while, as if they have to build up their courage to come back. But they always do."

"And that's why you had them at the portal when Ellen came in?" Jack asked. "To see if she was one of *them*?"

"Yes. Even the trucks that we use to move people and equipment have cats riding shotgun, you might say. Cats and thermal imagers."

His eyebrows went up at that, but all Naomi would say was, "You'll see." Then she stepped very close to him and said, "Jack, you're simply not going to believe what you see in there. Not at first, even after all that you've gone through." Taking him by the arms, she went on, "And from now on, we're not going to pretend that it's human. That was more for your benefit, Jack, because inside your head, you're still thinking of the woman from the FBI who came to your home. Even after shooting her point blank with a shotgun and seeing her get up again, your brain is still clinging to the fiction that she's human, because anything else is...madness. An impossibility. Right?"

Jack nodded. She'd hit the nail on the head with that one. He knew that Sansone couldn't have been normal, but there had to be some rational explanation for what had happened. Or did there?

"Just don't believe anything it says or does," she warned. "It will try to deceive you, Jack, in any way it can. I can't tell you how, but just be prepared for the unexpected."

He tried to swallow, but found that his mouth had suddenly gone bone dry. He really, really didn't want to see what lay beyond the blast door in front of them, guarded by the growling, hissing cats. "Let's do this," he rasped.

Giving his arms a last reassuring squeeze, she nodded and let him go, then stepped carefully through the cats to the door. Jack followed right behind her, surprised that the cats didn't crowd around the door to try and get in.

"They don't want to come in," she said. "It's like they know that they're here just to make sure it doesn't get out. They never come through the door."

She pressed an intercom button next to the door. "It's Naomi," she said, looking into a security camera located above the doorway. "I've brought Jack to brief him."

"Roger," a woman's curt voice answered. "Scan in, please."

Naomi stepped to the retinal scanner, holding her eye open for the blue laser.

"Confirmed," the woman, who Jack assumed was inside the antenna silo, said. The blast door began to cycle open toward them.

As soon as it was open enough for them to pass by, Naomi led him inside into what could most closely be described as an airlock.

"It's another man trap," she explained. "Although it's not designed to trap humans." Turning to another camera above them, she said, "We're secure. Cycle the doors."

"Roger. Doors cycling."

Behind them, the blast door, driven by another set of massive hydraulic rams, closed with a heavy *thunk* that Jack could feel through the steel floor plates, followed by the sound of the locking bolts sliding into place. Then the inside door, made of solid steel three inches thick, opened.

Naomi led him inside, and Jack stopped dead in his tracks at what he saw. As she had told him, the silo was a massive reinforced concrete cylinder almost thirty feet in diameter. The room they were now standing in was clearly a prison, but unlike any he had ever seen. There were three transparent cylinders, about eight feet in diameter, with walls and domed ceilings that were at least eight inches thick. Offset to the side in each one was a metal access hatch, easily six inches thick, that looked like the door to a bank vault. Jack could tell from the dull sheen of the metal that it was probably made of titanium. At the apex of the dome, which stood roughly ten feet above the floor, was an equipment cluster that included a variety of optical sensors, a pair of powerful remotely controlled gripping "waldos" that could reach anywhere in the enclosure, and something that looked like an oversized Taser in a small spherical turret.

Two of the enclosures were empty. The center one, however, was occupied, its prisoner watched over by three heavily-armed guards.

"Sansone," Jack breathed.

"Remember what I told you," Naomi whispered, touching his arm.

He batted her hand away. "Jesus, Naomi," he said, horrified, "what have you done to her?"

On the floor in the center enclosure lay Sansone, completely naked. Her body was covered with bruises, welts, and contusions. Jack was no medical expert, but he could tell from the pattern of injuries on her lower body that she had been sexually molested, brutally raped.

Remember, he tried to tell himself, *it's not human*. But in his mind he was no longer seeing Sansone, but Emily, his wife, just before she was murdered and tossed into a dumpster. The sight of Sansone tore his guts out.

"It's a lie, Jack," Naomi warned him, but he wasn't listening. He went up to the transparent wall of the cell and knelt down next to where Sansone lay on the inside, curled in a fetal position.

"Sansone," he called quietly, not sure if she would be able to hear him.

"Dawson?" she rasped, her voice coming from speakers somewhere above him. She lifted her head from the floor, painfully turning to face him. "Is that you?"

Jack fought back a wave of revulsion as he looked at her face, battered so badly that both eyes were swollen shut. "Yeah," he grated. "It's me."

"I'm sorry," she suddenly pleaded. "At the house. I'm sorry about what happened. We...we had orders to interrogate you. To bring you in." She paused, gasping for breath. "Then *they* came." She put a hand up against the inside of the clear wall, and he grimaced at the cuts he saw there, at the fingernails that had been ripped from her fingertips.

"Goddammit, Naomi," he snarled, turning on her. "Nothing justifies this! *Nothing!*" Two of the guards blocked his advance, their weapons leveled at his chest.

"It's a lie, Jack," she repeated calmly. Then, to the woman at the security console, she said, "Zap it."

"No!" Sansone screamed, clawing at the walls of her cell. "Jack, don't let them do it to me again. Not again! *Please!*"

Her outbursts momentarily drew the guards' attention. Before he realized what he was doing, Jack had darted forward to grab the barrels of both rifles the guards had trained on him, turning them up to point toward the ceiling. He savagely kicked one of the guards in the shin, knocking his leg out from under him and dropping him to the floor. He let the barrel of his rifle go, then turned and rammed his knee into the other guard's hip, throwing him off balance. Jack shoved him backward, wrenching the rifle from his grip as he fell. He took aim at the third guard, the woman who sat at the control console. Her weapon was out of its holster, but she hadn't had time to bring it up and aim it.

"Drop it!" Jack warned her. Glancing at Naomi, who hadn't moved, he said, "Tell her to drop it, Naomi, or I'll blow her fucking head off."

"Do it, Tamara," Naomi said.

"And tell these two clowns to move over there," he gestured with the rifle's muzzle to the small alcove on the right side of the sprawling room next to one of the empty cells. "You, too," he told Tamara.

The three of them did as they were told, the two men limping in pain.

"Thank you, Jack," Sansone whimpered. "Please, get me out of here."

"Get her out," he told Naomi. "Now."

"Jack—"

"Open it!"

Naomi moved over to the command console and looked back at him. Without saying another word, she pressed a control on the panel.

There was a sharp pop inside Sansone's cell, and then she began to screech just like she had at Jack's house when Alexander attacked her. He had tried to forget that sound, tried to suppress the memory of something that couldn't have happened in his reality. Yet here it was again.

Taking his eyes from Naomi, he turned toward Sansone and saw thin wire filaments trailing from the spherical turret in the top of the cell to a set of electrodes the weapon had fired into Sansone's back. She stiffened and then fell flat on her back onto the concrete floor.

"You Tasered her!" Jack shouted.

"Yes, I did," she replied calmly. The three guards made to move toward Jack, but she held up her arm, stopping them.

"Why...?" he asked.

It was then that Jack's thin hold on sanity fell away as he saw what was happening to Sansone. He stood there, rooted to the floor, as she began to change, to transform, into something that clearly wasn't human. Her features began to lose their detail, as if the flesh were changing into dough that merely resembled the human form. The color of her skin changed, as well, a sickly-looking swirl of yellow and purple covering her entire body like an enormous bruise. The cuts and bruises that had evoked such an emotional response in him faded, disappearing into the pulsating mass of tissue.

Then, like some hideous Phoenix rising from its protoplasmic ashes, multi-jointed appendages emerged from the devolving flesh, unfolding from what had once been Sansone's arms and legs. Her face disappeared, the faux visage oozing downward to join the bulk of tissue that had been her torso. A glistening green chitinous construct remained behind, a biological sensor array, an analog of the equipment mounted in the cell's dome. From the torso sprouted what Jack, had he been capable of speech at that moment, would have thought of as a biological Swiss Army knife. A big one.

Viewed as a whole, the thing reminded Jack of nothing so much as a giant cockroach that had been stepped on.

As the thing stood up on four spindly stalks that had unfolded from Sansone's legs, one of the "tools" from the pod shot forward against the side of the cell, hard enough that the reverberation from the strike shocked Jack into stepping backward.

As he looked at the indentation the thing had made in the wall of the cell, he felt a scream start to build in his throat. He suddenly saw an image in his mind of the cutting board in Sheldon's apartment after it had been ransacked, and the wavy groove that someone had cut into the hard wood. The pattern this thing had left in the wall was, if not identical, close enough that Jack knew that one of these things had been in Sheldon's apartment. And Jack had only missed encountering it by a couple hours, at most.

He dropped the rifle and backpedaled toward the door, a mindless scream on his lips.

Naomi was there to catch him. "Jack," she shouted as she tried to calm him, "this isn't a dream. It's real. But you're safe."

"No!" he cried, his heart thundering in his chest as he fought to get out, to get away from the horror behind him. "It's not possible! *This can't happen!*" He began to hammer at the door controls so hard that his hands began to bleed, cut by the unyielding plastic and metal.

"Listen to me," she told him, wrapping her arms around his chest, not in an effort to restrain him, but to reassure him. "Do you trust me?"

With one final slam of his fists against the controls, Jack shuddered. He had never been so terrified in his life, even after the horrors of Afghanistan, as he was now. His legs gave out, and he collapsed to the floor on his knees, Naomi still holding him tightly from behind. "Yes," he finally gasped as he fought desperately to keep from vomiting.

"Then listen to me," she said in his ear. "What you just saw, that *thing* in there, is what's real. It wasn't Sansone. Lynnette Sansone was a real person, but that thing killed her at some point and took her place. We just don't know exactly when. It showed you a tortured woman because it knew that would upset you, would get you to doubt what you knew, what we'd told you. They're incredibly good at deceiving us, Jack. I'm sure it knew about your wife Emily from its time mimicking Sansone at the Bureau. It found out what happened to her and tried to use that against you."

"And it almost worked," he rasped, horrified. "My God, I almost...I almost let it out. I almost..."

"No," she reassured him, "you couldn't have. There are safety interlocks that prevent the silo entry doors from opening after a cell door has been opened, unless it's been authorized from the command center. It might have escaped the cell, but it would have never left this room."

"It would've killed you and the others," he said. Shivering, he took hold of her hands in his. That was a burden of guilt, Naomi's death most of all, that he could never have lived with, even if the thing had somehow left him alive.

"Hush," she said, turning him around to face her. "That's not going to happen."

"Jesus, Naomi," he said, shaking his head, still trying to come to grips with the living nightmare he'd just seen. "Just what the hell are these things?"

With a grim smile, she said, "They're your little green men, I'm afraid. Come on, soldier," she told him, helping him to his feet, "it's time you got to know your enemy."

Twelve

As Naomi pulled Jack to his feet, he turned to the three guards and said, "Sorry, guys."

They just nodded, but he could see forgiveness in their expressions. Jack figured that just about everyone who came here to be "briefed" probably wigged out at first.

Then he turned to face *it*. The thing stood there, unmoving, with its eye stalks – *If that's what they are*, he wondered – fixed on him. Holding tightly to Naomi's hand, still unwilling to believe what his eyes were telling him, but unable to deny the truth of it, he followed her as she took him closer to the wall of the enclosure.

"We call them harvesters," she began. "We don't know what they're really called, or if they even have a name for themselves that we could comprehend, so we had to come up with something. Gregg coined the term, and it stuck."

"Haven't they..." Jack began, suppressing his revulsion at the thing's natural appearance, "...haven't they ever said anything about who they are or where they come from?"

"Nothing we were willing to believe," she said. "They're nearly perfect mimics, Jack, and they understand us better than we understand ourselves. We know they feel pain and discomfort, but beyond that we know almost nothing that we can really trust. We've tried every interrogation technique ever invented, using the carrot and the stick, but all we get is more of what they think we want to hear, or they just make that god-awful screeching sound."

"How do you know they haven't said something that was true?"

She shrugged. "I'm sure some of it probably is. The problem is sifting the truth from the lies. We have everything recorded, and there's a team at another site that has been trying to dig through all the crap to find the truth, but what we have is thin." Folding her arms, staring at the thing with undisguised loathing, she went on, "We're not sure how long they've been here. The UFO guys," she gave him a wry grin, "think they must have picked up our early radio signals and come running to find us. But then you have the issue of how many years it would take a radio signal to reach the nearest stars, the odds that these things live in any of those systems, and then the arguments start. They must have been here for decades, at least, to do the things we know they've done. But they could easily have been here for centuries, maybe longer. The honest answer is that we just don't know."

"There's no chance they could be, you know, from here?"

She shook her head. "Their cellular structure, especially of the malleable tissue, is so completely different from Earth-based life that there's not a chance they evolved here. I think they're genetically engineered themselves, tailored from their native form to be able to function on Earth." She turned to him. "All we know for certain is their mission here, which is to prepare our world for their kind, to transform our biosphere into something they can live in."

Jack, frowning, asked, "But if they were some sort of advanced extra-terrestrial race, wouldn't it be easier to just come in and blast us down to bedrock and rebuild things the way they want?"

"Would it?" she said. "Imagine how much went into reconstruction after the major wars we've had, the devastation to the planet if we tried to nuke an invasion force and they nuked us back, or worse. They think on a scale far larger than we do, Jack. We're lucky if we can plan something out a few years. We believe their time scale is measured in centuries for a project like this: they're willing to trade time for economy. Conquest is expensive; extermination isn't." She shook her head. "The irony is that we made it easy for them just by being who we are: they've been using our technology against us, injecting critical information at key junctures in our development to unwittingly aid in destroying ourselves. And here we sit, ignorant of what's happening in the shadows, thinking that we're smart and doing smart things, or perhaps stupid things but reaping enormous profits from it."

"And the corn Sheldon found, and the other plants like it, are the key," Jack said.

Naomi nodded. "Think of it as a type of pesticide, Jack. Once the engineered strains of the primary food crops like corn, wheat, and rice, and feed crops like alfalfa, are released into the market, there won't be any stopping it. It will cross-pollinate with native strains, carrying the retrovirus with it. We don't know what the retrovirus does yet, but whatever it is, it isn't going to be good for anything that currently lives on this planet. Except for *them*. Every person or animal that eats it, or consumes animals that have eaten it, will be contaminated. Once that happens on a mass scale, there probably won't be enough of us left to matter, and they can just march in and wipe us out with a flyswatter. And that's the least unpleasant scenario that we've come up with."

"I hate to ask, but what's the worst?"

She looked at him, her brown and blue eyes blazing. "The worst, Jack, is the sort of horror movie stuff you saw on the EDS web site: that we could be transformed into biologically compatible life forms. And you can bet that *homo sapiens* wouldn't be at the top of the food chain in a world ruled by them."

"How can they be killed?" Jack asked, forcing himself to look at the creature not through the eyes of a shocked and frightened human, but as a veteran soldier striving to learn his enemy's weaknesses.

"Their skeletal structure is tougher than Kevlar," she replied. "Assault rifles will kill them at close range, but you'll probably use up most of a magazine. That's why most of us carry them in here. Shotguns are dicey, depending on the ammunition: slugs are best. Any handgun short of a .44 magnum is useless unless you just get lucky. Aim for the center of mass, because you're almost guaranteed to hit something. If you aim anywhere else, you don't know if you'll hit the exoskeleton or their malleable tissue; if you hit the tissue, bullets just pass right through. And you have to be quick, Jack. When they move, they move *fast*." She turned to the thing in the cell and leaned closer. "Fire also works nicely."

Hissing, the harvester stepped back away from the cell wall. There were obviously speakers inside the cell, carrying their conversation to the thing.

"They're very afraid of fire," she explained, "and with good reason: they burn like wood doused in gasoline. We found that out with the first one we captured: we took samples of the malleable tissue and subjected it to a variety of tests, and it nearly blew up in our faces when it was exposed to an open flame. That's why Gary Woolsey burned down the lab where one of these things was, because if it even got close to the fire, it would be dead. It's one of the very few weaknesses they have."

"Yeah, but you can't exactly go wandering around in here or topside with a flamethrower," Jack said.

"Exactly," she said. "We have a well-designed fire suppression system down here, but fire's never something you want to turn loose in a sealed underground facility. It's hard to use as a weapon, but we know for certain that it'll kill them. Quickly."

"So what's the deal with the Taser?" he asked, pointing to the turret in the chamber that had swiveled slightly when the thing moved away from the wall, tracking its movements. "You used a stun baton on Sansone...*it*...at my house, too, didn't you?"

"The shock disrupts their ability to control the malleable tissue," she explained, "causing them to revert to their natural state. Shocking them also has a similar stun effect on them as it does on us, rendering them helpless for a few moments." She looked at Jack. "That's when they're most vulnerable and is the best time to kill them if you can't use fire."

"When you were at the house, one of the people with you – Tan? – had a syringe of something that he stuck in its chest after it got zapped."

"Formaldehyde," she told him. "Plain old formaldehyde injected into their central neural ganglion acts like an anesthetic. That was an accidental discovery with the second prisoner. It has to be done right after they've been shocked, but enough formaldehyde will keep them completely knocked out for hours. Eventually their system breaks it down and they revive."

"Christ," Jack whispered, looking through the wall at the thing. As he watched, a tendril uncoiled from its thorax near where the utility pod was located. "What's that?"

"The lance," she told him, stepping closer to Jack and pointing. "Remember when I told you that Sansone killed Woolsey in prison, that he died of a heart attack just after she interviewed him?" Jack nodded. "They can extend that stinger almost ten feet and stab through almost anything short of metal plate. Sansone must have reached out with it under the interview table, where no one could see it, and pricked his skin. He probably never even noticed, because even the tiniest dose would be fatal." She looked down at the floor. "The Kempf harvester lanced Sheldon. I'm amazed he made it as far as he did before it caught up to him."

As if in demonstration, the creature suddenly whipped the tendril at the wall, aiming right at Jack's rib cage. It struck with such force that the needle on the end of the lance penetrated nearly an inch into the hard plastic.

Both Jack and Naomi jumped back, and the guards stepped forward, their weapons raised.

"Shit!" Jack cursed as the thing yanked the stinger out of the wall.

"It's plenty strong enough to kill you just by stabbing," Naomi shakily explained. "But it's designed to deliver a witch's brew of toxins that are among the most lethal poisons on the planet, and death from it is hideously painful. We've been working on an antivenin, but we only have a tiny amount in the lab so far, and we haven't tested it on humans yet."

"How the hell did they get here, Naomi?" he asked. "There must be some sort of ship somewhere, right? Or some, I don't know, communications system. They have to be able to talk somehow with their..." His tongue tripped over the word *people*. "...with other harvesters."

"We don't know, Jack," she said, her frustration plain. "Some think there must be a ship hidden away somewhere, like maybe the myth of Area 51 is really true. Others think they were dropped here and left to fend for themselves, maybe with their superiors checking up on them every once in a while. The only thing we're fairly sure of is that they don't appear to have any way to replicate or breed, at least the three that we've been able to study. But we don't know if that's typical of their species, or if these are specialized variants." She paused. "Even with as much as we've been able to find out, there are still so many things we don't know, and I'm terrified that ignorance is what will kill us."

Without thinking, he put his arm around her shoulder and she leaned against him, wrapping her arm around his waist. Together they stared at the nightmare in the glass chamber, trapped like a monstrous insect in a gigantic glass jar.

"I think I've seen enough," Jack said.

Nodding to the guards, Naomi, her arm still around his waist, turned to lead him out of the chamber.

Just as the inner door was cycling open for them, Jack heard a voice that made his skin crawl.

"We can help you, Jack." It was Emily's voice, the voice of his dead wife.

His spine rigid with dread, he let go of Naomi and turned around to again look into the chamber of horrors. There, inside the clear-walled prison cell, stood Emily, just as he remembered her from the last time he had seen her alive. She was completely nude. Beautiful. Alien.

"We know who did it," the faux Emily said. "We know who killed Emily. We can help you find him, Jack."

"Don't believe–" Naomi began, clutching at Jack's arm, but he gently placed a hand over hers.

"You're full of shit," Jack said quietly to the creature, a cold rage blowing away the remains of his fear. As Sansone, the thing would have had access to all the files of Emily's investigation, and it had obviously done some research before coming to visit him the other night. The one thing that made his blood run cold was her voice: how could the harvester have replicated that unless it had heard her speak, or at least listened to a recording? He didn't want to know. "You already pulled my chain once," he said, thinking of how he had fallen apart earlier at the sight of Sansone's beaten body in the cell. "You're not getting another chance." Looking over at the female guard, Tamara, he said, "Zap it, please."

"Nooo!" the thing shrieked as Tamara hit the control to fire the Taser. Jack watched in satisfaction as the abomination that looked like Emily tensed up and fell rigid to the floor. He didn't wait to see it transform into its natural state before he joined Naomi and left the antenna silo behind.

Passing through the gauntlet of hissing cats, Jack retrieved Alexander, who shivered in his arms as they walked in silence through the long, empty tunnel that led back to the main junction, trailed by a frightened Koshka. Alexander quickly grew tired of being held, and Jack set the squirming cat down so he could limp along beside his feline friend, and the two cats stayed close to their human companions.

"I'm sorry, Jack," she said after a while.

"Why?"

"You've suffered so much," she told him. "Sheldon told me about what happened to you in Afghanistan, and about Emily. I'm sorry you got drawn into all this. You didn't deserve it."

Jack snorted. "My life was going nowhere, Naomi," he said after a moment. "When I came back from Afghanistan, there was just...nothing. I felt nothing, wanted nothing, except maybe to kill the fucking bastard who murdered Emily. But even that..." He shook his head. "There wasn't enough fire left in my soul to spark a match. Sheldon sort of kept me sane, but aside from him and another friend who was killed in the FBI lab explosion, the only other person I've felt close to since then is that goofy cat." He nodded in the direction of Alexander, who limped along beside them. "I don't know. Maybe falling down the rabbit hole into this crazy world of yours wasn't such a bad thing. I've got a purpose now. I have no idea where it might lead, but for the first time in years I feel like I've got a reason to live."

As they continued walking, it dawned on him that the harvester's masquerade, taking Emily's form in hopes of again manipulating him, ironically had helped Jack to finally put to rest the hold her memory had held over his life. He would always cherish their time together, but she was gone, and nothing he could do would ever bring her back. Emily had haunted his relationships with Jerri and the few others he had dated, and it was time to move on. He felt as if the chain to an emotional anchor had suddenly been severed, finally setting him free.

When he and Naomi reached the junction, they stopped and turned toward one another. Her room was close by, in the command center dome, while his was farther down the tunnel in Apartment One.

She looked up at him, her brown and blue eyes fixing him with a gaze that sent a hot flare through his chest. He wanted her, and could tell that she had more than a casual interest in him.

It's been so long, he thought, about to ask her if she wanted to go to "his place."

But before he could say anything, she told him, "I'll see you later, Jack. I've got some work I've got to get done." She leaned forward and gave him a quick kiss on the cheek, then turned and walked toward the entrance to the command dome, Koshka following behind her.

Jack stood there for a while, feeling foolish. Something brushed against his leg. He looked down to find Alexander sitting on the floor, staring up at him. The cat meowed unhappily.

"Tell me about it," Jack sighed as he bundled the big ball of fur into his arms and headed down the tunnel to his apartment.

Thirteen

Jack stood off to the side of the swimsuit-clad men and women who crowded the pool deck, gyrating to the dance music pumping from the speakers, loud enough to make the beer vibrate in the bottle he was holding. He wasn't wearing a swimsuit himself, but had opted instead for some comfortable jeans and a black knit shirt. He got plenty of looks from those around him. Many of them were looks of appraisal, some of scorn for not baring some skin. He didn't much care either way.

The music they danced to was Sheldon's, one of his many compositions, a product of his talent with music and electronic wizardry. Some of his songs had even become very popular on the web. Jack couldn't tell most of them apart, but was happy that his friend enjoyed himself and was getting some recognition for his talents outside of the rigid environment of the Bureau. He glanced over to where Sheldon stood, surrounded by a bevy of gorgeous women and a few equally handsome men, conversing in shouts and laughing at Sheldon's outrageous jokes. Tall and broad-shouldered, his golden-tanned face bearing a smile that was bright and quick to appear, he had a striking appearance that never failed to turn the heads of the ladies. But his good looks were more than skin deep: he was a genuine good guy, and an even better friend.

That was the only reason Jack was here. He hated parties or any other kind of social gathering. He hadn't always been that way, but since the jarring traumas he'd suffered between nearly being killed in Afghanistan and Emily's murder, things like this had no appeal for him. He'd much rather have been at home painting, but Sheldon had invited him. And as Jack had in the past when his friend had invited him, he had agreed without protest: Sheldon had always been there for him, the best friend he had ever had, and the least Jack could do was to make an appearance at his shindigs and pretend to enjoy himself.

In this particular case, Sheldon had told him he was going on a field assignment that might last a while, and he was holding a party to celebrate. It was a tradition he had, of having a bash any time he went out of town for more than a few days, which didn't happen very often.

Thank God, Jack thought with a wry smile.

As he drained his beer, a blond beauty magically appeared with another bottle, taking the empty away and pressing a full one into his hand with an inviting smile. She was a knockout by anyone's definition, and was clearly interested in more than just dancing. Jack smiled back, but gently shook his head. He was still flying solo and didn't have any interest in a casual romp. He glanced toward Sheldon, who was watching Jack to see what he would do. Sheldon rolled his eyes and shook his head in clear exasperation.

"Okay," the woman mouthed to him over the thunder of the music, then stood up on her toes and kissed him lightly on the lips to let him know the invitation still stood if he happened to change his mind. Then she disappeared back into the throng of party-goers, her hips swaying to the beat.

With a sigh, Jack watched her go, turning his attention back to his beer. This would be the last one he'd drink: he had a limit of two. Even though he was off-duty, he always carried his backup weapon in a holster strapped to his calf, and it wouldn't do for an armed FBI special agent to wind up drunk. There had been plenty of times in the last several years when he would have liked to get completely shit-faced, but he knew that it wouldn't make the pain go away or fill the emptiness in his soul.

He wasn't sure how long he'd been standing there, sightlessly staring into the crowd, before he noticed that the pounding dance music had stopped. Now there was what sounded like an orchestral piece starting up that seemed totally out of place after the previous song, but it didn't surprise anyone at the party, including Jack: Sheldon's taste in music ran the full spectrum, and one of the reasons his parties were so popular was that he was full of surprises. Unlike so many of the other songs Sheldon played, Jack happened to recognize this one: *MacArthur Park*, the original version recorded by Richard Harris.

"Did you know," Sheldon said, having broken away from his groupies to come stand by Jack, wrapping an arm around his shoulder, "that this is my all-time favorite song?"

"Yes, as a matter of fact, I did," Jack told him with a smile. "You've told me about a billion times, even though I've only heard you play it once or twice before. That sucks, because it's one of the only songs you've got in that big library of yours that I actually know."

Sheldon laughed, drawing looks and smiles from those around them. It was a soul-deep, infectious laugh that had been one of the things that had originally drawn them together.

"And you still remember what I want on my tombstone, right?" Sheldon asked with mock severity.

Jack rolled his eyes. Sheldon had told him a million times. It had become a sort of joke between them, but it was something that Jack knew, deep down, Sheldon was actually serious about. "Yes, I remember," Jack sighed.

"Well?" Sheldon prompted.

Jack looked up at the sky and said, "*If you love me only in my dreams, let me be asleep forever.*" Turning to Sheldon he asked, "Did I get it right?"

Sheldon's smile faltered for a brief moment, and Jack thought he saw a trace of wistful sadness that Sheldon had never let slip before. "Yeah," he said, giving Jack's shoulders a squeeze. "Just don't ever forget those words, Jack. Promise?"

Puzzled by Sheldon's sudden seriousness, Jack said, "I promise…"

***

Just don't ever forget those words, Jack…

Jack came awake with a gasp, sitting straight up in his bed.

Fumbling with the intercom, he finally figured out the right buttons to push to call the command center.

"Jack?" Renee answered. "You okay?"

"Renee," Jack told her, "I think I may have the pass phrase you've been looking for."

"Then get your ass up here," she said urgently. "I'll call Naomi."

Ten minutes later, the three of them were glaring in frustration at Renee's computer screen.

"I'm sorry, honey," Renee sighed, "but that isn't it. I've loaded up every possible permutation of the words in that quote and they all strike out. Breaking it down to random letter combinations will take a lot longer, but…" She shrugged.

"Dammit," Jack cursed. "I know that's it. It has to be. That was the only thing he ever made a big deal over that would fit what we're looking for. He thought far enough ahead during the time he was in the lab to figure that *they* would come after me, and that you'd eventually come for me. The data would be safe in the photo frame, but he had to use a key that only the two of us might know, and that I'd eventually remember. And it wouldn't have been just a simple name or something like that."

"Yeah, we've already tried all the typical things," Renee said, leaning back and folding her arms. "Your name every which way, his, the cat's, birthdays, all that stuff. And in combination. Zip."

"Sheldon would never have done anything that obvious," Naomi murmured, staring at the screen. "I agree, Jack, that he would've expected you to know the key, but what if it's not just a set of alphabetic characters?"

"Shit," Renee muttered, smacking her head with her hand before she leaned over her keyboard and started carefully typing in numbers. "I'll bet he used a basic substitution. He wouldn't have had time for anything really fancy. He had to do it in his head on the fly, but he could have easily replaced the letters with numbers in the sequence of the alphabet: 1 for A, 2 for B, and so on through 26 for Z."

The tension rose as she neared the end of the sequence, carefully double-checking the numbers as she typed.

"Have you found anything?" a woman's voice said.

They looked up to see Ellen and Tan standing there.

"We think we found the pass phrase for the file Sheldon super-encrypted," Naomi told her, her voice nearly shaking with excitement.

Jack kept his own expression neutral as he carefully watched Ellen. She smiled at Naomi's words, but there were clear lines of worry around her eyes.

"Shit!" Renee spat. "That doesn't work, either. Damn you, Sheldon, I thought the world of you, but if you were standing here right now, I'd kick you in the balls."

"Maybe we'll never know what the pass phrase is," Ellen said quietly.

"Yes, we will," Jack said evenly. "Renee, he knew this would eventually wind up in your lap. I know in my gut that quote is my piece of the key. It has to be. Whatever he did to change it, he knew you'd be able to figure it out, either from something that the two of you knew together, or some bunch of mathematical mumbo-jumbo. *But you can solve this*. I know it."

"Jesus, kid," she said, looking up at him, an expression of wonder on her face, "I think you're right. It's like a two-part key. Even if they got hold of you and got the pass phrase – that you didn't even know at the time – it wouldn't help them without knowing whatever else

Sheldon had done to it. But I can't for the life of me think of what it could be."

"I didn't either, remember?" Jack said.

"Why wouldn't the harvesters just destroy the file if they got it?" Tan asked. "Why should they bother trying to figure out the key to open it, when Kempf must already know what it contains?"

"It's not the harvesters Sheldon was worried about," Jack said quietly, looking at Naomi. "If that was the case, he wouldn't have super-encrypted this particular file. It was meant to keep one or more of us from seeing it."

Renee sat back, stunned. "Jack," she said slowly, "do you have any idea what you're saying?"

"Yes, I do," he said firmly. "The harvesters have someone here on the inside."

"We already had this discussion," Naomi said coldly, "and I thought we had agreed to let it go."

Jack held her gaze until Renee spoke again.

"I'm sorry, Naomi," she said quietly, her eyes focused on the domed ceiling as she concentrated, "but I think Jack's right. There's no other explanation that fits. Sheldon would've stuck to the plan unless he saw a good reason to deviate from it. And he had Ellen watching his back, so...Oh, God," she whispered, turning to stare at Ellen as she came to the same conclusion that Jack had about why Sheldon had stopped talking to Ellen in the lab.

"What?" Ellen, cried. "You think I'm a traitor? *Me?*"

"I won't stand for this, Naomi," Tan said fiercely as he scowled at Jack. "We risked our lives to save you, you bastard, and this is how you repay us? By accusing one of our most trusted people of treason?"

Jack said nothing. There wasn't much he could say. But he was gratified, in a tragic way, that he wasn't the only one who had seen the connection between Ellen and what had happened to Sheldon.

"That's enough," Naomi said icily before Tan could say anything more. "Jack, would you leave us, please? I'd appreciate it if you'd go back to your room and stay there." She didn't look at him.

Feeling like he'd been slapped in the face, he exchanged a glance with Renee, who still wore a horrified expression, before he turned and silently left the command center.

***

After Jack had left, Naomi had done her best to calm down Ellen and Tan, then sent them back to their room. Even though she was wanted for questioning by the FBI, Naomi planned to send her topside with Tan when his shift was up. Her photo hadn't been circulated outside of law enforcement channels, so it was unlikely she'd be picked up as long as she stayed at the house and out of sight for a while.

Turning her mind back to Jack, she was furious over his now-public accusation. Yet, a part of her brain had been circling around what he'd said, ruthlessly examining it for weakness, but so far had found none. She couldn't – wouldn't – believe that Ellen had been turned. And if she had, why had she come back? All she had to do was tell the harvesters where the base was, and they would take care of the rest. The truck park topside would have been swarming with federal agents or soldiers by now.

"Damn you, Jack Dawson," Naomi muttered as she shoved those thoughts aside and fought to concentrate on her work. She was examining the preliminary workups on the retrovirus, and didn't at all like what she was seeing.

Naomi didn't have the resources to completely map the genome of the harvesters, but she knew enough to recognize patterns of their DNA in the retrovirus. She looked over report after report that had been put together by the research team in the short period of time they'd had to analyze the samples Sheldon had died to obtain, but all she got for her effort was a splitting headache. She was one of the best geneticists in the world, but the retrovirus and the beyond-brilliant engineering that had gone into creating it mocked her own intelligence. All the reports boiled down to one simple and chilling conclusion: without a great deal more time to study it, the only way to find out what the retrovirus did would be to infect an animal host and see what happened.

"Vlad," she called to an exhausted-looking young man with limp brown hair who wore a rumpled lab coat, sitting at the computer next to her, "I want you to prep one of the rhesus monkeys. Grind up one of the specimens of the corn and put it in the food. Let's test the entire vector process from consumption to gene transcription and see what the devil this thing does." She would much rather have done a more detailed and controlled series of experiments, but she knew that time wasn't on their side. They had to find out what this thing was, and quickly.

"Right away, Naomi," he said with a thick Russian accent. After a few more mouse clicks to save what he was working on, he got up and began to shuffle toward the far side of the dome where the animal area was located.

"And Vlad," she called after him, "be damned sure you put it in one of the level four biosafety containment chambers. We don't want that monkey running around loose."

He gulped, trying to wipe the frightened expression from his face. "*Da*," he said quietly, bobbing his head in earnest agreement.

As Vlad went to fetch the test monkey, Naomi continued to stare at the mysterious gene matrix on the screen, wondering what horrors it contained.

***

Renee sat at her workstation, her mind spinning from the possibility that Ellen had been turned by the harvesters. They were good friends, and she simply couldn't believe that Ellen had turned traitor. *There was no reason for her to turn*, Renee thought. *What could the harvesters have offered her in exchange for Sheldon's life, and probably for ours, as well?*

On the other hand, Renee couldn't escape the conclusion that Sheldon had found something in the mysterious file that he hadn't wanted to reveal to Ellen. That was based on the assumption that what Ellen had told them of Sheldon's actions in the lab was true. Jack seemed to think it was, and Renee was inclined to go with him on that: she instinctively trusted him. But if it were true, everything they had struggled for, and their very lives, might now be in danger.

Naomi, angry and hurt after the scene with Jack and the others, had gone to the lab to lose herself in her work, leaving Renee alone in the command center while the others worked in other parts of the complex or got some sleep. As long as Renee had coffee, she had no problem staying awake and alert for a full twenty-four hour shift or even longer, although getting someone to spell her for a quick trip to the bathroom now and then was always a challenge.

Speaking of challenges, she thought sourly as she stared at the screen and the mocking dialog box asking for the pass phrase for the stubbornly encrypted file, which Sheldon had named "secret." *What did you do, Sheldon?* she begged her dead friend. *Jack's so sure I can figure this out, but I've tried everything I can think of, and—*

"Renee?"

She looked up to find Ellen standing there, next to her workstation. The young woman's cheeks were wet with tears. And she was holding a pistol fitted with a silencer, aimed at Renee's chest.

"Ellen..." was all Renee had time to say before her friend shot her twice in the chest. Her mouth forming an "O" of shocked surprise, Renee was knocked backward out of her chair, her limp body rolling to a stop near the steps to the command dais, face-down to the floor.

"I'm so sorry," Ellen murmured over and over as she dragged Renee's body by the ankles into the small utility room next to the conference room.

After making sure the door to the utility room was locked, Ellen ran to Renee's console and brought up the security monitoring system. Taking a thumb drive from her pocket, she inserted it into the workstation's USB port. Several keystrokes and mouse clicks later, she had electronically altered the security camera recording of Renee's murder. Anyone who reviewed the video would see Renee at her workstation for the next fifteen minutes, after which it would show Ellen entering the command center and shooting her. The other security cameras would show what they normally did: empty tunnels and the occasional cat or two. Ellen was gambling that no one else would show up in the command center before she could get back from what she now had to do. She was fairly certain no one would: everyone had been so upset about Jack's accusation that she was a traitor that they had all found some place or reason to be alone. No one even considered the possibility that she really was a traitor.

Except for Jack and Renee, of course. It had broken her heart to kill Renee, but she'd had no choice. She would kill Jack, too, but there were other things she had to do first.

She brought up the command systems for the portal elevator and blast doors, and neutralized their fail-safes. Then she did the same for the security systems in the prison where the harvester was being held. She nearly vomited at the thought of what she was doing, at what she had already done. Months ago she had released the second harvester that had been captured, but instead of trying to escape as Ellen had planned, it had tried to kill Naomi. Ellen had barely been able to cover her tracks that time. The harvesters had not been pleased with her, but Ellen had shown Kempf the security video of the battle the thing had chosen over escape, and that had mollified her and the others, whoever they might be. She hoped that this harvester, Sansone, would be smarter. She prayed it was, because Ellen knew that this was it. Not because she was afraid she would be caught, but because she was running out of time for the harvesters to fulfill their end of the bargain she had made months ago. She had sold her soul, but she knew in her heart it was a worthy cause, no matter the price.

She finished her work on the security systems, suppressing all the alarms. Then she found the file Renee had been trying to unlock and wiped it from the network drive and the backup systems. She knew what it was, courtesy of the Kempf creature: the names and a wealth of personal information on the humans who knew the true identity of the harvesters and were considered their human servants. Kempf had told her the list was kept as a form of insurance, with updated copies kept by every harvester: should any of the humans on the list decide to turn, they had more than enough information to hunt them down. Sheldon must have seen her name when he opened it after finding it on Kempf's laptop, which Ellen hadn't known would be in the lab. His fate had already been sealed, for he had been Ellen's gift to the harvesters after the one she had released had been killed in the base, but he had surprised them all. *Now*, she thought, *no one would ever know what was in the file.*

She looked at Renee's chair again, a sob escaping her lips as her mind replayed the sight of the older woman being flung backward by the muffled gunshots. *I'm so sorry, Renee*, she thought bitterly, *but I didn't have any choice. Please forgive me.*

What made Ellen feel even worse was that Renee would take the blame for everything that was about to happen. Ellen had spoofed the systems and deleted the copies of the secret harvester file under Renee's login, and any accounting of the network's activity would only show her hand at work. After finishing what she still had to do, Ellen would return to the command center, put Renee's body back in the chair, and sound the alarm just after the video showed Ellen killing her brilliant friend, whom the others would believe was the true traitor.

Biting back the hot bile that seared the back of her throat, Ellen dashed out of the command center and down the tunnel that led to the antenna silo and the harvester's cell.

Fourteen

Jack paced in his room like a caged animal, fueled by anger and a sense of helplessness that he hadn't known since he had been told of his wife's death while he was still bedridden in Afghanistan.

Alexander, perched on the bed, watched Jack with alert green eyes, but remained quiet in the atmosphere charged by his human's mood. Ironically, Koshka had chosen to accompany the big cat back to Jack's room, and Jack had taken perverse pleasure in the fact that the sleek feline had temporarily shunned Naomi.

Naomi, Jack fumed. "Why can't you *see?*" he suddenly shouted, startling both cats. Renee had made the connection with Ellen almost instantly. Naomi was so brilliant, but blinded by loyalty to her people, not believing any of them were capable of such treachery. Jack knew better: he had seen it before in Afghanistan. He had no idea what Ellen's motives were, but he had no doubt she was dirty.

Looking over the pathetic collection of things he had left from his former life, he saw the photo frame that Sheldon had given him. The thought that a woman, a fellow human, must have given Sheldon up to the enemy nauseated him. What made it worse was that it was probably the same person who had released the harvester that had almost killed Naomi. That this collaborator was here, being treated like a hero by the others, brought on a tide of black rage.

You can stay here like a child who's been put in time-out, Jack berated himself, or you can go out and try to open their eyes to what's going on.

"Fuckin'-A," he snarled as he stormed out of the apartment, the two cats trailing after him before the door closed.

Taking long, angry strides down the tunnel to the blast lock that was the gateway to the main junction, Jack tried to rein in his anger enough to confront Naomi with as much logic as he could muster. The last thing he wanted was to get into a heated shouting match, but if that's what it took, then that's what he'd do. He wanted some answers from Ellen, and he was going to get them. Tan might be a problem, but Jack was ready for him. He hoped.

He swiped his badge on the panel of Blast Lock #2, and was surprised that the thick door began to open before he had entered his code or done the retinal scan. Frowning, he called to the camera and microphone mounted on the ceiling, "Renee?" Nothing. "Is anybody at the security station?"

Again, nothing.

That shouldn't be, Jack thought. With a growing sense of dread, he ran the rest of the way to the main tunnel junction, encountering no one but half a dozen cats. He headed toward the command dome entrance, and was again surprised when the blast door opened just with the swipe of his badge, the retinal scanner nothing more than a shiny hunk of inert metal embedded in the wall.

Ignoring the living quarters on the first level, Jack vaulted up the spiral staircase to the command center above.

It was empty.

"Shit," Jack breathed. He knew there should always be at least one person on watch. Always. And he knew Renee had tonight's shift. He carefully made his way among the cubicles, then he checked out the conference room. Empty.

He was just about to check the other door next to the conference room when he heard a voice behind him.

"Turn around, Jack. Slowly"

It was Naomi.

He turned around, holding his hands away from his body. She held a .44 magnum revolver pointed at his chest. She looked at him with a devastated expression, her eyes welling with tears.

"How long have you been here?" Naomi asked him in a wavering voice as she moved carefully toward the security workstation where Renee should have been. "And what have you done with Renee?"

"I got here just before you did," Jack told her, exasperated. "You must have heard me running up the stairs. I came looking for Renee, and for you. Something's wrong, and I think Ellen's at the heart of it."

"We know Ellen, Jack," Naomi told him. "We've known her for years. We–"

"For God's sake, Naomi," Jack shouted, "*think!* She's the only link that ties everything together, from the time the last harvester escaped, to Sheldon's death, and to whatever's going on now. Did you notice that the security systems are screwed up? I was able to open the blast doors just with my badge!"

"What?" she asked, the blood draining from her face. "That couldn't happen, unless..."

With dawning horror, she looked at Renee's computer and the command interfaces for the security systems. They had been taken off-line. Leaning down, still keeping the gun pointed at Jack, she quickly brought up the internal surveillance systems and video feeds. Everything looked normal in the tunnels and the antenna silo where the harvester was being kept. *That's the most important thing*, she thought, her mind trying to come to grips with whatever was happening. "Why would Renee do this..."

"It wasn't Renee, dammit!" Jack insisted. "She—"

He snapped his mouth shut as he heard it, a muffled cry from somewhere behind him. Forgetting about the gun Naomi still had trained on him, he quickly moved toward the sound, which was coming from the utility room.

Without stopping to think, he kicked the door next to the lock, slamming his heel against the metal surface. Fortunately, neither the door nor the door frame were terribly sturdy, and on the third kick the frame gave way with a loud *crack* and the door slammed inward.

Jack plunged into the small room to find Renee on the floor, her arms curled over her chest as she cried in pain.

"Renee," he breathed. "Jesus, what happened to you?"

"Ell...en," she rasped. "Bitch...shot me."

"Oh, my god," Naomi whispered as she knelt down next to the older woman. Gently but firmly moving Renee's arms aside, Naomi pulled up her sweater to examine the wounds, shocked to see that there wasn't any blood.

Instead, she saw the dark lining of a bulletproof vest. She found where the slugs had hit, penetrating about halfway through the armor. With Jack's help, she quickly got the armor off.

"Ahhh," Renee cried.

"You probably have a couple of bruised or broken ribs," Naomi told her as she and Jack helped Renee up and back out into the command center, carefully settling her into her chair.

"I think I figured that part out, girlfriend," Renee rasped. "Jesus, that hurts."

"What happened?" Jack asked urgently.

Renee shook her head. "I was just standing my watch when Ellen showed up and shot me point blank with a silenced pistol. She didn't say a damn thing before she pulled the trigger." She looked at Jack. "I got the creeps about her after that little revelation you led us to, and decided it was time to try out that fancy body armor that Gregg bought for all of us that I used to turn my nose up at. Just in case." She grimaced as another wave of pain shot through her chest, and she gritted her teeth.

"Do you believe now?" Jack asked Naomi.

She nodded. "Yes, but what is she doing?"

"I don't know," Renee growled, "but you'd better sound the alarm."

"Right," Naomi said. Moving to the security station, she lifted the plastic cover from the big red alarm button and slammed her hand down on it.

Nothing happened.

"Shit," Naomi cursed. She hit the button again. Still nothing.

"Move aside," Renee told her. Jack pushed her forward to the console, and Renee began to type at the keyboard, trying to unravel what Ellen had done. "God," she whispered, "she must have been planning this for months."

"Why do you say that?" Naomi asked, glancing worriedly at Jack.

"Because what she did here you don't just sit down and do..." Renee paused as she continued to backtrack through the changes Ellen had made to the security systems. "Oh, no," she muttered. "Goddamn it."

"What?" Jack asked.

"She password coded all the security access routines," Renee said, her voice edged with frustration and a rising sense of anger at Ellen's betrayal. "She even locked out the communications system. Dammit!"

"But you have the master passwords to the system!" Naomi said.

"So does she," Renee told her grimly as her fingers continued to fly over the keyboard. "Whatever she plans to do, there's nothing we can do here without rebooting all the servers...Oh, shit." Turning up to face the others, she said, "She also deleted the file we've been trying to break into. She wiped all the copies. I can't retrieve them."

She looked at Jack, and he was shocked to see her angry expression transform into a satisfied smirk. "But I'll bet she didn't get the original."

"What," Jack said, astonished, "did you put the smart card back in that goofy photo frame that's in my room? Without deleting all the files?"

With a wink, she nodded at him. "Why should I delete the files? There wasn't any reason to."

"Let's go," Naomi said, putting a hand on his shoulder. As he turned to face her, she added, "And I'm sorry, Jack. I'm so sorry."

"Don't worry about it," he told her, gently brushing his hand against her face. "Come on."

"Where to?"

"We've got to bang on some doors and wake people up," he said, turning and heading for the stairs.

Naomi put a hand on his arm and stopped him. "Jack, it's the mid-shift, and there's no one downstairs. I'm the only one who lives in the command dome, except Gregg and a few of the other topsiders when they need to sleep over. Everybody else is in the apartments near the missile silos."

Jack's hopes sank. "We can't run all the way there to get help and still hope to catch Ellen."

"You think she's gone to get the harvester, don't you?" she asked.

"Nothing else makes sense. What else is here that would be worth killing Renee?" *And probably others*, he didn't add.

As they turned to go, Renee said, "Hey, kid, you might need this."

Jack took the .44 magnum pistol she held out to him.

Then he followed Naomi out of the command dome and they cautiously headed down the tunnel that led to where the harvester was held.

***

At that moment, Ellen was standing before the prison that contained the creature they had known as Sansone. It had assumed that shape again, and stood, nude, facing Ellen behind the cell wall.

Behind Ellen, the three guards were sprawled on the floor, unconscious. She had lured one of them outside on the pretext of helping her with the malfunctioning retinal scanner, then stunned him with a shock baton.

The other two she had stunned with a shot from the Tasers she'd brought, then kicked each of them in the head to make sure they stayed down. After that, she went out and dragged in the first guard. The plan was to make it look like the harvester had escaped, killing all three. She only had to make the guards helpless. The harvester would take care of the rest.

It's worth it, she kept telling herself, trying hard to believe the words.

"Your people made a bargain," she told the thing in the cell. "Will you keep their word? That your people will make a cure for Tan?"

"Of course," the woman-thing in the cell said, staring into Ellen's eyes as its face altered into a chilling smile. "Free me. Now."

Taking a deep breath, Ellen nodded, then hit the necessary command overrides on the security console. With a hiss, the door to the containment cell sprung open, and the Sansone creature quickly stepped through it.

"Remember," Ellen said as she turned around, "you'll need to kill these three after I've gone back to—"

The rest of her words were lost to a scream of searing agony. With horrified eyes, she looked down to see the Sansone-thing's stinger in her belly, the poison sack near the end contracting and expanding as it pumped its lethal ejaculate into her body.

Ellen stumbled backward toward the door to the tunnel, pulling the hard tip out of her flesh. "No," she moaned as the stinger disappeared back into Sansone's chest, the flesh of the faux breasts swallowing it up. "You...you promised!"

With an angry snarl, Ellen brought up her Taser and shot Sansone, who went rigid and collapsed to the floor.

Ellen turned and fled through the open door into the tunnel. Her gut was burning as the creature's venom quickly spread through her body, bringing paralysis along with it. Groaning in agony, she stumbled as fast as she could back toward the command center, hoping that the Sansone-thing would remain stunned long enough for her to make it. And that the poison wouldn't kill her first.

***

"Did you hear that?" Jack asked as he and Naomi moved quickly down the tunnel toward the harvester's prison. He cursed the designers of this Cold War relic for every one of the nearly six hundred feet they had to run from the command center to the antenna silo complex.

"Yes," Naomi said, raising her magnum. "It sounded like screaming."

"Yeah," breathed Jack as he picked up the pace. "Somebody's coming."

Ahead, they could see the tiny shape of a human figure moving toward them at a shambling, staggering run.

"Damn," Jack said. "It's Ellen!"

Suddenly the woman collapsed to the floor, writhing in pain.

Naomi sprinted toward her, with Jack cursing her stupidity as he tried to keep up with her.

"Ellen!" Naomi cried as she knelt next to the stricken woman. "What happened?"

"I'm sorry," Ellen cried, taking Naomi's hand. "I...I didn't have any choice."

"Talk some sense, girl," Naomi said softly as Jack knelt down, aiming his magnum down the tunnel toward the antenna silo. It was still so far away he couldn't make out the door in the strange optical illusion the long tunnel created.

"They promised me...they'd help him," Ellen panted, her face contorted from the burning pain that was spreading through her body.

"Help whom?" Naomi asked urgently.

"Tan," Ellen sobbed. "He's got...pancreatic cancer. Metastasized before they found it. Inoperable. He's...he's dying."

"And they told you they could engineer a cure," Naomi said, the words like ashes on her tongue.

Ellen jerked a nod. "Sansone...betrayed me," she whimpered. "I was...a fool. Thought I could trust it. Stunned it." She looked at Naomi with an expression that was as much emotional as physical agony. "I let the other one loose...never would have done that...if I had known it was going to try and kill you. God...I'm sorry!"

"Didn't you say there was a cure for the poison?" Jack asked. He couldn't muster any sympathy for someone who had conspired to kill her friends, even for the man she loved, but she must know critical information about the harvesters, and the only way they could get it was to keep her alive.

"There's an experimental batch of the antidote in the lab, but it's never been tested on—"

"No," Ellen breathed, shaking her head. "Not on me. I...don't deserve it. Tell Tan...tell him I love him."

She suddenly began to flail her arms and legs in a violent seizure, nearly knocking Naomi to the ground.

But as suddenly as it had come, the seizure passed. When Naomi turned Ellen's head to see her face again, Ellen's eyes stared up at her. Sightless. Dead.

"She's gone," Naomi whispered. "We need to get to the antenna silo and find out what happened to the guards and the harvester."

"I think you'd better rethink that idea," Jack said as an unholy racket erupted from the direction of the antenna silo. His guts turned to ice as he heard the hisses and growls of at least a dozen cats mixing with the shriek of the harvester. It was loose. He got to his feet and backed up, his gun pointed down the tunnel toward the sound of the enraged felines, pausing only to grab Naomi's hand and haul her up from where she still knelt on the floor beside Ellen's body. The last thing he wanted to do was face the harvester in the tunnel with only the two weapons they had. On top of that, no one else in the complex besides Renee knew anything about what had happened. "Come on," Jack told her. "Run!"

They had almost made it back to the command center when the lights went out.

Fifteen

"What the hell happened?" Jack whispered as he and Naomi blindly stumbled forward in the pitch-black tunnel, trying to reach the main junction.

"She must've rigged the power systems to fail to help that thing get out," Naomi told him. "Dammit!"

"What's wrong?"

"Nothing," she hissed. "I just banged my leg against the cable tray." The electrical cables serving the antenna complex were carried in a metal tray that jutted out from the side of the tunnel wall.

"Shouldn't there be emergency lights in here?" Jack asked. The tunnel was utterly dark, without a single ray or glow of light along its length. Jack shivered when the cacophony of the battle between the cats and the harvester abruptly ended in silence after several terrified squeals of pain.

"There are," she said, her hand tightening on his, "but everything's tied into the computer systems and the battery grid. There are redundant backups, but Ellen must have shut them all down."

"Great," he muttered as he forced himself forward through the darkness, dragging the muzzle of the magnum along the cable tray to help keep him from running into it. He held tight to Naomi with his other hand. "How fast can those things run?"

"Fast," she said shakily. "Faster than us."

"And I'll bet they can see in the dark, too," he said grimly.

"No, they can't," she told him. "We think they can see and smell about as well as we can. They also have a very distinctive and unpleasant odor when they're in their natural state. You'll know it if you smell it, trust me."

Jack yelped as something suddenly brushed by one of his legs. He almost fired at it before he realized what it was: one of the cats. An urgent mewling cry sounded in the darkness, and Jack felt a wave of concern as he recognized that feline voice. "Alexander, you idiot, what are you doing here?"

Just then his right shoulder slammed into something solid and unyielding, and he sprawled backward onto the floor, losing his magnum in the darkness. "Shit!" he cried, and heard Alexander's limping gait patter away into the void that surrounded them.

"The junction!" Naomi told him as she groped for him in the dark, helping him to his feet and dragging him into the connector to the left that led to the command dome. "We made it!"

"Good," he said, angry that he'd lost his weapon. His right arm was numb from the force of the impact with the steel support wall that stuck out slightly into the tunnel beyond the cable tray, defining the entry to the main junction. "Now let's get in the command dome and lock the fucking door behind us."

Naomi suddenly stopped. "We can't," she said bleakly.

"Why?"

"There's no way to open the blast doors without power," she told him. "They're far too heavy to open without hydraulics. Oh, God, we're trapped in here," she whispered, drawing close to him.

"Come on," he whispered urgently. "You know this place like the back of your hand. There has to be somewhere in a facility this big where we can hide!"

"Not here, there's nowhere in the junction! We can't open the blast doors to either of the domes without power, and we can't get through the blast locks to reach the apartments or the missile silos, either!"

"Wait," Jack said, already groping his way forward in what he hoped was a straight line across the junction to the tunnel that would take them toward the part of the complex where the apartments and old missile silos were. "Wait a second. There was something else in the main tunnel here, maybe a hundred feet from the junction and before the first blast lock. You showed it to me on the map, but I can't remember what it was called."

It took Naomi a second to realize what he meant. "The liquid nitrogen terminal," she said.

"Does it have a blast door?"

"No...no! Just a heavy metal door with a deadbolt, but I have a master key that'll open it."

"Come on, then," he said as a bone-chilling shriek filled the tunnel behind them as the cats and the harvester again clashed. *Close*, he thought, his skin breaking out in gooseflesh. *Too goddamn close!* He just prayed that Alexander and Koshka had the good sense to stay away from the thing.

Jack managed to head into the tunnel without knocking himself senseless on anything. He kept to the left side, which he remembered was where he'd seen the alcove to the old missile fuel storage area that was now used for liquid nitrogen. Trailing the fingers of his left hand as a guide along the conduits that lined the tunnel, he pushed himself and Naomi as fast as he could in the pitch darkness.

About a hundred feet past the junction, his hand swept into an empty space along the wall.

"Here!" he whispered, guiding Naomi into the alcove. After frantically groping for the lock, she inserted the key with shaking hands and turned it. Jack grabbed the handle and pulled it open, gasping in fear as the hinges made a horrific squeal in the utter silence around them.

Shoving Naomi in first, Jack followed right behind her before slamming the door closed and locking it. He felt her hands grab his shoulders and pull him back into the darkness until they came up against the rear wall of the small room that provided access to the forty-thousand gallon liquid nitrogen tank that resided here. Jack faced the door, trying to focus all of his concentration on what might be happening beyond it as she wrapped her arms around his waist and held onto him tightly, her body shivering in fear.

"God, Jack," she whispered hoarsely. "I hate those things. The last one came so close to—"

"Give me your gun," he said, and she handed him the magnum. He held it pointed in the direction of the door. "I won't let anything happen to you," he promised, knowing full well that if the harvester somehow managed to get through the door, it would probably get both of them. Even with .44 magnum bullets, he doubted he'd be able to kill the thing before it stung them both with a lethal dose of venom.

Everything was unnaturally quiet, the only sounds that Jack could hear being their shallow breathing and his own heartbeat. *They can be killed*, he told himself in a mantra, over and over. *And this gun can kill it. Aim for the thorax. They can be killed...*

He suddenly heard a deep growl just beyond the door, and his heart sank as he realized that it was Alexander. *No, you stupid cat!* he thought, afraid to speak the words aloud for fear the harvester might hear. He knew the thing must have heard the squeaking hinges, but Jack hoped it might not be sure this was where they'd hidden. Alexander was already slowed down by the injury he received during the fight at the house, and in the alcove beyond the door he'd probably be trapped. *Run, Alexander!*

The big cat hissed a feral challenge to the approaching monster just as a horrible stench assaulted Jack's nose. Naomi's grip around his waist suddenly tightened.

"It's here," she whispered into his ear as he fought not to gag on the horrific odor of ammonia and something burning. "Oh, God."

Alexander chose that moment to attack. A hissing, shrieking battle raged for a few seconds that felt like a lifetime to Jack, as he imagined his cat again facing off against the horrible thing that had come for them. His blood turned to ice as Alexander's furious assault ended in a brief feline cry of agony.

Shaking with rage, Jack wanted nothing more than to open the goddamn door and face the thing, to stick the snub-nose magnum in its squashed-bug innards and blow it to hell. If he had been alone, he very well might have, but he couldn't abandon Naomi. Cats were hardly known for their loyalty to the humans who cared for them, but Alexander had been an exception. In his own feline way, he had always been there for Jack when he'd needed comfort or a laugh. He fought the tears that came to his eyes, but gave up when he realized that it wouldn't matter: his vision was useless in this total dark, anyway. He let the tears flow.

"Come on," he hissed as he heard the thing move one if its appendages across the door, like someone scraping the tines of a fork across a dinner plate. "*Come on, you fucker!*" he screamed.

The thing suddenly hammered on the door, a rapid tattoo of powerful blows that set Jack's ears ringing. The hammering became even more frantic, and he heard the shriek of shearing metal as the door frame began to give way.

"Oh, God, Jack, don't let it get in here!" Naomi cried.

Jack had a sudden flashback to his last patrol in Afghanistan. The world was tinted an eerie green from the night vision goggles he wore, and a series of images and sensations cascaded through his mind in slow motion. The wraiths of Taliban fighters that seemed to appear right out of the rocks around him and his men. The sharp reports of automatic gunfire and machine guns, the explosion of grenades, the desperate shouts and agony-filled screams. The biting smell of the gun smoke, the nauseating stench of voided bowels, the coppery tang of blood. Then the hammer blows that sent him flying backward to the ground. The bullets that penetrated his body armor at point blank range, the night vision goggles torn from his face by an exploding grenade.

Until now, he had never remembered seeing the blanket of stars above him with his naked eyes as he lay there, thinking that the world was dying around him, and that the stars were so beautiful. So beautiful...

In the pitch dark, snapping back to the present, he had a moment of perfect clarity. He pulled Naomi's hands away from him and stepped forward. Something slapped against his free arm and he grabbed hold of it, knowing instinctively that it was the whip-like appendage holding the stinger. He curled his left arm around it as if it were a rope and heaved with all his strength. The door finally gave way completely, and the harvester slammed into him, its horrible stench overwhelming.

Instead of resisting the force of the impact, he pivoted, pulling himself against the creature, ignoring the sensations of gelatinous flesh and chitinous exoskeleton against his skin. The whip-stinger writhed and twitched in his left hand and he felt one of the thing's "arms" groping for his neck. He jammed the muzzle of the magnum deep into the mass of malleable tissue covering the bulging nerve ganglion behind the creature's utility pod and pulled the trigger.

The blast was deafening as the flash illuminated the thing in a grotesque shadow theater. Its screech tore at his eardrums and he felt himself being lifted off the ground as he fired again. And again. The .44 magnum revolver held five rounds, and every single bullet struck home, blasting through the Sansone-thing's naturally armored body to tear out its guts.

After the last shot, the creature suddenly collapsed on top of Jack, and he felt the malleable flesh begin to ooze over him as whatever neural control the creature exacted over it failed. Gasping, he shrugged it off, still holding onto the whip of the stinger until he was out from under the creature's body. Then he shoved the pointed tip into the gaping wound blasted by the magnum, embedding it deep in the creature's thorax.

He managed to crawl the few feet to the back wall before he vomited.

"Jack," he heard Naomi say through the ringing left in his ears from the gunshots. "Oh, my God, Jack." Then her arms were around him, holding him tight.

He wasn't sure how long they had been holding one another before he saw light flicker on in the tunnel outside. A few minutes later, the complex alarm suddenly blared, and soon they heard the sound of shouting voices and running feet coming down the tunnel.

They were suddenly confronted by two dozen men and women with assault rifles and shotguns raised and ready to fire.

"What's going on?" Tan asked sharply, his gun aimed right at Jack.

"The harvester escaped," Naomi told him as she and Jack got to their feet and moved out of the service room and into the tunnel with the others. "Jack killed it. Lower your weapons."

With looks of shocked disbelief at the gruesome body of the creature lying only a few feet away, they did as Naomi asked, although most of them kept their fingers on the trigger. They wouldn't trust that the harvester was truly dead, or at least fully immobilized, until its body was frozen solid.

"Ray," she said to one of the men, "get to the command dome and make sure Renee's all right. But don't go down the tunnel to the antenna silo." Ray looked at her strangely. "I'll explain later, but for now just secure the complex down to the junction."

Tan began to follow Ray and the others, but Naomi stopped him. "Tan, wait," she said, taking hold of his arm. "I want you to stay with me."

He simply nodded and stood close to her like the bodyguard he had been since Naomi had come to them.

Jack's heart went out to him, even though he knew Tan would never accept his sympathy. And then he saw a small, dark form lying very still on the concrete floor against the far wall of the tunnel, with a white cat, Koshka, curled up against it.

"Alexander," Jack whispered as he shoved the magnum in the back of his jeans and crossed the tunnel, kneeling next to his four-legged friend. The top half of Alexander's left ear had been torn off, and the white fur of his belly was matted with dark crimson blood that had run into a pool on the floor.

"I'm so sorry, Jack," Naomi whispered from behind him. "But we've got to–"

"Go on," Jack told her, his voice cracking. "I'll be with you in a minute."

With a squeeze of her hand on his shoulder, she and Tan left to join the others.

"You stupid little shit," Jack whispered. "Why didn't you run?" Lifting the limp body from the floor, he was startled to hear a weak cry of pain. Holding Alexander gently, Jack could see that he was breathing. Barely.

"Naomi!" he called as he turned to run after them, Koshka loping along behind him. "*Naomi!*"

Naomi and Jack, with Tan following behind, ran to the junction, and Naomi called to one of the women there. "Theresa," she said. "See what you can do for Alexander." Turning to Jack, she said, "Theresa's our vet who looks after the cats. She saved Koshka."

Theresa carefully took Alexander from Jack's arms and told him, "I'll do what I can," before rushing into the lab dome, Jack staring helplessly after her.

"Renee," Naomi called to one of the ceiling-mounted microphones in the junction. She wanted to go see her in the command center, but she had to tell, and show, Tan what had happened to Ellen first. "What happened? Did you bring the systems back up?"

"No," Renee's voice answered. "It was all programmed. She had one machine set up to reboot the others, then it reset the power control systems. The power came back on before the security systems, so the portal doors would've had power, but everything else went into lockdown until the security systems were released. I have to hand it to her: she did a hell of a job. Especially the little video bit she put in at the end of the command center recording where she makes it look like she blew me away just after the systems came back up, making it look like I was up to no good. You'll love it. She really expected to get away with this whole thing by making me the scapegoat."

"What about the cell block?"

"Scranton, Hatch, and Pearlman are dead," Renee said grimly. "There's...there's not much left of them."

"What is she talking about?" Tan asked, bewildered.

Naomi looked at him, her face a mask of sadness. "Something..." she began. "Something's happened to Ellen." Turning to Jack, she said, "I need your help with this." She nodded down the tunnel toward the antenna silo.

"Right," he answered, his elation that Alexander was alive tempered by the agony of the revelation they now had to make about Ellen.

"Tan, come with us," Naomi said. "The rest of you, double check the power and other critical systems to make sure everything's working." Then she turned and, Jack walking next to her, headed down the tunnel toward the antenna silo.

Tan went with them, slowing only momentarily when he caught sight of the limp body that lay sprawled in the middle of the tunnel.

"What happened?" Tan asked woodenly as he knelt next to Ellen's body. The venom the Sansone-thing had pumped into her had reduced Ellen's once-beautiful body to a mass of necrotic tissue that made her look as if she'd spent hours in the makeup chair for a zombie movie. Tan bunched his hands into fists, his forearms bulging with strain as he fought to control his emotions.

"She..." Naomi began, then stopped to wipe away a tear from her cheek. "She told us about your cancer, Tan. Somehow...somehow Kempf, when Ellen was at the lab in Lincoln, must have found out and convinced Ellen it could cure you if Ellen would help them. Ellen let the other harvester out a few months ago. She...set up Sheldon. And she helped Sansone escape." Glancing at Jack, who could only stare grim-faced at Ellen's ghastly corpse, she said, "I can't forgive her for what she did, Tan, but she had a noble reason." She reached out a hand to touch his arm, but it was like brushing her fingers against cold granite.

"She betrayed everything, all of us, for me?" he rasped, shaking his head slowly. "I never knew. Ellen..."

Before either Naomi or Jack could intervene, Tan calmly drew the pistol from its holster on his thigh, stuck the muzzle under his chin and pulled the trigger.

"*No!*" Naomi screamed as she was spattered with blood and gore. Tan's body slowly slumped forward over Ellen, his head coming to rest on her breast, blood spilling from the grisly wounds in his skull. "Tan! No, no, *no!*"

Jack pulled her to her feet and drew her into his arms as four men came charging down the tunnel from the junction, weapons at the ready. They skidded to a stop as they saw the two dead lovers and the pistol still firmly clenched in Tan's fingers.

Naomi was quivering against Jack, desperately trying to hold in the sobs of anguish that sought release. Her fingernails dug into the skin of his back through his shirt, so hard that they drew blood. He ignored that and everything else, focusing his attention on her, holding her tightly against him. "I'm sorry," he told her. "I'm so sorry, Naomi. If I'd had any idea what he was going to do..."

"You couldn't have stopped him," she whispered. "And he was already...dying. I think he would have preferred it this way, except for what happened with Ellen. My God."

There was nothing Jack could say, so he simply held her as she quietly wept for her dead friends.

Sixteen

Unlike an hour before, the command center was bustling with activity. Jack stood at the center of a small whirlwind of people who were talking, heading up and down the stairs, making calls, and typing frantically on their computers. They were trying to find Gregg Thornton and letting the other members of the Earth Defense Society know what had happened.

Jack wasn't yet trained on their systems, so he contented himself with watching over Renee's shoulder as she continued to work on breaking into the secret file that Ellen had tried to destroy. Renee had recopied the original from the smart card in Jack's photo frame to the base's internal servers. She also put it on an external secure server that she had hacked into, disguising it as an innocuous-looking system file, but making sure that Jack and Naomi knew where it was and how to get to it. Just in case.

"You'll figure it out," Jack told her.

"Yeah, right," Renee sighed, leaning back and rubbing her eyes. "I just hope Sheldon didn't think I'm smarter than I really am."

"You're brilliant," he said with a smile, patting her on the shoulder before moving over to where Naomi was staring fixedly at her computer screen.

"Still nothing from Gregg?" he asked.

"Nothing," she said, clearly worried. She had sent an emergency alert to a smart phone that Gregg carried specifically for secure communications with the base. "He's never taken longer than ten minutes to answer, for real emergencies or the weekly tests we do."

"What's that?" Jack pointed to a timer in the window showing Gregg's contact information on her screen. It read 00:02:13 and was counting down toward zero with every passing second.

"It's his dead man switch limit," she said. "Everyone who goes topside has to make contact with the base once every twenty-four hours using preset codes. One code is an all-clear, the other is a duress code, used when they're in trouble and being forced to use normal communications procedures."

"And if they don't call in before the twenty-four hours is up?"

"We assume the worst." She looked up at him. "Gregg's never been this far into the twenty-four hours before. My God, if something's happened to him..."

Jack was worried, too, but not just about Gregg. "Naomi," he said, "you've got to start thinking about evacuating the base."

She turned from the workstation and stared up at him. "Why?"

"Because Ellen probably compromised us," he told her bluntly. "She's been a willing accomplice of the harvesters for months, at least since she let the last one out of its cage. I find it hard to believe that she never revealed anything that might lead them to us."

"Ellen would have told us if she'd said anything," Naomi said. "She had no reason to conceal anything from us...at the end."

Jack shook his head. "Naomi, even if that's true, don't you think the harvesters might have been able to learn enough from her over the last several months to figure out where this operation is? I know it's not an easy thing to consider with everything that's been invested here, but it's a damn big assumption that she never even slipped up and dropped a clue."

"If they'd known before, they would have come already," Naomi countered. "And if they had found out after what happened in Nebraska, they would have come right away, even before she got here."

"Besides," Renee said into the sudden silence that had fallen over the command center as everyone picked up on their conversation, "it's not a simple matter for us to evacuate from here, Jack."

"Listen, I know you don't just pick up an operation like this and all the research you're doing and move it at the drop of a hat," he replied. "I get that. But if the harvesters have the sort of influence in the government that you seem to think they do, once they find out what's going on here, they'll come. And even this fortress won't hold them off forever. You've got to have a plan B for when that happens."

"You don't understand, Jack," Naomi told him. "If it were only a question of saving ourselves or the research here, the equipment, it wouldn't be a problem. If it was just that, Gregg would probably have set up shop in a warehouse or office complex somewhere. And we do have backup locations for the research aspect of what we do here."

"But the reason we can't just pick up and leave is because of what's in the missile silos," Renee told him.

"The freezers," Naomi clarified. "We have the world's largest collection of genetically pure seed here, especially varieties of the primary agricultural food crops."

"And don't forget the bees," said a middle-aged man with a dark complexion and jet black hair. "Even worms."

Naomi smiled. "And bees and worms," she said with a respectful nod. "This is Dr. Vijay Chidambaram. He pioneered a method of sustaining honeybee and other critical insect larvae and certain types of earthworms in cold storage for what we hope will be a long, long time."

Jack stared at her, uncomprehending. "Seeds, honeybees, and worms," he muttered. "Oh, my." Looking between her and the smiling Chidambaram, he said, "I'm missing something. I thought the main thing you were doing here is research to figure out what this retrovirus that Kempf engineered into the crops will do."

"We are, Jack," Naomi explained. "And if we're successful, hopefully we'll be able to halt or even reverse the effects of the retrovirus on the human and animal populations.

"But even if we can defeat the retrovirus in humans and animals, if the New Horizons seed is released, we'll still have to deal with infected crops in the biosphere," she went on. "Every successive generation of infected strain and anything it cross-pollinates with will still have the retrovirus. The only way we can defeat the harvesters' plan in the long term is to destroy the strains they're putting into our food supply, and any wild cross-strains, and replace them with genetically pure species."

"And to do that," Chidambaram told him quietly, "we have to have large quantities of pure seed stocks to work from, and the critical facilitators from the plant and animal kingdoms to enable pollination and breeding. There are over fourteen hundred germplasm genebanks in the world. Seed repositories," he went on. "But most of them are small, and even the large ones do not have nearly enough seed stock to quickly regenerate the major food crops. And we must assume that whatever effect the retrovirus has on the biosphere will adversely affect the insects critical to pollination, thus our focus on preserving them, as well."

"But if there are already a bunch of these genebanks out there, why make another one?"

"Because they're vulnerable, Jack," Naomi said. "Remember: they don't know about the threat we face. Most of them have little or no real physical security, and some are victims to lack of funding or subversion, which we know the harvesters have capitalized on. That's basically what happened to Bari, the largest genebank in Italy," she explained. "Back in 2002 the Italian government decided to merge it with research centers that were focused on genetically engineered plants, and created the Plant Genetic Institute. The new management, which was run mainly by the GMO researchers, largely ignored the genebank's original mission of germplasm conservation – the preservation of native seeds – and focused the institute's resources on genetic research."

"They even let the cooling systems for the seeds in the cold storage vaults fail and didn't repair them for months," Chidambaram added. "It's difficult to estimate what damage may have been done."

Naomi nodded. "The harvesters and their human collaborators took Bari out of the game through political maneuvering and calculated neglect. The same has happened to many of the other smaller genebanks."

"Most of the genebanks contain a wide range of species," Chidambaram said, getting back on the subject of Jack's question. "Ours focuses on core food crops for humans and livestock, plus supporting species that help protect against pests and weeds. This makes our job somewhat easier, as fewer than one-hundred and fifty species, albeit of many varieties, are used these days in modern agriculture. Those and some plants critical for livestock make up most of what is preserved in the silo vaults."

"So this place is the secret backup for the backups," Jack said, and Chidambaram nodded. "But how long would that take? I mean, if the harvesters got their mutated strains out there and everything went to hell in the food chain, how fast could you sort things out again?"

"Even with the combined resources of all the genebanks, it would take years, possibly decades, especially if the crops of commercial seed producers were contaminated." At Jack's puzzled look, Chidambaram explained, "Most farmers don't plant from their own seed, but buy it from commercial seed producers. If their seed is contaminated, many farmers will have nothing to plant." He looked at Jack with dark, sad eyes. "Beyond whatever the retrovirus itself may do, it is nearly certain that millions, many millions, would die of starvation before the balance could be restored."

"And it might take centuries to root out and destroy any remaining vestiges of the retrovirus in the biosphere," Naomi added bleakly, "especially if those strains cross-pollinate with any plants outside of the agricultural chain."

"Jesus Christ," Jack murmured. Now he had a grasp of the magnitude of what was happening, but suddenly wished he had remained blissfully ignorant. "Okay, so I guess we just hunker down here and hope for the best."

Naomi stood up, stretched, and hooked her arm in his. "Come on," she told him. "I need to go check on some things in the lab, and you can check on Alexander."

As they made their way across the junction linking the two subterranean domes, he asked, "Would it really be that bad? If something happens to the...native seeds?"

She nodded. "Yes. The harvesters have a good strategy for whittling us down, and it's going to be hard to beat. And if something's happened to Gregg..." She shook her head. "I can't fill his shoes, Jack. I'm not going to say we can't go on without him, because we will, but if he's...gone, it will be a catastrophic loss to our cause."

That made Jack feel guilty about the less-than-kind thoughts he'd had about Gregg Thornton during their brief acquaintance, and he had to admit to himself that he'd never in a million years have been able to conjure up all the things Gregg had. The front companies, this huge facility, and whatever else was out there that was part of the Earth Defense Society that Jack didn't even know about yet.

"I've got faith in you, Naomi," he told her, and she slipped her hand into his and squeezed it.

After they passed through the blast door into the lab dome, Naomi guided him toward the back where there was what looked like a small operating theater with movable panels forming temporary walls around it. Theresa, the vet, was there with another woman, talking quietly. Both wore surgical scrubs, but had their masks pulled down around their necks. Jack tensed up at the sight of Alexander, stretched out on the table, until Theresa turned toward them and smiled.

Jack blew his breath out, unaware that he'd been holding it.

"He's going to be okay," Theresa told him. "It looked worse than it was. He had a bad cut along his chest and probably a concussion. He lost a fair bit of blood, but he'll be okay. His scars won't be quite as impressive as Koshka's, except for the ear, I suppose."

"Hey, you big dummy," Jack whispered, leaning down to gently stroke the fur on Alexander's forehead.

The big cat's eyes were still unfocused from the waning effects of the anesthesia, but he slowly reached out with his tongue to touch Jack's hand.

"No more heroics, okay?"

Alexander answered by closing his eyes.

"He's going to need some rest for a while," Theresa told him. "Don't worry, I'll let you know when he's up and around."

"Okay," Jack said uncertainly. He had always hated leaving Alexander at the vet's office. The big cat always cried in the crate when Jack took him, and then cried all the way home, making Jack feel like he was guilty of animal abuse.

With a final look, Jack turned away and followed Naomi upstairs to the mezzanine level. Taking a few turns around stacks of crates and boxes, they came to a small walled-in section that wasn't easily seen from below.

"What's this?" he asked.

"It's our biohazard room," she told him. "It's not anything at all like what Fort Dietrich has in its labs for biological warfare research. Instead of trying to seal off the room completely, we use small self-contained biosafety containment chambers where we keep our specimens."

"And what sort of 'specimens' do you have in here?" Jack asked, hesitating as Naomi keyed open the door and stepped inside. He noticed that the door was hermetically sealed, but there were no biohazard suits in evidence. The only thing that struck him as odd about the room were the closely spaced sprinkler units on the ceiling.

"Anti-viral dispensers," she told him. "If there's any sign of a breach, everything in here will be flooded with a wash of a chlorine-based compound that will kill any viruses or bacteria if they're exposed to it long enough."

"Then what?" Jack asked. "What about anybody who's in here if that happens?"

"They stay in here, Jack," she told him grimly. "At least until we're certain there's no sign of infection. There's an airlock system to pass food in, and there's an independent water and waste system in here. Assuming you make it through the anti-viral wash and have a chance to worry about such things. Let's just hope that doesn't happen, okay? I don't really fancy having my skin blistered, or worse. That stuff isn't anything you want to mess around with."

Leading him up to one of four large cylinders lying on their sides, with integrated rectangular cabinets supporting them, she explained, "These are the biosafety containment chambers. They have externally controlled waldos and instruments that we can use to take many types of samples, and we can anesthetize the specimens, as well. And of course we can feed, water, and clean up after them, with the waste being collected in the unit's support cabinet where it's taken care of with a small incinerator."

"So who's the lucky occupant?" he asked.

"A rhesus monkey," she told him, picking up the chart and looking at the notes neatly written there. "Vlad, one of my assistants, infected it with a sample of the corn Sheldon found." She sighed in frustration. "We know a lot already about the retrovirus, but nothing that's going to tell us exactly what it does. I was hoping to be able to run a lot more tests before we got to this stage, but I can't help but feel like we're running out of time."

Jack nodded. He was well-acquainted with the sensation of being in free-fall, plummeting down the rabbit hole.

"This is interesting," she murmured as she compared Vlad's notes to the readouts on a computer screen built into a panel on the chamber.

"What is it?" Jack asked, looking over her shoulder, peering through the clear Lexan panel. From the tone of her voice, "interesting" didn't really mean interesting, it meant "bad." The monkey, a young male, stared out at him with wide, sad eyes. Several sensors were taped to its skin, and a clear tube full of blood ran from a shunt in its arm. He was surprised the monkey didn't just tear all of it away, but it seemed to have surrendered itself to its fate. After blinking twice at Jack, it turned its attention back to what Jack could swear looked like a banana sandwich that someone had made for him. He had eaten about half of it, but seemed to have lost his appetite. *Poor little guy*, Jack thought.

"Vlad prepped this monkey only a few hours ago," she told him, tapping away at the miniature keyboard embedded in the chamber's panel, "but it's already showing symptoms: its temperature is up three degrees and its heart rate is fifteen beats per minute above normal." She was silent as she pushed a few more buttons, then turned and sat down at a workstation along the wall behind them. "The chamber's equipped with a self-contained diagnostic unit that can perform quite a few different tests," she explained as she opened up several windows on the workstation that displayed a lot of data that Jack didn't understand.

"Some tests we can't do without anesthetizing the animal and doing a biopsy, but we can at least take a look at its blood serum. The system does that automatically. It usually doesn't tell us much for viral infections until the initial infection has run its course and we can screen for antibodies, but it's an...easy..."

Her voice died away as the display on the screen showed a succession of computer-enhanced images of blood cells, each image bearing a time stamp. The first ones showed normal red blood cells, or erythrocytes, that were a roundish shape and crimson colored. To Jack's untrained eye, they looked like tiny red cushions all bunched together.

About halfway through the images, however, other cells began to appear. Or, rather, they were red blood cells that had mutated into something else. Where the normal erythrocytes looked like round cushions, these looked to Jack like yellow sea urchins with stubby spines. Some of them were about the same size as the erythrocytes, while others were much larger.

"What are we looking at, Naomi?" Jack asked quietly as she intently studied the images on the screen.

"I don't know," she answered worriedly. "I've never seen anything like this. The mutated cells are somehow attaching themselves to otherwise healthy-looking erythrocytes," she glanced over at him, "then absorbing them to create more cell mass for themselves. And here," she pointed to the final four images that had been made over the last hour, where a torrent of cells that were about the same size as the erythrocytes but had a lumpy surface had appeared, "neutrophils, a type of white blood cell, are swarming in, trying to fight the mutated cells."

"And getting their asses kicked," Jack finished for her. The white cells were being skewered and absorbed just like the red cells: the neutrophils had absolutely no effect against the mutated predator cells.

Naomi looked over more data and ran some numbers in a scientific calculator that popped up on the screen. "At this rate, the monkey's entire blood supply will be converted to these new cellular forms in another hour, two at most." She shook her head. "They must still be facilitating oxygen transport from the lungs, somehow, though: oxygen uptake has actually increased."

"What does that mean?"

"It means that these new cells are doing a better job than the monkey's own red blood cells at getting oxygen from the lungs to the rest of its body."

While Naomi dove into more data that scrolled up on the screen, Jack turned back to the chamber and its quiet occupant. Through the Lexan, which made up about a third of the cylinder's surface to give a clear view of the chamber's occupant, he took a closer look at the monkey, who studiously ignored him. Its hair was a mix of tan and light gray, with the tan covering the crown of its head and cheeks, and most of its back, while the gray was predominant over the rest of its body. Periodically, the skin of its back would twitch, as if it were shrugging away an imaginary bothersome insect. It had given up any remaining interest in the banana sandwich, and sat at one end of the chamber, staring listlessly at the shiny stainless steel wall at the other end of its prison, perhaps looking at its reflection in the metal.

Jack was just turning away when he noticed something odd. Looking closer, he saw that a patch of the monkey's hair was discolored.

"Naomi," he called, but she was so engrossed in the blood work that she didn't hear him. "Naomi!" he called, louder.

"What is it?" she said, startled.

"Come here and look at this."

With one last glance at the data on the screen, she got up and came over to stand beside him to look in at the monkey.

"What's that?" Jack asked, pointing. "See, right there, on the left side of his chest? It looks sort of like a bruise. Is that from a biopsy or something?"

Naomi shook her head slowly. "No, it's not from a biopsy," she said, looking at the dark blue and purple patch of skin. "We haven't done any on this animal, and there's no procedure that we might do that would leave a mark like that."

Jack peered closer, nearly touching his nose to the Lexan. "Jesus," he whispered. "The hair looks almost like it's melted into the skin. Do you see that?"

Naomi leaned down for a closer look, concentrating intently on the nickel-sized area of skin. "Oh my God," she breathed, "you're right! What on earth is—"

The monkey suddenly shrieked and hurled itself at the chamber's observation window, its open mouth and exposed teeth smacking into the Lexan mere inches from their faces.

Both of them leaped back, with Jack instinctively shoving Naomi behind him. The monkey, gone completely berserk, bounced around in the chamber with such violence that the heavy unit wobbled slightly. After about fifteen seconds, it stopped.

"Christ," Jack breathed. "The little fucker scared me to death."

"Yeah," Naomi answered, her hands resting on Jack's powerful back. She may have been the acting leader of the society in Gregg's absence, and knew she was no coward, but Jack's protectiveness toward her had become a sense of profound comfort. "Me, too."

What she didn't tell him was what she had seen the instant before he pulled her away from the chamber and the monkey's ferocious challenge: the inside of its mouth and tongue were covered with the same blue and purple mottling as the mysterious patch on its skin.

She was about to say something to him about it when the base-wide loudspeakers came alive.

"Naomi!" Renee's voice boomed. "Naomi and all department heads, get your asses to the command center immediately. Something's happened."

Seventeen

"You'll never believe this," Renee said, her face pale from shock as she pointed at the main view screen at the front of the command center, which showed the frozen image of the global network news channel and a blond anchorwoman whose first name, Jack vaguely remembered from watching the news in the past, was Connie. "Hold on to your hats," Renee said grimly before hitting the control to resume the video playback.

"Ladies and gentlemen," Connie the anchorwoman said, her voice quivering, "we've just received breaking news of simultaneous terrorist attacks across the globe, with horrific explosions being reported within the last hour in the United States, Great Britain, Russia, China, India, and Turkey. While we don't have confirmation yet, the initial reports say that hundreds of people have been killed and many more injured. The attack here in the United States took place on the campus of Colorado State University just a few minutes ago, and we have Tracy Bowman live at the scene. Tracy, are you with us? Can you tell us what's happening?"

The scene shifted to a young woman with dark hair and a face blackened with soot. She had a cut on her chin that was still bleeding, leaving a crimson trail all the way down to the top of her blouse, which had once been white but was now a dirty gray. She was standing in the parking lot of what looked like a small restaurant with a number of shocked onlookers visible at the edges of the picture. Behind her was a street, then what looked like a running track in a park, or what was left of it. Beyond that was a gigantic pyre with flames licking hundreds of feet into the sky. Heavy smoke billowed from the conflagration, and more smoke hung like a dark fog over the park.

"Yes, Connie," the young woman said, her voice trembling as she spoke into a microphone that she clutched in bloody hands. She winced as a convoy of emergency vehicles went screaming by. "What you see behind me is all that's left of the National Center for Genetic Resources Preservation that is...*was* a part of the USDA's Agricultural Research Service. We were here covering this year's Mountain West Conference men's track and field championship at the Jack Christensen Memorial

Track when..." She suddenly put her hand to her mouth and squeezed her eyes shut, but managed to regain her composure after only a few seconds. Once again looking squarely into the camera, she went on in a shaky voice, "We were here covering the championship when the center, which is the largest seed storage facility in the United States, blew up in a...in a huge explosion. We were on this side of the track when it happened and only suffered minor injuries. But the bleachers for the spectators were right across the street from the blast..." She suddenly sobbed, unable to get out the rest of what she had to say.

The cameraman took the opportunity to zoom in across the street and the scorched grass of the track facility to where the bleachers had once stood. Jack winced and a few of the others in the command center gasped in horror at the hundreds of bodies strewn across the ground, most of them charred or blown apart. Some were still burning.

"There were hundreds of people there," Tracy rasped as the camera steadily panned over the devastation. A few survivors, some of them athletes who had come for the event, wandered dazedly around the field as the first emergency personnel rushed onto the scene. "Now...now I think most of them are dead. And there must have been heavy loss of life in the surrounding buildings. It looks like the general services and military science buildings were totally destroyed, with a lot of damage at least as far as Centennial Hall. As you can see, emergency crews are just getting here now."

"When did the explosion happen, Tracy?" Connie asked, tears in her own eyes.

"Only a few minutes ago," the young woman said. "Just a few minutes ago, all those people were alive."

"Thank you, Tracy," Connie told her, and the young woman's image was reduced to a small digital portrait on the back wall. "We'll be back to you shortly. But now, let's take a look at what happened. Ladies and gentlemen, younger viewers and those who don't wish to see graphic violence may wish to return to us in a few moments." After a deep breath, she said, "This is the footage of the explosion that Tracy and her cameraman recorded."

On the screen, Jack and the others were treated to a view of Tracy, not yet covered in soot and blood, eagerly interviewing a young athlete. In the distant background were the bleachers, crammed with hundreds of spectators. Athletes were spread around the field, engaged in their various events or practicing. Other people, most of them students, were busy walking around the area or standing and watching the events. Beyond the bleachers was the National Center for Genetic Resources Preservation building.

In the blink of an eye and completely without warning, the entire building disappeared in a titanic fireball. The camera caught a view of the flames and debris scything through the spectators in the bleachers before the cameraman, Tracy, and the athlete they were interviewing were knocked to the ground by the shock wave. The cameraman somehow managed to roll with the force of the blast, pointing the camera immediately back at the cataclysm.

Jack had seen many horrible things in his time, but this had to be the worst. Everyone in the bleachers, he knew, every single one of the hundreds of people there, along with most of the athletes on the field and nearby bystanders, had been killed instantly. Through the smoke and flaming debris, the pitiless camera showed scorched and dismembered bodies flung dozens of yards across the field. In only a few seconds, the aluminum bleachers became so hot that the metal deformed and, in a few places, started to flow like liquid plastic. Above the seed storage facility and the devastated buildings surrounding it, a column of smoke rose in the shape of a miniature mushroom cloud.

"Fuel-air explosive," Jack muttered. "Jesus." No one in the building could possibly have survived, he knew, and the body count in the surrounding buildings, packed with students and visitors here for the championship, would be horrific.

The camera panned to where Tracy knelt on the ground, screaming. The young athlete stood up and started moving into the smoke that now engulfed the field when he was hit in the head by a falling brick and went down, unconscious or dead. The cameraman grabbed Tracy and hauled her to her feet as more bricks, chunks of concrete, javelins of steel rebar, and other remnants of the building slammed to the ground in a deadly hail around them. Tracy looked up and was hit in the chin by a shard of concrete, and the cameraman grunted and momentarily stumbled as something slammed into him from behind. He got back to his feet and ran on, mercilessly dragging Tracy along. The camera was running all the while, capturing the horror.

"I can't believe they're airing this," someone muttered into the stunned silence in the command center. "The networks almost never show footage that's this graphic."

"Quiet," Naomi snapped.

Connie the anchorwoman reappeared, long streaks of mascara running down her face from the tears she had been unable to hold back. "I'm sorry, ladies and gentlemen," she apologized as she dabbed a handkerchief at her face. "We now have confirmed reports from the other countries I mentioned earlier – England, Russia, China, India, and Turkey – that similar attacks were carried out against major seed storage facilities, with major loss of life..."

"Turn it down," Naomi said quietly, her face ghostly pale. The audio was suddenly muted, but the horrific images continued, and a list of the targets that had been attacked scrolled along the ticker at the bottom of the screen.

"My God," Chidambaram, said, tears glimmering in his eyes. "We not only have lost the world's largest genebank, in Colorado, but the others, as well." He read aloud the names of the facilities as they marched across the ticker at the bottom of the screen. "The Millenium Seed Bank Project at Kew in England. The Vavilov Institute in Russia. The National Genebank in China. The genebank in Ankara, Turkey. And the one in Chang La in northern India. All gone, and hundreds if not thousands of people killed..." He fell silent as a video image of the smoking ruin of the Vavilov Institute in Saint Petersburg played across the screen, with dozens of scorched bodies in the foreground.

"Renee," Naomi said suddenly, "unmute the video."

The scene on the news channel had shifted to the White House press room, and the President had just taken the podium. Beside him stood the directors of Homeland Security and National Intelligence.

President Benjamin Fowler, who was normally quick to flash a photogenic smile, was uncharacteristically grim, and his skin was pallid under the harsh glare of the lights.

"My fellow Americans," he began without preamble, his deep voice rumbling into the microphone, "as you have just witnessed on the news, our nation has again been the victim of a vicious terrorist attack that has taken lives measured in the hundreds. This atrocity has been multiplied several times over in other nations around the globe, including some of our closest allies and largest trading partners. The directors of National Intelligence and of Homeland Security have received direct and damning evidence from the terrorist organization responsible, evidence that we have provided to the nation's news services to air as they deem fit."

"Jesus," someone whispered. "Why would they do that? They've never done that before."

"Look who just came in," Renee muttered. "That should answer your question."

Jack saw Vice President Norman Curtis glide into place at the President's left side. He wondered at the vitriol in Renee's voice until he remembered that Curtis was one of those "owned" by New Horizons. He was either under the harvesters' influence, or was one himself.

"The organization that has claimed responsibility is known as the Earth Defense Society," the President went on. "We believe this organization is also responsible for the murder of several agents of the Federal Bureau of Investigation, the kidnapping of another FBI agent, and the bombing of the FBI laboratory at Quantico and the resulting casualties there." He looked squarely at the camera, and there was no mistaking the suppressed rage in his voice. "I want anyone and everyone who has ever been associated with this organization to know that I will use every ounce of my energy, power, and authority to bring you to justice for what you have done. This nation will not stop, ever, until you answer for this wanton slaughter, and for destroying a completely benign treasure of all nations of the world in the form of these genebanks. We *will* find you."

And with that, the President turned and stepped off the podium, followed quickly by the vice president and the others on the stage.

The president's press secretary quickly stepped up to the microphone. "Ladies and gentlemen," she said, "as you can imagine, the president has a great deal to do. For now, let's please roll the video that was received by Homeland Security just minutes before the bombs went off."

The scene cut to a close-up head shot of a man everyone in the command center instantly recognized.

"Oh, my God," Naomi gasped, her eyes wide.

Jack, disbelieving, felt a trickle of ice run through his veins.

It was Dr. Gregg Thornton.

"To those receiving this," the image of Thornton said in a calm and measured voice, "know that what we do today is simply the opening salvo in a war to preserve our world from the plans of international government agencies that threaten all humanity.

"The genebanks that were destroyed today," he continued, "were not innocent storehouses of pure, native seeds as has been claimed, but were repositories of insidious, monstrous mutations, biological weapons that were intended to wreak devastation on our biosphere, to kill millions, particularly among the poor nations of the world that rely on the largess of the United States and other countries for their food. We of the Earth Defense Society could not allow this to happen." He looked reflective for a moment, as if pondering his sins. "We tried to warn you, the public, but no one would listen, and so we took action ourselves. We were able to destroy the largest of these so-called genebanks, but there are many more, my friends, that contain the seeds of our world's undoing. We cannot destroy them all on our own. We need your help.

"Let me also say that I deeply regret the loss of every innocent life that was taken today," he said, "and will not offer any platitudes that it was a necessary sacrifice. It was simply unavoidable, just as it was tragic, and I will carry to the grave the stains of their innocent blood.

"But now it is up to you, my friends. We have done our part. The governments of the world will try to convince you that we are your enemies, but we are not. Those who make and keep secrets are the true enemies in this war, and it is those you must rise up and fight before the 'haves' of our world leave nothing but a barren wasteland for the 'have-nots.' Godspeed."

The video then went back to the White House press room, which had erupted in a near-hysterical outburst of questions from the press.

"Screw this," Renee hissed before shutting off the news feed altogether.

"The best lies have a kernel of truth," Chidambaram murmured. "They blame everything on us, and in the same breath plant the idea in people's heads that it's a government cover-up."

"Just tell me that wasn't really Gregg," Jack said.

"The harvesters must have him," Vlad, who had slipped in during the broadcast, said in his thick Russian accent. "The replication was too detailed for anything but direct genetic sampling."

"I take that as a 'no,'" Jack said, turning to Vlad, "but what do you mean?"

"Harvesters can mimic any biologic form of similar mass from visual input, like photo or video, or direct observation" the young biologist explained. "But to replicate details accurately, from surface of skin to hair and color of eyes, it must have direct contact, be able to...take biopsy of human tissue, extrapolate map of DNA to be replicated." He nodded at the video screen. "Details on video extremely good, completely life-like. It was harvester."

"So, is Gregg dead?" Jack asked.

"Almost certainly," Naomi answered bitterly. "The harvesters don't have to kill us to replicate us, just make physical contact. But Gregg wouldn't have let himself be taken alive."

"I hate to say this," Jack told her, "but he might not have had a choice. Remember how you guys took down Sansone in my house. They could've surprised him and then interrogated him before they put on their little puppet show. They could be on their way here now."

Naomi shook her head. "Gregg had a suicide pill," she explained. "He had a false molar on the right side of his jaw." Renee and the others looked shocked. "I'm sorry. He made me promise not to tell anyone."

"You'd better promise me right now," Jack said, staring at her, "that you don't have one of those things."

"I don't," she whispered. "But I probably should."

Jack was about to tell her exactly what he thought of that idea when Chidambaram suddenly whispered, "Svalbard..."

Naomi's head snapped around to look at him. "What?"

"Svalbard!" he shouted. "They haven't gotten the seed vault at Svalbard, or they would have reported it!"

"Damn," Renee said, "he's right!" She started tapping frantically at her keyboard, searching through international video feeds.

"What the hell is Svalbard?" Jack asked, confused.

"It's what some call the 'doomsday seed vault,'" Naomi explained excitedly. "The other facilities the harvesters destroyed were genebanks, which are what you might consider regular conservatories for seeds. The facility at Svalbard is sort of like what we have here in the converted missile silos: it's a backup for the genebanks in case they somehow fail or are destroyed, or if there was a catastrophe that wiped out vital species in the biosphere that couldn't be restored from what was in the genebanks. The Norwegian government built it on the island of Spitsbergen in the Svalbard archipelago, in the Arctic Ocean about five hundred miles north of Norway. Even if the power there failed, most of the seeds would remain viable in the cold vaults for dozens, if not hundreds of years, and even longer for some species."

"But why wouldn't the harvesters have hit that, too?" Jack asked. "That would have been an obvious target along with the others, maybe even the most important one. Surely they didn't miss it?"

"There's why," Renee told him, and everyone crowded around her workstation. "Look at that monster."

On the screen was a weather map that showed an angry swirling storm that extended from the eastern shores of Greenland to Novaya Zemlya in Russia.

"Nobody's going to be flying in that mess," she said, quickly pulling up the international weather advisories from the Federal Aviation Administration. "Svalbard airport is socked in with winds gusting up to eighty knots and heavy snow. According to this, storms like this are fairly unusual this time of year, and this thing apparently blew in awfully quick."

"Thank God for climate change," someone muttered.

"So, if we rule out an attack by air, what about by sea?" Naomi asked.

"I'm not seeing anything that'll help answer that question," Renee told her as she continued to poke around on the web, looking for more information.

"I was on a fishing boat out in the Atlantic for a summer when I was in school," Jack told them. "We got caught in a storm that was probably a lot less powerful than this one, and if the sea right now around Spitsbergen is anything close to what I remember, any ship or boat that tries to put in to shore is going to be smashed to pieces, and there's no way they could get small boats in." He shook his head as he looked at the zoomed-in image of Svalbard on Renee's display. "If I was planning an op, I'd use aircraft. See, the seed vault is only about a kilometer from the Svalbard airport runway, up this slope that overlooks the airport and the bay. Land, secure the airfield, then take a little stroll up to the seed vault and blow the hell out of it. If you tried an assault from the water, you'd have to try and scale the side of the plateau that's at the top of that slope. That looks pretty damn steep, and even in good weather would probably be a bitch. The only real alternatives would be to either land somewhere along the coast near the airport, or farther into the bay at the town of Longyearbyen. That would probably draw a bit of unwanted attention, and it's four klicks away."

"Renee," Naomi asked, "how long do they think it'll be until the storm clears off of Svalbard?"

"If I'm reading this right," Renee said, "it looks like maybe ten to twelve hours before they expect the airport to open again."

"How far is Spitsbergen from here?"

"Mmmm..." Renee did some calculations on her maps, "about thirty-five hundred nautical miles."

"So about a seven hour flight in the Falcon," Naomi murmured as she stared at the screen, her eyes narrowed slightly.

"Wait a minute," Jack said. "You're not thinking what I think you're thinking, are you?"

Naomi shot him a puzzled expression and Renee snorted.

"Listen," Jack cautioned, "that's a damn long flight, even in a military aircraft. And in case nobody noticed, there's nothing around Spitsbergen for a good five hundred miles but the Arctic Ocean. There aren't any alternate airfields if we run into trouble or run low on fuel."

"I know, Jack," Naomi said. "We have a Dassault Falcon 7X that has the range and speed to get a team of us there. We can't just sit here and do nothing. You know we can't warn anyone: no one listened to us before the harvesters' trick mimicking Gregg, and they certainly won't listen to us now. If the harvesters don't have an attack force on the way to Svalbard now, they will as soon as they think they can get in to land." Her expression hardened. "They'll be able to walk right into the vault and blow it up if we don't get there first and stop them!"

Jack opened his mouth to argue with her, then shut it. She's right, he thought. Set your personal feelings aside for a minute and look at it from a military perspective. The harvesters have the initiative, and we've got to take it from them. We can't win just by playing defense. He was objective and honest enough with himself to realize that while there were certainly valid tactical concerns about mounting a quasi-military operation a few thousand miles away in the arctic, his real fear was that Naomi could be hurt or killed. That could happen here just as easily, he told himself, and almost has a few times now. Her best chance of survival – and yours – is to wipe these fuckers out, and you can't do that by sitting down here in this hole while the harvesters can act at will.

"Okay," he said finally. "What's the plan?"

"That would have been Tan's job," Naomi told him. "Now it's yours." Jack nodded. He'd been expecting that. "We've got a plane that can take a strike team of a dozen people to Spitsbergen with plenty of fuel to spare for a long loiter time if we have to wait out the storm, or fly round-trip without refueling." Turning to Renee, she said, "Alert Ferris and tell him to get the Falcon to Oroville Municipal airport. Tell him we'll have a full team aboard, and to get strike package A with the cold weather options loaded, along with max fuel."

"Strike package A?" Jack asked, surprised.

Naomi nodded. "We've been prepared for this for a long time, Jack," she told him. "We knew that the fight would come out in the open at some point, but we had no idea how it would present itself. So Tan and the others on our security team came up with a series of different options to cover most contingencies, then we pre-packaged as much as we could so we could move quickly. Package A is our 'armed to the teeth' option for a full twelve-person team." She locked gazes with him. "We can't fight a full-out war, Jack, but we'll have enough firepower to make them take notice."

"How long will it take the jet to get here?"

"Two hours, give or take," Renee told him, looking at Naomi. "We keep the plane at Oakland Metro in 'Frisco. The flight up here won't take long, but they have to load the equipment, fuel up, and do all the flight planning crap. Which brings us to the next item: Ferris needs to have a cover story to file the flight plan. We're going to have to fly through Canadian airspace, if nothing else, and we'll need clearance to get through or they're going to think we're up to no good."

"Norway," Jack said. "Set us up for a business charter flight to Norway, just pick an airfield that has a long enough runway and serves a major city that's on a close track with Spitsbergen."

"Then we could just declare an in-flight emergency and land there," Naomi said, nodding in approval, "with nobody being the wiser."

"And what's your purpose for visiting the fair and freezing country of Norway, Mr. Dawson?" Renee asked in her best customs official voice. "Business, or pleasure?"

"Business," he told her with a predatory smile. "Definitely business."

Eighteen

In the biosafety containment chamber, the rhesus monkey squirmed and whimpered. It was acutely uncomfortable, its body sending mixed signals of aching mingled with an odd sensation of numbness. The sounds through the speakers of its small prison that echoed the noises of its fellow monkeys in their distant cages, an attempt by its human keepers to provide their small captive with some sensory input, were now muted and dull as the monkey's hearing ability faded away.

Holding its hands up before its eyes, the monkey could see with its rapidly fading vision that its fur had been absorbed into its flesh, and that its skin had taken on a strange bruised look. Two of the monkey's left fingers had fused together, and the right hand had bent forward and was now stuck to the underside of its forearm, as if the bones of the wrist had gone soft and the skin had flowed together. It brought its left hand to its mouth, touching its lip with a finger, and was surprised when the flesh stuck together. When it pulled the finger away, it left behind nearly half its length, stuck to the monkey's lower lip. There was no pain or blood, no bone, just the strange-looking mottled flesh that now covered its entire body. The monkey sucked in its lips and was again surprised when they stuck to the inside of its mouth, parting around the still-hard teeth.

The monkey closed its eyes and curled up on the floor of the chamber. The discomfort gradually disappeared, to be replaced by a pleasant numbness.

As time passed, during which its human keepers did not make their normally appointed rounds, it was aware of only one thing. It was hungry. So very, very hungry.

Nineteen

For the first time since Jack had come to the base, he was heading toward the surface. He, Naomi, and four others had passed through the massive blast doors into the portal itself, a massive silo-like structure that Naomi had told him was thirty feet in diameter and seventy feet from the bottom of the shaft to the massive doors, which were over three feet thick, at the top. Looking through the wire mesh that encircled the elevator shaft framing, he could see the personnel stairs that wound their way around the inside of the huge shaft. He joined the others as they stepped onto the ten foot-wide elevator, which began to slowly take them to the surface.

They carried fake identification and passports, although they didn't expect to have to use them. Other than that, Naomi had instructed them to leave behind anything that could identify them. All of the weapons and gear they would need would be in the strike package that had been loaded onto the Falcon jet. Jack had expressed his concern about needing to check the equipment and make sure that everything they would need would be there. But after Naomi showed him the manifest of what this "package" contained, he couldn't help but be impressed. Tan and the others who had put the equipment together knew what they had been doing, and if the men with him were half as competent as he suspected Tan had been, their small team would be a force to be reckoned with.

He heard a loud whine and looked up to see the two leaves of the surface blast doors being pushed open by huge hydraulic rams.

"And this is the only way in or out?" Jack asked Naomi.

"Yes," she told him, "except for the auxiliary entrance at the antenna terminal. But the doors there are just as thick."

"Better hope those hydraulics never go out," Jack told her.

"We keep the doors very well-maintained, believe me," she said as the elevator came to a very gentle stop. "We filled in the old personnel entrance here at the portal with concrete. It would have been a lot more convenient, but it was far too vulnerable to a determined ground assault. With these," she nodded at the reinforced, steel-lined doors that were three and a half feet thick, "they'll have to knock a little bit harder if they want to get in."

The elevator rose into a large white room, brightly lit by overhead fluorescent tubes, that was large enough to accommodate the surface portal, along with a concrete apron leading up to the elevator. At the end of the apron was a set of vehicle doors that could easily accommodate a large delivery truck, but was currently occupied by a black limousine with dark tinted windows.

"You've got to be kidding me," Jack muttered.

"This is the secure room inside the truck repair shop," Naomi explained. "Nobody comes in here unless they're fully cleared."

"Isn't it sort of obvious if you just drive in or out of here?" Jack asked as he slid into the rear of the limo with two of the other men, while the remaining pair sat up front in the driver and passenger seats.

"Normally we don't," she told him as she strapped in beside him. "We usually bring people in by ones and twos, or we'll bring in several at night after the shop here is closed. But sometimes, like now, we have to take a risk."

The doors in front of the limo opened, revealing an expansive garage area that was occupied by several other similar limos and some SUVs.

"This is what we call the airlock," she told him as the limo quietly wheeled toward another set of doors. Behind them, the doors to the portal room closed, bearing a man-sized yellow sign that said "Danger! Extremely Hazardous Waste: Do Not Enter!" in heavy black letters with a skull and crossbones at each end. "We have another front company that runs a small limo service from here. All the limo drivers are fully cleared, so the only thing we really have to worry about is making sure the outer doors are closed any time the doors to the portal are opened. We use the SUVs for regular cargo and supplies. Anything larger than that, we usually haul in at night from one of the tractor trailer rigs in the truck shop next door." She pointed to yet another set of large doors in the opposite wall from where the portal was, with a sign overhead that read "Big Rigs ONLY."

"Then you can just drive right in or out, with passengers in the back behind tinted glass, and nobody's the wiser," Jack said, shaking his head. "Everybody'll just think it's another limo run. Slick."

"Glad you think so," she told him, smiling.

Looking out the window as they left the limo garage, he could see that the truck shop that occupied the rest of the building had four drive-through bays, each of which could accommodate a tractor and trailer rig with plenty of room to spare.

"The building covers up the most vulnerable points of the base from any direct observation," she said. "The portal and the intake and exhaust vents for the diesel backup generators. The vents have heavy blast valves up to four feet in diameter down below, but they'd be fairly vulnerable to a ground attack if someone could get into the shafts."

Jack watched as the limo wended its way through the orderly rows of trailers and rigs that were parked on the expansive property that had once been a Titan I missile base, here in the foothills of Sutter Buttes in California. He had never been here before, but wished he had some time to explore the area: the buttes looked like some beautiful country. Unfortunately, he could probably never again show his face outside of the Earth Defense Society without fear that he'd be turned in and arrested for crimes he never committed.

The limo glided past acres of orchards and farmland on its way to the Oroville Airport, about an hour's drive northeast of the base. He and the others spoke little on the way.

About halfway there, Jack was surprised to find Naomi's head resting against his shoulder: she was fast asleep. He breathed in the lavender scent that had come to be such a part of her in his mind. He envied her, because he knew he could use some rest, too, but was too keyed up about the mission. With a sigh, he stared out the window.

At last, the limo arrived at the airport and came to a gentle stop on the tarmac just off Chuck Yeager Way, parking right next to a sleek business jet with three engines near the tail.

"Hey, Sleeping Beauty," he said quietly, "time to wake up."

Naomi snapped awake, sitting bolt upright. "God, did I fall asleep?"

"Only for a few minutes," Jack lied as he opened the door and got out. He and the others wasted no time in boarding: they didn't want to be seen. It was just after four in the afternoon and there weren't many people around, but they didn't want to push their luck. If they'd had a choice, they would have waited until nightfall, but they needed to get to Spitsbergen and the Svalbard seed vault as quickly as possible. Jack had been concerned about whether they would be arriving in daylight or darkness, but at this time of year the sun never really set in the arctic: no matter what the hour, they would land in daylight, assuming the storm had passed.

He followed Naomi up the steps that had extended from the aircraft, noting that there were already another six men aboard, making up the rest of his twelve-person team.

"Girl, are you sure you want to do this?"

Jack looked beyond Naomi to see the pilot, a grizzled-looking bear of a man who must have been in his mid-fifties, with close-cropped gray hair and extraordinarily bright blue eyes.

"We have to, Al," she said firmly. "Gregg is gone. The harvesters have him, and things are accelerating faster than we'd anticipated. If we don't act..." She shook her head. "I can't live with that."

He raised his eyebrows, then turned his attention to Jack. "Don't believe we've met," he said, extending a paw of a hand. "Al Ferris."

"Jack Dawson." He shook Ferris's hand, noting that the other man's grip was firm without any attempt at a macho knuckle-crushing competition.

"Okay," Ferris said, raising his voice so the others could hear, "sit down and get strapped in. Once we get airborne, you can start unpacking your stuff."

As Jack sat down next to Naomi in a pair of seats facing a small table, he saw that there were packs and weapon cases arranged around the cabin, one for each passenger.

It wasn't long before the three engines on the jet, a Dassault Falcon 7X, had spun up and the aircraft began taxiing to the active runway.

Unable to help himself, Jack suddenly laughed.

"What's so funny?" Naomi asked.

"I always wondered what it'd be like to ride in a corporate jet," he told her. "All this had to happen just for me to get this stupid airplane ride."

She smiled and shook her head as Ferris smoothly pivoted the Falcon onto Oroville's runway 19 and pushed the throttles to the stops. The plane accelerated quickly, even with such a full load, and was airborne a few moments later. After clearing the local airspace, Ferris turned the plane north and climbed to its cruising altitude, heading for the distant Arctic.

Twenty

"Thank God, this damned storm is moving past," muttered Russian Army *Kapitan* Sergei Mikhailov as he stared out the windscreen of the Il-76 military transport, cursing the roiling storm clouds that had been responsible for an endless, bone-jarring ride.

The big four-engine jet transport had taken off from Pskov in northern Russia eight hours earlier, carrying Mikhailov's company of the 23rd Guards Airborne Regiment of the 76th Guards Airborne Division. The mission had come down directly from the prime minister in Moscow: secure the Svalbard airport and the nearby seed vault, both on the Norwegian island of Spitsbergen, from any possible terrorist threat. Mikhailov had been chosen to lead the mission because he had lived for three years at the Russian coal mining settlement at Barentsburg on the island, about fifty kilometers from the airport. Desperate for work, his father had taken a contract with the mining company there when Mikhailov had been a boy, and the two of them had gone there to live. Mikhailov had hated every minute of it: the company that ran the coal mine often didn't pay the workers, the settlement sometimes ran out of supplies and had to beg care packages from the Norwegians at Longyearbyen, and Barentsburg was so isolated that he had often felt he was at the very end of the world. He had never been so happy as when his father had earned enough money that they could finally return home to Saint Petersburg.

When Mikhailov was of age, most of the available career opportunities held no appeal for him, so he joined the Army as an officer cadet. He had quickly taken to what the Army had to offer, and had volunteered for the *Vozdushno-Desantnye Voiska*, the Airborne Troops, following in the footsteps of his great grandfather, who had become a Hero of the Soviet Union while serving in the 4th Airborne Corps at Vyazma during the Great Patriotic War.

Over the next several years, he had risen to the rank of *kapitan*, leading a company of airborne soldiers. He had never seen combat himself, but several of his non-commissioned officers had fought in Chechnya, and he had taken the opportunity to learn from them all that he could. Many of the lessons they had brought back with them from that bitter conflict, he had discovered, had been unpleasant, indeed.

When the division commander had personally tasked him to carry out the prime minister's orders, he had been eager to take on the mission, his first operational assignment beyond the routine exercises his unit engaged in. He knew that Russia and Norway had signed a treaty forbidding any military forces on Spitsbergen, but what could the puny Norwegian military do? Politely ask him and his men to go home? He had almost smiled at the thought while his division commander was talking, but assumed that the man would have misunderstood the expression.

"Yes, but they still refuse to give us clearance to land," the pilot answered as the big plane jolted upward, bringing Mikhailov back to the present as he was nearly driven to his knees. The flight from Pskov should have taken about five hours, but the storm had forced them to loiter for another three hours in buffeting winds before the airport was clear enough to attempt a landing. Mikhailov had considered making a combat jump until he and the pilot consulted the latest weather reports issued by the Svalbard airport: the wind gusts at low altitude were still brutal. The massive Il-76 could handle them, although it would be a hard landing, but the paratroops would have been swept away like dandelions in a tornado.

"We don't need any clearance," Mikhailov told him. "Just get my men on the ground."

The pilot grunted acknowledgement, and with the rest of the flight crew began to work through the landing checklists, while Mikhailov returned to the cavernous hold. He knew that his troops, some of whom were desperately ill from the hours-long roller-coaster ride, were eager to get out of this flying death trap and onto the ground.

The aircraft's loadmaster tapped him on the arm. His helmet had an intercom and he'd just received word from the pilot. "Five minutes!" he said, gesturing at the cargo ramp at the rear of the aircraft.

Mikhailov nodded and then began barking orders to his junior officers, who made the final checks of the men. It was more a formality at this point, because they had already checked their weapons and gear several times, but one more time never hurt.

"The men are ready, sir," his executive officer reported after making a personal inspection of every soldier.

"Very well," Mikhailov told him, moving down the aisle toward the cargo ramp. On the way, he stopped before a team of men who had come aboard at the last minute by order of the division commander. They were *Spetsnaz*, special forces soldiers. Mikhailov had worked with *Spetsnaz* troops several times in the past, but these were unusually aloof. When he had asked the division commander why they were coming aboard, he had only shaken his head.

"They have their orders, Mikhailov," he had said quietly. "And so do you. Just stay out of their way and don't interfere."

Mikhailov stood there a moment, looking at the four *Spetsnaz* men, all non-coms, who looked back at him with hooded eyes and bland expressions. None of them had said a word to anyone since coming aboard. The special forces soldiers he had worked with before had not been like this, and it bothered him. Unfortunately, he had no real authority over them, and if they hadn't opened up to any of the other men, it was unlikely they would do so with an officer.

He finally decided not to bother saying anything to them and moved on toward the rear of the aircraft, clinging to safety stays to keep himself on his feet as the big plane was shoved around by the winds.

The four men followed him with their eyes, but said nothing.

The loadmaster suddenly grabbed Mikhailov's arm and shoved an intercom headset into his hand. Putting the earphone to his ear, Mikhailov said into the microphone, "What is it?"

"There's another aircraft inbound to Svalbard," the pilot told him tensely. "It's a Norwegian Air Force plane. The tower told them of our approach, and they are warning us off."

"A fighter?" Mikhailov asked him, adrenaline suddenly shooting through his veins. The Norwegian Air Force was small, but potent: they had seventy-two American-designed F-16 fighters, which would make short work of the defenseless Il-76 if the Norwegians got trigger-happy. He suddenly, desperately, wanted to be on the ground.

"No," the pilot reassured him. "They identified themselves as a C-130 carrying troops. They must be right behind us, I'm guessing maybe five or ten minutes."

"Tell them we are here to provide counter-terrorist security and have no hostile intent toward them," Mikhailov told him. "We would welcome a joint operation with their ground troops."

"*Nyet*," another voice suddenly interjected.

Mikhailov turned around to find one of the *Spetsnaz* men standing close behind him, wearing the loadmaster's headset. The loadmaster stood there, quietly fuming.

"Only *Russian* military forces will be allowed on the island," the nameless *Spetsnaz* soldier went on. "You will not permit the Norwegians to land."

"Why?" Mikhailov asked hotly. "It's their territory!"

The *Spetsnaz* man stared at him, his eyes cold and hard. After a long pause, he said, "The Norwegian military has been infiltrated by the terrorists who conducted the earlier attacks. That aircraft may have agents aboard. You will not allow them to land."

With that, the man took off the headset and callously tossed it at the loadmaster as he headed back to rejoin his three companions.

Mikhailov was furious, but he wasn't about to disobey. He outranked the *Spetsnaz* soldiers, but he had no doubt who held higher authority.

Instead, he focused on the here and now. The Norwegians were right behind them, and he had to figure out a way to avoid a military confrontation. He was confident his company could win any battle with their Scandinavian cousins should things get out of hand, but if a battle broke out, it would be an international disaster. He knew they wouldn't turn around simply because he asked them to – it was their territory, after all – he had to find another way.

"Once we're on the ground," he told the pilot after a moment, "use the plane to block the runway." The Svalbard airport only had a single runway, without even an adjacent taxiway, and with the Il-76 sitting in the middle of it, the Norwegians wouldn't be able to land. "If they can't get on the ground, they can't cause us any trouble."

"Understood," the pilot said, although the tone of his voice made it clear he wasn't happy with the idea of using his billion-ruble aircraft as a runway barrier. "One minute."

Mikhailov held on tight as the big plane sharpened its already sickening descent, the pilot taking them in for a combat landing.

***

"*Faen!*" the pilot of the Royal Norwegian Air Force C-130J, named *Idunn*, cursed. "The tower says the bastards have blocked the runway!"

Kaptein Terje Halvorsen, with two platoons of his rifle company, KP1 of the *Hans Majestet Kongens Garde* (His Majesty the King's

Guard) Battalion aboard the plane, frowned but said nothing for a moment as he stared out the front of the C-130's bulbous nose at the rapidly approaching Svalbard airport. The Russians had beaten them by only a few minutes, and he silently cursed the luck that had delayed the C-130's arrival here. The flight from Oslo had been horrible because of the storm, and the pilot had been forced to detour to the west much farther than he'd expected to try and get around it.

On reflection, Halvorsen had been surprised at how quickly the prime minister had made the decision to send a military protective force to Spitsbergen, and even more surprised that he had not backed down from the bitter Russian diplomatic response after he had informed them that Norway was sending a small contingent of troops to the island. There were already reports coming in from the intelligence services before *Idunn* even took off from Gardermoen Air Station, north of Oslo, that Russian troops were being put on alert in response to Norway's "intransigence." In turn, the Norwegian military had also been put on alert. It was a bad situation that Halvorsen knew could easily spiral out of control, with worldwide tensions at an all-time high after the terrorist attacks that had swept across the globe.

"This is Norwegian territory," Halvorsen had tried to explain to the Russian aircraft, "and we have sovereignty here." After considering a moment, he had added, "We would welcome your support and would be happy to work together with you, but you cannot and *will not* refuse our landing."

Yet, they had. According to the tower controller, after a hundred or so Russian troops poured from the aft ramp of the Il-76 it had taxied to the middle of the runway's two thousand three hundred meter length and parked. A few minutes later, the airport's controllers had frantically reported that Russian troops had entered the control tower. After that message, the tower had gone ominously silent.

Now the Norwegians were close enough in their approach to see the big Russian plane squatting on the runway.

"Can you get us in there?" Halvorsen asked the pilot.

The pilot glanced up at him. "We can try," he said uncertainly. "We need a thousand meters to make a max effort combat landing. But if that fucker is more than a hundred meters closer to us than he looks, the people in Longyearbyen are going to be in for the fireworks show of the century."

"Do it," Halvorsen said. Both he and the pilot had seen combat, Halvorsen having served in the Norwegian mechanized company that had been deployed to Kabul in Afghanistan, and the pilot having done an exchange tour flying on American C-130s running support flights throughout that embattled country. Both of them had been in a few tight spots and were aware of the risks. Halvorsen didn't want a violent confrontation, but he was damned if he was going to let the Russians force them to go home with their tails between their legs. "And make sure Oslo gets a full report of what's happening here."

"Better get strapped in," the pilot said grimly. He had done several short field combat landings using what the Americans called a max effort approach. They were hairy under the best of circumstances, and with the winds still gusting near the ground, the chances of encountering low-level wind shear that could send the plane tumbling to the ground would make this approach even more exciting than usual. "This is going to be rough."

***

"What the hell is going on down there?" Ferris asked, astonished. He had called Naomi and Jack up to the cockpit to listen in on the chatter between the Russians and Norwegians in what was shaping up to be a shooting match on Spitsbergen. "I can't believe the Norwegians are gonna go for it. They've either got huge brass balls or shit for brains. Maybe both."

"They don't have a choice," Jack said. "If it was us, we'd do the same thing."

Ferris snorted. "Not if I was the goddamn pilot," he muttered.

Jack suppressed a smile. Naomi had told him a little about their curmudgeonly pilot on the long flight over the Arctic. He'd flown Combat Search and Rescue missions in both Iraq wars, earning a Silver Star and an Air Force Cross, plus two Purple Hearts. From that alone, Jack knew that Ferris had done more than his fair share of ballsy or shit-for-brains stunts. And had lived to tell about it.

"What about us?" Naomi asked.

"What *about* us?" Ferris snapped, turning to stare at her. "You're not thinking of dropping into the middle of that mess? Listen, girl, faking we have an in-flight emergency and dropping in to fight off a harvester or two was one thing. Sticking our noses into an international war zone is something else entirely."

"But, Al, we can't just—"

That was when they heard the Norwegian C-130's frantic mayday call, booming over the cockpit speakers.

***

Mikhailov was proud of his men. They had quickly and efficiently taken control of the airport without anyone being harmed. They had rounded up the airport personnel and the other civilians, a couple dozen tourists waiting for their airliner to be fueled for the flight back to the mainland, and confined them to the airport lounge. Speaking in broken Norwegian, which he had learned during the years he had lived on Spitsbergen, Mikhailov explained that he and his troops had absolutely no quarrel with Norway and its citizens, but had come to provide security for the Svalbard seed vault and the airport against a possible terrorist threat. He assured them that as soon as his men were in place and the area secured, he would see to it that they were sent safely on their way. And he meant every word of it.

That was when his men in the tower informed him over the radio that the Norwegian C-130 was continuing its approach.

"They're bluffing," Mikhailov said.

"Not according to our pilot," his executive officer told him. He had communications with the Il-76 from his position in the tower. "He says he has seen skilled pilots land and take off in these planes, C-130s, from very short runways."

"Do they have enough room to do this?" Mikhailov asked as he hurried out of the lounge and onto the tarmac. Looking down the runway, he could see the distant silhouette of the approaching Norwegian plane and the bulk of the Il-76 sitting in the middle of the runway. "Tell the pilot to move his plane to wherever he thinks it best to deter the Norwegians. I do *not* want them to land!"

"He knows this, *kapitan*," his executive officer said, "but–"

Whatever he was going to say died on his lips as they saw a small plume of smoke from the far side of the Il-76, and watched in horror as a shoulder-fired surface-to-air missile, a SAM, arced upward, straight at the approaching C-130.

***

"*Chto za huy!*" the loadmaster shouted as one of the *Spetsnaz* soldiers who had been assembling an SA-18 SAM stood up, perched it on his shoulder, and walked down the Il-76's cargo ramp onto the runway. Moving to a spot just forward of the port wing, he aimed it at the Norwegian transport, and fired. "Are you *insane?*" the loadmaster screamed at him.

The *Spetsnaz* soldier dropped the spent SA-18, turned around, and shot the loadmaster in the head with a short-barreled assault rifle.

A second *Spetsnaz* man emerged from the cargo hold, nodded to the first, and together they ran down the runway toward the terminal building.

They had gone a hundred meters when the Il-76 exploded.

***

"SAM! *SAM!*" the copilot aboard the C-130 shouted. "Twelve o'clock low! Flares away!"

Idunn's pilot didn't need anyone shouting in his ear: he could clearly see the pinpoint of bright flame heading straight at him as his copilot made a desperate mayday call, declaring an in-flight emergency.

At the rear of the aircraft, the flare dispenser pumped out a series of flares to try and deceive the incoming missile, but there was little hope. The SA-18 was resistant to such countermeasures, and the missile's super-cooled seeker stayed firmly locked onto its target: the inboard starboard engine.

"Get the gear up!" the pilot snapped as he jammed the throttles forward. He knew it would be an act of God for the missile not to hit them, but the C-130 was a tough aircraft. The small warhead carried by a shoulder-fired SAM was unlikely to bring them down right away unless it killed the flight crew or just got lucky. Had they been making a standard approach, he might have tried to continue his landing approach. Even if the missile took out an engine, he would have stood a better than even chance of getting the plane down in one piece.

But they were making a max effort combat landing, which was an altogether different situation. The C-130 was descending at nearly fifteen hundred feet per minute, far more rapidly than for a normal approach, on a steep glide slope toward the very end of the runway, with the thrust of the howling engines precariously balanced against the drag and lift of full flaps. It was one of the most difficult maneuvers a C-130 pilot could perform, with no margin for error. The pilot knew that if they lost an engine now, they'd be dead. Trying to gain airspeed and altitude was the only option he had. The plane began to slowly accelerate as the gear came up and the copilot began to retract the flaps.

The smoke plume of the approaching SAM grew larger and larger, until suddenly it blossomed into an explosion that consumed the inboard starboard engine and sent a torrent of hot shrapnel slashing through the cockpit, instantly killing the copilot. The pilot suffered half a dozen minor flesh wounds, but his hands never left the controls.

The big plane seemed to stagger in the air, but had gained just enough airspeed that the remaining three engines were able to keep it from plowing into the rapidly approaching runway.

The pilot alternately fought and nursed the controls, finally managing to level out near mid-field. He pulled *Idunn's* nose up bare meters above the Il-76 that had blocked the runway.

He was thinking they just might make it when the Russian plane blew up right under them.

***

Mikhailov stared in horror as the missile punched into one of the C-130's engines, blowing it completely off the wing. Miraculously, the plane managed to claw its way out of its steep descent, and he felt a huge wave of relief that it wouldn't crash.

His relief was short-lived, however: the Norwegian plane was just passing over the parked Il-76 when the Russian plane suddenly exploded, sending a huge gout of flame and debris skyward and gutting the already wounded C-130.

"It was those *Spetsnaz* fuckers!" spat *Starshiy Serzhant* Pavel Rudenko, the company's senior enlisted man and a veteran of Chechnya. "Look at them!"

Seeing the two special forces men running toward them, silhouetted by the flames of the Il-76, Mikhailov drew his pistol and was about to order Rudenko's squad, which had followed him out of the terminal, to open fire on them when Rudenko suddenly grabbed him and threw him to the tarmac.

Mikhailov's indignant protest was drowned out by a series of thunderous explosions that ripped through the terminal building behind them, killing everyone inside.

***

"Oh, shit," Ferris hissed as they watched the Svalbard airport turn into an inferno. He couldn't yet make out much detail, but it was easy to see that things there had gone to hell. The Il-76 was a flaming wreck of melting aluminum, the terminal building and tower had been blown to bits, and the C-130, its radio silent now, was streaming smoke and flame from its belly and starboard wing as the pilot fought to keep the doomed plane in the air.

"Get us down there, Al," Naomi ordered. "This wasn't an accident or misunderstanding. The harvesters arranged this, not just to destroy the seed vault, but to start a campaign of international tensions that will help mask their overall plan. We only have a dozen people, but now we might really make a difference here."

"Yeah," Ferris said sarcastically, "if we all don't wind up in a corporate jet flambé. And just where the hell am I supposed to land? In case you didn't notice, there's a big flaming pile of shit in the middle of the runway! And you realize, if we do manage to get down in one piece, we won't be able to take off in the amount of runway that's left."

"You'll find a way," she told him. "You always do. Come on, Jack, let's get strapped in."

Muttering a non-stop stream of expletives, Ferris started going through the landing checklist, wondering how in the hell he was going to pull this one off.

***

The Norwegian pilot's desperate efforts to keep *Idunn* in the air were interrupted by Halvorsen, who suddenly appeared next to him. The Norwegian captain had a gash down the left side of his face in front of his ear that had left a trail of blood down under the collar of his uniform.

"Help me!" the pilot cried, nodding to where the copilot's torn body still sat strapped into the right-hand seat.

Halvorsen hit the release on the seat restraints and hauled the copilot out of the seat, laying him on the blood and debris-covered flight deck. The wind roared in through the smashed sections of the windscreen, and he could clearly see the flames licking the starboard wing. Now there was only a mass of twisted wreckage where the inboard engine had been.

"Press down on the rudder pedal," the pilot shouted over the shrieking wind. The pilot had all three remaining engines at full thrust, but the drag and loss of thrust from the engine they'd lost was yawing the plane to the right. "Use your left foot. I can't hold her much longer. Shrapnel in my left leg!"

"Understood!" Halvorsen shouted back, pressing down hard with his left foot on the pedal until the pilot nodded. "We've got fire on this wing," Halvorsen said, "and a lot of damage to the bottom of the plane in the cargo hold." He didn't mention that he'd lost seven men and had another dozen wounded by the second explosion that had wracked the plane. He had assumed they'd been hit by another SAM.

"I know," the pilot said as he grappled with the wheel. "I'm going to try and get her up there," he nodded to the plateau off to their right. "It's flat and snow-covered. We might stand a chance. There's nowhere else to land."

Halvorsen looked at the plateau off the starboard wing. He knew it was only a few dozen meters above their current altitude, and he didn't hold out much hope that they'd make it. But if the pilot could get them there, at least it would put them in a good tactical position against the Russians: they would hold the high ground above the seed vault. If they survived the crash.

"Here we go!" the pilot cried. He knew he was racing against time as the flames began to spread on the wing: when the engine nacelle had been blown off, its fire suppression system had gone with it. *Idunn* was also losing hydraulic pressure, fast, from all the damage she'd taken. He only had a few more seconds during which he'd be able to control the plane. After that, simple physics would take over, and everyone on board would be dead. "Let up on the rudder!"

Halvorsen did as he was told, and his eyes bulged as the pilot brought the plane into what the infantryman thought was an insanely tight right-hand turn, straight at the side of the plateau. It was all he could do to keep from grabbing the wheel himself and hauling it back as far as he could.

Just when Halvorsen was sure the plane was going to smash into the snow-covered slope, the nose eased over the top by what must have only been a handful of meters. The entire fuselage shuddered violently as the airspeed fell off and the plane entered a stall, the air over the wings no longer moving fast enough to generate lift.

Cursing, the pilot eased the nose down, but *Idunn* was through flying. With a shuddering lurch the plane stalled and literally fell from the sky, slamming its flaming belly down onto the snow from an altitude of three meters. The tip of the left wing, heavier with its two engines than the right, canted down and dug into the snow, and the propeller on the outboard engine disintegrated as it chopped into the white landscape, still at full throttle. As the wingtip bit deeper, the plane was thrown into a tight ground loop, finally coming to a stop in a great geyser of snow.

"Get everyone out," the pilot gasped. "Quickly. Fire."

Halvorsen called back to his men, who were already busy trying to get the emergency hatches open. Then he turned back to the pilot and undid his harness. Dragging him out of his seat, he helped him off the flight deck and handed him off to a pair of his men.

A few minutes later, the survivors of his company had pulled the wounded from the plane and salvaged what equipment they could. Halvorsen stood next to the pilot, his wounds having been quickly dressed by the company medic. Unlike the mysterious explosion that took the Il-76, there were no spectacular pyrotechnic displays here. *Idunn* simply burned. Watching his plane being consumed by flames caused the pilot far more pain than the shrapnel had.

"We'll head toward the SvalSat station," Halvorsen ordered. SvalSat, short for Svalbard Satellite, was a satellite communications facility located on the plateau fifteen hundred meters away. It boasted six large satcom antennas and an operations building that would provide shelter for the wounded while the rest of the company dealt with the Russians. Halvorsen could clearly see the big domes covering the dishes from where he stood. "Once we get there," he told the pilot, "I'd like to leave you in charge of the wounded while I take the rest of the men to deal with the Russians." From the SvalSat station, the seed vault was another fifteen hundred meters to the east, in the direction of the pyre that was the airport. "We should be able to contact Oslo and tell them what's happened here."

The pilot nodded absently. The flames of his burning plane, fanned by the chill wind, were reflected in his eyes. "Then we'd better get going," he said.

***

Al Ferris concentrated on the view of the approaching runway while glancing at his instruments, trying to ignore the still-raging conflagration of the destroyed Il-76 directly ahead. Carrying such a heavy load, the Falcon was going to need over two thousand feet of runway, and if he was estimating the distance right, the Il-76 was at around the thirty-five hundred foot mark. That was the good news. The bad news was that the explosion that had consumed the Russian plane had sent burning fuel and debris hundreds of yards in every direction, including down the section of runway that Ferris needed.

"If we don't prang the nose gear or suck something into the engines," he muttered as he cycled the landing gear down, "it'll be a

goddamn miracle. Or we might get a SAM stuffed in our face. Jesus."
Over the intercom, he said, "Hang on, boys and girls!"

Normally he would have made his intended touch-down point a few hundred feet down the runway to provide a generous safety margin. Now he didn't dare: he needed every inch he could get. Sweeping in from the seaward side, he was aiming for the very end of runway 10.

The runway rapidly grew in the windscreen as he took the plane in, bringing it down as fast as he dared. "It's like a goddamn carrier landing in a thirty knot crosswind," he muttered.

At the last second he pulled back on the throttles and up on the control yoke, flaring the Falcon and dampening its descent just enough to keep from breaking the landing gear as the plane slammed into the runway, the main gear wheels shrieking with the stress and streaming plumes of smoke from the tires. He dropped the nose gear down to the runway, then activated the thrust reversers and rammed the throttles forward to help slow the plane. The Falcon shuddered, and he began tapping on the brakes, praying they wouldn't overheat.

Ahead of him, the view of the Il-76's inferno grew ever larger, and he winced as the Falcon's thin aluminum skin was hammered by debris thrown up by the wheels. He murmured a non-stop prayer that the engines wouldn't suck in any debris. If they did, he and the others might be able to walk away from the landing, but they'd be marooned here.

He continued to work the brakes, instinctively finding the best balance between slowing the plane and losing traction with the snow-dusted runway if the brakes locked, which would likely send the Falcon skidding helplessly into the burning wreckage of the Russian plane.

At last, with one final bang of something hitting the underside of the fuselage, the Falcon came to a stop a mere two hundred feet from the edge of the fire that ringed the dead Il-76.

"Jesus Christ," Ferris choked. He knew that he must have made more dangerous landings in combat, but he couldn't think of any off the top of his head. After taking a deep breath, he keyed the intercom and said, "Okay, you suicidal idiots, we've landed. Thanks for flying EDS Airlines. Now get your asses off my plane and go shoot somebody."

Twenty-One

Sergei Mikhailov was dreaming. It was a strange dream, unlike any he'd ever had before. Neither pleasant nor frightening, it was simply...strange. He could hear something – grunting, perhaps? – through a persistent ringing in his ears. In the dream, he saw concrete, heavily dusted with snow that swirled in a gusty wind that felt cold against his face. Tilting his head slightly, he could see feet, legs, and the buttocks of someone dressed in a camouflage uniform. There was a lot of blood on the man's legs, and he could see rips in the fabric of his pants and matching wounds in his skin. The man's legs and feet moved ponderously across the concrete in what Mikhailov suddenly thought was a comical dance.

He also saw an arm dangling down, and after a moment realized that it was his own. He was also wearing a camouflage uniform, and much of the material was blackened. With a sudden start he realized that this wasn't a dream. This was real.

"Stop," he croaked. His voice barely penetrated the ringing in his ears. "Put me down!"

He felt himself slowly falling backward, and realized that someone had been hauling him in a fireman's carry over his shoulder and was now setting him down. As he slid to the ground, he looked up to see Rudenko's scorched and blood-streaked face staring back at him with undisguised concern.

"*Kapitan?*" Rudenko shouted. "You were hit by debris from the explosion. Two of those *Spetsnaz* bastards planted explosives in the terminal while their buddies shot down the Norwegians."

"How many of our men survived?" Mikhailov asked grimly. The ringing in his ears was gradually fading, but he could still barely hear over it.

"Nine," Rudenko told him, "including you. A dozen more survived the blast, but the *Spetsnaz* bastards caught them by surprise and used guns and grenades on them. Our boys tried to take cover under that airliner sitting in front of the terminal, until the *Spetsnaz* blasted the shit out of it with an anti-tank rocket. Our men burned to death when the fuel in the plane's tanks caught fire."

"What happened with your squad?" Mikhailov asked, trying to come to grips with the extent of the disaster. "How did you manage to get away?"

Rudenko grinned, but there was no humor in the expression. "I thought those *Spetsnaz* shits were up to something from the beginning. I saw them run out of the hangar like their asses were on fire, just after the Il-76 exploded. That's when I threw you on the ground." He shrugged. "They thought we were finished. When they chased the other squad under the plane, we let them have it." The grin faded. "*Kapitan*...they must have some kind of new body armor. I saw both of them take at least half a dozen rounds and it didn't even slow them down." He looked down at his AKS-74U assault rifle, a version of the AK-74 in general use in the Army that had a folding buttstock and a shortened barrel. He had killed a number of men with this very weapon in Chechnya, and knew that those *Spetsnaz* soldiers should have been dead. "I *saw* the bullets strike. But I don't think it even pissed them off. Watching them kill our men...it was like they were exterminating insects. And I think they would have come for us, except that there was a pool of burning fuel that spread between us, and they didn't come anywhere near it. That was the only thing they seemed to have any fear of."

"Then what happened?"

"They joined their two buddies who shot down the Norwegian plane and grabbed some snowmobiles that were parked not far from the terminal. Then they headed that way." He pointed toward the eastern end of the runway, and Mikhailov saw four snowmobiles just making the turn to follow a winding road that led up the slope.

Toward the seed vault, Mikhailov seethed. "Well," he said, "now we know who our terrorists are, don't we?" Turning back to Rudenko, he said, "You saved my life, sergeant. I...there's no way I can thank you for that."

Rudenko's wolfish grin softened into a smile. He had suffered more than his fair share of despotic and idiotic officers whom he would have been happy to leave burn. Mikhailov, on the other hand, was a good man, and had been an officer worthy of his respect. "I figured you'd be good for a bottle of vodka," he said. "Oh, and one more thing," he added.

"What's that?"

"Another plane landed, not long after our plane exploded and the Norwegian transport crashed on the ridge," Rudenko told him, pointing toward the runway beyond the flaming wreckage of the Il-76. "We couldn't see it very well, but it looked like a small civilian jet."

"They picked a hell of a time to come visit Spitsbergen," Mikhailov said wryly as he got to his feet. He was still shaken, but he wanted the heads of those *Spetsnaz* men, and he wanted them *now*. Turning toward where the snowmobiles were churning up the road toward the seed vault, staring at the four men who had murdered most of his company, he told Rudenko, "Are there any other snowmobiles or vehicles? We need to—"

Mikhailov watched in amazement as the man riding the lead snowmobile suddenly blew apart into flaming chunks, as if his body had spontaneously exploded. Then the sound of a shot reached them, and he heard the sharp *crack* of a heavy rifle, firing from somewhere beyond the wreckage of the Il-76, near where Rudenko had seen the small civilian jet land.

The three other *Spetsnaz* men veered wildly around the flaming remains of their comrade. There was a puff of smoke from the front of one of the other snowmobiles and its rear flew up as if the machine had run into a brick wall, catapulting the rider forward. The entire control column and front steering skis were smashed. As smoke boiled from the engine, the wreckage cartwheeled into the path of the remaining two snowmobiles. One of them crashed straight into the stricken machine, while the other spun out and rolled.

"Now that's something new," Rudenko muttered. He had seen men killed by heavy machine guns and sniper rifles, but had never witnessed anything so gruesomely spectacular.

"Indeed," Mikhailov agreed. "It appears that the new arrivals aren't civilians after all." He turned to Rudenko. "I just hope we can get on their good side and they aren't simply shooting Russians on sight."

The three surviving *Spetsnaz* men sprinted into the curtain of smoke streaming from the two burning planes and the shattered airport.

***

Jack had spent a good deal of the flight getting to know the other members of his combat team, and the one he had been most impressed by was Craig Hathcock, the team's sniper. A fellow veteran of Afghanistan, Hathcock had served in the Canadian Army, and had sent more than his fair share of Taliban fighters to Paradise. In two cases he had done so at ranges of over a mile in gusty winds.

As soon as the Falcon came to a stop and Ferris opened the door with its embedded steps so they could get out, Jack led the team out onto the runway, where they formed a protective ring around the plane.

Hathcock had already been eyeing possible firing positions from his seat in the plane. He and his spotter, another former Canadian soldier, dashed to the south edge of the runway, taking cover behind some of the rocky outcroppings that protruded from the snow. Hathcock carried his favorite weapon, a massive Barrett Model 82A1 with a Unertl telescopic sight. The rifle fired the same size rounds as the vehicle-mounted .50 caliber M2 machine gun. The weapon's magazine was loaded with the standard rounds used by snipers who favored the Barrett, and which Hathcock hoped would be a very unpleasant surprise for the harvesters. It was the Raufoss Mk.211, which was named, somewhat ironically given the current situation, after the Norwegian town where it was manufactured. It boasted a nasty combination of armor piercing, high explosive, and incendiary capabilities. He had never had a chance to actually fight the harvesters, and he was eager to get a shot at them.

The smoke from the burning planes and airport terminal was streaming to the south, obscuring the slope where the seed vault was located. The only view he had was along the south edge of the runway. The hot smoke rose in the cold air just enough to make a "tunnel" that was relatively clear before being carried away by the wind toward the slope where the seed vault was located. Since there was nowhere else to aim, he pointed the Barrett along the runway's edge and put his eye to the ten-power Unertl scope.

"Son of a bitch," he muttered. Then, loud enough to key his voice-activated microphone, he said, "I've got four soldiers, Russians, I think, on snowmobiles heading for the road that leads up the slope to the vault."

Without hesitation, Jack said, "Take them out." There was no question that the Russians had started this fight by taking out the Norwegian C-130 with a SAM. The last they had seen of it, the C-130 had disappeared over the top of the plateau just as the Falcon was coming in for its hair-raising landing. Even through the smoke obscuring the area around the runway, Jack could clearly see another thick plume of smoke rising from somewhere on the plateau. The C-

130 hadn't made it very far. He didn't know why the Russian plane had blown up, but suspected that those four men on the snowmobiles somehow had a hand in this disaster.

"Roger," Hathcock replied. "Targeting the lead rider," he said to his spotter.

"Got him," his partner, George Claret, replied quietly. He was looking through a spotting scope, tracking the snowmobiles as they raced up along the snow on either side of the road that led to the seed vault.

Hathcock focused his concentration on the lead rider, who would be lost in the smoke in a few scant seconds. Holding his breath, his right index finger pulled back smoothly on the Barrett's trigger.

The weapon slammed against his shoulder, sending the index-finger size bullet downrange at over two thousand meters per second. He lost sight of the target in his scope as the weapon recoiled: keeping track of where his shots fell was one of the key duties of his spotter.

"Hit," Claret reported over the radio. Then, more softly to Hathcock, he said, "Blew the fucker into burning bacon bits, you did."

Hathcock got his sights back onto the three remaining targets, and decided that he didn't have time for finesse. Instead of aiming for the rider of the next snowmobile, he aimed for the machine itself. Again he stroked the trigger, and again the big rifle slammed back against his shoulder with an ear-shattering *crack*.

"Hit," Claret reported again as he saw the round strike the steering column of the lead snowmobile, the impact sending the machine spinning out of control. It careened into the other two snowmobiles and tossed its rider high over the small windshield, while dumping the other two Russians into the snow as they lost control of their own machines. "You earned some extra points with that one, mate. You pitched all three of the bastards into the snow with one shot."

Laying the gun's sights on where the snowmobiles lay wrecked, he cursed as the three white-clad soldiers disappeared into the curtain of smoke. "Shit."

"Damn good shooting," Jack said from behind him as he and the others moved up. The only one who would be staying behind was Ferris, who was busy turning the plane around and moving it farther away from the fires on the runway. "Let's get going. The vault is almost due south, just a kilometer away up that slope. We've got a chance to beat them, but we've got to move fast. You two," he said to Hathcock and Claret, "bring up the rear and cover our asses. Let's move."

Taking the lead, Naomi right behind him, Jack took his team single file through the snow toward the vault, their white winter uniforms quickly disappearing into the acrid black smoke.

***

The fifteen hundred meters from where *Idunn* still burned to the SvalSat facility was the longest march of Halvorsen's life. The snow that the storm had left behind was deep, and his men struggled to make their way forward as they dragged the wounded in makeshift stretchers.

He had heard the two reports of a large-caliber gun, which puzzled him: it had the distinctive sound of the heavy sniper rifles the Americans and some of the other allied forces in Afghanistan had used against the Taliban, but that made no sense. The Russians didn't use those.

It doesn't matter, he told himself grimly, *as long as they're not shooting at us.*

Finally, they made it to the control building, which sat roughly in the middle of the array of large "golf balls", the spherical environmental enclosures that protected the antennas, that together made up the SvalSat facility. The control building was two stories tall, with two deep blue garage doors on the front of the building, next to the personnel entrance. Nearby was the helicopter that was used to ferry the SvalSat crews to and from the station at every shift change. Halvorsen thought that was odd, because he knew that the scheduled shift change wasn't for at least another three hours, and the helicopter should have been at the airport.

Frowning, he tried the building's front door: locked. He hammered on the glass of the door, but wasn't about to waste time if no one answered immediately.

No one did.

With a nod to one of his men, Halvorsen stepped back as the soldier smashed the upper pane of glass in the door with the butt of his rifle, then reached in and unlocked the door. He pulled it open and Halvorsen stepped inside, followed by his men. They all held their weapons at the ready: he wasn't taking any chances, not after what had happened so far on this disastrous expedition.

"*Hallo?*" he called as he moved through the hallway toward the main control room, from where the satellite operations were managed. "Is anyone here?"

There was no answer but the moaning of the wind outside, and Halvorsen could feel the hair on the back of his neck stand on end.

"*Kaptein!*" one of his men called softly from up ahead, in what looked like the station's cafeteria.

Halvorsen quickly joined him, and visibly recoiled from what his soldier had found.

"What happened to him?" the soldier asked, his eyes wide as he stared down at one of the six people who normally manned the station during each shift.

The body, still in its clothing, looked like it had been bruised over every square centimeter of skin, which had then begun to...rot away. He had seen bodies in Afghanistan, some of which had been exposed to the elements for a time and had begun to decompose. But this wasn't like that. There was no bloating, and the tissue from the skin down to the bone seemed to be disintegrating.

"Could it be a virus?" the pilot, who'd hobbled in with Halvorsen, whispered.

"If it is," Halvorsen told him, "it's a bit late for us. We've already inhaled the air, and we don't have NBC suits." NBC was short for Nuclear, Biological, and Chemical, and the suits were designed to protect soldiers from coming in contact with or inhaling anything that could harm them. Unfortunately, they were bulky and heavy, and there had been no reason to expect to have to use them on a mission like this. Of course, there had never before been a mission like this, Halvorsen thought bleakly.

"Look, *kaptein,*" another soldier said, pointing to the table. Food and coffee had been laid out at three places. Halvorsen took off one of his heavy gloves and felt one of the coffee mugs. It was still warm.

"There's no sign of a struggle," he murmured. "What the devil could have happened to him?"

"There's a body in here, too, *kaptein,*" a soldier called quietly from the women's bathroom farther down the hall before he turned away and retched onto the floor.

Halvorsen checked on the woman who lay dead in the bathroom, and saw that she was in the same condition as the first body. "That's two," he said grimly. "There should be six people here, plus the helicopter pilot. Let's find the rest." He turned to his senior surviving NCO, who was next in the chain of command. "Get some men upstairs and check things out. Remember that these are our countrymen. Check your targets."

The man nodded sharply before leading six soldiers up the stairway to the second story, their boots thumping quietly on the floor in the otherwise silent control building.

Halvorsen was faced with a difficult decision: the rest of his men, including the wounded, were still outside in the wind and cold. He wanted to get them into the shelter of the building, but the gruesome discovery of the bodies gave him pause.

You don't have a choice, he realized. Help would have to come from the town of Longyearbyen, which was only six kilometers away as the crow flies. Unfortunately, there was only one road leading up to SvalSat, and it was impassable from the snow left by the storm. Plus, he thought grimly, the Russians no doubt had control of the road where it branched off near the airport. The only other ground access was by snowmobile, and there was no way of telling how long it might be before help might arrive, assuming anyone from town could slip past the Russians. No, he thought. Regardless of what had happened here at the station, he had to get his men inside before they began to suffer from hypothermia.

Turning to one of the other soldiers, a *korporal*, he said, "Find something to wrap the bodies in and put them in the garage, then get the rest of the men inside and make them as comfortable as you can. You three," he said to the soldiers behind the *korporal*, "check out the garage. The rest of you, follow me to the control room."

Upstairs, *Sersjant* Lars Solheim uneasily led his men along the corridor of the second story of the control building. The sound of the wind was louder here, and the footfalls of his men, careful as they were trying to be, seemed deafening in the otherwise silent building. He was relieved when he heard the *kaptein* order the rest of the men brought inside: if the company commander had thought there was any serious threat here, he would never have done that.

They carefully checked the few rooms, which were mostly used for storage, on this level, until they came to the last one at the end of the hall. It looked like a utility closet. Solheim and the others covered the door with their rifles. One of the men gripped the doorknob gently, then suddenly twisted it and kicked in the door, ducking out of the line of fire.

As the door flew open, Solheim was presented with the totally unexpected scene of a young blond woman, staring up at them with terrified eyes from behind stacked-up boxes of bathroom supplies.

Blowing out his pent-up breath in relief, Solheim lowered his weapon, gesturing for his men to do the same. "Miss," he called. "It's all right. We're here to protect you. You can come out of there now. Please." He shouldered his rifle and extended a hand toward her.

"Are you all there are?" she said quietly as she stood up, her terrified demeanor fading away. She was completely nude and quite generously endowed, and the seven soldiers gawked.

"No, miss," Solheim managed, trying to keep his gaze fixed on her deep brown eyes, "there are more of our men downstairs."

"Good," she said. She stepped around the boxes, her hips swaying suggestively. "I was hoping you'd say that."

Solheim was thinking of how to respond when he saw the flesh of her stomach ripple as *something* emerged, rapidly snaking out of her abdomen. Too late, he recognized what it was just before it struck him in the throat: a stinger.

Downstairs, Halvorsen and his men had swept the control room and found four more bodies. Three of them were in similar condition to the two others they'd found.

The fourth was different. In addition to the awful appearance of the others, its left leg was gone. It hadn't been amputated, but had been dissolved below the hip joint.

"Good God," he murmured. To his men, he said, "Cover them up and put them with the others in the garage."

All hell suddenly broke loose on the second floor above, with men shouting and a flurry of shots being fired. There were muffled screams, several heavy thumps, and then silence.

"Upstairs, *now!*" Halvorsen ordered as he led his men back down the main corridor, carefully jumping over the wounded who were crammed everywhere on the first floor.

He had just run up the first half dozen steps to the second floor when he came face to face with Solheim, his face a mask of terror.

"Get out!" he screamed. "It's a trap! One of the rooms was booby-trapped – there's a bomb!"

"What–" Halvorsen began, and then froze. He suddenly smelled the tell-tale odor of gas. The facility used propane for heating, and if the lines had been severed to let the gas into the air-filled spaces of the control building, even the smallest spark would blow the building and everyone in it to pieces. "Get the men out!" He shouted as he turned and ran back down the stairs, past the pilot, who flattened himself against the wall to stay out of the way. *"Now!"*

While his heart was hammering with fright, both for himself and his men, Halvorsen couldn't help but be proud as he watched his soldiers grab their wounded comrades and drag or carry them out, even as the stench of the gas grew stronger. Unless the enemy – it had to be the Russians, he thought bitterly – had badly miscalculated, only a few would get out before the building exploded. He had already given himself up for dead: he would not leave before the last of his men was out.

He didn't notice that the pilot, a frown on his face, had hobbled up the stairs, ignoring the offers of assistance from one of the soldiers to help get him out of the building.

Solheim, Halvorsen saw, had already made it outside, and was dragging two of the wounded to safety in the snow. He was glad: Solheim was a happily married man with three children, and had always been a fine soldier. If any of them deserved to live through this, he did.

The pilot suddenly rushed down the stairs, ignoring his injured leg. Without a word, he charged directly at Halvorsen, driving him backwards through one of the large glass windows along the west side of the building.

The last thing Halvorsen remembered was the sound of shattering glass and the disorienting sense of falling, weightless, to the snow-covered ground before the world exploded around him.

Twenty-Two

Jack heard the thunder of an explosion somewhere on the plateau above them, but he couldn't see anything. He paused for a moment, giving the others a chance to catch their breath. The climb up the slope toward the vault hadn't looked very daunting from the airport. They had made good progress for the first two hundred meters, even slogging through the snow.

Beyond that, the incline had steepened and the snow had given way to ice-covered rocks that were torturous to climb.

"Jack," Naomi choked. The smoke from the fires at the airport was noxious, and made their struggle that much more difficult.

He turned to face her, relieved to have even a momentary break himself. He had set a brutal pace, but there was no choice: the Russians had farther to go, but only had to deal with the snow on the road that would take them straight to the vault. "What is it?"

"We need to go left," she told him. "There's a cut through the rocks there," she pointed to a barely-visible cleft at Jack's ten o'clock position that looked like nothing more than snow, probably covering some ice. "That should take us up." She shook her head. "We can't keep climbing like this...or we'll be exhausted." *Or fall*, she didn't add.

"Okay," he told her. "Come on." He changed course, stomping through the snow into the cut. The going was still difficult, but not as treacherous as on the rocks.

"I knew..." he heard Naomi mutter behind him, "I should have...done more...aerobics..."

Jack grinned, then coughed. His throat was raw and his eyes were burning from the smoke, and he knew it could be an ugly, close-quarters fight at the top, with visibility under a few dozen yards, if that. Assuming they could beat the Russians, who were no doubt double-timing it up the road.

Sucking in another lungful of smoky air, he pressed forward, hoping they could make it in time.

***

"Are you crazy?" Mikhailov asked. He was gaping at Rudenko, who sat in the driver's seat of a fuel truck that had been parked behind the airport's hangar building. The hangar itself hadn't been damaged, and the truck had miraculously escaped the earlier fireworks that had destroyed the rest of the airport. "Haven't we had enough burning things to deal with?"

"*Moi kapitan*," the NCO told him, "it has the keys in it, it runs, it will carry all of us, and it's big enough to get through the snow on that road. Unless you want to chase those *Spetsnaz* fuckers on foot, this is the best way to go."

Mikhailov would have agreed to all of Rudenko's claims except that the truck would carry them all: the cab would fit three, but the remaining men would have to cling to the vehicle's exterior. *Then again*, he told himself, *it wasn't that far different from riding on the back of an infantry combat vehicle*. And those, too, were highly flammable.

"*Bozhe moi*," he muttered as he climbed into the cab next to Rudenko, who seemed to be enjoying himself tremendously. Another soldier got in next to Mikhailov, and the rest of the squad clambered onto the rear and held on as best they could.

"Here we go!" Rudenko cried as he put the truck into gear and pulled away from the hangar. Once clear of the debris of the airport terminal and the destroyed airliner, he floored the accelerator and raced across the runway toward the road the *Spetsnaz* men had taken up the slope toward the seed vault.

Beside him, with nothing to hold onto but the dashboard, Mikhailov gritted his teeth, praying that no one would shoot at them.

"Look at it this way, *kapitan*," Rudenko told him, reading his mind. "If we get hit now, we'll probably never even feel it when this big bastard explodes."

"Thanks for the reassurance," Mikhailov replied sarcastically. He grimaced as the truck bounced and jolted over the snow as Rudenko turned onto the Vei 600 road that would take them to the access road leading to the vault.

Beside Mikhailov, the *starshiy serzhant* smiled. But his mind was on the *Spetsnaz* soldiers somewhere up ahead, and the pleasure he would take in blowing their fucking heads off for what they'd done.

***

Halvorsen snapped awake to the sound of flames crackling nearby and the stench of smoke. He sat up, and saw the pilot lying next to him. Halvorsen thought he was dead, but the man's eyes suddenly flickered open. His lips moved, but Halvorsen couldn't hear what he was trying to say. He leaned closer, bringing his ear to the man's lips.

"Not...Solheim," the pilot rasped.

"What?" Halvorsen said, confused. Pulling away for a moment, he took a closer look at the pilot, and his heart sank. A bright crimson stain was spreading rapidly through the snow beneath him: he was losing blood, and fast. "Be still, let me see if I can–"

"No...time!" the pilot said, weakly batting Halvorsen's hands away. "It wasn't Solheim," he repeated. "The man who came down the stairs was...an imposter. Found Solheim and the others...dead upstairs. Torn apart."

Halvorsen shook his head, sure the pilot was hallucinating. "You're imagining things, my friend."

"Solheim had a long gash down the back...of his left leg," the pilot wheezed. "Saw it when he went up the stairs. Man who came back down...didn't." He gulped for air. "That's why...I went up. To see. Made no sense."

And it still doesn't, Halvorsen told himself, but what the pilot was saying began to churn around in his mind. He had seen Solheim dragging two of the other men to safety, but couldn't remember the details. He'd been a bit worried about other things at the time.

"Come on," Halvorsen said, getting unsteadily to his knees. He and the pilot had fallen into the snow that lay alongside the control building, escaping the worst of the blast that had swept over them. The building itself was little more than smoking wreckage, with debris blown as far away as the big antenna domes a hundred and fifty meters away. "I've got to get you out of here.

"Too late," the pilot whispered, shaking his head. "Watch...your back."

The man's eyes turned away to stare into the sky. He was gone.

Halvorsen looked at the name tag on the pilot's uniform. BREKK, it read. After their brief introduction when Halvorsen had boarded the plane, he had forgotten the pilot's name. "Thank you for saving my life," he whispered as he took his glove off and closed Brekk's eyes.

With a sigh, he got to his feet and waded through the snow and debris to what used to be the front of the building. The bodies of his men were strewn everywhere like burned and bloody rag dolls. A fierce rage was growing in him as he reached down and picked up a rifle that one of his soldiers no longer needed. He looked to the northeast, in the direction of the seed vault, and saw a figure moving through the snow. He couldn't make out any details, but he knew it must be Solheim. He was alone.

Halvorsen found proof of what the pilot had told him as he followed Solheim's trail: eight soldiers lay dead in the snow, several of them starting to show the same rotting skin condition as the bodies they'd found in the control station.

"This is impossible," he whispered. Whatever the hell was going on, Solheim – or someone masquerading as Solheim – was right in the middle of it.

Putting the rifle, a Heckler & Koch HK416, to his shoulder, he centered the gun's red-dot sight on the imposter.

He didn't pull the trigger, because even without the magnification of a telescopic sight he could tell that it clearly *wasn't* Solheim. It didn't even look human.

Halvorsen lowered the rifle, sure that he was hallucinating. He rubbed his eyes, then squinted against the glare of the snow at the figure roughly two hundred meters away.

His eyes weren't deceiving him. Whoever, or whatever, it was, it clearly wasn't human. It was too far away to make out details, but whatever it was moved on more than two legs, low to the ground, much as an insect might. A huge insect.

Halvorsen was tempted for a moment to try and take a shot from this range, but didn't. The men around him had fired their weapons before they died: he could see a few of the expended cartridge cases where they had sunk into the snow. They could not all have missed at what must have been point blank range. Whatever it was that had killed them was either extraordinarily resilient or heavily armored. Plucking a pair of grenades from the web belt of one of the soldiers and attaching them to his own, he decided that he would have to get closer. Much closer.

Absolutely sure that he had lost his mind, Halvorsen gripped the rifle tightly and set off as fast as he could after the thing.

***

By Jack's estimation, they had made good time, and he was sure they must have beaten the three Russians to the vault.

He was wrong.

"Down!" Naomi cried as she grabbed Jack by his web belt and hurled him into the snow just as an assault rifle sent a spray of bullets right where Jack would have been.

Behind her, the others opened fire, shooting blindly into the smoke that concealed both the access road and the entrance to the vault.

"Dammit!" Jack cursed. "How the hell did they beat us?"

"They can move fast, remember?" Naomi reminded him as she snapped off a few shots in the direction of the vault. She had only caught a quick glimpse of one of the things before it had tried to shoot Jack. The vision had been macabre: human-looking arms held the Russian assault rifle, but the rest of the thing was in the harvester's native form. "They've got the high ground and can keep us pinned down here!"

"The hell they can," Jack told her fiercely. "Chalmers! Gomez!" he called to two of the other men on the team. "Lay down some Willie Pete – two o'clock!"

A few seconds later, a pair of white cylindrical grenades sailed off into the smoke in the direction of the seed vault. Dull *whumps* sounded as the grenades exploded, sending up a brilliant fireworks display.

Unlike regular grenades, whose destructive capability was mostly in their shrapnel, Willie Petes were incendiary weapons that hurled burning bits of white phosphorus when they exploded. The white phosphorus would stick to whatever it touched, and would burn until it was totally consumed or was deprived of oxygen. It had often been used in past wars against troops in bunkers or other positions that were difficult to get at with more traditional weapons. Its effects on human beings were horrific.

On the harvesters, the results were spectacular. The one that had fired at Jack shrieked as a brightly burning glob of white phosphorus stuck to its exoskeleton and malleable flesh like white-hot molasses. It hurled itself into the snow as its flesh ignited, but its efforts were in vain: the snow couldn't dampen the burning particles, and the creature turned into a gyrating torch. It soon lay still, its body crackling like frying bacon as its flesh was consumed by fire. A few seconds later a second one rose from the cover of the snow, screeching as it burned.

"Two down," Jack muttered. Turning to the others, he shouted, "Make for the access road, and be damned careful you don't touch any of that stuff!" The biggest problem with using such weapons in a situation like this was that it was indiscriminate, and would burn his people, even through the soles of their boots, with the same zeal as it had the harvester.

Jack led them up onto the snow-covered road, Naomi right behind him, through the still-burning maze left by the white phosphorus. The entrance to the vault loomed through the smoke ahead: a slab-sided concrete monolith about eight feet wide and twenty feet tall that disappeared into the snow-covered plateau. A set of amazingly ordinary metal double doors marked the entrance.

Jack pulled off his gloves and quickly stuffed them into his parka. "Grenade," he snapped, holding out his hand. Ordinarily, he wouldn't have used this approach because there would have been civilians here. But with two harvesters on the loose inside, the chance of any of the workers here still being alive was remote, at best.

Naomi slapped a grenade into his palm, then moved over to the door while the rest of the team covered the entrance with their rifles. Jack pulled the pin and nodded. Naomi opened the door a few inches, just enough for Jack to toss the grenade down the entrance tunnel, before slamming the door shut again.

The doors shuddered with the explosion of the grenade, the doors reverberating with the pings of shrapnel.

"*Go!*" Jack shouted. Naomi pulled open one of the doors while another team member yanked open the other, and Jack and the others charged inside, weapons at the ready.

"They already hit the power," Jack said into his microphone, seeing that the overhead lights were out. "Switch to thermal." He flipped down the T14 thermal imager that was strapped to a mount that fit over his head and flicked it on. It was a monocular device that now allowed his right eye to see the darkened corridor in shades of artificially enhanced gray. The walls of the tunnel, which was kept at zero degrees Fahrenheit, showed as a ghostly white, with warmer objects showing as various shades of gray. Hot spots caused by the grenade's explosion and shrapnel showed up as black. Jack normally would have preferred one of the more typical night vision devices for a situation like this, but they couldn't distinguish between a human and a harvester. The thermal sight could, because their malleable tissue showed up as being "cold" compared to a human's signature.

The team moved swiftly but cautiously down the tunnel, half of them hugging the right wall, the others the left, to prevent them from bunching up and making one big target.

About thirty meters in, they passed from the concrete entrance structure into a larger rock-walled tunnel about five meters wide that had been carved from the plateau that rose above them.

"Hathcock, Claret," Jack called to the sniper team. "Hold here and watch our backs. Check your targets before you shoot, as there might be civilians coming up to check on the vault, but if you're not sure..."

"Blow the fuckers away," Hathcock finished for him.

"Right," Jack replied grimly. "The rest of you, let's go."

Hathcock quickly extended the bipod legs of the Barrett rifle, then dropped prone to the freezing floor behind it, snugging the stock up to his shoulder as he sighted on the door they'd just come through. Claret knelt near the tunnel wall, covering the door with his G36C rifle.

Behind them, the rest of the team moved on through the dead-quiet tunnel, deeper into the vault.

Another sixty meters brought them to a set of doorways on the right side of the tunnel.

"I think that's the refrigeration room," Naomi said, tucking in behind Jack along the wall near the doors. Gomez and two of the others stood farther back, their rifle muzzles covering the three doors.

Jack looked at her, nearly smacking her head with the thermal sight that stuck out several inches from his face. "A refrigeration room?" he asked. "In *here?*"

"The colder the seeds can be kept, the longer they'll last," she explained quickly. "The permafrost will keep the vault cold even if the power fails, but not cold enough to keep the seeds from deteriorating over time."

The old joke about selling refrigerators to Eskimos came unbidden to Jack's mind. "What about those?" he asked, pointing down the tunnel to a set of double doors in a bulkhead that formed the end of the tunnel about ten meters from where they stood now.

"Those doors lead to the vault," she said. "The harvesters must be in there already."

Jack was tempted to forget the doors here along the tunnel wall that included the refrigeration room. But if he had learned anything in Afghanistan, it was to never leave a place behind you where your enemy could hide.

"Clear the rooms here," he ordered, "then we'll do the vault."

One of Jack's men yanked open the first single door, revealing a small room that contained equipment, but nothing more threatening.

The second door led to a larger room at the end of a short hallway that, again, held nothing more than equipment and electrical boxes.

They moved on to the double doors further along the wall, closer to the doors that led to the vault proper.

"Go," Jack ordered tensely.

Two men pulled them wide as everyone tensed on their triggers.

Nothing. It was a larger room that held the cooling equipment, which was now silent with the loss of power. But it was large enough that someone could hide, so they had to go in and make sure it was clear.

The lead man into the room, Gomez, didn't see or feel the thin filament that was strung across the entryway as he passed through the doorway.

The filament was connected to an OZM-4 antipersonnel mine, a Russian version of what was once called a "bouncing Betty." Jack happened to be looking right at it when it went off, the small propellant charge that popped the mine up from the floor about two feet appearing as a malignant dark blot in his thermal imager. Without thinking, he slammed Naomi to the floor as the mine exploded, sending fragments slicing through the air into the corridor about waist high.

The men who had gone into the room didn't stand a chance. They were within a few feet of the mine when it went off. While their body armor protected their torsos and the helmets protected their heads, their lower bodies were lethally exposed. They fell to the floor, their legs and lower abdomens shredded.

"Goddammit," Jack hissed savagely as he ran forward, but was suddenly held back by Naomi's restraining hand.

"No!" she cried. "Let the others do it, Jack," she told him. "There might be another trap."

"I don't care," he said, angrily shrugging off her hand. *We should have been more careful*, he berated himself, ignoring the other voice in his head that told him they had no time. There was no telling what the harvesters were doing.

"They're gone," one of the other men said after checking the bodies. He himself had taken several pieces of shrapnel in his upper right arm as he'd dived to the floor, and was now awkwardly carrying his weapon in his left hand.

Jack stared helplessly at the men who lay dead in the room, their bodies already beginning to fade from dark to light gray in the thermal imager as their bodies cooled in the freezing air.

***

Kapitan Mikhailov held on grimly as Rudenko expertly guided the fuel truck up the winding mountain road toward where the vault's entrance lay. They had passed by the wreckage of the snowmobiles taken by the *Spetsnaz* men they were pursuing, but hadn't caught sight of them.

"I used to drive a logging truck in Siberia before I joined the Army," Rudenko explained as he spun the wheel with one hand and smoothly down-shifted with the other, taking a particularly tight hairpin turn to the left that had Mikhailov looking out over a field of snow-covered rocks far below. "Trust me, *kapitan*, this is nothing!"

Five hundred meters and three turns later, the concrete entrance to the vault flickered in and out of sight through the smoke.

"*Huy!*" Rudenko cried as the windshield suddenly shattered, bullets slamming into the dash and the seat cushions. He spun the wheel to the left, away from the drop-off, and jammed on the brakes. The big truck lost traction on the snow and skidded to the side, coming to a jarring stop just off the road.

"Everyone off!" Mikhailov shouted, following the other soldier who had been riding in the cab out onto the ground. "Get away from the truck!"

"Whoever's shooting isn't one of ours," Rudenko told him as they dashed for a small rock outcropping. "It sounds like a NATO weapon, not an AK. Good thing they're not using incendiary rounds." To the other men, he called, "Does anyone see them?"

A chorus of tense *nyets* answered his question.

One of the men made a dash forward up the road to get to better cover. A shot rang out, and he dropped to the ground, clutching his leg. Then more shots *spanged* into the fuel truck.

"I saw his muzzle flashes," Mikhailov said, pointing. "Look, just above the road right across from where the vault entrance goes into the mountain."

"I don't..." Rudenko began, then stopped. He saw something through the intermittent smoke, but it didn't look like a man. He wasn't sure what it was. The only thing he could tell for certain was that it wasn't one of the *Spetsnaz* men. Shrugging, he raised his rifle to his shoulder. His weapon was tailored more for close-in combat and was unlikely to hit the target at this range, but...

"Hold your fire, Rudenko," Mikhailov said.

"What? Sir?" Rudenko looked at him, bewildered.

"It's got to be one of the Norwegians from the plane that crashed," he told him. "We're not going to shoot him."

Rudenko looked at the wounded man still writhing in the road, then back at Mikhailov, wondering if the young captain had lost his mind. "Then what would you suggest, *kapitan?*"

"Let him reach the vault," Mikhailov explained. "Maybe he can help us deal with our *Spetsnaz* friends." He didn't like the idea of letting the Norwegian soldier fall into a trap, but there was no way to communicate with him and not get shot. Mikhailov only wished he could warn the man that there were others already lying in wait for him.

None of them noticed the white-clad figure following about a hundred meters behind the first.

***

Jack had expected another booby-trap at the double door through the bulkhead that separated the main tunnel from the vault area, but there was nothing.

Well, there was something, Jack grimly acknowledged: four bodies, some of the civilians who'd worked here at the vault. All of them were riddled with bullets.

"Keep moving," he ordered, and the surviving team members, minus Hathcock and his spotter who had been left behind to cover the entrance, carefully moved forward along the remaining fifteen meters of the main tunnel before reaching a T-junction.

"Which way," he softly asked Naomi.

"There are three vaults," she whispered. "Vaults One and Two are there," she pointed down the tunnel toward the left. "That one," she pointed to the right, where about ten meters away was a bulkhead and double door, "is Vault Three."

"We'll take number three first," Jack said.

Quickly moving down the tunnel toward Vault Three, Higgins and Preston gripped the door handles, while Jack and Naomi held their rifles ready.

"Now!" Jack said.

They flung the doors open. There was nothing but a space like an airlock, about two meters long, leading to a set of inner doors.

"Shit," Jack muttered. "Let's do it again."

They did, and when the doors opened, Jack and Naomi quickly moved inside, followed by the other two men.

They were in a massive ice-rimmed cavern that had been carved from the rock, nearly ten meters across and almost the same high, and roughly thirty meters long. Before them stood large, extremely sturdy open-frame metal shelves, more like what one might expect to find in a warehouse for heavy equipment than a place where seeds would be stored. And on the shelves were hundreds, thousands, of equally sturdy-looking boxes of various sizes.

Good news and bad news, Jack thought. The bad news was that the vault was a maze that gave their enemy plenty of hiding spots. The good news was that the harvesters would stand out like a sore thumb in the thermal imager. He switched the imager's polarity, so that instead of being darker, warmer objects would appear lighter in his display. A human being or a harvester would show as nearly white.

"Spread out," Jack ordered, "but stay abreast of one another as we move down the aisles. I don't want them slipping by us."

They were halfway through when Naomi suddenly said, "Stop!"

"What is it?" Jack said, dropping to one knee and aiming in her direction across the tops of the boxes on the lowest shelf.

"Just a minute," she whispered. He heard her scoop up something from the floor. "They look sort of like shell casings, but they're not. They look familiar, but I can't see well enough with the thermal imager."

"Let's finish clearing the room, then," he told her.

A few moments later, the four of them emerged at the back of the vault.

"Nobody here," one of the others said.

"One down," Jack said. "Let's hit number two."

They went back out and quickly moved down the tunnel to the second vault.

Things went fine until they opened the inner door. A flurry of automatic weapons fire erupted from near the back of the vault, the shots appearing as brief white streaks in Jack's imager as the bullets slammed into the rock walls near the door.

Jack's team returned fire, driving the harvester behind one of the shelves.

"Go!" Jack shouted as he dashed down the center aisle. Naomi moved down the one to his left, while the two other men took two of the other aisles.

"Taser it if you can!" Naomi shouted back at him.

Jack snorted. That would be a mean trick while the harvester was armed with a rifle.

A man-sized white blob suddenly darted out in front of him, and his finger was already pulling the trigger of his G36C, sending a stream of 5.56 millimeter rounds slamming into the creature. While every member of the team carried extra magazines with incendiary ammunition, none of them was using it: they were hoping to capture at least one of the harvesters alive.

"Taser out!" Naomi cried as she fired at the harvester, which had been driven back against the rear wall by Jack's bullets.

He saw the thing tense into paralysis and then fall, rigid, to the floor. Higgins was instantly astride it, driving a huge hypodermic into its thorax.

"Behind you!" Preston cried, firing at another harvester in an adjacent aisle. His bullets went over Naomi's head as she dove to the floor.

Jack instinctively fired in the same direction as he moved to cover Naomi, blasting seed-filled boxes from the heavy shelves and scattering their contents across the floor. The two streams of bullets converged on the wildly dodging creature, which shrieked in rage and pain.

"Taser out!" Higgins shouted. He was on the far side of the creature from where Jack and Preston were firing.

Unfortunately, he was also within striking range of the harvester's stinger, and he went down with a gurgling cry as it rammed the spike into his chest, pumping the deadly venom into his heart.

"Fuck this," Jack muttered. He hit the magazine release on his weapon, then slammed one of the magazines loaded with incendiary bullets home. He caught sight of the harvester darting further down the aisle and fired.

The thing burst into flame, burning so hot that his thermal imager was rendered useless. But his left eye, staring out into what had been darkness, could see just fine in the shimmering light of the creature's burning flesh. He pumped some more rounds into it, just for good measure.

Finally, satisfied that it was dead, he knelt beside Higgins to check on him, but he was gone. With a weary sigh, Jack made his way back to Naomi and Preston.

"At least we have something to show for our troubles," Preston said as he knelt beside the harvester while it shuddered under the influence of the formaldehyde he had injected into its system.

"I'm sorry about Higgins," Naomi said quietly. Preston only nodded. Naomi was about to say something more when she saw something on the floor down the aisle the harvester had been in. "Oh, my God," she breathed as she stood up and went to look closer.

"Naomi?" Jack called, following behind her.

"Oh, no," she muttered. "Oh, no!"

"What, dammit?" Jack demanded.

"This," she said, picking up from the floor what looked like a ridiculous toy ray gun that would have been a perfect movie prop for any of the "B" science fiction movies from the nineteen-fifties. The only difference was that this one was connected by a hose to a cylinder about a foot and a half long and six inches in diameter.

"What the hell is that?"

"It's an SJ-500 gene gun," she told him, nearly in tears. "Those cartridge-like things I picked up in the first vault? They were cartridges, all right: for this." She looked up at the storage boxes, the hundreds, thousands, of boxes around them. "They've been in here, infecting some of the seeds with whatever's in these cartridges."

"The retrovirus?" he asked.

She shook her head. "No, not with this. This is used to inject genetic material into cells. The retrovirus is handled differently. The tank holds highly pressurized helium that shoots the gene material into the target animal or plant. We'll have to take the cartridges back to the lab and analyze them, but if I had to guess, I'd say that it's either a kill gene, a gene that will cause the next generation of plants to spontaneously die, or maybe will create some sort of flora that's native to them, like a food source beyond the...protein we know they consume." She took a tool out of her pocket and disconnected the gun from the hose.

"They haven't been in here very long," Jack observed. "They couldn't have infected very many."

"That may not be true," Preston said. "Look at this."

Jack and Naomi came back over to look at their captive harvester.

"It's wearing civilian clothes under its uniform," Preston said, pulling up the camouflage shirt to reveal a thick gray sweater. Undoing the belt and fly, he pulled the thing's uniform pants down to expose insulated blue pants.

"Oh, my God," Naomi whispered. "It's been masquerading as one of the workers in here."

"Then it must've put on a Russian uniform, maybe to escape with the other harvesters after they finished with the vault," Jack surmised.

Naomi looked up at Jack. "There's no telling how long it's been contaminating the vaults. It could have been here for weeks, months. Or longer." Leaning back against one of the tall shelves, she said, "Every seed packet in these boxes is now suspect. We can't let any of them be used. Ever."

Jack had a sinking feeling in his stomach. "So their plan wasn't really to destroy this place," he said. "They *wanted* the world to need the seeds that are stored here. Seeds that were contaminated, and that nobody would have known about." He paused, the ramifications hitting home. "And now we have to destroy it. All of it."

Naomi nodded as she angrily stuffed the gene gun in her backpack. "And that leaves the little question of how we do that, doesn't it?" she asked.

"Yeah," Jack sighed. "But first things first: we have to clear the last vault. You stay here and watch our little buddy. Preston," he called to the other man, "you're with me."

"Jack," Naomi called after him.

He turned to look at her, her face flickering in the dying light of the still-burning harvester.

"Be careful."

***

Claret had turned around briefly at the sound of gunfire echoing down the tunnel from far behind them, but Hathcock never took his eyes off the closed door at the entrance.

As if on cue, the door flew open and a man stumbled inside. He wore a tattered uniform that both of them recognized as Norwegian from their time in Afghanistan.

"*Hallo?*" the man called hoarsely as he collapsed against the side of the entrance, the door standing open behind him, his rifle clattering to the floor. "Is anyone here?"

"Stay where you are," Claret called. "Keep your hands where we can see them!"

"There are Russians, coming behind me!" he shouted. With a sob, he added, "Those fuckers shot down our plane. I am the only one left. *The only survivor!*"

"Check him out," Hathcock said quietly as he centered his aim on the man's chest. "Stand up!" he ordered the Norwegian.

The man, his uniform literally in rags and covered in blood, managed to get to his feet as Claret moved closer. He was within a couple meters of the Norwegian when Hathcock suddenly remembered.

"Use your imager!" he called, but it was too late.

The "Norwegian" dodged to the side as Hathcock pulled the Barrett's trigger, blasting a huge divot out of the concrete wall where the thing had been just an instant before. With his other eye, the one not glued to the big weapon's scope, Hathcock saw the stinger suddenly uncoil from the faux soldier and strike out at Claret.

Claret was incredibly lucky, as the sharp biological dagger slammed into the stock of his rifle, the point sticking in the hard plastic. The harvester wrenched the weapon away from him, and Claret was reaching for his sidearm when the tunnel suddenly boomed with the sound of a weapon on full automatic.

Hathcock watched in fascination as the harvester, caught between its human and natural forms, did a dance of death as it was shot from behind by another figure that stood silhouetted in the doorway. The creature was slammed against the wall, not far from where it had originally fallen, and Hathcock stroked the Barrett's trigger. The tunnel entrance lit up briefly from the muzzle flash as the .50 caliber round blasted the harvester into flaming pieces that spattered to the floor around them.

The silhouette in the doorway resolved into a Norwegian soldier who looked like he'd been recycled through Hell half a dozen times. Claret, his thermal sight over his right eye now, turned and nodded to Hathcock. The man was human.

"*Kaptein* Terje Halvorsen," the man said as he stared at the creature's shattered exoskeleton and burning, fatty flesh, an unmistakable look of hatred in his eyes, "at your service."

***

Several minutes later, Jack, Naomi, and Preston came back out of the tunnel, dragging the harvester they'd captured. They were surprised to see yet another harvester corpse awaiting them.

"It must have infiltrated the SvalSat station," Halvorsen explained after they'd all introduced themselves, "I suspect as the helicopter pilot that transported the shift crews. The thing impersonated one of my men after killing him, then blew up the station." He was silent for a long moment. "First the Russians shot us down, then that thing killed the rest of my men."

"I don't think it was the Russians," Jack told him. "There were four of these things, masquerading as Russian troops. I'll bet they're the ones who shot down your plane."

"About that," someone said quietly from behind them, just outside the entrance, causing everyone to spin around, raising their weapons, "you would be correct." The man stepped forward, looking calmly at the rifle muzzles pointed in his direction. "I am *Kapitan* Sergei Mikhailov of the Russian Army," he said in excellent English. "These *svolochi*," he said, nodding at the nightmare forms on the ground, "shot down your plane. They also destroyed ours, and killed most of my men when they blew up the airport terminal." He looked at Halvorsen. "We did not come here to fight you. We were ordered to protect the seed vault from terrorist attack."

"You blocked the runway with your bloody plane!" Halvorsen shouted.

Mikhailov nodded. "Yes, because we were lied to by...*them*." He was still in denial about the biological impossibility that smoldered on the floor, and the other one that looked like a smashed cockroach that the Americans had dragged up the tunnel. "When we saw you come in here after this...thing, we could have killed you. We did not." He looked at Jack and Naomi. "What are these...creatures?"

"That's a long story," Jack breathed, worried now that it wouldn't be long before the locals started showing up, and probably more planes from Russia and Norway. He and his team needed to be gone long before then. "We'll tell you what we know, but first we have to figure out how to destroy everything in the vault. These sons of bitches contaminated the seeds."

"That, I think," Mikhailov said, "is something we can help with."

Fifteen minutes later, they all stood around the entrance, watching as the burly Russian NCO, Rudenko, happily pumped nearly three thousand gallons of Jet-A fuel down the tunnel.

"My lady?" Mikhailov said, extending a signal flare to Naomi while Rudenko pulled the tank truck away to a safe distance. "Would you prefer the honors?"

Numbly, she nodded and took the flare. Lighting it, she stared down the fuel-drenched tunnel before throwing the flare in as far as she could. With a loud *whump*, the fuel ignited, and in a few seconds was burning so hot that the metal entrance doors began to warp on their hinges.

"Come on," Jack told her, pulling her away and shielding her from the intense heat of the flames that were now roaring out of the entrance, "let's get the hell out of here."

Twenty-Three

Back at the base in California, something stirred in the bio-safety containment chamber that had once held a rhesus monkey infected with the harvester retrovirus. The monkey was no more. Every cell of its body had been converted to a new use, given a new purpose. To feed. To grow.

The organism had no thought, no awareness, only a biological imperative to seek out what it needed to satiate its raging hunger. It was guided neither by sight, nor sound, nor smell, but by receptors on the surface of its body that were able to sense and sample on a molecular level all that they touched.

This new life, risen from the old, had no shape, no specific form. It moved by flowing, and was able to cling to any surface it touched.

Spreading tendrils from its central mass, it probed its immediate surroundings. It found the food dispenser the monkey had used, and its body swarmed over it, secreting powerful enzymes that rapidly reduced the fruit and vegetable slices into molecules it could easily absorb.

The creature's tendrils pushed farther up the enclosure, encountering the thick rubber seals that kept the enclosure airtight. There were seals around the hatch and seals around the other penetrations into the chamber, all rich with rubber...and carbon.

It rapidly consumed the rubber, its digestive enzymes quickly dissolving it, breaking down the chemical compounds into what it needed. Then it oozed through the gaps left where the rubber had been, making its way farther into the innards of the chamber. There, it fed on the housings for the medical sensors and camera, the analysis equipment, and the other components that contained carbon. It left behind as excreta those elements it didn't need for growth, by squeezing a dark mass of viscous liquid from its body.

In the course of its feast, as it continued to probe and digest the carbon-rich components of the chamber, it ate its way to freedom.

***

Vlad had spent the hours since the team had left for Spitsbergen helping the other scientists on the team prepare another batch of seeds to go into the vaults that had been built into the old missile silos. It was tedious work, but had to be done. Everything depended on it, and he relied on that for his motivation when he would rather have been at his microscope.

With that necessary chore done, he was finally able to return his attention to the biopsy samples he had taken from the strange lesions that had appeared on the rhesus monkey. A part of him felt guilty at having had to do that, for he loved animals. But he knew it was a necessary evil: they had to know what the retrovirus did, and the only way they would be able to find out was to see it in action. He only hoped the effects wouldn't cause the monkey much pain.

An exhausted sigh escaping his lips, he sat down at his workstation and called up the results for the series of tests he had programmed the biosafety chamber to carry out on the tissue samples from the monkey.

While the results were being loaded, he took a quick scan of the monkey's blood work, which had been run every hour using the intravenous shunt in the monkey's arm. He saw that the white cell count had increased gradually in the beginning, with a spike about three hours ago, followed by a rapid drop to nearly zero. Frowning, he looked at the results for the other major blood components, all of which showed gradual changes during the first hours after the animal had been infected, then major spikes or drops three hours ago before falling off to near-zero. The only exception was the red blood cell count, which gradually tapered off to zero half an hour ago, when the test monitor reported an error because the flow of new blood for sampling had terminated.

"The needle must have come out," Vlad murmured to himself as he tried to make sense of the readings. What he was seeing should be impossible: the monkey should have been dead long before the red cell count reached zero. There wouldn't have been enough red cells left to transport oxygen from the lungs to the rest of the body.

Oddly enough, aside from an initial fever about an hour after the monkey had been infected, its body temperature had remained nearly constant. Even now, it was half a degree above normal.

Then he saw the respiration and heart rate data, and sat back in his chair in shock: the monkey had stopped breathing about the same time as the spikes in its blood work three hours ago, and its pulse had declined along with the red cell count until that, too, had stopped about ten minutes ago.

"*Yob tvou,*" he cursed under his breath, snatching his smart phone from his belt. It should have sounded an alarm when any of the monkey's vital signs had passed certain thresholds. Pressing the button to activate it, it gave him a brief "low battery" warning before automatically shutting off. He was so tired that he had made the simple mistake of forgetting to charge it.

Putting the phone away, he looked at the biopsy display as it came up on a second monitor window. It showed a mass of cells that looked nothing like what he was expecting to see. All had a spherical nucleus, but were of varying sizes and amorphous in shape, as if the cell membrane had no discernible boundary. There was a hazy look to the image, and Vlad's shock grew as he bumped up the magnification to 1,000X and saw filaments, tendrils, joining the cells together.

"No," he breathed. "This is not possible!" He had seen this before: it was the malleable tissue of a harvester, and these morphing cells gave the creatures their ability to change shape and color.

But there were several other cell types visible in the mass, cells he hadn't seen before in the detailed autopsies and analyses that had been done on the captured harvesters. He could only guess at their functions until he had time to run further tests.

Shaking his head in wonder, he brought up the webcam showing the inside of the biosafety containment chamber to see what the monkey's physical condition was.

The image was blank. The camera must have malfunctioned.

Muttering a stream of expletives in Russian, Vlad got up and headed for the mezzanine level and the sealed room with the biosafety containment chambers.

***

Renee had only gotten a few fitful hours of sleep after the team had left for Spitsbergen. She could normally drop off to sleep quickly and rarely dreamed, but sleep hadn't come very easily this time. When it finally had, it was full of very intense, violent images that she couldn't remember now. Thankfully.

"I'm going to die of coffee poisoning," she muttered darkly as she took another swallow of the strong brew.

The command center was fully manned now. Renee, being the senior person, was in charge of the base in Naomi's absence, and she sat at the circular console that overlooked the rest of the command center. She had received a call from Ferris on the plane's satellite phone to let her know that they'd landed safely – more or less – after a huge fireworks show at the airport on Spitsbergen, and that the team was heading up the mountain toward the vault.

After that, Ferris had dutifully called back periodically to report on what he was hearing from up the mountain slope, but he couldn't see what was happening with all the smoke. Naomi and Jack both had satellite phones, but neither had tried to call, and Renee had orders not to call them unless it was an absolute emergency. Renee had wanted to pick up the phone half a dozen times, but knew they were probably a tad busy. The last thing they needed was the phone ringing while they were trying to kill a harvester.

"Dammit," she grumped. She hated not knowing. She felt like her kids were out there and in terrible trouble, and it was tearing her up.

The world situation wasn't looking any better. Not only had the Earth Defense Society received top billing for the most wanted organization in the world by everyone from local sheriffs to Interpol, but there was a growing amount of finger-pointing going on between various countries in the aftermath of the attacks on the genebanks. Russia and Norway were already waging a war of words over sending military forces to Spitsbergen, with both sides claiming the other was responsible for the sudden outage of the critical SvalSat communications facility there that had cut off communications to hundreds of thousands of people. Renee didn't have to hack into anyone's computers to know that both countries were mobilizing troops along their mutual border: it was all over the news.

Making things worse was that Norway was a member of the North Atlantic Treaty Organization, NATO, which had originally been founded to counter the Soviet Union during the Cold War. While the Soviet Union and its puppet Warsaw Pact were long since gone, Russia still felt very threatened by NATO, and knew that the other NATO countries were bound by their treaty obligations to come to Norway's aid if she were attacked. None of the other NATO countries had yet put any troops on alert, but the news had reported that the senior NATO command staff had been called in for an emergency meeting at Norway's request. That had further angered the Russians, and the news services were claiming that there were unverified reports of more Russian troops on the way to Spitsbergen, along with Russian warships from the Northern Fleet getting ready to put to sea.

The reports from other parts of the world were just as bad, if not worse. Despite the televised claims of the *faux* Gregg Thornton laying responsibility for the attacks on the Earth Defense Society, India was blaming China for the destruction of their seed vault in Ladakh in the far north of the country. It had been near the Line of Actual Control, a disputed boundary since the war India fought, and lost, with China in 1962. China, in its turn, blamed India for the destruction of their genebank in Beijing, asserting that if India had not committed the act itself, it had acted as a conduit for the terrorists who had. There had already been two minor skirmishes between army units patrolling the borders, with three reported fatalities.

It's going to get really ugly, she thought, and she wasn't sure how they would be able to stop it, if they could at all.

That was when it struck her: *You're in charge*, a little voice in her mind, the one she had hated since she was a child, whispered. It sent a chill down her spine, because she had never considered herself a leader. She was strong-willed and as tough as anyone, but she was a follower and always had been. But now...

Gregg was almost certainly dead. Naomi and Jack were fighting for their lives on some God-forsaken island in the Arctic, and the world was quickly going to hell around them. She knew she couldn't wait much longer for certain things to be done. *Get some balls, woman*, she berated herself. *We're at the tipping point now. You can pray all you want that Naomi and the others will make it out alive and hopefully succeed. But you have no idea when that will be, and certain things have to be done now, or it may be too late.*

That's when she looked up and saw the others in the command center looking at her expectantly. They had all come to the same conclusion, and knew that they had to prepare for what Gregg had intended the base to do: act as an ark to help guarantee humanity's long-term survival in a war that was finally erupting into the open. The biggest problem was that what they were about to do would raise the base's signature to anyone looking closely for them, drastically increasing the chances that they'd be discovered. If that happened too soon, the game would be over.

"Shit," she muttered. "Get the Phase One protocols going," she ordered. "Send out the personnel recall. Burn the single-use phones." Every EDS member was supposed to carry at all times a special phone whose sole purpose was to receive a single text message, a unique code sent to each of them informing them of an emergency recall, after which the phone was to be destroyed. Many members would be coming to this base, but Gregg had purchased and renovated several other Cold War missile facilities across the country as survival shelters for the other EDS teams and their families. But this base was the only ark, the only seed vault. "And get the nitrogen tanker in here. We're going to need to top off the coolant for the vaults. What's our diesel fuel level?" she asked the woman at the logistics station.

"We're at a hundred percent," she said. "The tanks were topped off last week just after the weekly generator test. All the other power systems are on-line, backups are ready. Food stocks are at ninety-eight percent, and I've already scheduled a delivery to bring that up to one hundred within two hours. The deep water wells are in the green, with the water tanks continuously topped off. Everything else – spares, weapons, ammunition, equipment, medical supplies – is ready."

"Intel?" Renee asked.

"Aside from the world going down the toilet, as you well know," a young man said, nodding his head toward the newscast, "we've had a huge spike in web searches for EDS and our leadership staff, mostly from U.S. government agencies, but also from computer IP addresses located in several other countries. But there haven't been any active pings or attempted intrusions against our networks so far: hiding behind the front company firewalls seems to be working. As long as nobody knows where to look for us, they're going to have a hard time finding us."

"Good. But just make sure you keep a damn close eye on outbound activity," Renee cautioned him. He was a bright kid, but tended to get a little cocky. "They turned Ellen against us. It's possible it happened to someone else, too, and I don't want anybody giving away the show. I limited transmit access from the network to the machines here in the control center, so if you see so much as a single damn packet going out from any other machines, or anything fishy from here, I want to know about it right away. Ditto for phone calls, cans and string, whatever. Got it?"

"Yes, ma'am," the young man said, nodding.

Cocky, maybe, but he took his job dead serious, she told herself. As we all need to now. "Security?"

"Nothing unusual going on topside," drawled a middle-aged man with receding hair who carried a long-barreled .44 magnum revolver in a shoulder holster. "The ground sensor grid is active with one hundred percent coverage, with all sensors up and functioning properly. I just did a manual check of the blast valves: all of them checked out fine, and the base is in hard condition." In the Cold War days, "hard" meant that everything was closed and locked down in case of a nuclear blast. Any time the blast valves or the portal doors topside were open, the base was "soft," where the overpressure from a blast could potentially destroy the base. While all of them hoped that they would never have to worry about nukes, the principle was still the same: the site would be a lot tougher to get into with all of the topside doors and valves closed. "I also checked the hardened sensor array and the external camera: they're ready to go, too, if we need 'em." The base had a set of large tubes, about a foot in diameter that contained a variety of instruments. They normally were kept retracted, flush with the concrete at ground level not far from the portal entrance. The original sensor arrays had been designed so they could be raised like periscopes to take samples of the atmosphere after a nuclear attack. The old instruments had been replaced with far more sophisticated devices that could not only measure nuclear radiation, but could take biological and chemical samples, as well. The camera the man had referred to was in a similar retractable tube. They normally never used it, because it was actually inside the truck repair shed above them, which had its own video cameras in various places for surveillance of the portal entrance area. This camera would only ever be used for real if the sheet metal building above them was blown away.

"Okay, then," Renee breathed, nodding her thanks to the man for his report. "Let's get our people inside and button up. Make sure everyone is armed and has a basic load of ammunition." The others nodded gravely. "In the meantime," she eyed the seemingly endless stream of bad news on the main display panel, "let's see how this crap plays out."

As the others went about their tasks, she turned her attention back to what had stymied her since Jack's arrival: Sheldon's damnable super-encrypted file. She hated to think of how many of her brain cells had probably died trying to figure out this riddle, and grinned in dark-humored amusement as she imagined millions of her neurons hurling themselves into frustrated oblivion.

She stared at the pass phrase Jack had given her. She had already tried everything else she could think of to transpose the letters or words of the quote into a pass phrase that would actually *work*.

"It had to be something Sheldon could have done in his head," she muttered to herself as she stared at the screen. It would have been something tough, maybe impossible, for someone without his knowledge to do. But he was...had been incredibly smart. "And it has to be something he thought I could figure out."

She glanced up at one of the smaller monitors on the front display that showed various figures about the base's status. It contained a table, columns and rows of numbers.

"Wait a minute," she whispered, trying to suppress the tingle that had suddenly sparked into life in her lower spine. The table reminded her of the ASCII, or American Standard Code for Information Interchange, which were numbers that represented text characters in computers and communications equipment. Every letter had a corresponding ASCII number, starting with 65 for capital *A* and running through 122 for lower-case *z*.

She tried a direct substitution for the pass phrase, typing in the numbers instead of the letters for the pass phrase, but that didn't work.

"Shit!" she cursed. She knew she was close. She had to be.

Then something Jack had said came back to her: Sheldon had wanted the quote on his tombstone...

Tombstone. Sheldon had written a song with that title. He'd given her a copy of all of his scores, because she enjoyed music (including his, they had both discovered with some surprise), and had once been half-decent on the piano herself. She remembered *Tombstone* as one of the few songs he'd written that she had absolutely hated.

"Sheldon, you son of a bitch," she whispered to herself. "This had better be it." She quickly looked up the musical score for the song, pulling it up on her screen.

Try addition, she thought, quickly setting up a spreadsheet with the letters of the pass phrase, then transcoding them into ASCII numbers. Below the numbers, she put the number of the notes, from one to eight for A through G, corresponding to the notes at the beginning of the song. Since most of the notes went with words, not individual letters, she had to make some educated guesses, carrying the additive numbers across several letters to line up with the corresponding musical notes, or in some cases having several notes for a single word to match the song. She had the spreadsheet add the two numbers, then punched them into the password box for the file.

Access Denied, it told her.

"Okay, be that way, you son of a bitch," she said. "I'm not done yet."

She ran the same thing again, but used subtraction instead, taking away 1 through 8, depending on the note, from each ASCII character.

Holding her breath, she carefully typed in the resulting numerical sequence into the password box.

The box disappeared, and the encrypted file opened to reveal that it wasn't just a file, but a folder containing several documents.

"Hot damn!" she cried. She'd finally done it.

***

Vlad stepped into the biohazard room, carefully closing and sealing the door behind him. Everything seemed normal, with the four biosafety containment chambers just as he had left them last.

He moved over to the one containing the rhesus monkey and peered through the Lexan panel into the animal's living space. It was empty. Then he noticed that the Lexan, an extremely tough polycarbonate plastic, wasn't just clear, it was *gone*. Vanished.

"Not possible," he breathed as he quickly opened the chamber, then stepped back as it fell apart in his hands. Everything should have had thick rubber seals, and there had been a variety of plastic parts: all of them were gone. All that was left was bare metal and various little bits and pieces that weren't made of plastic. Peering inside at the electrical connections, he could see bare copper wires, with all of their insulating coatings gone. He caught a glimpse of something in the bottom of the systems cabinet that should not have been there. It was a small, greasy-looking pool of liquid that had a foul, chemical odor. It clearly wasn't feces, but he had no idea what it was, and he wasn't about to touch it.

"*Gdye vy?*" he called to the monkey. "Where are you?" The room was small and it couldn't have gotten far.

He checked the other chambers, and was shocked to discover that they were in exactly the same condition as the first: all the plastic components – everything that contained a significant quantity of carbon, he realized – was simply gone.

He stood in the middle of the lab, hands on hips, completely bewildered. That's when he saw that the computer at the workstation in the corner of the room was now nothing more than a jumble of metal, wire, and circuit boards, as if all the plastic had been dissolved away. Just like in the first biosafety chamber, there was a puddle of foul-smelling, viscous liquid on the table.

"*Chyort voz'mi*," he breathed, unable to comprehend where the monkey had gone, and wondering what had happened to the equipment in the room. "You cannot have just disappeared..."

He searched among the neatly stacked boxes of medical equipment and disposables like rubber gloves and replacement modules for the chambers, again noting that everything made of plastic or rubber was simply gone.

And there was no sign of the monkey.

There were no other places to look, and he knew from the monitor logs that no one else had accessed the door. There was no other way out of the room than the door through which he'd entered. The only other access points were the small airlock for food items and the vent in the ceiling.

The small airlock wasn't an option for a simian escapee, as it was locked and opened only from the outside. That left the ceiling vent and its filtration system.

Frowning, he looked up...and screamed as a shapeless mass dropped onto his face from the vent above, where it had just feasted on the rubber seals of the biological filter.

No one heard Vlad's brief, tortured struggle in the closed room.

Twenty-Four

Jack's satellite phone chimed as they all stood near the hangar, watching the industrious Rudenko use a bulldozer to scrape away the last bits of the smoldering Il-76 from the runway so the Falcon could take off.

"Shit," Jack muttered as he took the phone out of his parka and looked at the calling number in the display, one of the numbers they used through one of the front companies that masked the call's true origins. "It's Renee." He had meant to call her earlier, but he had completely forgotten in their headlong rush to get back to the airport and clear the runway so they could leave before any other military forces showed up.

Jack turned away from the noise of Rudenko's bulldozing so he could hear what Renee was trying to tell him.

Watching Jack for his reactions, Naomi continued her conversation with Mikhailov and Halvorsen. She had been trying to convince them to come with her. "If you stay," she said, "the harvesters won't let you live. We don't believe there are very many of them, and for them to have sent so many of their kind here was an indicator of just how important this place was to their plans. There may be more of them among the relief forces that are coming."

"Perhaps," Mikhailov told her. "But if we leave, who will explain what happened here?"

"More importantly, perhaps," Halvorsen said, "who will explain what did *not* happen." He glanced at Mikhailov. "Russian troops did not shoot down our plane, nor did they kill my men."

"And the Norwegians were not responsible for the deaths of my men, or the destruction of our transport," Mikhailov added. "But other troops and aircraft that come will not know this. If we leave, more good men will die, fighting over a lie. It is worth risking our own lives to save theirs."

Naomi couldn't argue with their logic, or their courage. "I understand," she said. "I had to ask."

"You will take the live creature back, then?" Halvorsen asked, nodding toward the tightly wrapped man-sized bundle that Naomi's surviving team members were shoving into the Falcon's small baggage hold. "You should leave it here. Let the world see it and know them for what they are."

"They'd only see the lie," Naomi told him. "Just like I did the first time. Even if you see it transform before your eyes, the first time you simply can't believe it's possible. And on television? No one would believe it was anything but a hoax using special effects." She shook her head. "They're too dangerous to place in the hands of anyone who doesn't really know them." *We've had to learn that lesson ourselves the hard way,* she thought bitterly.

"And they will believe a dead one?" Halvorsen asked without sarcasm. They had brought back what was left of the thing that had impersonated Solheim to show the incoming troops. "Some fools will claim these creatures washed up from the depths of the arctic sea."

"I know," Naomi answered. "No one will believe it at first. But if enough people see it, a few reputable scientists might come forward to challenge what they'll think is a fake. You've just got to do whatever you can to get it in front of the media. And keep yourselves alive."

Mikhailov snorted. "The first should not be difficult. I am not so certain about the second."

"At least this one won't kill anyone else," Halvorsen said quietly, looking at the Solheim-thing.

"Listen," Naomi told them as Ferris gestured impatiently from the door of the Falcon. The plane's engines were already spun up, and he was impatient to leave. "If you ever need to contact us, you can reach us through these email addresses and telephone numbers." She handed both men small slips of paper with the information written in her neat script. "Just dial the number, leave your name, then hang up, or send an email with just your name. We'll find you."

Halvorsen accepted the piece of paper gratefully. The future, not just for himself, but for his country and perhaps the world, had suddenly become very uncertain, and he was happy to have any allies he could.

By contrast, Mikhailov took his with obvious skepticism. "How will you find me in Russia?" he asked, as if his country were in fact on a different planet.

Naomi smiled. "We have people there, too," she said as Jack finally rejoined them, his face locked in a neutral expression that worried her. Holding out her hand, she shook Mikhailov's hand, then Halvorsen's. "Good luck to you and your people."

Jack shook their hands as well. "Watch your backs, guys," he told them. The two soldiers both nodded gravely in return.

Rudenko strode up to the two captains as Jack and Naomi boarded the plane and turned to wave. The three soldiers waved back, then watched as the two Americans disappeared inside the jet and the door retracted closed behind them. A few moments later, the sleek Falcon roared down the runway, then gracefully lifted into the sky.

It wasn't long after the Falcon, flying low over the ocean, faded from view that they heard the sound of jet engines overhead.

"Fighters," Halvorsen sighed, knowing the sound well from his time in Afghanistan. He had been hoping that transports would get here first and put troops on the ground, someone they might be able to talk to face to face and show the other form of sentient life that they now knew inhabited the Earth. That hope had been incredibly naïve, of course: both Russia and Norway knew that *something* had happened here, something that had caused the C-130 to send out a mayday and the Russian transport to stop responding. The gunslingers would be sent in to investigate first, not more defenseless troop transports.

"*Da*," Mikhailov said, looking up as two Norwegian F-16 fighters streaked low over the airport, pumping out flares and chaff behind them to help draw away any SAMs that might be fired at them. Much higher in the sky, he could see the contrails of six more F-16s. Their Russian counterparts, he was certain, would not be far behind.

He handed the portable radio Naomi had given them to Halvorsen. It was a stroke of genius on the Americans' part that they had brought it, for all the communications equipment at the airport had been destroyed. He and Halvorsen would have had no way to try and talk sense into their comrades in the air. "I hope you are very convincing, my friend," Mikhailov said as he watched the F-16s bank sharply around the side of the plateau, disappearing from view. "For all our sakes."

"Me, too," Halvorsen muttered as he keyed the microphone, hoping his words could avert war in the Arctic.

***

"What is it?" Naomi asked Jack as soon as they were strapped in. Ferris was already accelerating down the runway, loudly complaining to himself about fools and idiots. "What did Renee tell you?"

"She figured out the pass phrase to Sheldon's file," he told her as they were pressed back into their seats as the Falcon left the ground. Jack expected Ferris to climb, but he didn't: he gained enough altitude to bring up the gear and then flew straight out over the waves beyond the runway. They were flying so close to the ocean that Jack could swear some of the wind-whipped whitecaps almost reached his window in the fuselage. The ride with the winds still trailing the storm was rougher than the worst rutted road Jack had ever driven on, and it was difficult to speak without cracking his teeth together as the plane battered its way through the rough air. "Jesus!" he exclaimed as the plane suddenly dropped what must have been a dozen feet and everyone cried out. "*Ferris!*" he shouted to the pilot. "What the hell are you doing?"

"Trying to keep us from getting shot down," Ferris growled over the intercom as he wrestled with the plane's controls, keeping it as low as he dared. Unlike many modern military aircraft, the Falcon wasn't equipped or designed for low altitude flight at high speed, and he had forgotten how physically and mentally taxing it was to fly low and fast in a stock civilian aircraft. "If the Norwegians or Russians are sending fighters to Spitsbergen, the only thing that might save us is to fly low and stay in the ground clutter. Otherwise we'll stand out like a sore thumb and get our asses blown off. So shut up and let me fly."

"God," Jack hissed as the plane lurched again. Turning back to Naomi, he continued his tale from Renee. "So, there's good news and bad news."

"Just spill it, Jack," she said. "I'm a big girl, I can handle it."

Jack smiled and said, "I know. That's one of the things I like about you."

She grinned back, reflecting his own happiness at simply being alive after what they'd gone through. Both of them keenly felt the losses they'd suffered during the battle, and they both knew it had been a victory for the harvesters. But they had managed to kill six of the creatures, which had to be a devastating blow in return.

"There's a list of names," he explained, "just like Ellen Bienkowski said there would be. All the people who have connections to New Horizons that you told me about, from the Vice President on down, are on there, along with a lot more, in the U.S. and other countries. New Horizons was just the tip of the iceberg."

"We suspected that," she told him. "But aside from trying to track senior executives in the GMO industry moving into key government positions, it wasn't much more than guesswork."

"Well, you don't have to guess anymore: there are three hundred and twenty-seven names on that list, minus Ellen. Renee checked the names against EDS personnel: Ellen was the only one. So it looks like we don't have any more traitors in our midst. For the moment, at least."

Naomi breathed a sigh of relief. That's what she'd been most afraid of.

"There's also another list," he told her, leaning forward, and Naomi looked at him expectantly. "Rachel Kempf and Lynette Sansone were on it, along with Martin Kilburn, who worked at the FBI lab and was probably the one who blew it up." *I'm going to find you, Kilburn,* Jack promised himself, *and I'm going to roast your smashed-cockroach body for what you did to Jerri and the others.*

Naomi gasped as another gust of wind slammed into the plane, knocking them all sideways. "There's a list of the *harvesters*?" she said, incredulous. "But why would they keep a list of themselves?" Naomi wondered. "That would..."

"...leave them potentially vulnerable to what we're going to do to them," Jack finished for her as the Falcon at last began to climb. The other members of the team cheered Ferris, who grumbled back at them. "It makes sense, in a way," he went on. "How the hell are they supposed to know who's a harvester and who's not except when they can physically meet? There have to be times when they communicate remotely. And if they change identities, they have to let all the other bugs know, and that's not a who's-who list that you want to make a mistake with." He shrugged.

"What sort of people were on it?" Naomi asked. "Did she have time to say?"

"No details, really, aside from those few that we recognized. What they *don't* seem to do is masquerade as people with a lot of public visibility. They let their human lapdogs do that."

"How many?" Naomi asked, afraid of what the answer might be. "How many are left?"

"If that list is all of them, there are thirteen more, including the one we're bringing back with us, whichever one that is."

"My God," Naomi breathed. "We're that close. Thirteen away from wiping them off the planet." She looked at him, her eyes narrowing. "You said there was good news and bad news. I take it that was all the good news, such as it is. What's the bad?"

Jack's expression turned grim. "The corn samples that Sheldon found were prototypes, all right, but they weren't the only ones," he told her. "Kempf was a busy bug after you left: she perfected strains for rice, wheat, and soy, as well."

"But with the LRU lab under quarantine by the FBI, they won't be able to put the prototypes into the field," she said.

He shook his head slowly. "They never quarantined it. Once they gathered the crime scene data, the FBI was ordered out and the lab was reopened for business. Renee found out from digging through the FDA's network that they quietly cleared the new grains for production and sale yesterday. New Horizons is gearing up for production on a massive scale, and all the international distributors are companies with a lot of people on the list of humans in the harvesters' employ."

"Sweet Jesus," Naomi whispered as she turned to look out the window at the bright green of the Arctic Ocean, far below. She felt as if she were in a movie, watching herself and those around her from afar. It was a strange, uncomfortable feeling, her inner self seemingly detached from her body. She and Gregg had hoped beyond hope that they might be able to catch the genie before he escaped from the bottle. But there wasn't just a single genie: there were millions, if not billions of them in the form of every single grain New Horizons would be shipping.

"There's worse," Jack went on. "Just a couple hours ago, the news networks announced that an extremely virulent strain of influenza has broken out in the U.S., India, and China. The CDC in Atlanta is still trying to firm up the threat, but the talking head experts are claiming that this strain may be similar to the one that drove the flu pandemic in 1918 that killed somewhere between fifty and a hundred million people. The term biological warfare came up more than once from the news commentators. Between the attacks on the genebanks, the resulting international tensions, and this flu outbreak, people are running scared."

Naomi found she was holding her breath. She knew from the look on Jack's face there was more. And even worse. "What else?"

"A New Horizons affiliate, a pharmaceutical company, is claiming they've come up with a genetic shield from *all* strains of influenza, delivered by retrovirus. They claim it's been kept under tight wraps to prevent industrial espionage, but jointly announced it with the New

Horizons line of crops engineered to deliver just such a cure. It won't cost much more than regular grain seed, and a lot less than traditional inoculations. And the cure will be permanent." His stomach churned at the thought. *It'll be permanent, all right*, he thought. "The President is going to Congress to request a special subsidy to lower the price to make it available as widely as possible, and Congress is ready to sign."

"My God," Naomi groaned. "Everyone will want the New Horizons wonder seeds, driven by fear that the world is going to hell. The company won't be able to ship them fast enough."

"They won't be able to ship them at all," Jack promised her, "because we're going to blow them to hell first."

Twenty-Five

"What a load of horse hockey," Special Agent Carl Richards muttered between mouthfuls of a thick pastrami sandwich, followed by a long swig of dark, bitter ale as he watched the news on the television. He was sitting in his prized leather armchair, alone in his apartment as was his habit on the few hours each day he wasn't at work. He had no social life, nor did he want one. He lived for his work, and had never questioned the value it gave to his existence. The things that many considered sacrifices he had made – a wife, children, family, friends – were things that had never really mattered to him. Work was his life, his fellow agents were his family, and the men and women he brought to justice helped to ease the cries of the ghosts of his brutal childhood.

He was still bitterly annoyed at the Lincoln Research University crime scene being reopened without a more thorough on-site forensic analysis. Even with the disaster at the FBI lab that followed on the heels of Sheldon Crane's murder in Nebraska, Richards knew that more should have been done before the lab was cleared for operation again. But the word had come straight from the Director of the FBI herself, and that was that.

As he sat there, his mind steadily churned through the information he had absorbed. He made no claim to being an analytic genius like he believed Jack Dawson to be, but no one would ever mistake him for a fool, either. Looking back, now that he had a little time to really focus, the wrap-up at the New Horizons lab had seemed rushed, and even the investigation at the FBI lab scene had been disturbingly half-assed.

No, he thought suddenly. *Things had been directed, orchestrated. There was something artificial about the investigation there.* What stuck out in his mind the most was the strange treatment of Dr. Martin Kilburn, one of the lab survivors, the one who had fingered Dawson's former girlfriend as the bomber and Dawson as an accomplice. Richards had wanted to interview him about Dawson's visit there that night. But he hadn't been allowed access to Kilburn, or even been permitted to submit questions for him to answer later. After a very public interview (*If you considered a few hundred FBI agents the public,* Richards thought sourly), Kilburn was whisked away. As

Richards discovered by using his main gift of being a relentless pain in the ass, it was again on the director's orders.

Then there was the whole thing with Dawson. Richards would do his duty to his very last breath and hunt Dawson down without a shred of mercy, but he couldn't deny that everything about the man being associated with terrorists felt wrong. Richards knew he wasn't a people person, but he *knew* people, understood them, extremely well. Dawson simply didn't strike him as someone who'd blow up a lab full of his colleagues and a former lover with whom he was still close friends, then run away to join a terrorist group that had sprung up out of nowhere. It didn't make sense.

On the boob tube, which he alternately relished and reviled, President Fowler, accompanied by a smiling Secretary of Defense, was glad-handing a bunch of high school kids and parents at a political rally in Madison, Wisconsin. It was an election year, and even with the world going to hell in a hand-basket, the politicos had to be on the stump, kissing babies and pimping votes. Richards thought the whole thing was ridiculous: democracy for him meant voting Republican, and that was that. But he enjoyed the speeches and the mudslinging the same way that people enjoyed football games.

The news commentators, who simply couldn't shut up long enough to leave a single second of silence in the broadcast, revealed the obvious: that Fowler's speech had been rewritten to focus on recent world events, and the attacks that had wrought destruction on American soil. The Secretary of Defense wasn't expected to say anything, but his presence alone was intended to help reinforce the President's message.

There won't be any good backbiting in this speech, Richards thought, disappointed.

As the television showed President Fowler mounting the podium, he let the campaigning politician's smile fade and put on a suitably grim and determined expression. "My fellow Americans," he began.

Then the transmission from the high school suddenly terminated, the view cutting over to one of the cameras in the news room.

"Ladies and gentlemen," one of the commentators said smoothly, "we seem to be having technical difficulties. We're trying to get another video feed in from a local affiliate. Ah, here we go...*Oh, my God!*"

The beer bottle and what was left of Richards' sandwich hit the floor as he leaped out of the chair, snatched up his holster and coat, and dashed out the front door, not even bothering to lock it behind him.

On the television screen the camera showed a billowing cloud of black smoke and flaming debris where the high school auditorium had been.

***

"You guys need to hear what just came up over the satellite radio broadcast," Ferris suddenly called over the cabin speakers in a trembling voice.

Naomi, Jack, and the others turned to look up toward the speakers on the ceiling, as if they could see the words coming out.

"...repeat, just moments ago there was a massive explosion at the high school where President Fowler, accompanied by the Secretary of Defense, was giving a campaign speech today. We don't have any confirmation from the Secret Service, but eyewitness reports indicate that the auditorium where the President was giving his speech was leveled in the blast, and hundreds are feared dead. We're looking at the video footage here in our studio, and there's literally nothing left but rubble and bodies. My God, this is terrible! We don't know–"

"Turn it off," Jack called hoarsely.

With a grunt, Ferris switched off the audio. Everyone sat still for a moment, stunned.

"It shouldn't come as a surprise," Jack said after a few moments.

"Why do you say that?" one of the other members of the team asked.

"Because the Vice President is one heartbeat away from the Presidency," Jack told him. "And we know who controls him. If there were any major obstacles to whatever they're trying to do before, they're gone now."

"It's just us now," Naomi whispered as she looked up at Jack, her blue and brown eyes glistening.

"Maybe not," Jack said. "Ferris!" he called. "I need to make a call over the plane's satellite phone..."

***

The carnage at the FBI lab had been bad enough, Richards thought grimly, but it didn't hold a candle to the high school where the President had been speaking. It looked worse than the devastation at the Colorado State University campus. The Secret Service hadn't made it official yet, but Richards knew there was no way the President or anyone else in the auditorium could have survived.

"Goddamn them," he hissed at whoever had done this. "*Goddamn* them!"

He was speeding at almost one hundred miles per hour down I-95 toward Washington, the red bubble stuck to the top of his black Impala flashing as he headed toward Ronald Reagan International Airport where a chartered airliner was being loaded with every agent within an hour's drive of D.C. More, many more, would be following behind on other planes, and every field office east of the Mississippi would be emptied out within the next few hours, all converging on the latest disaster to strike the nation.

His cell phone rang, and he immediately reached out and punched the hands-free talk button on his stereo. "Richards," he barked.

"Guess who this is," a familiar voice said from the speakers around him.

Richards, totally surprised, almost lost control of his car. "Dawson," he grated, "when I find you, I'm going to skin you alive. The other things you and your whacko friends did were horrific enough. But killing the President? We'll never stop hunting you. *Never.*"

"Listen to me, Richards," Dawson told him evenly. "I couldn't have killed the President, because I'm on a plane a few thousand miles away. My 'whacko friends' and I just had a firefight with the real bad guys, the ones who are behind all this. We've been trying to stop them. So was Sheldon Crane. That's why he was killed: because he found out things no one was supposed to know."

Richards had a sharp retort on his tongue, but paused. His gut instinct about Dawson was warring with his sense of duty, and it was one of the very few times in his life that he'd been so deeply conflicted that he couldn't even speak.

"I can prove it," Jack pressed, sensing that the other man was at least giving some thought to his words. "But we need your help. Things are going to get worse, much worse, if we don't stop them soon."

"Who's 'them?'" Richards asked. "Little green men from Mars? I don't believe in little green men."

"Neither do I," Jack told him. Richards would have laughed were it not for how dead serious Jack's voice was. "They're not little or green, but they're deadly as hell. We've got one with us that we captured during the fight at Spitsbergen." He paused. "You need us, Carl, you just don't know it yet. And we sure as hell need you."

"God help me," Richards muttered to himself, "I can't believe I'm even listening to this!"

"Richards, I swear on my murdered wife's name that I'm telling the truth."

Those words took Richards by surprise. Like most of the agents who'd worked with Jack, he'd heard the story of his wife's murder, and knew that Dawson would never have said such a thing unless he was deadly serious.

Shaking his head in disbelief that he was even thinking of anything other than collaring Dawson and dragging him off to trial, Richards said, "Okay, Dawson, what do you want?"

***

Aboard the plane, Jack breathed an audible sigh of relief. "The first thing we'll need," he said, glancing at Ferris, "is clearance back into U.S. airspace."

"Where are you now?" Richards asked.

Naomi shook her head, and Ferris grimaced, but Jack went ahead and told him. "We're over Greenland, heading toward the east coast. If you check the international news, you'll probably see a story pretty soon about a battle involving Russian and Norwegian troops on the island of Spitsbergen. That's where we're coming from. We didn't have a flight plan back, and with the murder of the President the FAA has closed our airspace, and the Canadians didn't want to let us through, either."

"All right, Dawson, I can swing that," Richards told him, picturing in his mind a pair of F-16 fighters escorting Dawson's plane in. "What else?"

"I want to meet up with you and show you who the real enemy is." Naomi's eyes flew wide. "Wait one," he told Richards as Naomi covered his microphone with one hand.

"Jack," she told him urgently, "we can't risk showing that thing to anyone outside of the confinement chambers at the base."

"It's knocked out with formaldehyde, right?" Jack asked pointedly. "As long as you can keep it unconscious, we'll have to risk it. Listen, this guy's a hard-ass and he's not going to be easily convinced. He's going to want real proof, and we've got it right here with us. If we can get him to believe what's going on, he'll be a huge help to us. But he's not going to just take my word. I'm shocked he even agreed to talk to me at all."

"Dawson, you still there?" Richards snapped irritably.

"Yes," Jack told him, gently removing Naomi's hand from the mic. "So what do you say?"

"If I can get you cleared through Canadian and U.S. airspace," Richards asked, "how long will it take you to get to Baltimore-Washington International?"

Jack glanced at Ferris, who held up his hand, thumb and fingers spread. "Five hours," Jack told him, nodding for Ferris to make it happen.

Ferris shrugged and punched some navigation data into the Falcon's console, then nudged the throttles forward to its maximum cruising speed

"I'll be waiting, Dawson," Richards told him. After a brief pause he said, "If you're lying to me, you'd better make sure I'm dead before you walk away, or I'll spend the rest of my life hunting you down. You'll never have a chance to rest again for whatever miserable life might be left to you. *Never.*"

"Don't worry," Jack told him. "We'll be there. Just keep an open mind about what you're going to see."

"Five hours," Richards said, then the line went dead.

Blowing out a deep breath, Jack tore the headset off, feeling as if it weighed a hundred pounds. Just like that, exhaustion left behind by the stress of combat hit him like a hammer.

"Come on," Naomi told him, helping him to his feet and leading him back to the seats in the passenger cabin. "I'll call Renee and let her know what we're doing. Then let's get some rest while we can."

***

There was standing room only in the EDS base's command center. All eyes were fixed on the horror transpiring on the screen, where Vice President Norman Curtis was being sworn in as President of the United States. No one in the underground base had any doubt that the deputy Secretary of Defense, a known puppet of the harvesters, would be moved up to take the now-dead secretary's job.

The world had watched through the lens of a video camera as a single bloodied Secret Service agent had somberly carried a body bag from near where the podium had been. His burden was light, for there had not been much of the President's body left after the blast.

Now, Norman Curtis, a known agent of the harvesters, was holding up his right hand as a local judge in Alabama, where Curtis had been campaigning, read him the oath of office.

After talking to Naomi and hearing Jack's plan to show their captive harvester to Special Agent Richards, she had double-checked the files Sheldon had stolen: Richards wasn't on either of the lists. The FBI Director was on the list of human conspirators, but Renee hadn't had time to verify the rest of the collaborators; she had focused on the harvesters first. They turned out to have taken the guise of sufficiently public personalities that much of their activity could be monitored through the Internet. Not surprisingly, almost all of them had very recently gone "on vacation."

As she stared at the news display, Curtis finished the oath of office: "...and will to the best of my ability, preserve, protect and defend the Constitution of the United States."

Muttering in disgust, she stood up and gently shouldered her way through the silent crowd around her. She'd seen enough, and felt like vomiting. "I'm going for a walk," she said to no one in particular as she went down the stairs, then out through the dome's blast door and into the main junction.

Once alone, she began to cry. "Please, God," she sobbed. It was the first time since she'd learned the truth of what was happening that her faith and resolve had faltered. As she watched Curtis being sworn in, she felt completely crushed and dispirited, as if she and the others no longer stood the slightest chance of succeeding. She would be so glad when Naomi and Jack returned. She hated being in charge, especially now, because she knew she couldn't let the others see her this way. "Please, God, give us just a little help. Just a little."

After a few moments she recovered her composure, wiping her tears away on her lab coat and accidentally smearing mascara across the pristine white fabric.

"Goddammit," she cursed. Then she laughed at herself. "The world's falling apart and you're worried about your damned mascara. Idiot."

Sighing, she decided it was time to get some sleep, if she could. But first she wanted to check on the lab and see if anything interesting was going on.

***

The thing that had once been a rhesus monkey moved silently along the mezzanine level of the lab dome. It had left the confines of the biohazard room by consuming the rubber gaskets lining the door and squeezing its gelatinous body onto the metal decking beyond. It was growing rapidly as it broke down and reformed the material it had consumed, yet it remained hungry. It needed more.

As it grew, triggers in its DNA commanded the formation of an ever larger array of specialized cells. The thing had no awareness, but its ability to focus on the food it required was sharpening. It was no longer a random act, but a search directed by highly sensitive receptors that formed along the outer layers of soft, flowing tissue. The receptors guided it in the direction of the storage area, and it silently feasted on the cardboard and plastic boxes and their contents.

But all too soon the feast was over, and it ran up against a metal wall that had no easily consumed gaskets through which the beast could force itself. Moreover, its feasting had triggered more changes from its complex DNA: it was nearing saturation, almost ready for the next step in its life cycle.

Almost.

That was when its receptors focused on chemical signals from directly below, through the grates in the metal floor: complex organic matter. It quickly withdrew from probing the infernal metal wall and silently oozed through the holes in the decking to fall into the lab animal storage area.

***

Alexander was jarred from a drug-induced sleep by a riot of screeching and howling that suddenly erupted from the other animals nearby. He had been sleeping in a large crate, padded with a soft blanket, as he recovered from the wounds he had received while fighting the creature to which his kind were especially attuned.

Mewling in pain, he got to his feet and turned to look in the direction of the other animals. They were in cages inside a much larger cage-like enclosure, and *something* was after them. Alexander didn't know what it was, in the fashion that his kind recognized other creatures, but he instantly knew it was a threat. Backing against the opposite wall of his crate, he arched his back and his fur stood on end, and he bared his teeth in fear.

He heard a deep growl nearby, and he glanced over to see his companion cat, white to his black, on a table across from his crate. She, too, was baring her fangs at whatever writhed in the cage among the shrieking animals.

He watched with eyes dilated wide open as a shapeless form swept down from above onto the rabbits, rats, mice, monkeys, and a pair of small pigs. They all shrieked in terror, but their cries were short-lived: in only a few panting breaths they were nothing more than quickly dissolving lumps in the roiling mass of mottled flesh.

After the thing finished with them, it slowly began to move out of the large cage. Toward Alexander.

Ignoring the pain from the wounds that the *other* thing had given him earlier, he turned and desperately clawed at his own cage, crying in fear as the thing oozed along the floor toward him.

His white companion hissed and drew back on the nearby table, then suddenly fled to a safer spot halfway to the door that led out of this place. She could not help him.

He bloodied his paws as he scratched against the slim bars of the cage, trying to get away, and blood oozed from his reopened wounds as his terror drove him far beyond the pain.

Then a shadow fell upon him as the thing rose up, a pillar of pulsating and undulating matter that was utterly alien to his instincts and feline understanding, now standing high enough to block out the light from above.

Shivering, Alexander backed into the corner of his cage, panting in fear as he waited for Death to take him.

***

Renee went through the security process to enter the lab dome, stepping wearily through the entryway as the blast door swung aside. As she had both expected and hoped, it was empty. Everyone was over in the command center.

Except Vlad, she thought. She hadn't seen the young Russian over there. "Vlad?" she called.

No answer.

Then she heard a sound that turned her blood to ice: the snarl of a terrified cat. Then two. But what bothered her even more was that there wasn't a single sound from any of the other animals, especially the monkeys, which were normally a very boisterous lot.

With the hair standing up on the back of her neck, she drew her pistol and cautiously moved deeper into the maze of work benches and equipment toward the animal storage area.

Koshka, Naomi's white cat, suddenly ran past her and darted behind the lab bench on Renee's right. Renee could tell the cat was terrified. She could hear another cat hissing and snarling, and the sound of what must have been its paws desperately clawing at the crate: Alexander.

"Jesus," she whispered hoarsely. She knew that she should just turn and run to get help, but she couldn't bring herself to abandon Jack's cat. *Stupid, stupid, stupid!* she cursed at herself, even as she continued to move forward.

She couldn't see Alexander's crate yet, as it was around a bulkhead that protruded from the left side of the dome that made up the inside wall of the animal storage area.

Alexander suddenly stopped hissing, and all Renee could hear in the silence of the dome was the big cat's rapid panting.

Taking a deep breath, Renee tightened her finger on the snub-nose .44 magnum's trigger and quickly stepped to the right between two lab benches so she could see Alexander's crate and whatever *else* was there.

***

The thing sensed yet another source of nutrients just ahead, easily in reach, but it paused. It had consumed a great deal, gorging itself on organic matter, and the complex chemical and biological processes that dictated its life cycle triggered yet another set of commands to its rapidly changing body.

Expelling a large pool of unneeded material, it began to seek a dark, silent place where it could molt. Slithering up one of the mezzanine support pylons along the inside of the dome, it made its way back to the upper deck and silently began to probe around for a suitable place.

It quickly found the intake tunnel that fed fresh air to the diesel backup generators. It flowed through the grate in the locked safety bulkhead into the dark space beyond, finally coming to rest under the air filtration system that was mounted just before the outer concrete bulkhead and the blast valves that led to the air intake vent.

There, in the warm dark, it lay still and quiet. Changing. Becoming.

***

Renee's finger was so tight on the trigger that later she wondered why the pistol hadn't just gone off, but there was nothing to shoot at.

Alexander was in his crate, coiled in one corner and staring fixedly up toward the mezzanine above him, but apparently unharmed.

She stepped closer, her gun still at the ready, until she saw what was in the animal holding area. Or, rather, what was missing.

"Shit," she breathed as she looked at all the empty cages. Every single animal was gone, disappeared. All the snaps were still on the cage doors, and the bars and mesh on the various cages weren't bent or disturbed. Looking closer, she noticed that there was no waste, blankets, or toys in any of the enclosures, either: they were all nothing but bare metal. "Vlad?" she called again, nearly choking on the young man's name. "Vlad!" she shouted, louder.

As before, there was no answer.

She started to move away, intending to check the biohazard room, when a deep and desperate cry stopped her. Turning, she saw that Alexander had shoved himself up against the door to the crate, one paw stretched out to her as if begging for her not to go. She had never seen a cat look so terrified before, even during the two battles they had experienced with the harvesters here in the base. *But if there was a harvester here*, she thought, *why weren't the other cats gathering, drawn by whatever unfathomable instinct that had made them such good organic alarm systems? And how the hell could it have done...whatever happened here?*

Looking into the crate, she saw that Alexander was again covered with blood, and noticed that a few of his stitches had been ripped out, no doubt while he had thrashed around, trying to escape.

"Okay, boy," she murmured, putting the gun back in her holster. She was reassured slightly by Koshka, who was now right behind Renee's legs. But the white cat, clearly still spooked by something, was staring up at the mezzanine, just as Alexander had been. Renee suddenly decided that going up there alone maybe wasn't such a good idea.

Opening the door to the crate, she took gentle hold of Alexander as he leaped out and clung to her like a terrified child. She grimaced as the big cat's claws penetrated the fabric of her lab coat and sweater to lance her skin. He was shivering as if he had a terrible fever.

"It's okay, big guy," she told him, ignoring the pain of his claws as she cradled him. "I've got you. Now let's get the hell out of here and go get some help."

As she turned to go, she caught sight of something above her on the mezzanine level, an indistinct shadow through the grates in the flooring. But before she had time to think about setting down Alexander and drawing her weapon, it had disappeared.

Into the air intake tunnel.

Backing out of the lab, keeping her eyes on the mezzanine, she carried Alexander to what she hoped was the relative safety of the main junction. Then, with Koshka safely out of the lab dome, she closed the blast door behind her.

Twenty-Six

Ferris guided the Falcon to a stop next to the executive jets at BWI's general aviation facility in the northeast corner of the airport. Jack dropped the stairway to the tarmac before Ferris shut down the engines.

A few yards away was a black Chevy Impala. Special Agent Carl Richards stood stiffly beside it, his fists tightly clenched at his sides.

"Stay here," Jack told the others. "Let me talk to him first."

"We'll cover you," said Hathcock as he brought up an H&K submachine gun.

"No," Jack told him sternly. "We've got to convince this guy we're the real deal. We're not going to kill him. Got it?"

Hathcock shrugged and lowered his weapon.

With a last glance at Naomi, Jack went down the steps and walked quickly toward Richards.

Behind him, Hathcock raised the H&K again and held it steady, the sights centered on Richards' chest. Naomi nodded in approval, then turned her attention back to Jack.

Moving into handshaking distance with Richards, but not extending his hand, Jack said, "The F-16s were a nice touch. What'd you have the Air Force tell the pilots?"

"That you were carrying precious cargo and needed protection," Richards replied. "You'd better not make a liar out of me, Dawson. The country has gone completely nuts over internal security, as you might imagine. Pulling off this little stunt cost me a lot of favors."

Nodding, Jack told him, "Come on. You need to know what we're up against."

"Aren't your friends going to come down and help with the alien autopsy gag?" Richards asked sarcastically.

"No. It's just you and me," Jack told him. "Believe me, this is one show and tell you're not going to like at all."

"I can't believe I'm laying my career on the line for you," Richards told him as Jack opened the luggage door, revealing a tightly-bound bundle that was roughly the size of a man. "I think I've simply gone insane."

"No," Jack told him solemnly. "You're here because you're trusting your instincts."

Jack quickly undid the bindings of the bundle's heavy plastic tarp. He paused before pulling back the plastic to reveal what was underneath.

"You're not going to believe what I'm about to show you," Jack told him. "I sure as hell didn't when I first saw one of these things, with it up and moving around, and it almost got me to let it escape. But it's *real*, Richards. And this thing and others like it are trying to take over our home, our world, and kill us all in the process."

Frowning with impatience, Richards pushed Jack aside and tore back the flap of plastic.

"God," he gasped, briefly turning away. "What's that smell?"

"That's how they smell in their natural form," Jack told him as Richards turned back to look more closely at the thing in the plastic. "They're shape-changers, Richards. They can control this stuff," he pointed to some of the bruise-colored malleable tissue that had pooled around the thing's head, "and change their shape and color to anything that's about the same size. Like a person. And when they do, the smell goes away. We don't know why. Here," he said, handing Richards a pair of disposable examination gloves. "Put these on, then you tell me if you think this thing is just a bunch of latex and rubber."

Richards didn't hesitate. He grabbed the gloves, expertly snapped them on, and then began to probe at the creature's flesh, his fingers disappearing into the mottled, slimy surface, then running over the exposed and glistening skeletal structure, even its mandibles.

The body suddenly convulsed. Both men leaped back, their hands going instinctively to their weapons. They put their hands on the grips, but didn't draw the guns; they didn't need any unwanted attention from airport security. Richards' eyebrows shot up when he caught sight of Jack's gun, a massive .50 caliber Desert Eagle strapped under his left arm.

"What's with the cannon, Dawson? Penis envy issues, maybe?" Richards asked sarcastically as he warily eyed the thing in the tarp.

"No," Jack told him nervously, his eyes fixed on the harvester, which again lay completely still. "Their skeletal structure is like an organic carbon fiber material that's incredibly tough, stronger than Kevlar. That dinky 9mm you're carrying would barely scratch it." He glanced at Richards to make sure he had his attention. "I had to empty five .44 magnum rounds into one of these things at point blank range to stop it, and even then it was a close call. After that, I got myself a bigger gun." He gestured Richards closer. "You haven't told me you think this is a Hollywood stunt."

"I'll tell you what I think, Dawson. I think I'm still back in my apartment, having a nightmare after eating a bad pastrami sandwich and seeing our President blown to bits on TV. And when I wake up, I'm going to find you and knock your block off, just on principle." He looked at the thing again, but didn't touch it. Then he peeled off the gloves and shoved them in his coat pocket. "Dawson," he said, his voice suddenly losing its usual tone of arrogant self-assurance, "this can't be real. It just *can't* be."

"It can be," Jack told him, "and it *is*. We don't know where they came from, and as far as we know there's no mother ship or any of that garbage. But we do know they've got a lot of human collaborators in high places, and they plan to transform our biosphere with the help of genetically engineered crops from New Horizons."

Richards glanced sharply at him. "Those are the guys with the cure for the sudden virus outbreak, right? I thought that was a little too coincidental."

"Naomi worked for New Horizons, remember," Jack said. "She worked for one of *them*, but she didn't know it until they tried to co-opt her. And when Crane investigated EDS, she showed him the truth and he believed. That's when he went underground, went rogue. EDS needed someone to penetrate the Lincoln Research University lab, because that was where the crop strains were being created. Sheldon was perfect for the job. He got in, found out what they were doing, and *they* – the enemy, the harvesters, we call them – killed him for it."

"And you got suckered into this same mind game?"

Shaking his head, Jack told him, "There wasn't any mind game about three special agents coming to my door and trying to kill me the night of the lab explosion, looking for information that Sheldon had sent electronically but that I didn't even realize I had. One of the agents, Lynette Sansone, was one of these things." He gestured at the creature. "Naomi and some of the others rescued me." He stepped closer to Richards. "Carl, their objective is to *wipe us out*. And there are humans helping them to do it."

"Oh, come on," Richards said. "Why would anyone do that?"

Jack shrugged. "Greed? Power? Who knows? It's not like human beings haven't tried to wipe out other human beings before. Why not help somebody else do it? For all we know it could be some sort of brainwashing, but I don't think so." Thinking of Ellen Bienkowski, turning traitor in return for the promise of a cure for Tan's cancer, he went on, "I think the harvesters are using leverage of some kind on most of the people they've subverted. All that matters now is that we stop them, and the New Horizons seeds are the key: we think they're at the center of what's been going on, the critical element of their operation. The terrorist attacks, the virus outbreak..." He paused. "Even the assassination of the President. It's all part of the plan to destabilize things and get those seeds in high demand and out into the world, and it's working."

"What are the seeds supposed to do?" Richards asked, wrinkling his nose as he caught another whiff of the harvester's odor.

He's starting to believe, Jack told himself with a huge inward sigh of relief. "We've got people working on that, but the honest answer is that we don't know yet. But you can bet it's nothing good."

He closed the plastic over the harvester and shoved the reeking thing back into the luggage compartment, then locked the door. Turning to Richards, he said grimly, "There's one more thing. The FBI's been penetrated by at least one collaborator, and you're not going to believe who it is."

"Something tells me I'm not going to like hearing this," Richards grated.

Jack shook his head. "No, you're not. It's the director herself. There may be more, we have a list of the human collaborators and are trying to pin everyone down, but EDS has known about the director for some time now." He sighed. "There's worse."

"Oh, please, bring it on," Richards told him sourly as he leaned back against the plane.

"The new President is a collaborator, too," Jack told him, "and I'd wager my next year's pay – if I had a job anymore – that he was involved in putting together the assassination this morning."

That struck Richards like a hammer, and his face blanched. For a moment, Jack thought the man might actually pass out on the tarmac.

"You okay?" Jack asked.

"What kind of a stupid question is that?" Richards snapped as he rubbed his hands over his bald head. "Of course I'm not okay.

Everything I've believed in my entire life has just been turned upside down, and the thing that's really making me angry is that I'm actually believing this ridiculous, absurd...*shit!*"

"Nothing that you believe has been turned upside down, Carl," Jack reassured him. "It's just that we're being lied to and led down a path toward our own destruction. These things," he gestured toward the closed cargo compartment where the harvester lay, "may not even be from another world for all we know, although the biologists in EDS believe they must be, because their DNA is so different from ours. But that doesn't matter. What matters is that they're a threat to our country and our world, and the people we've spent our lives defending. That part of your life, the part that's been the most important to you, hasn't changed at all. Only the source of the threat has."

Richards blew out a deep breath and looked out across the runway for a long moment, his face unreadable and still except for a vein pulsing at his temple. On the other side of the airport, a Boeing 737 roared into the sky from one of the commercial runways.

As the airliner quickly shrank to a glitter of sunlight reflecting from the jet's wings, Richards turned to Jack and said, "All right, hotshot. What's the plan?"

"That," Jack told him uneasily, "is a damn good question."

***

"I want them found." President Norman Curtis sat behind his desk in the oval office, glaring at the members of his National Security Council. In what was an unusual circumstance in many respects, he had also instructed the Director of the FBI, Monica Ridley, to attend. Among the other men and women in the room, he was aware that she knew The Secret. The terrible, wonderful Secret. "The people who did this, these Earth Defense Society people. I want their heads on a platter, and I want them *now!*" Turning to the Secretary of Homeland Security, Jeffrey Komick, Curtis said icily, "What actions have you taken, Jeffrey?"

Leaning forward on one of the sofas that suddenly seemed incredibly uncomfortable, Komick took a deep breath before answering. Curtis had never been a well-liked member of the former President's team. He was an extremely savvy politician and was quite competent, but he had about him an aura of cold arrogance and a fierce temper that had always been well-masked in the presence of his former boss, but would become, Komick and several other cabinet members feared, the norm for the country's new leader. Komick suspected it wouldn't be long before he'd be in search of another job, and the greater part of him was already looking forward to it as a relief. However, like the others gathered in the room, he put the needs of his country first, and he would weather whatever Curtis brought to bear on him. For now.

"Mister President," Komick began, his rasping voice filling the now-silent room, "starting where the President..." he paused a moment, his mouth hanging open as his mind replayed the horrifying scene of the explosion that killed his longtime friend and hundreds of others, "...where the President was killed, we've locked down concentric rings around Madison, Wisconsin, blocking all road and air traffic with the help of the National Guard."

The Secretary of Transportation shifted uncomfortably, but kept her eyes firmly fixed on Curtis. When Komick had said that road and air traffic had been locked down, he meant it quite literally: there was an unprecedented gridlock forming around the now-beleaguered city of Madison that was spreading like a tsunami, particularly through the nation's airspace. On the ground, tens of thousands of people were marooned in their cars, unable to move, and the news had already reported a number of small-scale disturbances that would soon build into riots.

Curtis merely glanced her way, then dismissed her with his eyes. "What else?" he said to Komick.

"We're searching everywhere and everyone in the area," Komick went on, "and of course we have every available member of the law enforcement community combing the area, looking for witnesses and clues. The various agencies under Homeland Security have received thousands of tips already and we're coordinating with the Intelligence Community," he nodded his head at the Director for National Intelligence, "but so far we've come up empty."

"How about the FBI?" Curtis asked, turning to Monica Ridley.

Far more relaxed than Komick, Ridley explained, "We've got three hundred agents in Madison, with more on the way. They've been conducting a thorough forensic examination of the scene, but our analytic capabilities have been seriously hampered by the destruction of the FBI lab at Quantico." As Curtis opened his mouth to speak, she went on smoothly, "But that hasn't stopped us from putting some pieces of the puzzle together." Turning to her notes, she went on, "The bomb appears to be very similar to the ones used by EDS in their earlier attacks on the seed storage facilities: it was an improvised fuel-air explosive that was detonated in the basement of the auditorium where the President was speaking. It was the same chemical composition as the others, and roughly the same size."

"That's impossible," Komick interjected. "How did anyone get something like that past the Secret Service protective detail?"

"No one got past them, Mr. Secretary," Ridley said. "The perpetrators were *in* the detail, not outsiders. We believe that at least two of the Secret Service agents assigned to the President's protective detail that day were associated with EDS. I doubt it was a coincidence that both of them were on duty in the basement when the bomb went off."

"They were suicide bombers?" someone else asked. "That's ridiculous."

"That's not what I said," Ridley said, clearly irritated. "I said that we believe at least two had ties to EDS: they both had received money some time ago from Gary Woolsey, a known EDS terrorist who burned down a New Horizons lab, killing the occupants, and who died in prison shortly after his conviction." She looked up. "We haven't found the bodies or remains of the agents in the rubble, and at this point we have every reason to believe they escaped after initiating the bomb, releasing the fuel-air mixture into the basement, but before it detonated."

"Jesus!" Curtis exploded. "You mean those bastards infiltrated the Secret Service?" He turned to the Secretary of the Treasury. "I want every agent assigned to my protective detail re-checked and re-cleared. Today." Turning to Ridley, he ordered, "You handle it. I don't want this particular investigation accidentally handed over to any moles. Get someone who knows what the hell they're doing. We don't need any more screwups."

"Mr. President!" The Secretary of the Treasury, under whom the Secret Service operated, blurted. "Sir, I must protest! The Secret Service is not infested with traitors! The director here so much as said she doesn't have any direct evidence: this is all pure speculation. And–"

"Enough!" Curtis shouted. Leaning forward, he fixed the man with a glare. "The President of the United States, who was a close friend of mine for the last thirty years, was assassinated this morning. I don't plan on being the next victim, or have my family fall prey to these...savages. If it causes your department some discomfort to be investigated, too bad. Let's face it: the only logical answer is that it had to have been an inside job. That school was swept and cleared multiple times, just like every other place that's visited by the President. Some guy dressed up as a janitor didn't just wheel a bomb in there." Softening his voice slightly, he said, "This week has already seen enough tragedies. I don't want any more. I expect you to give Director Ridley your full cooperation." Looking around the room, he added, "And that goes for all of you. The gloves come off and the brass knuckles go on. I want these EDS people found."

"And then what?" Komick asked quietly.

Curtis compressed his mouth into a thin hard line before he spoke. "And then," he said, "I want justice done."

***

After Curtis brought the meeting to a close, he ushered everyone out but Ridley. Collapsing onto the sofa beside her, he tiredly rubbed his hands over his eyes.

"I ran a marathon once," he said quietly. "For two days I felt like I'd been steamrollered. I feel now like I've just finished a dozen marathons."

Ridley glanced around the Oval Office, a look of concern on her face. She'd only found out the day before that Curtis was in on The Secret, but hadn't expected him to speak openly about it.

Curtis chuckled, knowing what she was thinking. "I've received assurances from our friends that we're secure here," he told her. "But it always makes me wonder what was really said during those eighteen and a half minutes missing from Nixon's Watergate tapes. I'll bet they know."

"It makes me wonder if we should be speaking at all," she told him bluntly. It was true that he was the President now, and her boss, but they had a very unique relationship because of their shared knowledge of The Secret.

"We don't really have a choice," he told her. "Things have gotten out of control, and we have to be able to coordinate our efforts more closely. And the first part of that is that we have *got* to stop these EDS bastards. The terrorist attacks were bad enough, but what they did this morning..." He shook his head sadly. Curtis had no illusions that he could be a cold hearted son of a bitch, but the man who had died that morning on the podium had indeed been a close friend. Curtis had hoped to someday reveal The Secret to him, because the President had been a man of vision, a man of dreams. And The Secret, once it could truly be unveiled, would be a dream the likes of which humankind had never known. "We need to find them, Monica. I don't care how you do it, but we've got to make sure they don't interfere with the rest of the plan."

"Is New Horizons ready?" she asked.

He nodded. "Yes. I hate to say it, but the terrorist attacks and the recent virus outbreak have been catalysts we can take advantage of. I've received confirmation from Dr. Kempf that the final retrovirus variant is ready. She told me what's in it: a full-scope cure for almost every disease we have! I can't believe what *they* can do," he said in unabashed awe. "It will cure people of everything from cancer to the common cold! And so easily!"

"Maybe it's too easy," Ridley said quietly.

"No," he said firmly. "Years of research and billions of dollars have gone into this. This wasn't something that just popped out of thin air. It took our technology a while to catch up to their genius, their almost instinctive understanding of genetics, but now..."

"Now we can play God," Ridley filled in for him. "Or have *them* play God for us. Even our brightest scientists don't understand much of what they're doing. You realize that, don't you?"

"What difference would it make?" he asked. "Would my daughter be alive today if it wasn't for them? Would you?"

Ridley looked down at her clasped hands. Shortly after she'd graduated from the FBI Academy at Quantico, she was diagnosed with an extremely aggressive form of amyotrophic lateral sclerosis, or ALS, that threatened to destroy her life, her future. It was more commonly known as Lou Gehrig's disease, and affected the nerve cells of the brain and spinal cord that control voluntary muscle movement. The diagnosis was even more shocking because it was most commonly found in people who were in their forties or older; Ridley was in her early twenties. The thought of what her future held was unbearable, and she had begun contemplating suicide to avoid the hellish life that she saw looming before her.

In a coincidental encounter, she met Dr. Rachel Kempf, who told her that her company was conducting some top secret government-sanctioned genetics research that might be able to stop the progression of the disease, or even cure it altogether. Ridley was certain that even an experimental treatment that could possibly kill her was better than the inevitability of the disease that would slowly destroy her.

Kempf invited her to a small lab in San Diego, California, for treatment. Kempf's company, a pharmaceutical firm that Ridley had never heard of, would pay all the expenses: Ridley was simply to play tourist and enjoy herself while the experimental miracle cure worked its magic.

And it did. In only a few days, the early onset symptoms of the disease that Ridley had been experiencing – weakness in her hands and a slight but noticeable slur in her speech – disappeared. Kempf showed her the MRI scans from before and after the treatment, where the abnormalities she had identified in Ridley's brain and spinal cord before the treatment were completely gone. Ridley was cured. Permanently.

It was the most emotional moment of Ridley's life, and that's when Kempf chose to reveal what she truly was, taking the form of a humanoid being that was half again as tall as Ridley, with smooth white skin and a bright red feathery crest along her elongated spine. Looking down at Ridley with tremendous almond-shaped eyes, she told Ridley The Secret, that what they had done for her, they hoped to do for all humankind. But a secret it must remain, for there were many who would oppose what Kempf and the others like her sought to bestow upon humanity.

Ridley had no choice but to believe, for she was living proof. She became a convert, a zealot. And every day of her life since then had been devoted to making that dream come true for everyone.

Yet, she couldn't avoid a gnawing sense of doubt as time went on. As she steadily climbed the ladder in the Bureau, Kempf and a few others of her kind exposed more and more of their plans to her so she could better guide events around them. Most of what she'd come to find out was benign, but there were disturbing discrepancies, such as the unfortunate deaths of several of Kempf's chief researchers in a car accident a year ago, followed by the disappearance of Dr. Naomi Perrault. Ridley still believed the story that Perrault hadn't been able to accept The Secret, and had instead believed it to be an insidious plot to destroy humanity. But having worked for over twenty years in the FBI, Ridley couldn't help but analyze the data she had seen, and doubt had steadily encroached into her vision of a halcyon future.

Looking up at Curtis, she knew that his daughter's story wasn't far removed from her own. The girl had been diagnosed with inoperable brain cancer at the age of ten, when Curtis had been a junior senator. Kempf had paid him a visit and offered an experimental therapy that might cure his daughter. That the girl had cancer wasn't yet known to the public, and Kempf's one inviolable condition was that if the treatment was a success, it was to remain a secret.

With no hope forthcoming from the world of conventional medicine, Curtis readily agreed. Like Ridley, his daughter was miraculously cured in a matter of days, and today was enjoying a very healthy and successful time at Harvard University. After Curtis was convinced that his daughter was indeed healthy and cancer-free, Kempf had revealed herself and The Secret to him. He, too, had become a ready and willing convert.

That chapter of the Curtis family's life had been carefully orchestrated to make sure that the public never knew the true nature of his daughter's medical condition. The official story had been that she had been diagnosed with a serious but fully treatable liver ailment.

Ridley had only found out that Curtis knew The Secret the day before through Kempf, who had also told Curtis of her story. Keepers of The Secret were rarely introduced to one another, Kempf had explained, but she had felt they both needed to know in order to more effectively run EDS to ground. It had come as a shock to Curtis to learn that Ridley had been in on The Secret for over twenty years, and it had made them both wonder just how long The Others had been on Earth, working on their miracle cure. But Kempf's only answer to that question had been, "A very long time."

Curtis sighed, interrupting her reverie. "I think everyone who knows has doubts," he told her quietly. "But I can't deny what they've done, what they can do. And I can't deny the joy every parent with a dying child would know if their child could be saved." He was silent for a moment, before he went on, "When we found out that Kathleen had cancer and the doctors couldn't do anything, that she didn't even have a chance..." He shook his head, and she could see tears brimming in his eyes at the memory. "Just the knowledge of it nearly destroyed me. We couldn't have another child. She was all we had, all we would ever have." He fixed Ridley with a pitiless gaze that chilled her. "I would have done anything to save my daughter. *Anything*. And so far, nothing that Kempf and her kind have asked of us has been outrageous."

"That's what bothers me," Ridley said. "They haven't asked for anything but our silence and to help them make our world a better place. Maybe I've just gotten cynical, but can they really be that philanthropic? They're going to make all our ills go away just because they're nice, without asking anything in return?"

"Wouldn't we, if we could?" Curtis asked. Ridley only offered him a doubtful expression. "It's true, Monica," he told her emphatically. "Listen, the United States spends almost thirty billion dollars a year on foreign aid. Sure, a huge chunk of that's for weapons, but a lot isn't. A lot of it's medical aid. Every time there's a disaster somewhere in the world, even in countries that hate our guts, we send them tons of money and aid supplies. And now, with the subsidies Congress is going to approve, we can help poor countries afford the New Horizons seed. And we've already paid for development of the seed itself. If what Kempf and her kind are offering was something that we could send out overtly without people going berserk over some sort of idiotic alien conspiracy theory, I'd gladly put my signature on a bill that would send it to the entire world and happily pay every penny of the cost. And nobody's ever accused me of being a liberal-hearted sap."

Ridley had to smile at Curtis's last remark. While it was a Republican administration, the former President had been able to work well across the aisle with the Democrats in Congress, and Curtis had been able to cater equally well to the more conservative members of the party. It had been a winning combination at the polls, and the unlikely team had been very effective in office. But Curtis was universally known as a hard-ass, and beyond a very small circle of close friends, no one would ever have expected to see tears in his eyes over anything.

"So, no, I don't think their philanthropic claims are ridiculous," he told her. "But Kempf and the others are right," he conceded. "People wouldn't understand if they knew what was happening, just like these fools in the EDS don't. Unless you've experienced the miracle, you can't believe in it. We'd be burned at the stake as heretics, even though we're offering people salvation. That's why we have to help the world without people knowing it."

Twenty-Seven

Jack, Naomi, three other heavily armed men and one woman stood tensely in front of the blast door to the lab dome, weapons at the ready. It had been a long, tiring flight back to California after their meeting with Richards in Maryland, capped by the dangerous procedure of getting the captive harvester from the airport to the base, and then into one of the cells in the antenna silo complex.

While everyone would have liked to take a rest, Jack and Naomi insisted on finding out what had happened in the lab dome, and to Vlad.

"We don't need any mysteries like that," Jack had told Renee after she finished relating the story of what had happened when she had gone into the dome those long hours before.

"Open it," Naomi ordered.

"I'll go first, if you don't mind," Hathcock said easily. Jack nodded: even though the man was only carrying a G36C assault rifle instead of the massive Barrett sniper rifle, he was by far the best shot and had more combat experience than anyone else in the base, including himself.

As the massive door thrummed open, Hathcock quickly scanned the expanse of the room over his gun sights before stepping inside. Jack and Naomi followed right behind him, covering to the left and right, scanning high and low between the mezzanine level and the ground floor.

"No contacts," Hathcock called clearly as he moved deeper into the maze of lab equipment and work benches. "I'll take the upper level."

"Roger," Jack said from behind him, motioning for two men to follow Hathcock up the steps to the mezzanine. He, Naomi, and the last of the search party, Carla Torres, a woman who'd also served in Afghanistan as an intelligence specialist, moved carefully along the ground floor.

Jack had them sweep wide to the right, checking the far side of the dome from where the animal storage cage was, to make sure nothing had crept over there. It was clear.

Spreading out, they then moved back to the other side of the dome, finally coming to stand in front of the animal area where Alexander had been trapped.

"It's clear down here," he called up to Hathcock. *Yeah, it's clear all right*, he thought, *too damn clear*. "Jesus," he said aloud. "What the hell happened here?"

Naomi moved forward far enough to reach out and open the latch on the doorway to the enclosure.

"Keep your eyes on the mezzanine," Jack told Torres, who nodded uneasily. "Renee said that she thought she saw something moving up there."

Torres stepped back a few paces so she could get a better view of the support structure for the upper level and scanned the length above where Jack and Naomi were standing. Then Jack stepped into the animal enclosure to look around, but there wasn't much to look at.

"Nothing," he said into the quiet that surrounded them.

"That's what's so odd," Naomi muttered as she joined him, leaning over to inspect the monkey cage more closely. She ran her hands across the metal inside the cage, the bottom and the mesh sides. "We keep the animal cages clean, Jack, but there's not a trace of anything but metal here, not even a tiny scrap of food caught in the mesh. And the metal's shiny, like it's been polished." She looked around at the other enclosures. "It's like the entire room's been given an acid bath that scoured everything away."

"What could have done that?" he asked, a shiver running up his spine as he looked at the floor for any trace of liquid. "Wait a minute. What's that?"

Naomi turned around to look where Jack was pointing. Under the table that had once been home to a dozen lab rats was a large pool of...something. "Don't touch it," she warned.

"No worries," Jack told her, edging back to give her more room as she knelt next to the puddle.

"Torres," she said, "grab a handful of specimen vials and some swabs from that table there, please."

Torres grabbed several vials and some swabs, quickly handing them to Naomi. Then she backed up to where she could watch the mezzanine.

Naomi carefully dipped a swab in the liquid and dropped it into the vial before sealing the lid. Then she slipped the vial into an empty pocket. Standing up, she called out, "Hathcock!"

"Here!" he answered instantly.

"Watch for any puddles of liquid up there," she told him, "and keep well clear of them. The cages down here look like they've been bathed with some sort of acid, and I don't want you stepping in any of it." Naomi didn't think the liquid here was acid, as it hadn't reacted to the materials in the swab, but there was no sense in taking any chances.

"Understood," he called back. "We're moving into the biohazard room now..."

"There's nothing else I can see here," Naomi conceded.

Nodding, Jack turned away and led her and Torres back toward the steps leading up to the mezzanine.

They found Hathcock emerging from the biohazard room, a perplexed look on his face.

"Bugger if I know what happened in there," he said, nodding back over his shoulder, "and there's no sign of our Russian friend. But look at this." He pointed to the edge of the door to the room. "There should be a heavy rubber seal here, and a matching gasket on the wall. They're gone. And all the rest of the seals are the same way. And look at this." He pointed to what had once been a computer, but was now an eerie-looking pile of shiny metal and silicon bits. "Every bit of rubber and plastic in the room is gone. Just disappeared."

"What about the monkey?" Naomi asked, moving past Hathcock to look inside the room.

"What monkey?" Hathcock said, following her to the first biohazard containment chamber. "There's nothing in any of these. They're all empty. And the lower parts of them have just fallen apart."

Naomi peered into the first chamber where the rhesus monkey had been. Just like the animal housing area, it had been scoured clean. The metal door to the lower part of the chamber that contained all the mechanisms was on the floor.

"Shit," Hathcock swore. "Plastic hinges. They're gone."

"Along with everything else in the unit that wasn't metal," Naomi said, peering into the guts of the cabinet with the aid of the flashlight on the end of Jack's rifle. "And guess what? There's another puddle in here." Using a vial and swab, she took a sample, marking the top with her pen so she'd know where the sample had been taken from.

"So what happened?" Jack asked. If anything, he was more spooked now than he had been down below.

"Whatever happened," Hathcock told him, "it was behind a locked door." He poked the door to the room with the muzzle of his weapon. "This was secured when we got here. I had to pry it open." Nodding to the keypad inside the door, or what was left of it, all the plastic and rubber components having mysteriously vanished, he said, "Now I know why."

"Naomi," Torres called from around the corner in a tense voice. "You should see this."

Followed closely by Jack and Hathcock, Naomi joined Torres and the others on the walkway that led past the biohazard room to the storage area.

"What is it?" she asked as she scanned the next segment of the mezzanine that led from the air intakes for the diesel generators around to the exhaust tunnel on the opposite side.

"The supplies," Torres said. "The stacks of boxes. Half of them are gone."

"Bloody Christ," Hathcock muttered as he moved forward into what had been the storage area, "she's right. But look at this." He probed the toe of his boot through a scattering of detritus, all of it metal, foil, or ceramic, on the metal grating. "This is stuff from some of the spare parts boxes," he said. "But some of it," he reached down and picked up a ceramic cylinder, "isn't something you could even take apart: this is part of a water filter with a cast plastic housing. You couldn't even cut it off without damaging the ceramic filter. Yet here it is."

"And where's the rest of the stuff that should be here?" Jack mused. "There must have been at least a dozen good-sized boxes."

"Look at this one," Naomi pointed to a box that was stacked atop several others along the dome wall. "It's been half...melted."

As they stood there uncertainly, Jack's mind began to weave together the bits of the puzzle that he and the others had seen. The conclusion he was coming to was too terrible and bizarre to contemplate, but it seemed to fit all the facts they had at this point.

"I don't think it was melted," he said quietly, "at least as we're thinking of it. I think everything that's missing was *eaten*." The others looked at him in shock. "Don't ask me by what, but look where we're standing." He gestured to the grated metal flooring on which they stood. "Right above the animal area." He turned toward the biohazard room. "I think this started with the monkey. Remember the weird lesion or whatever it was that we saw on it before we left for Spitsbergen? I think that was the first visible sign that the retrovirus was transforming it into...something. And that *something* started eating all the plastic and other stuff, even the animals that are missing."

"Carbon and other organic compounds," Naomi murmured, her terrified mind flying along the trajectory of Jack's reasoning. She suddenly gasped. "Oh, my God! Vlad!"

Nodding grimly, Jack said, "He must've come up here to check on the monkey, and it was already out of the chamber."

"Then the fucker got him," Hathcock continued. "But how did it get out of the biohazard chamber?"

"The harvesters are shape-changers," Naomi said. "Maybe...maybe this is some sort of a larval form that's made up mostly or entirely of the malleable tissue. Perhaps it didn't have any skeleton developed yet."

"What," Hathcock said, "so it just oozed its way out through the gaps that were left after it ate the rubber seals?"

"I don't know," Naomi said, "but it got out of there somehow. It got Vlad, then it must have come over here..."

"...and when it was done snacking on the supplies, it dropped down onto the animals." Jack shuddered. *Had it dropped a few more feet to the right*, Jack thought, sickened, *poor Alexander would've been finished.*

"After that," Jack said, "Renee said that both Alexander and Koshka were staring at something up here, and she thought she saw something go into the air intake tunnel."

"Naomi, Jack, I hate to be a spoilsport, but trying to ferret this thing, whatever it is, out of that tunnel isn't going to be a piece of cake. Because it's not just a simple tunnel, it's a three story-high air filtration complex. There are nooks and crannies in there big enough to hide a Volkswagen."

"Could it have already gotten outside?" Torres asked worriedly.

Naomi shook her head. "No, all the blast valves are kept closed except when the generators are running," she said. "And there aren't any rubber seals on them for this thing to eat so it could escape to the outside: it's all hardened steel. They were designed to hold back the heat and overpressure from a nuclear blast, remember?"

"The other minor detail," Jack said heavily, "is how do we kill it? It's not a harvester, at least not like the ones we know, or the cats would be going berserk more than they already are with the one cooling its slimy jets in the antenna silo. If it's some sort of oozing thing, would our weapons have any effect on it?"

"Fire?" Hathcock suggested.

"Maybe," Naomi answered, frustrated, "but we just don't know. And using fire in here isn't the greatest idea, anyway."

Hathcock frowned, but said nothing. From the look on his face, it was clear that he'd be happy to take his chances using a flamethrower against whatever new threat they were facing, and damn-all to the risks.

"So what do we do?" Naomi asked as she peered down the dozen or so meters of tunnel that led to the air intake complex. It was well-lit, but the intake and exhaust tunnels had always made her feel uneasy, even under normal circumstances.

"Seal up this tunnel," Jack told her. "I assume we've got some spare metal plating in storage somewhere in the complex that can be used for repairs?" Hathcock nodded. "Get a team together and weld some plates over the mouth of the intake tunnel here. That'll at least contain whatever-it-is for now until we can figure out a better solution."

"What if we have to start the generators?" Naomi asked. "If we need anything more than battery power, we'll have to open the lab dome's blast door so they can have access to the air in the rest of the complex. But running them would asphyxiate us in minutes."

Turning to her, he said, "Then let's just hope we don't need to run them."

***

Naomi sat back and rubbed her eyes. She'd been staring at the screen for what seemed like days, and she was only upright because of the evil brew of coffee that she had ordered Renee to keep shoving in front of her. She wanted desperately to rest, but she had to know what had happened since they'd left for Spitsbergen, and the only thing that might tell them was what was in the residue samples she'd taken from the lab.

"How's it going?" she heard Jack's voice from behind her.

"It's...strange, Jack," she said, turning to look up at him. "Very strange. Let me show you what I've been looking at.

"This is a chromatogram of the sample of the liquid from the biohazard chamber where the monkey was kept, telling us how much of which elements are present in the sample." She pointed to the screen, which showed what looked like a chart of vertical spikes of varying height along the horizontal axis. Jack looked at her blankly. She punched a few commands into the workstation's keyboard, and the graph was replaced by a list of elements: hydrogen, oxygen, and a long list of others, arranged in alphabetical order, with a number next to each. "Not that it came as a surprise, but this isn't a homogeneous sample: it's a mish-mash of different compounds, so the readings here are only telling us what elements are present. But do you notice anything missing?"

Jack looked down the list, frowning. "I never claimed to be a chemistry whiz, but I would assume that carbon should probably be in there somewhere."

"Bingo," she said. "There's no carbon in this liquid, Jack. None. I've run this test several times already, and there's not a single carbon atom that I can find in a liquid that's otherwise a witch's brew of nearly everything else, including traces of several heavy metals that were probably in the electronics the thing...consumed."

She hit more keys, and a new graph appeared, this time with the list of compounds displayed next to it. A few more keystrokes, and the original list of elements she'd shown him appeared alongside the new list. "This sample is from the animal storage area. See anything different?"

His eyes darting from one list to the other, he said, "The second list is definitely longer, with more elements listed. And...carbon is there now, along with some elements that weren't in the first sample. There's also a ton of hydrogen and oxygen. Water, maybe?"

"I'd have to run more tests, but that's my first guess," Naomi told him.

"So, what does all that mean?"

"I think that whatever we're dealing with used up almost everything it came in contact with at the start, when it was in the biohazard room," she said slowly. "And the liquid residues that we found were the things it didn't need. It simply flushed them out. In the monkey's bio-safety chamber, the residue was very viscous and had a limited number of elements, because the thing needed almost everything it consumed."

"And by the time it got to the animals," Jack interjected, "or after it finished with them, it had most of what it needed, and flushed out a lot more. It was becoming saturated?"

Naomi nodded. "I think so. Everything in the residue it left behind was simply elements and compounds it didn't need or couldn't use." She sat back. "And all the missing plastic and rubber makes sense now: those materials have a very high carbon content. It absorbed all of it, every single bit, when it first escaped, and by the time it finished with the animals, it didn't need any more and flushed out the excess."

"But what would it need so much carbon for?"

She turned to him, looking grim. "What makes a harvester so hard to kill without fire?"

Jack's face turned ashen. "Jesus," he said quietly. "The thing's growing a reinforced carbon skeleton, isn't it?"

Naomi nodded silently, her eyes reflecting the glow of the unwelcome revelation shown in the workstation's displays.

Twenty-Eight

"According to the information I've been able to dig up," Renee told the people gathered in the command center's conference room, "the seed is being produced and prepared for shipment at a newly-constructed building complex about twenty miles northwest of Lincoln." An image of the facility appeared, showing a large central building that looked like a warehouse, and several smaller support buildings. "They located it here," the picture shifted to an overhead image of the area, a patchwork quilt of green and brown Nebraska farm land, "right between the towns of Ulysses and Staplehurst. The location is fairly isolated, for what that may be worth." She looked around the table, her eyes lingering on Naomi and Jack. "That's the good news, such as it is. The bad news is that they've already prepared nearly ten thousand tons, and it's going to start shipping tomorrow."

"*What?*" Naomi gasped. "How could they have done that so quickly?"

"I don't think they did it quickly, Naomi," Renee told her. "I couldn't get past some of the company's network firewalls – they've really tightened up on that, by the way – to the information I wanted, but based on the shipping manifests I was able to find, I think they've been preparing this stuff for at least the last six months. That corresponds with the time they opened this facility."

"We just happened to catch them at LRU as they were about to fold up shop there," Jack surmised. "They were already getting the seed ready for production."

Renee nodded.

There was silence around the table. Ten thousand tons, Jack thought, with every single seed representing a potential ecological disaster.

"How can we deal with that?" Dr. Chidambaram interjected. "All of our planning was based on interrupting the harvesters before they got to this stage, of destroying the threat before it materialized. Now...ten thousand tons..."

"Can't we just burn it?" Jack asked.

Chidambaram shook his head. "It's very difficult to burn closely packed seeds, as these will be, in bags or in bulk trucks or rail cars," he said. "Not enough oxygen can get in to assist in the burning process. Much of the seed would go untouched."

"What about a fuel-air explosive," Jack asked, "like the harvesters used on the genebanks? That seemed to work pretty well on them."

"It is a different situation, Jack," Chidambaram explained. "Seeds in the genebanks are generally stored in small quantities, in separate sealed packets and boxes. There may be many samples, but they are not closely packed together. With seeds tightly packed in bags, and thousands of bags stacked together, a bomb such as you describe would disperse many of the seeds they have stored in that facility out into the surrounding fields where they might take root."

"And we have no idea if any of the retrovirus particles would be carried away in the smoke," said one of the other women in the room, a biologist who had come after Renee sent out the emergency recall. The woman looked at Naomi. "We would have to assume at least some of those particles might remain viable."

"Then I guess we'll have to go in and neutralize it bag by bag," Naomi said firmly.

"Naomi," Jack told her, shaking his head, "that's impossible. You're talking, what, a few hundred thousand bags, figuring a hundred pounds a bag?"

"Four hundred thousand," Renee corrected quietly. "Give or take a few."

"That would take us forever," Jack went on, "and the harvesters aren't going to give us that sort of time. Look at that," he pointed to a lighter colored strip surrounding the facility, and small, squat buildings at the entrances. "Those are security fences and guard posts. They moved their operation here because they think it's secure. We'll be lucky if we have an hour before we've got a cage dropping around us, assuming we can force our way in there in the first place."

"There's no other way, Jack," Naomi told him stubbornly. "There's just no other way to be sure that they're destroyed."

"Yes, there is," Jack said after a long pause. He was looking down at the table now, careful to avoid Naomi's gaze.

Everyone, including Naomi, stared at him.

"Spill it, Jack," Renee said bluntly.

He looked over at Chidambaram and said, "A nuke would do it, wouldn't it?"

"For God's sake, Jack!" Naomi blurted. "You can't be serious!"

"Would a nuke work?" Jack pressed, staring now at Chidambaram, who was distinctly uncomfortable.

"Yes," the group's leading agricultural expert admitted. "The heat and radiation would come as close as we humanly could to completely destroying even that quantity of seed, and the retrovirus particles, even with a small explosive yield, but..." He held out his hands in a gesture of helplessness. "Jack, you cannot set off a nuclear weapon in the middle of the country!"

"Jack—" Naomi began angrily.

"*Listen!*" Jack shouted, silencing her and shocking the others. "The only way we have of stopping this is to destroy those seeds, right? *Right?*" Heads slowly nodded around the table. "Looking at Renee's research and our discussion here, we've already eliminated just about every other means we have that might work, either because we can't be sure the seeds will be completely destroyed or because we just won't have time. Right?" More grudging nods, except from Naomi. She stared fixedly at the wall on the opposite side of the room. "People, we're running out of options." He looked again at Chidambaram. "Doctor, I've fought for and bled for this country," he told him, "and the last thing I would ever do is put any of its people in harm's way. But if that's the only option we have, then that's the one we have to take."

"Aren't you forgetting one minor detail?" Naomi said, turning to glare at him. "This may be an old missile base, but they didn't happen to leave any nukes lying around here when they closed it up. Where do you think you're going to find a nuclear weapon? The local hardware store?"

"No," Jack told her, "but..."

"We're thinking about this all wrong," Renee suddenly said, a sly look on her face.

"What do you mean?" Naomi asked her.

"We're focused on trying to destroy the seed before it gets shipped, right?" she told the others, and everyone nodded. That much was obvious. "But we can't." Jack opened his mouth to argue, but Renee held up her hand to him. "We *can't*, Jack. We can't burn it or even blow it up safely, and we can't wave a magic wand and miraculously come up with a nuke to vaporize it, even if it didn't kill a bunch of people. Besides, the seeds are going to start shipping *tomorrow*, remember? Does anybody have a clue how to get a nuke delivered by overnight express?" She shook her head. "No. None of that's going to happen, at least not between today and tomorrow."

"So what are you proposing that we do, Renee?" Jack asked, sharing a questioning glance with Naomi.

Renee smiled. "We steal the seed right out from under their noses."

***

"We've got something." A special agent hurried over to where Richards sat at his desk, trying to look busy while actually doing nothing but worrying. The young woman handed him a printout, and his stomach fell away as he saw what was typed there.

"Our Legat in Moscow got this from the FSB," the woman said, barely able to restrain the excitement in her voice. Richards automatically translated the alphabet soup in his head: the Legat was the Bureau's Legal Attaché office in the U.S. Embassy in Moscow, which had gotten the information from the Russian *Federal'naya Sluzhba Bezopasnosti*, the modern-day successor to the infamous KGB. "It's a report by one of the Russian soldiers involved in the incident on Spitsbergen. Apparently, there was a civilian aircraft there–"

"I can read, Special Agent Dobbs," Richards snapped as he again scanned the damning information. *It's a lead, all right*, he thought numbly. The Russians had eyeballed the tail number on the Falcon jet that Dawson and the others had taken to Spitsbergen, and had obviously tracked down its country of origin, which would have been easy enough. And with that, not only did the FBI, which was led by a collaborator, have the next best thing to a glowing neon arrow pointing to where the EDS was located, but they'd also find out that Richards himself had been conspiring with them. He'd managed to keep secret his little stunt of getting Dawson clearance to fly back into the States, but he'd known it would catch up with him sooner or later. He just hadn't expected it to be quite this soon. Once his agents began to dig into the information on the plane, it wouldn't take them long to discover the link back to him. He knew most of them considered him an asshole, but he had trained them well. "Take this up to Assistant Director Clement right now," he told Dobbs, shoving the paper back at her.

"Me?" she gulped.

Richards fixed her with an astonished glare. "Did I stutter? Yes, you! Personally." Dobbs, who had graduated from the Academy only two months before, just stood there. "*Now*, Dobbs!"

She nodded and hurried from the room, clutching the printout in her hands.

Richards waited until she'd gone before he stood up from his desk. He felt his eyes tearing up as he took one last look around the place that he'd dedicated his life to, knowing he could never come back.

Blinking his eyes clear and cursing himself for a sentimental fool, he slipped on his coat and left.

***

"We'll have them soon," Monica Ridley told the President over the secure phone. "We have a trace on a plane that was in Spitsbergen where the Norwegians and Russians nearly came to blows."

"Those idiots," Curtis told her. "We gave both of them information that EDS was targeting Spitsbergen, and they made a complete fiasco out of it when we could have had the bastards in our hands."

"At least one good thing came of it," she reassured him. "We've already pinned down the plane's flight activity, and where it went after it returned from Spitsbergen." She paused. "It first landed at Baltimore Washington International."

Curtis sat forward in his chair in the Oval Office, nearly spilling his coffee. "What? How the devil did they get clearance to reenter our airspace?"

"One of my most senior and trusted agents," she said, trying to mask her frustration, "decided to go rogue on us. I found out that he made arrangements for the Air Force to pass the plane through, without clearing it with anyone higher up in the Bureau or Homeland Security."

"Are *any* of your agents reliable, Monica?" Curtis said acidly.

"Yes, Mr. President," she replied, carefully forcing out the words, "but this man was one of my best. He was conducting the investigation at Lincoln, and would've been my first pick to send in after the EDS when we find them."

"If we find them, you mean."

"No, Mr. President," she said, allowing a measure of pride and certainty back into her voice. "When. Because we know where that plane went to after it left BWI, and after analyzing its flight plans for the last six months, we know where its primary airport is."

"Where?" Curtis asked, a flare of excitement washing away some of the aggravation.

"Oroville Municipal Airport in California," she told him. "We have agents on the way there as we speak, and it's only a matter of time – a short time, I believe – before we find our EDS friends."

"Good," Curtis said, nodding to himself. "That's good. Just don't screw it up, Monica."

"I won't," she reassured him, then hung up.

***

Monica Ridley pulled up to an expensive condo in downtown Alexandria that wasn't too far from Jack Dawson's house, and parked her black BMW Z4 in its designated space in the basement garage. It was nearly ten o'clock at night, and aside from the security attendant at the entrance, the garage was deserted. She walked across the concrete to the elevator, the clicking of her heels echoing from the white-painted walls. The fact that she was a woman walking alone in a deserted garage may have caused some to cast a worried glance around them. But Ridley was unconcerned. Like her field agents, she was well-armed, and had survived her own trials by fire earlier in her meteoric career. She wasn't afraid, only weary.

Taking the elevator up to the eighth floor, she turned down the hallway and went to the door for her condo. Using her magnetic key on the lock, she opened the door and stepped into the dark entry hall, flipped on the lights, then entered her pass code into the security system, which turned from a blinking red to a peaceful green.

After dropping her purse on a stand in the entryway, she was about to turn on the light in the living room when a voice from the darkness behind her, somewhere in the kitchen, made her freeze.

"Why did you betray us?" was all the voice, a man's voice, said. It was a voice she had heard before several times, from a man whom, before today, she had trusted and respected.

"I could ask you the same question, Richards," she replied, turning on the light. She didn't bother asking him how he'd gotten in. Any security system could be defeated with the right knowledge, and Richards had spent part of his career working as a physical security specialist. Her household alarm system would hardly have been a challenge for him. She held her hands away from her sides, making sure he could see they were empty, as she turned around to face him.

"How much did your EDS friends pay you to turn traitor? How much did they pay Sheldon Crane? Or Jack Dawson?"

"You can't buy men like Crane or Dawson," Richards snapped as he moved further into the light, "or me, for that matter." He held a snub-nose revolver, a .44 magnum, aimed right at her heart. "They just showed me the truth. They showed me one of the things that you're collaborating with, the things that want to kill us all, and that have been behind the attacks and the death of the President." He shook his head slowly. "You've betrayed your entire species."

"*What?*" Ridley said, genuinely surprised. "You've seen them? The Others?"

"One of them," Richards replied, nodding. "They captured it when some of the things tried to destroy the seed vault at Spitsbergen. They put it into some sort of stasis so they could transport it to wherever they're going to lock it up."

"Lock it up?" she asked, dismayed. "The fools! Don't they realize what the Others are trying to do?"

"They're trying to exterminate us, for the love of God!" Richards shouted.

"No, Richards," she said fervently, shaking her head and taking a step toward him. "That's not true at all! They're trying to *heal* us, all of us. I'm living proof of their intentions. I was diagnosed with Lou Gehrig's disease right after I graduated from the Academy, and they cured me, Richards. They cured me! That's what this is all about: they want to give all of humanity the same gift."

"Then why all the mystery?" Richards snapped. "And what about the President and the terrorist attacks? Why did they do that?"

"The Others didn't do it! Perrault and EDS did," Ridley snapped right back. "I would've thought you had figured that part out already."

He shook his head. "I don't think EDS had anything to do with the President's death," he told her, "at least not directly. They couldn't have: Perrault, Dawson, and a team from EDS were a few thousand miles away over the Arctic when the president was killed."

"What do you have as proof?" she spat. "Their word of honor?"

"No," Richards told her. "I have as witnesses a pair of F-16 pilots who picked up the EDS plane off the coast near Maine and escorted it to Baltimore where I talked to Dawson and saw the...thing. And I just don't buy the idea that a bunch of crackpots that nobody's ever heard of suddenly put together a terrorist organization that could strike multiple targets around the globe simultaneously and then manage to kill the President of the United States." He moved from around the kitchen counter to come stand closer to her, still holding the gun toward her chest. "Explain how they could possibly have pulled any of that off and I'll hand you my weapon and turn myself in right here and now."

Ridley knew that Richards actually meant his last words, that they weren't mere sarcasm. She was shocked to see that the look on his face in that moment was almost pleading. *He wants to believe EDS was to blame*, she thought. *But he's right*, the analytic side of her mind whispered. *How could they have possibly done all that The Others have accused them of?*

The answer, she realized with paralyzing clarity, was simple: they couldn't have. The only alternative conclusion, unfortunately, was one that she couldn't bear to contemplate. Instead, she focused on the clock in the kitchen behind Richards. If she could just keep him talking for a few more minutes...

"So," she said, her mind shearing away from the chasm that Richards had opened for her, "are you planning to kill me? If you are, then just get it over with. Otherwise, get out so I can make myself some dinner. I'm starving."

"Is the new President in on this, too?" he asked, ignoring her. "That's what Dawson told me."

"Well, if he said it, it must be true," she said acidly, but she knew her body language must have given her away as she saw Richards' expression harden, his mouth turning down in a deep frown. "Richards," she said, softening her voice, "please, listen to me. They're not bad or evil, no matter what Dawson or Perrault might have told you. They're trying to help us. They're—"

There was a knock at the door. Richards turned his head, his attention drawn by the sound, and Ridley threw herself to the floor and screamed, "*Gun! In the kitchen!*"

A second later the door crashed inward, the frame splintered as Ray Clement's powerful body hammered into it. He rolled to the floor in the hallway and came up, gun in hand, aiming to the right and into the kitchen.

Even though he was caught by surprise, Richards had always been regarded as a cool-headed bastard, and with good reason. Without hesitation he fired through the wall separating him from the entry hallway, guessing where his opponent might be. He was rewarded with a cursing roar from Clement, who came around the corner like a bull elephant, his 9mm spouting fire in Richards' direction.

Richards dodged back behind the counter separating the kitchen from the living room where Ridley was, Clement's 9mm slugs chipping into the sleek granite counter and ricocheting into the dark cherry cabinets behind him. Richards fired again, hitting Clement in the chest and knocking him backward over the sofa.

As Richards moved back around the counter, trying to make it to the hallway, Ridley fired several shots at him from behind the corner of the sofa, and he was stung with fiery pain as a slug nicked his shoulder. He aimed his weapon at her, had her face right in his sight picture even as she was shooting at him, but at the last second changed his aim slightly. Even in this life or death moment, he couldn't bring himself to kill his director. He fired, the .44 magnum bullet blasting into the parquet wood floor right in front of her, sending shards of wood into her face. Screaming in pain, Ridley pulled back behind the sofa.

Two shots left, Richards told himself automatically as he sprinted for the hallway.

Just as he turned into the hallway he heard a blood-freezing screech behind him. Turning, unable to help himself, he stared, transfixed with horror, as one of the creatures, a harvester, rose up from behind the sofa. *Clement*, his mind gibbered. *He was one of* them.

A long tendril, tipped by a stinger, uncoiled from the creature's thorax and arrowed toward Richards. It would have hit him right in the chest, except the two remaining bullets that Richards fired were far faster. Both slammed into the harvester's center of mass, driving it backwards, insectile limbs flailing, into the living room, where it crashed into Ridley's glass coffee table.

Richards didn't wait to see if he'd killed it. Clutching his bleeding shoulder, he turned and ran.

***

"Hold still!"

Ridley heard Clement's voice from above her. She was blinded by the blood that had flooded into her eyes from the hail of splinters Richards' shot had sent into her face. Most of them had sliced into her forehead and scalp, but she was terrified that some had hit her eyes. She felt something daubing at her face, then Clement's voice again.

"Your eyes are okay," he reassured her, carefully wiping the last of the blood from her eyelids with a hand towel he'd grabbed from the kitchen. "You can open them."

She did as he told her, blinking away the last of the blood. "Jesus," she hissed as he helped her up onto the sofa, pain searing her scalp from the dozen splinters lodged there. Blood still streamed freely down her face, but she ignored it. Looking at Clement, she said, "I heard...something horrible. What was it?"

He shook his head. "Probably just me screaming, bellowing like a mad cow," he told her, forcing a smile. The smile faded. "Or more likely it was you screaming. That and the sound of the shots in a confined space would certainly mess with your hearing." He looked at her more closely. "You were damn lucky, Director. If he'd had slightly better aim, we wouldn't be having this conversation."

Ridley was about to tell him that Richards hadn't missed: she'd seen him shift his aim, the big bore of the revolver moving ever so slightly just before her world had exploded in a cordite glare as Richards pulled the trigger.

But before she could say anything more, there was a stampede of shouts and footsteps out in the hall.

"I'm just glad we'd scheduled this meeting," she said hurriedly. She had decided on her own that she was going to bring Clement in on The Secret, and had set up a meeting with him here, where she could show him her medical records as proof. He was her lead man now in the hunt for the EDS, and she felt he needed to know, to understand, everything that was going on in order to aid his search efforts.

Unfortunately, that would now have to wait. The shock was wearing off, and the pain from the wood shards was nearly unbearable. She considered herself to be tough, but her body was shivering in agony. "I just wish I'd had time to tell you what I wanted to," she whispered. "You really need to know—"

"We'll have that conversation soon," he reassured her, gently holding her hand as a pair of cops carefully moved into the condo, weapons ready and shouting for Clement to identify himself, "but first we've got to get you to the hospital." Holding up his badge, he turned to the cops and shouted, "Federal agents! I need paramedics in here right now!" Turning back to Ridley, he said quietly, "In the meantime, I'm going to find that bastard Richards and run him down."

Twenty-Nine

"What the hell was he thinking?" Naomi demanded angrily after Jack told her what Richards had done.

Jack had just spoken to him over a secure voice link through the Internet that they had set up for use in case of an emergency. Jack had known the day would soon come when they would have to use it, but hadn't expected it to be quite so soon. He had been totally surprised that Richards had done something so spontaneous, but in retrospect he should have known: the senior agent had been shaken to the core, far more so than Jack, by the revelation that the FBI Director had been an agent of the harvesters. Richards could never have simply walked away from such an insult to the institution that had been his life for almost twenty years.

After hearing Richards' brief but pointed description of the encounter with Ridley and Clement, Jack had offered to send the Falcon to fetch him, but Richards had tersely informed him that he had made his own travel arrangements.

"Take that plane and get rid of it," he had advised Jack. "They made the connection between you and the jet, and there are going to be agents swarming into California to track you down. I'll get to you on my own. Assuming you're still alive."

Then he had hung up.

Returning his attention to Naomi, Jack said, "I had no idea he'd do something like confronting the director. And finding out that Clement was a harvester..." He shook his head. "He wasn't on either list!"

"He must have been replaced recently," Renee said. It was just the three of them at the conference table in the command center. "Remember, the list we have was just a local copy from Kempf's laptop. It was a snapshot. There must be a master copy somewhere on a server that all of them can get to that has current information."

"It doesn't really matter now," Jack told them. "We're out of time."

Sighing, trying to shed her anger, which was more a manifestation of fear of what the coming hours might bring, Naomi asked, "Are you ready, Renee?"

"We've got everything lined up," she answered.

"I just hope this works," Jack told her.

"Me, too," Renee said in a voice that suddenly sounded small and vulnerable. Jack knew that she felt confident in her plan, but the world was literally on Renee's shoulders now: if this failed, there was no backup option, no "plan B." The Earth as they knew it would very likely die.

"Then let's get to it," Naomi said, getting up from the table. She let Renee go through the door to the command center first, then lingered for just a moment. "Jack..."

His arms were suddenly around her, drawing her to him, and her lips met his. It was only a moment, but it was something they both needed.

"For luck," she whispered as they reluctantly separated and followed Renee.

The command center was fully manned, but was quiet, tense. This was Renee's show, and she took her place in the central command console like the conductor of an orchestra. All eyes looked to her, then to the main screens as she began to initialize her plan.

"Since we can't destroy all the seed at the source," she muttered, as if she were talking herself through it all again while she typed commands into the computers linked to her console, "the next most logical step is to intercept it during shipment. Or," she said with the hint of a grin as she hammered a few last commands into the keyboard, "take control of it right from the plant itself."

Half of the main screen at the front of the room echoed what she was seeing on her computer console: windows spawned on the screen showing logins for a dozen shipping companies.

"I couldn't hack into the New Horizons computers at the plant," she said. "Their security was too good. But the trucking companies they've contracted with were another matter."

With a final tap on the keyboard, the logins in the open windows began to flicker, filled and refilled with letters and numbers as Renee's hacks began to work their magic. One after another, her software gained access to the systems of the companies that New Horizons had contracted to ship the seed.

"Then," Renee muttered as she typed more commands, "we reroute the trucks to go where *we* want. New Horizons is having a huge media event over this, so they're sending out the first batch of seed in a wave of eighteen wheelers."

Vehicle tracking and delivery schedules appeared on the main screen, and Jack had a hard time following everything Renee was doing: windows were popping into existence, data scrolling rapidly, then suddenly disappearing as she took control of the companies' routing schedules.

Blinking his eyes clear of the mass of information on the right half of the screen, he focused his attention on the left half, which he could actually understand. It showed a map of red pinpoints clustered around the New Horizons plant in Nebraska: a huge fleet of trucks coming in empty, and leaving with a full load of genetically modified seed.

"Now," she went on, her fingers still on the keyboard, "the trucks should receive new dispatch instructions after they leave the plant, rerouting them to new destinations." Another map window popped up, zoomed out to show the entire country. "We're getting teams together at each of these sites," she highlighted five locations, scattered over as many states, "to isolate the seed so we can properly neutralize it."

"How are they going to do that?" Jack asked as he watched data flow across the screen. "And isn't someone going to get suspicious about the changes in the destinations?"

"She's diverting the grain to other deep underground facilities we have," Naomi explained as she watched the swarm of glowing icons moving across the map. "Three of them are abandoned mines. The other two are other Cold War bunkers, smaller than this one, but still big enough to safely house the New Horizons seed until we can properly dispose of it. If nothing else, we'll be able to keep it out of the environment."

"As for someone noticing the change," Renee added with an uncomfortable shrug, "that's always possible. But most of these guys," she nodded toward the map, indicating the truckers, "don't get paid to ask a lot of questions. They get paid to haul cargo. All they'll see is a destination change in their shipping orders on the trucks' computer displays." She looked up, catching Jack's eye. "We know from the contract specifications I nabbed that all the trucks had to have computer connectivity with a New Horizons central dispatch system. That way the trucks could be tracked with GPS, and New Horizons could send them routing updates or destination changes. Since New Horizons deals with crops and not trucks, they contracted out for the central dispatch service, which I was able to hack into." Looking back at the screen, she murmured. "Now we wait and see if it works."

Five minutes went by, then ten. More and more red icons, more trucks, dispersed from the New Horizons plant, bearing their lethal cargo.

"Come on," Renee whispered, glaring at the map on the main screen.

A wave of the red icons suddenly turned yellow.

"That's it!" Renee called to the men and women manning the other consoles. "The first set of updates has been sent out. Make sure every one of those damn trucks diverts from its original route."

On her own workstation, she zoomed in closer to the map, following the icons for three trucks she'd chosen at random that had turned from red to yellow. The computer had plotted their most likely path to their original destinations in red, and the projected path to the new destination in yellow.

"Turn, you bastard," Renee murmured as the first truck neared the projected turn.

Jack and Naomi watched over Renee's shoulder, their attention riveted on her computer screens. The yellow icon of the first truck slowed, then turned onto the new route. The other two, trailing about a quarter mile behind one another, followed.

"Yes!" Renee shouted jubilantly. "It's working!"

Leaning down, Jack gave her a quick kiss on the cheek. "You're bloody amazing," he whispered.

"Thanks, sweetheart," Renee told him, "but you can give me a big smooch after we've accounted for every one of these bastards. We're still a long way from being out of the woods."

"And then, of course," Naomi said, "we have to deal with the little problem of the facility itself."

Jack frowned. That was the one part of the plan that he hadn't liked at all, but Naomi had made it clear that Jack was staying put. Staying here. "Hathcock's a good man. He and his team will take care of it."

Hathcock and eight other men had boarded the Falcon on a quick turnaround from the nearby airport and had headed back to Nebraska as fast as a grumbling Ferris could fly them after they'd gotten back from Baltimore.

Jack glanced at the time displays running along the bottom of the main screen. "They should already be in position. Once the last trucks are away..."

"They'll turn that place into an inferno," Naomi concluded softly.

***

"Ladies and gentlemen," President Curtis was saying, "this is truly a historic day." He was standing behind the podium in the White House press room, a broad smile on his face. Beside him was the CEO of New Horizons, Aaron Steinbecke, who wore a matching expression.

One of the members of the EDS command center staff was tasked with monitoring the news channels for relevant information, and it hadn't taken long to find plenty. It had been six hours now since the first trucks had rolled out, and the last of them had been shown leaving the plant just as President Curtis had begun his news conference. A real-time video feed of the plant was being shown in the lower right corner of the news screen as Curtis continued, "I have here with me Aaron Steinbecke, the CEO of New Horizons, a company that is going to literally change our nation and our world. Mere hours ago, a fleet of trucks was sent out–" the lower corner video feed cut to an earlier scene near daybreak that showed a stream of tractor-trailer rigs rolling out of the New Horizons facility as the sun rose behind them, "–that are carrying what very well may be the most important cargo ever delivered: grain that will not only provide us nourishment, but that will also protect us from disease, including the outbreak of a new virus that some scientists believe could rival the influenza pandemic in 1918 that killed millions.

"But instead of producing vaccines that are both expensive and often difficult to distribute, New Horizons has been able to engineer a cure into the very crops that we grow for food. And this morning I am submitting a bill to Congress requesting the necessary funding to subsidize the cost of these new strains of wheat and other food crops to keep the price at current market levels." He looked into the camera, his expression one of caring and compassion. "This salvation, born through years and billions of dollars in research, will be for all mankind, and we will make it affordable for every country in the world."

Jack turned his attention from the President's speech as the handset for one of the phones in the command console beeped. Picking it up, he said, "Dawson."

"We're ready," Hathcock told him.

Jack looked at Naomi, who nodded. "Blow it."

***

After hanging up, Hathcock motioned to Claret, who flipped open the protective cover over a red button of the remote detonator he held. Hathcock raised a pair of binoculars to his eyes and looked at the New Horizons plant that stood half a mile away.

He and his men had taken a page out of the harvesters' play book and had put together a fuel-air explosive bomb, but this one was much larger than any the harvesters had used on the genebanks. *Much* larger. His team had rigged a trailer with tanks containing six thousand gallons of gasoline and high pressure air tanks to disperse it into an aerosol inside the building. After that, a single spark would blow the place into oblivion. Hathcock, however, wasn't content with something so mundane as a spark: the trailer also contained ten bricks of C-4 explosive, connected to a remote detonator.

He shook his head, still astonished at their luck. He and Claret had hijacked one of the trucks contracted for New Horizons and driven it to the facility, fully expecting it to be a suicide mission.

Much to their surprise, while New Horizons was worried about security of the seed itself, they weren't inspecting the incoming trucks and their empty trailers. When the two men arrived at the outside perimeter gate, fully expecting a shootout with the guards and a heroic dash into the building that would end in a fiery demise, the guards simply checked the truck against their list and waved them on through.

"Right, then," Hathcock had told them, barely able to conceal his surprise as he put the semi into gear and joined the line of trucks entering the big building.

Once inside, Hathcock faked a mechanical breakdown with some imaginative use of the clutch and gear shift, and the harried loading supervisor angrily directed them off to the side of the loading area to get out of the way of the other trucks waiting to pick up their cargoes.

After that, New Horizons security personnel had unceremoniously shepherded the two men out of the building and off the compound, not wanting a pair of truckers gawking around the facility. The truck was to be towed away later, once the loading operation was complete.

One phone call later, Hathcock and Claret were picked up by a team member in a pickup truck, who brought them here to their designated observation point inside a barn that had a clear view to the facility from the hay loft. While it had been a huge temptation to simply blow the facility to bits right away, they had orders to wait until the last of the trucks had cleared out. It had been a long wait, but the time had finally come.

"Armed," Claret said. A green light glowed on the remote detonator, showing that it was communicating with its counterpart that was connected to the bomb in the truck.

"Initiate aerosol," Hathcock ordered.

Claret flipped a switch on the detonator and was rewarded with another green light. "Initiated."

Half a mile away, servos actuated, opening valves to the gasoline and high pressure air tanks in the trailer they'd left behind, turning the liquid gasoline into a fine aerosol mist that sprayed out vents cut in the roof and floor of the trailer.

***

The creature that mimicked Dr. Martin Kilburn stared impassively at the humans who had loaded the trucks. Because of the losses his kind (although he technically was not a "he," as the adult form of his species was neuter) had suffered at Spitsbergen, he had been sent here from FBI headquarters to help ensure the final processing and loading of the seed went according to schedule.

Kilburn was not the only one. All the other creatures like him were here, save the one now imprisoned by the Earth Defense Society after the unfortunate incident on Spitsbergen, and another in Washington, D.C.

Looking down from his perch, he saw one of his genetic kin wearing the body of the one called Rachel Kempf, running diagnostics on one of the computers that controlled the various machines on the loading floor. His kind had no leader as the humans would understand. But if they had, it would likely have been Kempf. "She" had been central to their planning, and had been the one to understand how best to motivate the humans to assist in their own destruction.

Kempf glanced up at him, her face betraying no emotion before she returned her attention to the computer.

None of them had human emotions, although they could mimic them well. As he surveyed the loading docks, where thousands of bags of the precious seed were being loaded into the stream of trucks, Kilburn displayed an air of satisfaction. Aside from the unfortunate breakdown of a single truck inside the facility, everything had gone smoothly in loading the seed.

The seed. It was the key to everything, to the very survival of his ancient and nearly extinct species. His kind could not procreate directly, as could the other species on this world. He knew that this had once been possible, dark ages ago, but their form had mutated over time, and this adaptive trait had been lost. Those like him were old, very, very old, so ancient that he had no memory of what had once been, other than indistinct dreams and visions. He no longer remembered where his race had been born, on this planet or another. But at one time, he knew, there had been many of his kind. Now only a few remained, all but two of which were in this building, ensuring their future.

For that future lay in genetic transmutation of other species, spreading the building blocks of his kind like a virus, using a virus. This was the only form of reproduction that had been left to them. But this required technology, technology that had required centuries to develop with the help of the humans. They had guided the efforts of the humans as best they could, but they were slow, so slow, to learn what his own kind knew by instinct, by genetic coding. And his kind had learned over time that it was unwise to take matters into their own hands, to push the humans too far or too fast: many had perished at the hands of humans after revealing too much of themselves. The nightmare creatures popular in human myth and legend were not all entirely the stuff of fantasy. Many of his ancient kin had been burned at the stake, beheaded, or worse.

Soon, he thought, looking at the humans recovering from the hectic labor of loading the many trucks that were now on their way to distribution centers across the country, *these creatures will be nothing but incubators and food for our species, and this world shall be ours.*

"Hey!" someone down on the loading floor suddenly shouted. "What's that?"

Searching the work area, Kilburn found the human who had shouted, and saw that he was pointing at the broken down truck that still sat at the side of the loading area.

A heavy mist was pouring from the top and bottom of the big trailer, billowing out into the facility.

Then Kilburn caught the first whiff of the unmistakable odor of gasoline. *It's a bomb*, he realized instantly, having been among those of his kind who had designed similar devices to destroy the world's primary genebanks.

Even though he was standing on a supervisory platform thirty feet off the ground, he didn't hesitate. There was no time to warn his genetic kin who still worked below, and his kind was not given to self-sacrifice.

He saw Kempf suddenly look up toward him, just before he pivoted around and hurled himself through one of the windows at the back of the platform.

Kilburn knew that she and the others would not survive.

***

On Claret's remote, another light winked green. "Aerosol discharge complete," he said, his thumb now hovering over the red button that would set off the C-4 explosive and detonate the vaporized gasoline.

"Det..." Hathcock began to say, then abruptly stopped. "Son of a bitch!" he cursed as he saw a person fly from one of the windows set up high in the building. Except by the time it reached the ground, it clearly wasn't human. "Rifle!" he snapped, tossing aside the binoculars. One of his team members handed him the Barrett sniper rifle. They had brought it along, just in case.

"Should I detonate?" Claret asked urgently.

"Stand by," Hathcock said tensely as he brought the Barrett to his shoulder and lined up the magnified sight picture in his right eye with the wide field of view in his left. The creature, clearly a harvester, was dashing on four multi-segmented legs across the compound toward a nearby stand of trees. "Mother of Christ," he hissed as he tried to keep the thing centered in the Unertl scope.

"The bloody thing's moving like a cheetah," Claret said quietly, having grabbed up the binoculars to act as Hathcock's spotter. "If it reaches those trees..."

Hathcock had only seconds, not only to stop this harvester from escaping, but to finish off the others still in the building before they realized what was happening and tried to escape, too. He would only have time for one shot.

Eliminating all distractions from his mind, Hathcock focused his entire being on the eerie form that danced in the scope's sight picture. Holding his breath, he waited until he was between heartbeats before he gently stroked the big rifle's trigger.

***

The Kilburn-thing ran in its natural form, all concerns about revealing its true self gone. It knew that the humans and its kin would die in the blast that must come at any time now, but it was determined to survive. It had survived the explosion at the FBI laboratory. It would survive this.

It was five yards away from the safety of the trees when the bullet from Hathcock's rifle speared it through the chest. The bullet's incendiary filling detonated, igniting the creature's malleable tissue and blowing it into flaming chunks.

***

"Detonate!" Hathcock ordered as he lowered the rifle and looked from the smoldering pyre of the harvester back toward the New Horizons facility, where people were just starting to pour out the doors. He knew that a lot of innocent civilians were about to die. Hathcock wasn't a heartless man, but having been through the hell of war himself, he knew that it happened. "God forgive us," he whispered as Claret pushed the button on the remote detonator.

***

On the news channel showing the White House press room, President Curtis was just turning to invite Steinbecke to the podium to speak when the video feed in the lower left that had been showing a close-up of the New Horizons plant suddenly flared a brilliant orange and went dark.

Even though the main view showed Curtis continuing to speak, his words were overridden by a news anchor who suddenly interrupted the broadcast from the White House.

"Excuse me, ladies and gentlemen," the man said, "we seem to have...wait a moment." He put his hand to his ear as if unable to believe what he was hearing.

Then a new video flashed up, this time taking up the entire screen: it was the New Horizons plant. Or, more accurately, what was left of it. The view on the television suddenly split, showing the massive conflagration that had consumed the plant on one side, and the White House press room on the other.

Curtis paused in his introduction of Steinbecke as an aide rushed up and whispered in his ear. The President's smile faltered, then was quickly replaced by shock as he audibly asked the aide to repeat his message. The man did, and Curtis turned back toward the hushed audience, his face a mask of undiluted rage.

"My fellow Americans," he said in a voice that was so quiet that it was little more than a whisper. But it made up in anger what it lacked in volume. "Once again, we have been attacked. Many of those watching this broadcast must have witnessed what we here have not yet seen for ourselves: the destruction of the New Horizons plant, just a moment ago."

Another aide, holding out a smart phone of some kind, rushed up to Curtis's side. Curtis watched it for a moment, seeing the miniaturized broadcast of the plant exploding in a massive fireball, before gesturing for the man to move away.

"As of this moment, my friends," he continued to the stunned audience in the press room and millions of television and Internet watchers across the nation and the world, including Jack, Naomi, and the others at the EDS base, "we are at war. This is no longer terrorism as we've known it in the past. Those who are committing these atrocities, who I believe are members of the so-called Earth Defense Society, or EDS, aren't fighting for a political or religious ideal. They're trying to destroy humanity's future, and this is the last time they'll strike, here in America or anywhere else." Curtis stared into the camera, and Jack felt a chill run down his spine at the President's expression. "We'll find you," Curtis promised. "And when we do, you'll be shown no mercy."

With that, he turned and stormed out of the press room without another word.

Thirty

"We found them," Ridley announced as she strode into the emergency meeting of the National Security Council in the White House Situation Room. President Curtis had called the meeting after she had informed him that there had been a major break in the pursuit of the EDS.

Ray Clement followed her in and sat in a seat along the wall behind Ridley as she took a seat at the table.

"My God, Monica," Jeffrey Komick, the Secretary for Homeland Security, gasped as he saw the bandages covering Ridley's forehead and the right side of her face. Like the others in the room, he'd heard that she'd been injured in a shootout, but he hadn't realized that it had been that close.

She spared him a glance, but nothing more. "As we suspected," she went on, "they're in California, in the Sutter Buttes area, not far from Beale Air Force Base."

That sent a stir through the group that was silenced by an impatient wave of the President's hand.

"We were able to make the connection between the plane and a series of service contracts and companies, even a local wind farm, that seemed to have a common controlling interest," she said, giving a broad overview of what the hundreds of special agents who'd been scouring the area and every database and information source that the Bureau, Intelligence Community, and Homeland Security agencies could access, had managed to finally piece together through thousands of man-hours of investigation and analysis. "My agents finally pinned down the physical location of the EDS hideout by piecing together leads from truckers who'd seen some unusual things going on at a repair facility located in central California."

Clement handed out photographs from a folder that had been tucked under his arm. The satellite images showed a very busy truck repair and trailer storage business. Semis and trailers were parked all over the compound.

"They're in *here?*" Curtis asked, bewildered.

"More precisely," Ridley told him, "they're beneath it. That's the site of an old Cold War ICBM base. They must have made it at least partly habitable, and used the truck repair company as a front."

"Maybe the trucking guys didn't even know," Komick murmured. He glanced up to find everyone looking at him. "Stranger things have happened, you know."

"Actually," Ridley said, "you're probably right. The truck business is completely legitimate. That's part of the reason it took so long to track them down. But once we had several leads pointing us at the trucking business, we interviewed everyone we could who'd had anything to do with it. We also had the lucky break from the Russians about the plane, without which we would never have gotten this far." She shook her head in grudging admiration. "They didn't make it easy to find them."

"Did you find the plane?" the Director of National Intelligence asked.

"No. It had taken off earlier on what we know now was a bogus flight plan. We're not sure where it is, but we'll find it."

"To hell with the plane," Curtis spat, holding the satellite image in shaking hands. "What are we going to do about *this?*"

"We've already got an assault team ready to go in," Ridley told him. "All they need is your go-ahead."

"A team?" Curtis said angrily. "A *team?* I want bloody overwhelming, irresistible force!"

"A hundred and fifty heavily armed FBI agents is 'bloody overwhelming, irresistible force,' Mr. President," she replied evenly. "And remember, sir, that those men and women are very...motivated, shall we say. After the bombing of the FBI lab, not to mention the betrayals by Dawson and Richards, they want payback."

"Payback?" Komick asked quietly. "What about justice?"

"Is there a difference, Jeff?" Curtis asked caustically. "What justice did the hundreds killed in Colorado have? Or the workers in the New Horizons plant? Or any of the other people who've been blown up lately? Not to mention all the people who may die of disease in the time it takes New Horizons to rebuild that plant and get production of those seeds going again." He glared at Komick. "They poured everything they had into that plant and had everyone who'd been involved in the project there to make sure there weren't any screwups." He shook his head in disgust. "It was a disaster for which there can never be any *justice*."

Turning back to Ridley, he said simply, "Go."

***

"My God!" Richards cried over the intercom as the Hughes MD520N helicopter dodged through the ravines along the northeast edge of Sutter Buttes, the landing skids occasionally thwacking against a tree branch. He had always hated helicopters, and he hated flying low even more. And Ferris was flying really, really low. "You're going to get us killed!"

"Shut up," Ferris muttered as he pulled the nimble helicopter up and to the left, rolling into the next ravine. He had seen over a dozen helicopters approaching the Buttes behind them, no doubt from Beale Air Force Base to the east. They had the unmistakable sleek profile of military UH-60 Blackhawks, and Ferris had a good idea where they were going. The Blackhawks had a speed advantage, but if they were laden with troops, which he knew they must be, they wouldn't catch him with the head start he had on them.

After dropping off Hathcock's strike team in Nebraska, Ferris had landed the Falcon at Sutter County Airport in Yuba City, about fifteen miles southeast of the EDS base. He had landed there after Naomi had called to warn him that the FBI had issued an alert to local law enforcement agencies about the Falcon, and that Oroville airport was probably swarming with police and FBI agents. Renee had a helicopter chartered and waiting for him, and Richards was there, too. Ferris almost cried when he looked at the Falcon one last time as he took off in the helicopter: he had come to love that plane, but knew he would never fly it again.

And Richards...if Naomi hadn't ordered him to pick up the obnoxious FBI man and Jack hadn't vouched for him having saved all their asses when they'd returned from Spitsbergen, Ferris would have kicked him out of the chopper. He'd done nothing but moan and complain about Ferris's flying, but Ferris was too much of a professional to fly even lower and faster just to piss off Richards even more.

Well, mostly, Ferris thought to himself as he yanked the helicopter almost vertical out of the last ravine before making a beeline for the old Titan base.

"Renee," he called over their secure radio, "we're coming in! But be advised: we've got some unwelcome guests hot on our asses. I'm guessing a hundred plus troops, maybe five minutes behind us."

"Roger," Renee replied instantly. "We'll be ready."

With another glance over his shoulder to check the position of the approaching Blackhawks, Ferris angled the Hughes in for a hard landing just outside the base's fence line, as the inner compound was too crowded with trucks and trailers to land.

"Come on!" he shouted to Richards as he quickly undid his safety harness and hopped out. He sprinted for the repair building, not even bothering to shut down the chopper.

***

"Is everyone topside away?" Naomi asked.

The man in the video screen nodded, just as he was joined by a panting Ferris and a clearly disoriented Richards. "I sent all the uncleared workers home," the man said. "The rest of us are ready to come below."

"Stand by," Naomi said. "The portal is opening now."

Behind the small group of men and women who stood around the man in the video, the cadre who worked in the truck repair shop and who knew its true nature, the door to the secret room where the portal entrance lay slid open. They all went through it, and as it closed behind them, the massive blast doors of the portal elevator shaft opened.

Naomi watched on the security console as everyone piled into the big elevator, then she hit the control to bring down the elevator and close the portal's blast doors above them.

A few minutes later, Ferris and Richards entered the conference room.

"You're all crazy," Richards blurted.

"You tried a little face off with the Director of the FBI in some kind of macho stunt, and you have the balls to call us crazy?" Naomi shot back.

"That's not what I mean," Richards told her. "This place is a death trap!" He looked at Jack. "There's no other way out of here, is there?"

Jack shook his head.

"If you thought that," Naomi snapped, coming over to face him, "why did you bother to come here?"

"Excuse me, kids," Renee cut in sarcastically, noting that Jack hadn't dived into the verbal slugfest, but had his attention riveted to the wall displays showing maps and video images of the surface level compound, "but I think we've got bigger problems than your hormone levels."

"Here they come," Jack said grimly as dozens of troops in black uniforms slid to the ground from ropes tossed out the doors of the Blackhawks that now hovered above the maze of trucks and trailers. They landed in a ring around the outer part of the truck parking area, then began to move inward toward the repair building.

"Oh, no," Richards muttered as he got a better look at some of them when they passed by one of the hidden cameras. They had "FBI" stenciled in large letters on the back of their uniforms, with smaller stencils on the front. He and Jack exchanged a sick look.

"Don't worry," Naomi reassured them. "They're not going to have an easy time getting to us."

"They'll never reach the portal," Renee said, but her voice held nothing but dismay and regret.

"I'm not worried about them reaching us," Jack told them. "It's just..."

"The idea of killing fellow agents isn't exactly appealing," Richards finished for him quietly.

"I'm sorry," Naomi told them, putting a hand on Jack's shoulder. Looking at the map of the compound and the red dots that represented the approaching agents, she picked up a headset and handed it to Richards. "You can try to warn them off."

From the tone of her voice, Richards knew that she didn't expect him to have much luck. He shook his head, but reached for the headset anyway. He slipped it over his head, putting the microphone close to his lips. Naomi hit a control and gave him a thumbs up. "Agents of the FBI," he said firmly. The men and women moving through the compound paused as the public address system in the repair shop boomed out over the compound. "This is Special Agent Carl Richards. This facility is heavily defended and you will *not* succeed in breaching it. I know...I know what you're feeling. I know you have a job to do. But if you come any closer, many of you may die. And it will be for absolutely nothing. Just...just quarantine this facility. Cordon off the perimeter..."

He stopped talking as the agents, most of them visibly shaking their heads, and a few of them making obscene gestures, continued to move forward.

Gently, Naomi took the headset back. "I'm sorry," she told him.

"Now what?" Jack asked in a raspy voice. All the spit in his mouth had dried up and he was clenching his fists as the agents, no doubt some of whom he'd worked with before, moved closer to the repair building.

"It's not going to be pretty, Jack," Renee said shakily. "Tan was in charge of setting up the physical security for this and the other sites we have." She glanced up at him. "He was a ruthless bastard."

"Just get on with it," Naomi ordered. "None of us want to do this, but we can't allow them to get in. We've got to stay on-line until all the trucks are accounted for. We're also the last major genebank in case any of the New Horizons seed does get out." Folding her arms as if she were suddenly chilled, she said, "Do it."

Renee nodded, then started clicking controls in another window on her workstation. On the map display at the front of the room, a cloud of green icons bloomed across the compound. Jack could see that many of them were out in the open and assumed they were mines, but there were others that were clearly in or on some of the trailers parked on the surface.

The result was instantaneous and overwhelming. The video feeds of the compound were suddenly shaken by dozens of near-simultaneous explosions as bounding anti-personnel mines, often called "Bouncing Bettys," were triggered. Much worse were the booby-trapped trailers: they were fitted with long strips of explosive with embedded ball bearings that, when detonated, were like enormous Claymore mines. In an instant, tens of thousands of small ball bearings scythed through the ranks of the FBI agents.

"Christ," Richards moaned as he watched the cream of the Bureau massacred in a hail of metal. He had no idea how many died in that first wave, but he was filled with a painful mix of fierce pride and emotional agony as those who survived refused to break and run, but continued to move forward.

Proud and determined or not, they couldn't stand against the base's defenses. In twos and threes, and sometimes larger groups, they were mowed down by the thick barrier of mines through which they had to move to get to their objective.

Jack was numb as he watched the carnage, noting absently that Naomi, Renee, and several others, including some men, in the command center were crying. He knew that defending the base was necessary and that people would die in the process. But he also knew that there would be a special place reserved for him in Hell for his part in this.

At last, the remaining agents finally gave up valor for discretion and began to pull back.

"Turn off the mines behind them," Jack said hoarsely. "Let them get out."

"It's already done," Renee managed as she tried to dry her tears on her sleeve.

They watched in silence as the special agents retreated, the survivors heading out through the front gate. *So few*, Jack thought. He counted less than thirty men and women still on their feet, and half of them appeared to be wounded. He was only thankful that Renee hadn't turned on any of the audio pickups that he was sure were up on the surface. He didn't know what he would have done if he'd had to hear the screams of the wounded and dying.

"We're not out of it yet," the young man on one of the other consoles called out about five minutes later. He was watching the display from the small air search radar that was installed on top of the repair building, its housing disguised as a battered exhaust fan cowling. "Looks like we have a pair of fast movers inbound..." He managed to pick them up by slaving a video camera to the radar track. The command center staff was rewarded with a jittery view of what Jack identified as a pair of F-15E Strike Eagles. "They're going straight for the repair building."

"Don't tell me you have SAMs?" Richards asked. He was still pale and shaken.

Naomi shook her head. "No," she said, "we don't have anything that sophisticated. We'd hoped to never have to do what we're doing now: our best defense was secrecy."

A hail of black objects separated from the Eagles as they streaked overhead.

Down below the surface in the command dome, Jack and the others felt and heard nothing, but the video feeds and other information from the surface suddenly disappeared from the displays. The repair shop, the mines, and probably most of the trailers that still had any explosive strips had just been wiped away.

"Damn," Naomi whispered. Turning to Jack, she said, "Do they have any bombs that can reach us down here?"

"A BLU-109, maybe," Ferris piped up before Jack could say anything. "It's a two-thousand pound bunker buster bomb that might be able to penetrate the blast doors on the silos and the portal, but I don't think they have anything that can reach us down here."

"But if they can breach the surface blast doors," Naomi said worriedly, "they could destroy the silos. If they do..."

Ferris shook his head and shrugged. "I can only tell you what I know, girl," he said quietly.

"Do we have any eyes left topside?" Jack asked.

"We've got the periscopic sensor array and camera," Renee confirmed. Clicking some controls on her workstation, she said, "There..."

The video camera on the sensor mast rose from its submerged storage sleeve and showed them a scene of utter devastation: the repair shop was gone, blown into wreckage that was strewn across the compound. And there, moving quickly through the still-smoking remains of the building and vehicles, were the surviving FBI agents.

"Persistent buggers," Renee said, her voice a mixture of admiration and fear.

"The good news is that we probably won't get bombed while they're here," Jack said. "The bad news is that it looks like they're heading straight for the air intake opening." The vent, hidden under a thick grate in the back corner of the repair shop, had been covered with an armored manifold. But the manifold had been blown open: one of the Eagle pilots had gotten lucky with a bomb.

Naomi shook her head. "Even if they can get through the surface vent, they won't be able to get inside," she said. "The blast valves are closed, and they couldn't get through them without heavy explosives."

"See those satchels a couple of those guys are carrying," Richards said, pointing to a pair of agents who were clearly being protected by the others. "There's your heavy explosives."

"I'm not so worried about them getting in," Jack said darkly. "I'm more worried about what might get *out*." He looked at the others. "Remember what we have trapped in the intake chamber."

"What?" Richards said, looking from Jack to Naomi and back.

"God," Naomi said, the blood draining from her face. "We can't let them get near it!"

"Near what, dammit?" Richards shouted angrily.

"What we think is now a harvester, or becoming one," Naomi explained. "It killed one of my people and our test animals. We think it went into the air intake tunnel, and we barricaded it in by welding steel plate over the tunnel mouth. As long as the blast valves are intact, it can't get out..."

"But if those guys manage to blow them open," Richards finished for her, understanding now, "if the blast doesn't kill the thing it could take the place of one of them, just like it did Ray Clement."

"We've got to stop them," Jack said. "We've got to go topside and fight them off."

"Jack, no!" Naomi exclaimed. "I won't allow it!"

Turning to her, Jack said, "The only alternative is to tear down the plating covering up the intake tunnel so we can go in and kill...whatever is in there." He nodded his head toward the ceiling. "I'd rather take my chances fighting a kind of opponent I understand."

"Let's just get this done," Richards growled. "Anybody have a weapon and some body armor?"

***

"My God," President Curtis said into the silence of the White House Situation Room. "This is a disaster."

The Predator drone orbiting over the EDS base had shown the massacre of the FBI assault team in high definition video detail on the room's main display screen. No one in the room, with the exception of the senior military officers who were all veterans of both Gulf Wars, had ever seen such carnage.

The FBI SAC for the raid had been in an orbiting Blackhawk, and had been given the authority to call in an air strike as a last resort. No one had expected the "last resort" to be necessary in the first few minutes of the operation. And the air strike hadn't even touched the Titan base itself.

Seeing that there might be a way into the base through a hole blown in some sort of vent, the SAC, shaken though he was, ordered a team in to take advantage of the situation.

"If this doesn't work," Curtis said, "I want something ready that *will*." He turned and looked directly at the Chairman of the Joint Chiefs of Staff, General Daniel Coleridge, United States Marine Corps.

"If this," Coleridge nodded at the video display showing the agents now clustering around the hole blown in the massive vent, "doesn't work, we can use the BLU-109 penetrator bomb. It's a two thousand pound weapon that was designed to deal with hardened underground structures. We think it will penetrate the blast doors on the surface, but–"

"General," Curtis said quietly, cutting off what the older man was going to say, "we've known each other long enough that there's no need for bullshit." The old Marine's expression hardened. "I don't want to hear the word 'should.' All I want to know is, will it work or won't it?"

"We don't know, sir," Coleridge said flatly. "One weapon won't be enough: the facility is huge, and even if the weapon was able to penetrate, we'd need at least two dozen to make sure we destroyed all the major structures." He paused. "But there's a good chance we'll have to drop a lot more. My people have been studying that Titan base from what they could turn up in the short time we've had since I gave the original warning order. It's amazingly tough and would take a lot of punishment. But if we drop enough of these bombs, we'll eventually kill everyone down there. That I can guarantee."

Clement, who had been sitting quietly behind Ridley, suddenly snatched the secure smart phone attached to his belt as it began to vibrate. Looking at it for a moment, he gasped, then leaned forward and whispered something in Ridley's ear. She snapped her head around to look at him, her eyes wide with shock. Then she turned to Curtis and said, "Mr. President, may I have a word. In private."

Curtis frowned, but from the look on her face and the tone of her request, he suspected that whatever she had to say – and what the senior agent with her had said – had something to do with The Others.

"Very well," Curtis said quietly. "I'll be back shortly. Keep an eye on this debacle." He nodded toward the screen at the head of the room.

Ridley and Clement, trailed by two Secret Service agents, followed Curtis to one of the complex's smaller conference rooms. "I'm fine, guys," he told the Secret Service men after ushering Ridley and Clement into the room. "Just wait outside, if you would, please."

Nodding, but clearly unhappy, the two agents took up positions on either side of the door as Curtis closed it behind him.

"What is it?" Curtis asked Ridley.

"He has a message for us," she said, her eyes fixed on the big man who'd accompanied her to the meeting. She had mentioned his name earlier, but Curtis couldn't remember it. "He told me that he's one of them. One of The Others."

"Jesus," Curtis breathed. Kempf was the only one of their kind that he had ever been in contact with.

"Yes, Mr. President," the creature who mimicked Ray Clement said, inclining its head. "Do you require additional proof?" It extended its right hand, which quickly lengthened into the slender finger-like digits, porcelain smooth and white, as the Kempf creature had been when she had revealed herself to him years ago.

"I believe you," he said, unable to keep the awe from his voice. "But...why are you here? Why now?"

"Mr. President," the Clement-thing said urgently, its hand returning to its state of human mimicry, "we are very...concerned about the situation. You do not know this, but the situation is far worse than you or your people suspect." It nodded toward the video display where the FBI men were still working on getting through the surface vent. "Just a moment ago, there in the other conference room, I learned that the Earth Defense Society has been conducting genetic experiments at this base." It paused. "They have perfected a genetic weapon that could damage or destroy this planet's biosphere. If the containment of this weapon is breached by these bombs you plan to use, if it is released into the atmosphere, it would spell disaster for your species." It offered him a pitying look. "Our kind is highly adaptable and would survive, but humans and all creatures like you would not."

"What the devil is it?" Curtis asked, his stomach suddenly churning with acid.

"We do not know," the Clement-thing said. "We suspect it is either an aerosol or microscopic particulate. Either could be weaponized easily, but even accidental release would spell the doom of most forms of life now on Earth, and there is nothing we could do to prevent it."

"How do we destroy it?" the President of the United States asked.

"With nuclear fire," the creature told him.

Thirty-One

"This is suicide, Dawson," Richards said quietly as they rode the portal elevator toward the surface. "You realize that, don't you?"

Jack looked at him and forced a grin. "You didn't want to live forever, did you?"

Richards shook his head. "Idiot," he muttered.

Around them were a dozen men and women, all wearing combat gear that was nearly identical to what the FBI agents wore. Most had G36C assault rifles. Some, like Jack, had shotguns. They also had a load of grenades. Jack had insisted, not so much to use against his fellow agents, but on the off chance that the whatever-it-was that was trapped in the tunnels somehow got past the blast valves.

"Jack!" Naomi's voice suddenly sounded through the radio receiver in his ear as, above him, the massive doors to the portal entrance began to cycle open. She and the others in the command center had their eyes glued to what the FBI agents were doing. "They've gotten through the surface vent. They've sent one...now two men down."

"That'll be our friends with the satchel charges," Richards pointed out unnecessarily.

"Aren't there any defenses built into the vent structures?" Jack asked.

"No," Naomi told him. "Tan had talked about it, but it never happened."

"Right," Jack said, shoving the *It would have been nice* thought aside as the elevator reached the surface. "Here we go."

As the elevator cage reached the top of its travel, the frame rising above the level of the massive concrete casing, they immediately came under a hail of rifle fire from the FBI agents circled around the vent only one hundred fifty feet away.

"Smoke!" Jack shouted, and instantly three smoke grenades sailed through the air to a spot between them and the FBI agents. In fifteen seconds there was enough smoke that the agents were totally obscured. Which also meant they couldn't see Jack and his people. "Go!"

Richards led the way, leaping from the portal casing to the right as Jack led the way to the left. The agents were still pouring a hail of fire in the direction of Jack's people, but they could only hope to get lucky.

And they did. Two men to Jack's left grunted and dropped to the ground as they were hit.

"Leave them!" he yelled as others knelt to help the wounded. "We'll get them on the way back." *If we make it back*, he thought as he ran forward as fast as he could into the smoke, his weapon at his shoulder, ready to fire.

Behind him, the portal elevator sank out of sight, and the massive blast doors closed behind it, protecting the entrance to the base. Naomi had fought against it, but Jack had been insistent: if they lost the fight out here, he didn't want the agents to have a free ride down the portal.

As soon as the smoke thinned enough for him to make out the vague outline of the agents, who had now spread out in a defensive skirmish line, Jack dropped to the ground and yelled, "Grenades!"

His team hurled half a dozen grenades at the agents. Before any of them went off, he heard and felt the explosions of more grenades thrown by the team led by Richards. *Cocky bastard*, Jack thought, *but good in a fight*. The grenades had found their mark, and the fire from the FBI team slacked off.

"*Go, go, go!*" Jack screamed as he leaped up and charged forward, firing in controlled bursts at the agents. There wasn't any finesse in what he and the men and women with him were doing now: they needed to kill their opponents, and do it quickly. There was an unknown danger lurking below that might be released by the agents with the satchel charges, but Jack was also worried about death from above. He knew there must be Predator drones orbiting the base, and he knew that Predators weren't just equipped for surveillance. They could kill, too.

Three more of his people went down under heavy fire, but then he and his team were in among the few surviving agents.

"Surrender!" Richards boomed. An agent who was down on the ground, shot in the thigh, raised his rifle to point at Richards, and Richards kicked the rifle away and butt-stroked the agent into submission. "Dammit, we won't hurt you if you surrender, you idiots!"

The remaining four agents finally gave in. Dropping their weapons, they slowly raised their hands.

"You men down there," Jack shouted into the shaft at the two agents who'd gone down. "We promise you safe passage if you come back up right now...with the charges intact. Otherwise you'll be staying down there with them." He leaned a little further to try and see them, and was rewarded with a half dozen rifle rounds *spanging* off the metal of the vent cover. "Grenade," Jack said grimly, holding out his hand.

"The charges might go off if you drop this," Richards said, handing him a grenade.

Nodding in understanding, Jack told him, "Get everyone back to the portal." Then, to the men below, he pulled the pin on the grenade and shouted, "Last chance, guys! Come up right now or you'll get a grenade down the throat. We'll haul you–"

His last words were swallowed by a fusillade of shots from below, two of them hitting him in his chest armor, knocking him backwards and spilling the grenade from his hand. The striker level flew off, igniting the fuse, and the egg-shaped weapon rolled right next to his face. Eyes wide and gasping from the pain of the ribs bruised by the bullets that struck him, he managed to bat the grenade away, and watched with relief as it fell through the hole into the gaping air intake vent.

"Stupid assholes," he gasped, trying to roll to his feet. He caught sight of Richards dashing toward him just before they were both tossed through the air like wads of paper by the explosion of the two satchel charges, which detonated when Jack's grenade went off.

***

In the darkness at the bottom of the air intake chamber, the creature had finally *become*. Uncoiling for the first time in its adult form, it flexed its limbs. Gathering its strength, the creature stood erect before taking its first step, then another. It paced the length of its lair, a long dark recess, the bottom of a great cylinder laid on its side. None of its kind was here with it in this place, but it could sense that one of them was somewhere close, and another far, far away. It did not know how or why it knew this; its mind had not yet matured enough to form such questions.

At one end of its lair were five large, round openings. It was just probing them with its claws when the shock from an explosion on the far side knocked it to the floor.

***

"The radiation and the extreme heat of a nuclear detonation will ensure that the genetic weapon is fully neutralized," the Clement-thing explained calmly to a shocked President Curtis. Monica Ridley watched the exchange, her face a mask of silent horror. "There is no other way to ensure its destruction. They must not be allowed to vent it into the atmosphere, or all will be lost."

"There's no time," Curtis said, shaking his head as he glanced back at the video feed from the Predator over the EDS base. "It would take hours to get a weapon ready..."

"And to evacuate the local population," Ridley interjected, finally regaining her composure. "We can't just drop a bomb in the middle of California without giving people warning!"

The Clement-thing looked at her dispassionately. "You must," it said flatly. "There is no other way." It turned back to Curtis. "And it will not require hours. An aircraft is armed and in the air not far from Beale Air Force Base. All you need do is issue the necessary orders to deliver the weapon."

"A plane is flying around with a live nuke aboard without my authorization?" Curtis shouted in dismay. "How the hell did *that* happen?"

"Sir, are you all right?" A Secret Service agent stuck his head in the door, his right hand under his left arm, holding his weapon.

"Yes, Eric," Curtis said, calming himself with great difficulty. "Please, wait outside."

With a pointed glance at Ridley and Clement, the agent nodded and closed the door.

"It happened because we wished it to be so," the Clement-thing said in answer to Curtis's question. "Remember that in 2007, six cruise missiles armed with live nuclear warheads were loaded onto a B-52 bomber at Minot Air Force Base in North Dakota and flown across your country to Barksdale Air Force Base in Louisiana, all without proper authorization." It paused. "This is not the first time this has happened, nor was it the last. It was merely an event we...made possible that, unfortunately, was discovered." It shrugged, an all too human gesture that sent a chill down Curtis's spine. "We have had people such as you in certain positions in the military to...enable such contingencies in case an emergency like this arose. We knew we were close to finding our enemy, your enemy, and thus we made preparations. We now have the opportunity to stop them. We must take that opportunity." Its eyes, suddenly not quite so human, fixed on Curtis. "*You* must take it, President Curtis. In the name of humanity."

Curtis simply stared at it.

"If it is any consolation," The Other went on, "there will be a minimum of civilian casualties. The B83 nuclear bomb with which the aircraft is armed should be powerful enough to destroy the base and the EDS weapon, but the radius of heavy damage will only affect lightly populated agricultural areas to the north. The Sutter Buttes will shield the more densely populated areas to the east and south."

"I..." Curtis began, then snapped his mouth shut. He exchanged a look with Ridley, who silently shook her head.

"This is all wrong," she said quietly, moving away from Clement. "There's no way EDS could have created such a weapon. *You're* the only ones who understand genetics enough to create such a thing." She glanced at Curtis, then back at the creature. "And I don't think any terrorist group that had no prior record could possibly have managed everything that you claim EDS has done. It doesn't make sense."

"We saved you, Monica," the creature said softly, sadly. Turning to Curtis, it said, "And your daughter. These gifts we gave freely. They could also be taken away," it added darkly.

"Then they weren't gifts," Ridley told it harshly. Turning to Curtis, she said, "We've been taken for a ride, Mr. Pres–"

In the blink of an eye, faster than Curtis could follow as he stood rooted to the floor with fear, the thing that wore Ray Clement's clothes leaped at Ridley, drawing her into a tight embrace with one arm while its free hand clamped over her mouth to muffle her scream. Her eyes bulged in shock and pain, then quickly relaxed to stare sightlessly past Curtis. The Clement-thing carefully placed her in one of the chairs along the wall, looking for all the world as if she'd fallen asleep.

"Soon, when she awakens," it told Curtis, "she will be as she would have been had we never given her our gift." It paused. "We will do the same for your daughter if you do not do what you must. And you realize what that will mean."

"I'll call in the agents who are outside and have them arrest you," he said with more bravado than he felt as his mind's eye showed him his daughter dying, clutching her head in agony as the tumor rapidly swelled in her brain. He looked at Ridley: even now he could see her muscles twitching, twisting her limbs as her body withered under the assault of the Lou Gehrig's disease that The Others had removed from her years before. It was as if the Clement-thing had somehow accelerated the process, and the disease was making up for years of lost time in only minutes.

"It will be very painful for your daughter, and for you," the harvester told him quietly, following his gaze. "She will lose her thoughts, her memories. Her mind will perish as the tumor overwhelms her brain, bringing unimaginable pain. Then she will die."

Curtis's insides melted into the same clutching, deathly fear for his daughter that he had felt when she had first been diagnosed. At that moment, the most powerful human being on the planet was reduced to a father, terrified for his only daughter's life.

"You promise that there won't be many civilian casualties?" he heard himself say, as if his voice was being controlled by some other intelligence.

"Most likely a few hundred will be killed outright, with a few thousand more suffering serious injury," the Clement-thing reassured him. "But you will be saving the entire world, Mr. President. That is what you must focus on. Far greater sacrifices have been made by far lesser men."

Curtis nodded, his mind and body numb. "What about her?" he asked, nodding toward Ridley. "What…what should I tell the others?"

"You can tell the truth: her injuries are taking a toll on her, and she needed some rest before rejoining us."

"But when they find her…"

"Her condition will be a mystery that no human will be able to explain," it told him smoothly.

Gathering himself, Curtis nodded, then turned toward the door. "Clement" followed him.

"Director Ridley needed some rest," Curtis told the agents outside as he pulled the door closed behind Clement. "The injuries she suffered are taking a toll on her, so make sure she's not disturbed."

"Yes, Mr. President," one of the agents said. He stayed by the door while Eric, the senior agent on the President's protective detail, escorted Curtis back to the main sitroom, with Clement right behind.

"I need the Secretary of Defense, General Coleridge, and Colonel Mathay," Curtis ordered brusquely. "Everyone else clear the room." The gathered members of the National Security Council froze at the mention of Mathay's name. "*Now*," Curtis snapped.

That started an organized stampede toward the door.

After the others had left the room, a tall, lantern-jawed man in the uniform of an Air Force colonel stepped in, followed by two grim-faced Secret Service agents. They wouldn't be ordered outside for this one. The colonel's nametag said Mathay, and he carried a large leather briefcase that was secured to his right wrist by a length of chrome chain that ended in a locked handcuff. It was popularly known as the "football," a device that allowed the President to send launch orders to America's strategic forces.

"Shut the door," Curtis ordered the Secret Service agents before gesturing for Mathay to come to the table and set down the briefcase.

"What's going on, sir?" Coleridge asked huskily, his pale gray eyes fixed on the football.

Thomas Wilburne, the recently-promoted Secretary of Defense, glanced at the case, but his expression didn't reveal any surprise. Then he looked at Clement and nodded his head respectfully.

He knows, Curtis thought. *He's in on The Secret, too.* With a sinking sensation he suddenly understood that the deaths of President Fowler and the former Secretary of Defense had been a bit too convenient. *Ridley was right.* But that confirmation wouldn't sway him from what he had to do. He might burn in Hell for it, but he'd do anything to save his daughter. *Lord, forgive me*, he begged.

"I've received what I believe to be absolutely reliable information," Curtis told them, "that there is a weapon in the EDS base that poses a clear and immediate danger not only to the United States, but to the world at large." He looked directly into Coleridge's eyes. "If this thing gets out, if it's exposed to the atmosphere, it will contaminate the world's biosphere and end life as we know it."

"I'll order the Air Force to prepare the penetrator bombs," Coleridge said, reaching for one of the phones along the wall, "and–"

"No, general," Curtis told him. "Conventional weapons will only increase the likelihood that this thing that EDS has created will be accidentally released into the atmosphere. It has to be completely contained. Sterilized." He nodded at the case. "And there's only one way to do it."

"Mr. President," Coleridge began carefully, "sir, may I ask where this information is coming from?"

"It's from a deep penetration agent we've had inside of EDS for the last month," Clement answered before Curtis could say anything. "It's one-hundred percent reliable." He glanced at Curtis. "We've gotten details of the weapon, a retrovirus suspended in an aerosol form. It was just confirmed." He gestured at the phone on his belt. "There's no question, general."

"Sir," the old Marine said to Curtis, "we...we can't just drop a nuke. We haven't been attacked on a scale that–"

"We *have* been attacked!" Curtis shot back angrily. "Why the hell do you think I'm standing here instead of Ben Fowler, our former Commander-in-Chief? Remember him? He was blown up, along with your former boss and a few hundred high schoolers. And how about the hundreds of people who were burned to death in Colorado? Not to mention the ring of explosions around the world, all of which EDS publicly took credit for." Despite his guilty knowledge that The Others may not have been as white as snow, he was nonetheless filled with righteous anger at the outrages that had been visited on the country and the world. "Ring any bells, General Coleridge?"

"Yes...yes, sir," Coleridge said quietly.

"All I want to know, general," Curtis told him coldly, "is if you're going to carry out the orders I give you. If not, consider yourself relieved and I'll summon your deputy to see if he has the balls to get this job done."

"No need, sir. It's my job. I'll do it.

That was when the Predator's video feed, which had been running uninterrupted on the front screen, suddenly flared with a tremendous explosion from where the FBI agents had been engaged by a defensive team that had come to the surface from the subterranean base.

They all turned to look at the scene.

"We're out of time," Clement said urgently, watching as smoke roiled out of what must have been a ventilation shaft leading into the base. "It may already be too late."

"Colonel Mathay?" Curtis ordered.

Without a word, as if this were nothing more than a routine communications exercise, Mathay opened the case, revealing a heavily protected device similar to a laptop. With a few keystrokes, he activated the football's console.

"Your orders, sir?" the colonel said, looking at Coleridge.

"Initiate an operational alert," Coleridge said after a long, uncomfortable moment. He looked at Curtis. "What attack option did you have in mind, sir?" he asked. "We don't exactly have anything to cover this in the SIOP." The SIOP was the Single Integrated

Operational Plan that was the blueprint for how the United States would employ its nuclear weapons.

"It's an ad-hoc mission," Wilburne, the new Secretary of Defense, said. He looked up at Coleridge, then at Curtis. "And there's already an asset available."

The President's expression hardened at the reminder that one of the nation's nuclear weapons had been loaded aboard a strike aircraft without his knowledge or consent. But that was an issue he would deal with later.

"BLUE MAX?" Coleridge asked. "That was a nuclear strike training exercise. The planes don't have operational weapons on board."

"One of them does," Wilburne told him flatly, but he was looking at Clement.

"You've known that our planes have been carrying nuclear weapons without my authorization?" Curtis asked him, aghast.

Wilburne nodded, his eyes still on Clement. "I coordinated the weapon deployments," he said. Turning his gaze to Curtis, he added, "I was…ordered not to inform you or President Fowler, sir."

"God Almighty," Curtis breathed. "All right. Use it," he said, looking at the video feed and the rising plume of smoke from the EDS base. His blood chilled at the sight as he wondered if even now, particles of the weapon were escaping into the air. *If the weapon's even real*, a part of his mind whispered.

"Your authentication, please, Mr. President?" Mathay asked.

Curtis reached into his coat pocket and withdrew a plastic card about the size of a credit card that was nicknamed "the biscuit." On it were printed the authentication codes that would allow the nation's nuclear weapons to be armed and used. He read off a string of letters and numbers, which Mathay carefully entered into the football's console.

"Mr. Secretary?" the colonel said, looking at Wilburne. In order for a valid nuclear weapons order to be issued, the President's order had to be confirmed by the Secretary of Defense.

Wilburne already had his biscuit out. "I authenticate…" And he read out a set of random letters and numbers, which Mathay again entered into the console. They were rewarded with a set of illuminated buttons on the console changing from red to green.

"The target, General Coleridge?" Mathay asked.

"Here," Clement said, handing Mathay a small slip of paper that held the latitude, longitude, and surface elevation of the EDS base.

Mathay glanced at Coleridge, who turned to look at Curtis.

"Enter it," Curtis said flatly, and Mathay punched in the information into the console.

"Mr. President," Mathay said finally, "do you authorize the nuclear mission execution order?" His finger hovered over a rectangular red button that said EXECUTE.

Curtis swallowed hard, the full meaning of that single word glaring from the button striking home. "Yes," he said, forcing out the words. "I authorize the execution of this mission."

Mathay nodded, then pressed the button. In a few seconds the display on the console reported that the order had been issued and received by the designated strike aircraft.

"It's done, sir," Mathay said.

"May the Lord forgive us," Coleridge whispered, his face pale.

***

"Martin, if you're making this up I'm going to bust your ass," Major Elaine Harris growled over the intercom. She was the pilot in command of a B-52H *Stratofortress* strategic bomber of the 5th Bombardment Wing out of Minot Air Force Base, and she was not happy. Not happy at all. What had begun as a nuclear strike exercise, something they rarely seemed to get to do these days and had spent weeks preparing for, had gone awry. Harris's aircraft had pulled out of the training mission they had been flying in isolated desert areas of Nevada and ordered into a holding pattern in cleared airspace west of Beale Air Force Base in California. No explanation, no nothing. They'd burned up thousands of pounds of fuel doing nothing but blasting holes in the sky in a racetrack pattern over the mountains of Tahoe National Forest, and Harris was ultra-pissed.

"Major," Lieutenant Martin Borichevsky, the plane's navigator told her tensely. "It's an action message, all right. I've already confirmed it. Twice. It's a valid exercise order."

"What kind of crap is that?" Harris's copilot muttered as he looked at the target plot the bombardier had punched into the plane's systems. "The target's just outside of Beale?" He was from California, and could imagine them being ordered to attack the base itself as part of an exercise, but not a bunch of orchards in the foothills of the nearby Sutter Buttes. "This is just a simulated release, right? I can't believe they're going to have us live-drop a training weapon outside of a bomb range!" he said.

"Negative," the bombardier said firmly after briefly conferring with the navigator. "Martin's got it right: it's an actual release. We've got the go-ahead."

The copilot looked over at Harris. "This doesn't make any sense, major. We're not actually going to do this, are we?"

Harris regarded him for a moment. They'd only flown twice before and she didn't know him all that well. She unsnapped her mask and killed the intercom so the rest of the crew couldn't hear. "What the hell do you think we get paid for?" she snapped. "If the action message is valid and we've confirmed it, we follow our orders. I don't give a shit if those orders are to drop a nuke on the White House. If you can't handle that, you should've stayed in the Boy Scouts." She stared hard at him. "This aircraft is mission capable, mister. Are you?"

Slowly, he nodded, then turned away.

Harris snapped her oxygen mask back on and clicked over to the intercom. "Weapon?" she called to the navigator, trying to dismiss her copilot's concerns as she began to run through the extensive pre-strike checklist before the bomber would be ready to do what it had originally been designed for: delivering a nuclear bomb. Only in this case, it wouldn't be a real one.

"The strike order calls for a single B83," the bombardier called out. The plane carried four training weapons that, aside from blue markings designating them as such, looked, weighed, and handled just like real B83 nuclear gravity bombs. Except, of course, that these didn't have an actual nuclear weapon in the bomb casing. "Setting it for...three hundred kilotons. Air burst at five hundred meters above ground level."

"Flight profile?" Harris called.

"Low-high-low," the navigator responded. That would bring the plane in at a low-altitude run toward the target. Then they would pop up in a rapid climb to release altitude to drop the bomb. As the bomb fell to earth, slowed by a parachute that would deploy after it was dropped, Harris and her crew would dive for the deck and get the hell out of the area so they wouldn't be obliterated by the simulated nuclear explosion. "Turn to course two-eight-one," the navigator called, and the indicator on Harris's navigation display moved to the right, settling on the new course. "Recommend an altitude setting of five hundred feet in terrain following mode."

Harris smiled behind her oxygen mask as she hauled the B-52's nose around to the west and started the descent into the mountains that separated her plane from the target. She was looking forward to the reaction from the 9th Operations Group weenies at Beale as her BUFF, the acronym for the B-52's unofficial nickname of Big Ugly Fat Fucker, suddenly roared overhead.

Maybe this mission won't be such a dog after all, she told herself.

***

Monica Ridley's eyes fluttered open. She was still in the conference room. It took a moment for her to understand that it wasn't all a nightmare, that what had happened with the Clement-thing, The Other, had been real.

With adrenaline flooding into her system, she tried to stand up, but instead collapsed to the floor in a heap of unresponsive limbs. She whimpered at the pain that suddenly shot through her abdomen, and looked down to see a spot of blood that had welled up from where the *thing* had jabbed her with something, like some sort of needle.

It must have injected me with something, she thought, something that's bringing back the disease.

"Oh, God," she cried softly, biting down on the fear that threatened to overwhelm her. *You've got to do something*, she told herself sternly. *You're not just going to lie here and whimper*. No one had come for her yet, which gave her an opening.

She looked up at the wall behind the chair where she had been sitting. There was a secure phone in a recess in the wall. She just needed to reach it.

It took five minutes of agonizing effort to push and pull herself back into the chair, fighting against her increasingly useless limbs. She felt as if her body was decaying, withering away with each second.

At last, panting with exertion, she managed to knock the phone off its cradle and into her lap. Then, with painstaking care, for she knew she had little time left, she punched in the numbers for the secure line to the FBI's watch center.

The call was picked up after the first ring. "Watch center, Special Agent Ramirez," came the sharp, no-nonsense voice of the woman who answered.

"This is..." Ridley began, shocked at the sound of her voice. It sounded like it was coming from a wheezing child. Forcing a deep breath into her lungs, she tried again. "This is Director Ridley," she said, her voice sounding like it had some authority now.

"Ma'am," Ramirez asked, "are you all right? Are you ill?"

"No, I'm fine," Ridley lied, her growing fury battling against her body's increasing helplessness. "I need you to patch me through direct to the SAC for the Sutter Buttes operation. Now."

"Yes, ma'am," Ramirez replied. "Stand by."

If only I could, the FBI's Director thought bitterly as she looked at the useless legs that would never stand or walk again. As the seconds ticked past, she prayed she could get through to her people in time.

Thirty-Two

A low boom echoed through the complex, the only outward sign of the explosion that had thrown Jack and the others to the ground on the surface above.

"No," Naomi whispered as the video feed showed him flying through the air to land hard on the concrete where the truck repair shop had been. He lay very still. "Please, God..."

Then the full significance of the explosion hit her. *The blast valves in the air intake complex.* They were the only thing keeping the harvester, or whatever it was, from getting out. "Renee," she called, "is the air intake complex still secure?"

After a moment, Renee said, "The indicators are showing that the valves are all closed," she said, then quickly added, "but I'm getting a warning light on valve three."

"Will it come open?" Naomi asked, trying not to give all her attention to the screen showing the topside video feed, where a stunned Richards was up now and stumbling-crawling toward where Jack lay.

"It won't open," Renee told her, "but it may not completely seal against any more blasts."

"I don't think we have to worry about that," Naomi said, "at least for a while. They took enough of a beating. What else–"

An alarm suddenly began to whoop.

"External power is down!" the woman at the power systems station called out, shutting off the alarm. "We're on battery power now."

"Go into power conservation mode," Naomi ordered. The woman nodded and turned back to her console. Throughout the complex, lights and other electronic equipment that weren't essential were shut off.

"Come on, Jack," Naomi whispered, clutching the edge of her workstation as she watched Richards kneel down next to him. "Come on..."

"What the hell?" Renee blurted as something suddenly dropped down from the top of the view in the video feed. It was a helicopter, a Blackhawk. As everyone in the control center watched, eyes wide, it landed hard, slamming onto the concrete apron around the ruined air intake vent right next to where Richards was trying to revive Jack.

Amid more exclamations of surprise, the Blackhawk's crew leaped out, hands in the air. One of them, from the troop compartment, rushed over to Richards, who pointed a pistol in the man's face.

***

"Special Agent Richards?" the black-clad special agent shouted above the dying roar of the Blackhawk's slowing rotor blades as the pilot made a hasty shutdown.

"That's right," Richards snapped back, barely hearing the man but able to read his lips. His ears were still ringing from the blast of the satchel charges. But his aim was steady enough. *If this guy so much as sneezes,* he thought coldly, *I'll blow his brains out.* "What do you clowns think you're doing?"

"We're surrendering," the man told him, ignoring the gun. He gestured for two of the helo's crewmen to help with Jack, and they immediately knelt down, gently picking him up. "I'm Special Agent Franzman, the SAC. I have new orders straight from Director Ridley."

Richards suddenly caught sight of the other FBI agents who'd survived the initial massacre but who hadn't come along in the attempt to use the satchel charges. They were carrying their wounded comrades and moving as fast as they could toward the portal. None were armed, and all had confused and frightened looks on their faces.

"What in blazes is going on?" Richards demanded.

"We're about to get nuked," Franzman said, deadpan. He clearly didn't believe it, but like Richards, he was a professional who followed orders, especially if they came straight from the director herself. His expression made it clear that he expected Richards to laugh or reassure him that the director had gone mental. Having to suddenly turn himself and his agents over to two men, Richards and Dawson, who moments before had been the FBI's two most wanted criminals, was causing him some serious indigestion.

Instead of laughing, Richards grabbed Franzman's arm and ran as fast as he could toward the portal. "How long?" he shouted as he ran.

"She didn't know," Franzman told him. "She just said we were in 'imminent danger.'"

"God," Richards moaned as he dashed the last few meters, passing by the men laboring with Jack's unconscious weight. Richards stopped at the first of his team members he came to, snatching off the man's headset. His own had been blown off by the blast.

"Naomi!" he shouted into the microphone. "Open the portal! They're going to nuke us!" To the rest of his team, who had their weapons aimed at the other FBI agents approaching from the direction of the main gate, he yelled, "Drop your weapons. They're friendlies now. We've got to get back inside!"

Impatiently, they all gathered around the thick blast doors, waiting for them to open.

***

They're going to nuke us. Richards' words hit Naomi and the others like a punch in the gut. Had it been anywhere else or any other time, she would have laughed at the bad joke. Now...

"Naomi!" Richards shouted again.

"Stand by," she told him. "We've lost utility power and we can't open any of the blast doors on batteries alone – the hydraulic rams for the doors need too much power." Turning to Renee, she said, "Start the backup generators." They were the only thing that could provide enough electricity to drive the hydraulic actuators.

Renee stared at her. "We can't," she said. "The intake tunnel is blocked by the steel plating we welded on to hold in the...the thing!"

Naomi sat back, her warning to Jack about welding the intake tunnel shut echoing in her mind, but there had been no other choice.

Just as there was no other choice now. "Open all the internal blast doors," she ordered, "then start the generators. That should give the diesels enough air from inside the complex for the time it'll take to get the portal open and closed again."

"*All* the blast doors?" Renee said. "Even the antenna complex?" The harvester they had captured from Spitsbergen was contained there in one of the cells. It had been dormant since they'd returned, and there had been no time since then for anyone to do more than make sure it didn't get into trouble.

"Yes," Naomi said. "We've only got one shot at this, and we can't afford to run out of air or we're dead. We should get most of our air back once there's a clear airway up through the portal when the surface blast doors are open."

"You're the boss," Renee said quietly as she began to open all the blast doors, a shiver going up her spine as she hit the control to open the one to the antenna complex. "You're clear, power!" she called to the woman in charge of the complex's power systems.

"Starting the generators now," the woman said uncertainly.

Even here, upstairs in the command dome, they could hear the deep roar of the two massive diesel generators in the lab dome as they coughed into life.

Naomi had to pop her ears right away as the big engines began to suck in hundreds of cubic feet per second of the complex's air. Huge as the base was, the air wouldn't last long at all.

They had to endure an agonizing wait while the voltage on the generators stabilized before the woman at the power console shouted, "The generators are on line! We've got power!"

"Naomi!" Richards called again. "Open the goddamn door!"

"Open the portal doors and get everyone below, *now!*" Naomi shouted.

***

"Christ," Jack gasped, blinking his eyes as he finally came to. He slowly sat up, holding his arms across his chest where the Kevlar vest had stopped the slugs that otherwise would have killed him. It gave him a chill, how closely the shots matched the rounds he'd taken in Afghanistan years ago. Fortunately, the FBI agents had been shooting 9mm weapons that couldn't penetrate his vest. But it still felt like someone had hit him in the sternum with a sledgehammer. "That hurts."

"Nice of you to join us," Richards snapped, kneeling down to make sure Jack was okay. "I guess you'll live, at least for the next minute or so."

"What the hell's going on?" Jack asked, looking with bewilderment at the gaggle of FBI agents standing around them and the Blackhawk helicopter sitting nearby.

"Nothing good," Richards told him tersely as he helped Jack to his feet. "Naomi!" Richards shouted angrily. "Open the goddamn door!"

As if on cue, the huge concrete and metal doors of the portal began to open, the two leaves slowly rising upward. There was a curious sucking noise as the doors opened that Richards didn't remember it making when they'd come up to the surface.

Once the doors reached their fully open position, the elevator appeared, and Richards ushered everyone on.

"Can I ask what the rush is?" Jack said as he stood on the concrete lip of the portal, not wanting to step onto the elevator. As large and strong as it was, it was clearly overloaded, and he didn't relish plunging the seven stories to the bottom.

From the east there came the faint sound of a large jet, and everyone turned to look. The aircraft was barely visible, trailed by black sooty exhaust. It was making a steep climb, and if it kept on its current course, it would fly right over the base.

"That!" Richards shouted as he shoved Jack onto the elevator. "Naomi," he said through the microphone. "Get us down! Now, now, *now!*"

"Oh, shit," Jack whispered to himself as he finally put together the things that Richards hadn't had time to tell him. He recognized the plane, even though it was difficult to make out any details at this distance. He had seen B-52s in action in Afghanistan, and once you'd seen one and what it could do, you never forgot.

Slowly, so slowly, the portal elevator began to descend.

"Yeah," Richards told him, his eyes riveted on the plane as it ballooned skyward, still heading right toward them. "That about sums it up."

At last, after what seemed a lifetime, the massive portal doors began to close over them, and that's when Jack made out the roar of engines somewhere in the complex. *The diesels*, he knew. *They had to start the backup generators. The air...*

The last thing he glimpsed before the doors sealed shut was a tiny speck falling away from the B-52.

***

"Bomb away!" the bombardier cried. "If that isn't right in the bullseye, I'll eat the pilot's undies."

"You wish," Harris quipped back as she hauled the big plane around in a diving left turn. This course would put the buttes between the plane and the bomb when it 'went off,' and might also give her a legitimate reason to do a flyby over Beale. The air traffic controllers in the area were having a complete cow, but if her orders were to simulate a bombing of Sutter Buttes, she was going to do it right: they'd just have to clear any traffic out of her way.

"Get your blast curtain closed!" she snapped at her copilot. The cockpit had thick curtains that were pulled shut to prevent the crew from being blinded by a nuclear blast.

"Major," he snapped, "you can't be serious! We're at five hundred feet flying at almost five hundred knots, with air traffic all over the place out there!"

"Close them!" Harris shouted. *As soon as we get back to base*, she vowed, *I'm going to kick your ass off my crew.*

Muttering under his breath, the copilot did as he was told, yanking the heavy curtain closed.

"Time to detonation?" Harris asked.

"Fifteen seconds," the bombardier said, estimating the time until the bomb would reach the proper altitude above the target before it electrically simulated detonation. But there wouldn't be so much as a puff of smoke, he lamented as the timer wound down. "Ten... nine... eight..."

***

"Shut down!" Naomi cried as soon as the elevator reached its stops at the bottom of the portal shaft.

The woman at the power console hit the kill switch, and the droning of the big engines suddenly ceased.

"Get the surface sensor array down!" Naomi suddenly remembered that the array would be blown away if it was still protruding above the ground.

"Already done," Renee said as the screen at the front of the room faded to black.

Naomi didn't hear her. She was dashing down the steps to the lower level. "Jack!" she cried. "*Jack!* Everyone get in here, fast!"

Jack followed the others out of the portal into the main junction, pausing just long enough to slap the button that would close the portal blast door before running headlong into the command dome and into Naomi's waiting arms.

The portal door closed and locked just as the bomb detonated.

Thirty-Three

What had been an intact B83 thermonuclear bomb microseconds before was transformed into a tiny sun shining above the scrub-covered base of the Sutter Buttes, briefly reaching a temperature of nearly ten million degrees at its core.

Set for a yield that was the equivalent of three hundred thousand tons of TNT, the explosion obliterated everything to a distance of two miles north of the buttes. The crops and orchards were set alight by the thermal radiation, and then ripped from the earth by the blast wave that followed. Homes and buildings half a mile past North Butte Road, nearly two miles from ground zero, were first ignited by the thermal radiation, then crushed by the blast wave. At a distance of nearly five miles from ground zero, people, animals and birds were killed or injured throughout the Gray Lodge Waterfowl Management Area. The town of Live Oak, nine miles to the west, suffered minor damage, with several hundred people temporarily blinded by the flash. The areas to the south, as the Clement-thing had predicted, were largely shielded from the blast by the intervening buttes.

After the flash heralding the bomb's detonation, everyone in a radius of nearly twenty miles was treated to the chilling sight of a mushroom cloud rising over the buttes, which themselves had been scoured clean of life.

***

The old Titan complex had been built to withstand the blast and overpressure of near-misses by the megaton-range warheads developed early in the Cold War. But a three hundred kiloton blast five hundred meters directly above the entry portal would not so easily be shrugged off by any structure ever built by the hands of Man.

In the fraction of a second that the blast wave took to reach the ground, the huge blast valves in the exhaust complex, still open from when the generators were being run, snapped shut, holding back the enormous overpressure.

The valves in the intake complex were already closed, but one of them had suffered minor damage from the satchel charges used by the FBI agents. A small gouge in the edge of the lowest blast valve, no wider than a dime, allowed enough of the blast overpressure through to blow open the door at the rear of the filtration area and tear off one of the steel plates that had been welded to the intake tunnel entrance.

The young harvester in the air intake complex, just recovering from being stunned by the earlier explosion of the satchel charges, was hurled to the rear of the air intake complex where it lay still.

***

Jack felt as if a god from Greek mythology had taken the entire world and given it a vicious shake. He held on tightly to Naomi as the walls of the command dome rang like a huge bell, the concrete vibrating and warping. They were tossed around on the floor, but the base designers had been careful to mechanically insulate the floors: that was the purpose of the huge gaskets around the edges of the floors and walls.

A small crack suddenly zipped along a section of the dome wall, but the old structure held together.

Deafened by a roar from a hundred freight trains, Jack's ears popped as the pressure spiked, and he saw in the flickering light that the dome's blast door hadn't fully closed behind them. The temperature, too, suddenly shot up, and he caught the scent of something burning. He hoped that they weren't about to be seared by superheated air.

The main lights flickered out, to be replaced by emergency lighting along the ceiling of the command dome's lower level. The intense beams provided a surreal shadow theater of dust, smoke, and bits of debris from the ceiling that had been shaken loose to rain down on Jack and the others.

As he lay on the floor, Naomi pressed tight against him, he realized that the roar was gradually fading.

"Naomi," he said, his voice sounding distant, muted. "Naomi!"

"I'm okay," she said, pulling away from him slightly, blinking some of the dust from her eyes. "My God, I can't believe they...that they did this!"

"I can't believe we're still alive," Jack said, giving silent thanks to God that he was still capable of thinking or believing anything.

"We may not be around for long if we don't get power back and find whatever's burning and put it out," Naomi said, shakily getting to her feet. There was a thickening layer of smoke drifting through the door from somewhere out in the main junction. Jack joined her, and they began to help the others up.

"You know, Dawson," Richards told him, "I think right now I'd rather be outside thinking you were still a bad guy, rather than in here waiting to be slow cooked."

"I love you, too," Jack said, clapping Richards on the back.

"Renee!" Naomi called, carefully moving up the stairs.

"We're here," Renee called down, "but I think we're back to using slide-rules for a while."

"We just have to get the power back on," Naomi said. "The main breakers must've tripped."

Renee, her hair covered with white dust, shook her head. "It's not just main power. The command systems all have uninterruptible power supplies, so the computers are still up, but they don't have anything to talk to beyond the command dome. I think the network fiber must've been severed somewhere." She spat out a mix of spit and dust, then waved her hand in front of her face to ward off the thickening smoke. "We'll have to get into the lab dome. All the power systems are there, and I should be able to get control through one of the workstations, assuming there's not too much damage, and track down where the network cabling's severed. And we need to get the air handlers going to bring in some outside air and pull out the smoke."

"Have you people ever heard the term 'fallout?'" Richards chimed in. "We're right under a mushroom cloud, in case you hadn't noticed. Sucking in a bunch of that nice radioactive air may not be such a bright idea."

Renee looked at him as if he were a turd stuck to the bottom of her shoe. "We have NBC filters, you moron," she snapped. "That would be nuclear with an 'N', biological with a 'B', and chemical with a 'C.' Think your pea brain can handle all that?" As she pushed by a gaping Richards, she turned to Jack and said, "Find somebody smarter the next time you need a sidekick, will you?" With a last glance at Richards, she added, "And get somebody better-looking, too. With hair."

Jack shared a grin with Naomi at Richards' expense before catching up to Renee. "No you don't," he told her as she made to squeeze through the blast door, frozen partway open, to the junction. Except for the portal door, the other inside blast doors hadn't fully closed before the main power had gone out when the bomb detonated. "You wait until we give the all-clear. You're the only one who can get all this stuff running again, and we can't afford to let anything happen to you."

"I'm touched," she said sarcastically, just before she bent over and vomited on the floor. "Fucking nerves," she whispered, angrily wiping her mouth with the back of her sleeve as she stood up, still unsteady. Looking up at Jack, she said, "I'm fine. Let's get this over with."

Jack exchanged a glance with Naomi before he squeezed through the blast door. Naomi and Renee followed behind.

In the main junction, the emergency lighting was on, but the junction remained dim: the lights were near the ceiling, and much of the light was being swallowed by the smoke.

"The smoke's coming from the lab dome," Jack said over his shoulder as he carefully crossed through the junction.

"We need to go make sure the others are okay," Naomi told him, referring to the complex's other personnel who'd been in the apartments next to the three missile silos. "I've also got to check on the silos. If they're not intact..." She shook her head. "All this could be for nothing."

Jack wasn't happy with her making the trek down the long tunnel to the silos, even in company with other armed men and women.

"I'll take her," Richards told him quietly.

"We'll help," Franzman, the FBI agent who'd formerly been in charge of the assault on the base said.

Jack nodded gratefully. "Keep her safe," he said. To Naomi, he said, "Be damn careful. We should have the power back on soon so you can get through the blast locks. And watch out for any metal that might've been connected or exposed to anything on the surface. The heat..."

"I know," Naomi told him with a wan smile. Then she turned and headed off down the dim tunnel. Richards took the lead, with Franzman and nine other agents forming a protective circle around her.

"Come on, Romeo," Renee told him. "Let's see what the damage is in here."

Jack and two agents who had come with Franzman squeezed through the open blast door into the lab dome, not sure what they'd find.

Behind them, the remainder of the command center crew returned to their stations, hoping that soon they'd be able to bring the base back to life.

***

"Criminy, what a mess!" Renee exclaimed after she'd managed to finally squeeze her way through the door to the lab dome.

The main floor was a disaster area, with equipment and tables knocked over, and everything covered with paint chips and dust. Jack had to swallow his fear as he saw cracks in the dome wall that zig-zagged like lightning bolts toward the ceiling, disappearing into the smoke above his head. "Make it fast, Renee," he told her. "I don't think this place is going to–"

A hunk of concrete as big as Jack suddenly fell from the obscured ceiling, plunging out of the smoke to shatter on the floor with a jarring crash, nearly hitting the pair of FBI agents.

"Shit!" Jack cursed. There was no point in risking more lives than necessary if the dome collapsed. "You men!" he called to the agents. "Get out of here. Go back to the junction and help the others." Giving Jack an unsure look, the two men didn't question his orders and made their way back out of the dome. Turning back to Renee, he said, "Let's get this done."

"Here, help me move this," she told him, gesturing at a pile of equipment and debris blocking the door to the electrical systems area.

After a few minutes of grunting and heaving, the door was finally clear and Renee opened it.

"Well, that's some good news," she said guardedly.

"What?" Jack asked, looking around the pitch black room. The only thing he could see was a large bank of red and green indicator lights off to the left.

"The batteries are okay," she told him, moving toward the lights. "Like I thought, the breakers went, but that we can fix. Here, help me with these."

In the glow of the indicators, he saw her move toward a set of six large equipment cabinets, each of which had a set of large buttons and a single large handle. "Pump each one of these three times," she told him, pointing to one of the handles, "then the handle should lock."

Jack followed her directions, pumping and locking the handles. "There's too much power flowing through there for a simple mechanical switch," she explained as she pushed buttons and flipped breakers on one of the other panels. "So we get to do it the fancy way."

"Done," Jack told her, slamming the last handle home.

"Okay, here we go..." She pushed one of six large buttons on the console before her, and the first cabinet made a loud thunk. They were rewarded by the main lights – what few were left undamaged by the blast – flickering back on around the periphery of the dome from where they were suspended under the mezzanine level.

"Oh, shit," Renee hissed.

"What is it?"

"Look what we're standing in."

Jack looked down in the flickering light and saw that the floor was wet. "Water. So?"

She shook her head and moved back away from the electrical panels. "It's not water, Jack. It's diesel fuel. Can't you smell it?" She looked up at the wall just below the mezzanine level, where the tunnel into the exhaust complex was. There was a trickle of liquid down the wall. "At least one of the tanks or lines must have been ruptured by the blast." As they watched, the trickle grew into a steady flow.

Jack could smell it now, even over the stench of the smoke. And he remembered Naomi telling him that there was enough fuel in the tanks up there to power the backup generators for a couple months.

"Christ," he cursed, looking again at the shimmering pool that was quickly spreading across the floor. "Once that hits those breakers..."

"Yeah," she told him. "The breakers will arc and ignite the whole shebang." She looked at the other five breakers that needed to be reset.

"Don't even think about it," he warned her, taking her arm and pulling her back. "We've got to get out of here. Right now."

"We need the power, Jack," she protested, but she didn't struggle against his insistent grip.

"It's not going to do us any good as soon as that fuel hits the first live circuit," he told her. "This place is going to turn into an inferno, and we need to be long gone when that happens."

Jack turned to head back toward the door to the junction, and that was when he saw the cats. He momentarily felt guilty for not even thinking about Alexander since the trip to Spitsbergen, yet here the big furball was. Koshka was with him, as usual, and so were three others. He leaned down to try and shoo them toward the blast door and out of the dome, then realized that all of the cats were staring in the same direction: toward the air intake tunnel on the mezzanine level.

Where the larval harvester had been trapped.

Alexander suddenly arched his back and stuck up his tail, growling. Koshka and the others joined him, and all at once they scattered, taking cover where they could behind the debris strewn across the floor of the lab dome.

"Renee," he called quietly over his shoulder as he scanned the mezzanine. He couldn't see the mouth of the intake tunnel through the smoke.

"What?" she said from close behind him.

"We have to go," he told her, drawing his pistol, the big .50 caliber Desert Eagle, and snapping off the safety. He hadn't thought to bring a rifle with him. "Now."

"What *else* could be wrong?" she asked, trying to make a joke. Then she saw the cats: silent, intent, as if waiting in ambush. Or trying to not draw the attention of a much more ferocious predator. "Oh, God," she whispered, realization of their predicament suddenly dawning on her.

"Come on," Jack told her quietly as he began to edge toward the blast door leading to the main junction.

"Jack, wait," she said suddenly, pointing at a white refrigerator that was still standing along the dome wall, not far from where the animal storage area was. "The antivenin is in that refrigerator. We should get that before—"

"No," he said, catching sight of a powerful, alien limb slowly descending from the smoke that wreathed the mezzanine level stairway. The creature was much closer to the door than they were. "There's no time. Move! Now!"

Pushing her in the direction of the door to the junction, he moved toward the stairway and the creature that was now fully revealed: a harvester, its black exoskeleton shimmering in the glow of the lights while the malleable tissue oozed around its core as if unsure of what shape it should take.

Praying that firing his weapon wouldn't ignite the diesel fuel, Jack raised the big pistol and took aim at the harvester's center of mass. Just as he pulled the trigger, the cats broke from cover, yeowling and hissing at the creature.

The harvester reacted with lighting fast reflexes, leaping back up onto the obscured mezzanine. Jack's shot blasted a chunk of concrete from the wall where the harvester had been, and the cats darted for the door, their desire to survive overriding the instinct to fight the creature.

"Go!" Jack shouted at Renee, "Get the hell out!"

"I'm stuck!" she cried. She had forced her way into the gap between the blast door and its frame, but one of the straps on her body armor had caught on an exposed bolt in the door's locking mechanism. "Help!" she cried into the junction, which was now empty, the two FBI agents who had been with them earlier having followed Richards and Franzman down the tunnel toward the silos. "*Help me!*"

Jack tried to free her with one hand, holding the pistol with the other. He couldn't. "Goddammit," he growled, shoving the Desert Eagle back into its holster so he could use both hands, "hold still!"

But no matter what he did, the strap refused to come off the head of the bolt. Renee's fierce struggling had only succeeded in wedging her body in more tightly, and at just the wrong angle. She was well and truly stuck.

Giving up on using his bare hands, he reached down and pulled out the flip-out utility knife that he always carried. "Hold still or I'm going to cut you!" he shouted at her.

That finally got her attention, and her struggles ceased. Jack shoved the blade under her armor where the straps connected and began sawing through them.

He was almost done when he felt one of Renee's hands squeeze his shoulder in a death grip.

"Jack," she whispered, her eyes wide with terror. "*Behind you...*"

***

"Thank God," Naomi breathed as she took the brief casualty reports from the leaders of the three apartments adjoining the missile silos. Renee had restored the power to the blast locks just as Naomi and the others had arrived at the first lock, allowing the others to get out. The worst casualty had been a young woman with a broken leg. Other than that, bruises and abrasions were the worst they'd suffered. "What about the arks?"

"All intact," said Wade Livingston, one of the engineers who had helped design and build the nitrogen-cooled seed storage units inside the silos. His face was lit only by the reflected light from a dozen heavy duty flashlights the others carried. The tunnel and the rest of the complex beyond the first blast lock were still without power and lights, except for the short-life battery backups in each of the silo complexes. "There's a lot of heat bleeding through the silo doors, but the radiant barriers and ceramic insulation are coping with that. It'll cost us some extra nitrogen to keep the temperatures down, but not as much as I'd thought. The silo batteries are all intact, so we've got backup power for a while until we can get the mains back on."

"What about radiation?" Naomi asked, worried. She was concerned for her people, but the arks were even more important. They'd poured millions of man-hours into preserving genetically pure seed, and the last thing she wanted was for any of it to be compromised by radiation from the bomb.

"All the dosimeters are showing radiation well below any danger levels," he told her. "We certainly took some, but I'm happy that the designers of this complex were as lavish with concrete as they were. And that whoever decided to paste us used an air burst and not a ground burst."

Richards snorted. "If they'd used a ground burst, we wouldn't be having this conversation," he muttered. A ground burst would have sent a shock wave through the ground that would have shattered the concrete. It would also have produced a huge amount of radioactive fallout, which apparently was something even the harvesters and their minions hadn't wanted to do.

"Other than that, damage was fairly light," Livingston went on. "We had some breaks in the utility lines and some other minor things. The only serious damage was the tunnel past Blast Lock One: it partially collapsed. I've got a team shoring it up, but that'll take some work to fix." Suddenly breaking into a ragged cough, he told her, "I think the biggest problem right now is air. We've got to get this smoke cleared out."

"Renee is working on that," Naomi reassured him. "But we've got to get the mains back on-line first, and—"

"What are you idiots doing here?" Richards suddenly snapped at the sound of approaching footsteps. The agents he'd left to guard Jack appeared in the flashlights that were suddenly turned their way.

"Dawson sent us to see if we could help," one of them explained. "Chunks of the ceiling were falling inside that dome they went into, and he ordered us out. So here we are."

Naomi saw Richards' face contort in anger. He opened his mouth to give the agents a tongue lashing, but didn't get the chance as the unmistakable sound of a gunshot boomed down the tunnel from the direction of the main junction.

"Oh, no," Naomi moaned. "*Jack!*"

Richards bolted down the tunnel in the direction of the sound, his rifle at the ready. With sick looks on their faces, the other FBI agents turned and followed him.

***

"Behind you!"

Jack reacted instinctively. Dropping the knife, he slid his right hand to the grip of his pistol, holstered under his left arm. He knew he wouldn't have time to draw it and turn around, so he leaned over and twisted his torso, pointing the gun's muzzle behind him before pulling the trigger while the gun was still in its holster. He had no idea if he'd hit anything, but the muzzle blast might startle the creature and at least give him a chance.

He fired, and was rewarded with an ear-piercing shriek. Drawing the gun, he turned around and dropped to one knee so he could take more careful aim.

The harvester had been shoved backward by the impact of the big .50 caliber slug, one of its "arms" shattered by the bullet just above the lowermost joint.

It launched itself at him, the chopping blade in its thorax slicing through the air toward his face.

He waited until it was right on top of him, the muzzle of the Desert Eagle nearly touching the glistening blade before he pulled the trigger. The creature staggered backward, and Jack saw tissue and chunks of exoskeleton blasted into the air behind it. He fired again, blowing a ragged hole as big as his fist all the way through its thorax, then again.

Shrieking in agony, the thing dodged to one side to avoid the last bullet, and its stinger shot out, aimed at Jack's face. He ducked, and heard Renee scream as the deadly lance *spanged* into the metal door less than an inch from her face, venom spattering from its tip.

The creature withdrew its lance and turned to flee, taking great leaps toward the steps leading up to the mezzanine.

"Oh, no you don't!" Jack shouted, bolting after it.

"Jack!" Renee called after him. "Jack, don't!"

He heard her, but didn't listen. He wasn't about to let this thing get away.

Even injured as it was, it flew up the steps, faster than any man could run. Jack paused to take aim, firing at the thing as it reached the mezzanine. The harvester twirled in mid-leap, the bullet just nicking its misshapen head. Screeching again, it dodged around the biohazard room before disappearing down the intake tunnel.

Jack followed right behind. *Two shots left*, he warned himself as he moved past the metal plating that had been ripped off by the nuclear blast, then entered the tunnel that led to the air intake complex. He could barely see anything in the thick smoke, and he covered his nose and mouth with the sleeve of his left arm to help him breathe. Ignoring the stinging of his eyes, he crouched low to get below as much of the smoke as he could.

He reached the end of the tunnel, which opened into the rear section of the intake complex, where he found a gigantic squirrel cage fan that was at least twelve feet across and so high that it disappeared into the smoke. Jack had never seen anything like it, and was thankful it wasn't turned on.

He moved through an access door, then up a ladder, heading closer to where the blast valves were. The smoke was thicker here, and it was getting much more difficult to breathe. He passed more giant-sized equipment as he went deeper into the complex, which was like a large cylinder placed on its side.

Hathcock was wrong, he thought, when he said you could hide a Volkswagen in here. You could hide a goddamn Cadillac.

The smoke was so thick on the platform that he nearly fell off the edge when he reached the end. He could barely make out the round shapes of the five blast valves, each of which was four feet across. They were closed, except for one where he could see a tiny glow of heat where the metal was white-hot. He couldn't see the bottom of the complex, but figured it must be a good ten or fifteen feet below the platform he was on. *That would've been a bad fall, Jack*, he thought grimly.

As he turned, intending to go back, he caught sight of something on the platform behind him. He dropped flat onto the metal flooring, where the air was slightly clearer.

It was the harvester, moving stealthily toward him. He couldn't see its body through the smoke, only its insectile feet, stepping closer.

"We think they can see and smell about as well as we can," Naomi had told him, what seemed like ages before. The harvester knew he was here, but the smoke was blinding it and it didn't know enough to get down low.

With only two shots left, Jack couldn't risk firing blindly into the smoke. He had to be able to see his target. Which meant bringing it down to the floor. Close.

He waited until the thing was practically on top of him before he kicked its feet out from under it with one of his legs. Screeching and flailing its limbs, it fell to the floor right beside him. Before he could shoot, it had him, its arms around his chest, pulling him to its thorax and the deadly mix of organic weapons there.

"No!" Jack shouted, bringing his knee up to block the chopping blade that suddenly extended from the creature's chest. The harvester's claws dug into his flesh where they gripped his waist below the body armor, and Jack gasped with pain.

The harvester suddenly rolled on top of him, its face right above his, and its mandibles parted to reveal rows of serrated teeth. It lunged at his neck, but Jack was ready: instead of tearing out his throat, its mouth closed over the muzzle of the Desert Eagle.

"Fuck you, you bastard!" Jack shouted as he pulled the trigger. The big bullet blasted out the back of the harvester's skull, and the creature rolled away from him, limbs flailing as a wet rasp issued from its throat.

Jack pinned the thing against the wall of the chamber with his foot and stuck the pistol against the harvester's chest before pulling the trigger on his last bullet. It blasted through the creature's exoskeleton and tore into its vital organs.

After a final shudder, the harvester lay still. Dead.

"Jack?" he heard a strangely muffled voice calling a few moments later. "Jack, where are you!"

"Here," he managed, trying to hold back the coughing that threatened to take hold of him.

A moment later, he saw lights moving in the smoke, and then hands were pulling him to his feet. Naomi and Richards.

"Renee?" he asked.

"She's fine," Naomi reassured him.

"She needs to go on a diet," Richards complained as he pulled a smoke hood over Jack's head so he could breathe easier. "It took both of us to pull her big ass out of that door."

Jack took one last look through the smoke at the harvester's oozing mass before he followed Naomi and Richards back into the tunnel to the lab dome.

Thirty-Four

"Christ Jesus," President Curtis whispered, his face ashen as he stared at the Predator drone's video footage of the enormous mushroom cloud that rose over Sutter Buttes in central California. The yield of the bomb that was dropped on Hiroshima had an explosive yield of about fifteen kilotons. The one that Curtis had ordered dropped on his own country had been twenty times more powerful.

"It had to be done," the creature masquerading as Ray Clement soothed. "There was no choice."

Curtis turned from the horror on the screen in the situation room to stare at the thing. General Coleridge, who had no idea what Clement really was, glared at him. The Secretary of Defense, Wilburne, looked ill.

"Don't patronize me," Curtis growled. Then, turning to Coleridge, he said in a calm voice, "General, it would probably be a good idea to let the military know that we weren't just nuked by the Russians or Chinese."

"Sir," Coleridge said, then quietly left the room.

As the door whispered shut, Curtis went on to The Other, "I made the decision and I'll take the responsibility, but don't tell me there was no other choice. If there was a mistake, it was that I trusted in you to be omnipotent and omniscient, that you and your kind could keep us away from disasters like this. And make no mistake: this *is* a disaster. We believed in you too much, and this is the price we have to pay." *And it's just too goddamned high*, he cursed himself, *even for my daughter's sake.*

Just then the door burst open. It was his chief of staff, Paul Rochelle, followed by half a dozen Secret Service agents with guns drawn.

"Mr. President!" Rochelle exclaimed as the agents gathered around Curtis, intending to manhandle him to safety, if necessary. "NORAD reported that we've been attacked with a nuclear weapon! There was an explosion just moments ago in Calif–"

"I tried to stop them, Mr. President," Coleridge said, storming into the room behind the agents, "But they wouldn't listen."

"Listen to what?" Rochelle shouted. "We've been attacked!"

"No, Paul," Curtis told him quietly, motioning for the Secret Service agents that he didn't need their assistance. "It was...I ordered it. It was the Earth Defense Society base. There wasn't any time and we had to be sure we took them out. They..."

He stopped, shaking his head. As if he were a balloon that had suddenly deflated, Curtis slumped down into his chair at the head of the table. "Casualties," he muttered miserably. "Do we have any estimates yet?"

"No...no, sir," Rochelle replied, stunned. "How could we? We just found out. I...Mr. President, I don't understand. How...?"

"Tell the governor of California that we'll provide any and all assistance they require," Curtis told him, holding up his hand to forestall any more questions. "Get the staff going on that right away, and get FEMA moving. Then get the press secretary in here so we can get an explanation of this out to the public." He glanced at the Clement-thing. "But right now, I need a few minutes alone."

Everyone made to move toward the door except Clement.

"I said *alone*," Curtis snapped.

Nodding respectfully, or at least making a good show of it, "Clement" followed the others out.

In the sudden silence after the door closed, the President stared at the roiling, glowing mushroom cloud that now towered over Sutter Buttes and the devastated wasteland around it.

Then Norman Curtis, the most powerful man in the world, put his face in his hands and wept.

***

"Sir!"

Paul Rochelle had just closed the door to the President's conference room when a Secret Service agent called from the door to the next conference room down the hall.

"What is it?" Rochelle asked dully. His voice was still weak as he fought to grapple with the nightmare reality into which he and the rest of the country had just been plunged. He still couldn't believe that what had happened had really happened.

"FBI Director Ridley, sir," the agent said, gesturing into the other room. "I was supposed to make sure she wasn't disturbed, she needed some rest, the President said after they spoke earlier. But after what happened, I checked on her, and..." He looked into the room, then back at Rochelle, shaking his head in disbelief. "I'm sorry, sir, but you need to see this."

Rochelle cursed under his breath and walked quickly to the door, looking where the agent pointed.

Ray Clement watched the exchange impassively, then turned and quickly walked out of the situation room complex.

"Oh, my God," Rochelle said as he rushed into the room to kneel next to the twisted, motionless woman who lay on the floor. "Call the medical unit and get somebody down here right now!"

"Already done, sir," the agent replied, his eyes riveted on Ridley, who lay curled in a fetal position where she had fallen from a chair along the wall. A secure phone was still in her hand, but her fingers no longer had the strength to hold it. There was a trace of blood on her blouse, just above her waist.

"Director Ridley," Rochelle said quietly, lowering himself so he could see her face, afraid to roll her over in case she'd injured her back or spine. "Director, what happened? How badly are you hurt? Talk to me!"

Her eyes were open and fixed on him, and she tried to move her lips, but no words came out.

"What is it?" Rochelle asked, bending closer, her lips now right to his ear.

"Clement...imposter," she breathed. "Stop...him..."

"Who's Clement?" Rochelle asked, not recognizing the name. He looked up at the Secret Service agent. "Do you know who she's talking about?"

"He was a senior FBI agent accompanying Director Ridley," the agent said. "A big guy, African-American, with–"

"Find him!" Rochelle barked. "And for God's sake, don't let him get near the President!"

As the agent ran from the room, gun drawn and microphone to his lips to alert the rest of the White House protective detail, Rochelle turned to Ridley and said soothingly, "Don't worry, help is on the way. You'll be okay."

The only answer she could give him were the wordless tears that crept down her cheeks.

***

Clement walked briskly toward the entrance used by tourists, rather than the one for official visitors, planning to lose itself in the crowd. Had it truly been human, it might have smiled at the convenient timing of an incoming group of people streaming through from the visitor center.

But it wasn't human. Its outward expression was impassive as it strode past the goggling tourists. It contemplated thoughts in the way of its species, altogether indecipherable to humankind.

"Everyone on the floor, *now!*"

The sudden order was followed by the sound of running feet and the metallic clicks of weapons being taken off safe.

"Down! Down! Down!" the same voice boomed. Around Clement, the humans noisily fell to the floor, crying and cursing in fear.

"Freeze, Clement!"

The creature stopped, then slowly turned to face the human who had spoken to it. It was a Secret Service agent who stood with a dozen more, all of them with guns leveled at Clement's chest.

"On the floor. Now!" the agent growled. "I won't ask you a second time."

The creature stared at him. It felt no fear, for emotions were simply another facet of the mimicry that allowed it to blend in with its prey, or avoid the rare true predators that walked among this species. It understood fear, for it had seen it on the face of Ray Clement as he died: the creature had replaced him the night Sheldon Crane had infiltrated the Lincoln facility, hoping that in the guise of Clement it could help regain control of what Crane had taken.

"Clement" – it had taken the name as well as the DNA of its victim, for it did not have a name as a human might understand it – knew that it had failed, as had the others. Of all those on The List, only one would soon remain. Clement could still sense it, knew that it was alive. The others had all perished at the New Horizons facility.

It expressed no sadness, no frustration or regret at their deaths, its worldview one of ultimate nihilism. Yet it knew that the trucks carrying the precious seeds were on their way into the world. Its species would yet survive.

Returning its attention to the Secret Service agent, it said cryptically, "There will be others."

Then it launched itself at the humans.

***

"Mr. President," Rochelle said urgently as he struggled to keep up with Curtis's angry stride, "you don't have time for this!"

"Yes," Curtis snapped, "I do. This is the one thing in the world right now that I *must* have time for."

Striding into the visitor center, he was confronted with a bloody scene. Four Secret Service agents lay dead, two of them looking like they'd run into a chainsaw, while the other two had died in contortions of unimaginable agony. Three more writhed on the floor, screaming in pain, with doctors and nurses from the White House Medical Unit doing what little they could to ease their suffering.

Miraculously, none of the civilians had been hurt, despite the dozens of rounds the agents had fired, shots that had snapped Curtis out of his melancholy reverie in the Situation Room. The far wall of this room, where he now stood, was peppered with bullet holes. He wrinkled his nose at an incredibly foul odor beyond the sharp stink of the gun powder that permeated the room.

One agent stood alone over a sheet-shrouded mass about the size of a man that was soaked with an ichor fluid. He was still holding his weapon trained on whatever was under the sheet, his expression a mixture of rage and fear.

"Show me," Curtis said quietly.

Looking at him with haunted eyes, the agent nodded. But instead of turning back the sheet, he pulled his Uzi tight into his shoulder, aiming it at the object of Curtis's interest as another agent stepped closer and gingerly pulled back the soaked covering.

"What the devil," Curtis whispered as he beheld the misshapen creature, or what was left of it, that was revealed when the sheet was pulled back. It looked nothing at all like the beautiful alien that Kempf had revealed herself to be, and for a moment he wondered if they were two totally different species.

"How can this possibly be..." he murmured before admitting the truth to himself: The Others had lied about everything, and had preyed upon the emotional weakness of Curtis and people like him to advance their own agenda. Part of him still recoiled from the possibility that his daughter would have the gift The Others had given her taken away. But the rest of him seethed at having been taken for a fool and turning down a path that would leave his name in the halls of infamy, as the President who had dropped a nuclear weapon on his own country, who had killed thousands of those he had sworn to protect.

In that moment of clarity another truth struck him: all this time, the Earth Defense Society had indeed been working to defend their world and humankind. The terrorist attacks, the strange goings-on that had been reported in the genetic engineering industry, all of it had been the work of The Others. Only the so-called lunatics of the EDS had seen the truth and had tried to fight back. And he had done everything possible to exterminate them.

After a long moment of staring at the mottled mass of oozing flesh and exoskeleton, dark and glistening where it had not been smashed by bullets fired by the Secret Service agents, he nodded to the agent holding the sheet, who gratefully put it back over the body.

"Burn it," he ordered grimly. "And sterilize this room. I don't want a single damned molecule of that thing left when you're done."

Then, kneeling down next to one of the doctors struggling to control the agony of one of the wounded agents, he asked, "How is he?"

"He won't make it," the doctor told him, his features drawn downward by the weight of resignation that he would lose these patients. "Whatever...it was, it hit him and the others with some sort of stinger and injected them with a toxin of some sort. None of us have seen anything remotely like this, and none of the drugs we've given them is even touching it. There's nothing I can do to save them. I can't even ease their pain," he finished bitterly.

"Just do what you can," Curtis said woodenly, grasping the doctor briefly on the shoulder.

Turning to Rochelle, he said, "I want to see the staff and General Coleridge in the Oval Office in five minutes." He glanced out a window as a white-topped Marine Corps Sea King helicopter settled onto the White House lawn, summoned by Rochelle as soon as he'd learned of the nuclear strike. It was known as Marine One when the President was aboard, which he would be soon. "And alert Air Force One at Andrews Air Force Base to be ready to take off as soon as I get there. I'm heading to California."

Thirty-Five

"We don't have a choice," Naomi said grimly. "We've got to get out of here. And there's only one way we can go: through the antenna complex."

The inhabitants of the old Titan base were gathered in the smoke-shrouded junction between the command and lab domes. Renee and some of the others had restored additional power by making a dangerous trek back into the lab dome, but their fix wouldn't last long: the flood of diesel fuel from the enormous storage tanks in the exhaust complex had continued unabated, and it was now spilling out onto the floor of the junction, covering it in a slick of the stinking liquid and filling the air with fumes. The partially restored power had allowed Livingston, the engineer, to close the blast locks that led to the missile silos that contained the seed vaults. Even if the rest of the complex was consumed by fire, the vaults would be safe.

Unfortunately, restoring partial power hadn't gained them the one thing they needed more than anything else: the ability to open the portal's surface doors. The inner door connecting the portal to the junction had opened after power had been restored. When Renee had tried to open the surface doors from the command center, however, it became clear that no one was going to be leaving that way: the mounting of one of the hydraulic rams used to push the leaves of the door upward gave way with an ear-splitting *crack*. The sudden increase in load on the other rams resulted in a complete failure, and the doors, which had risen a total of two inches, slammed back down with a thunderous boom.

After that, Naomi had sent Livingston to check on the power leads to the antenna complex, to see if they could use the auxiliary elevator to escape.

"There was no way we could get there," Livingston explained after he and the two men who went with him returned early. "The smoke was so thick that we couldn't see at all, and I got separated from the others. I found them, finally, but it's just not safe down there, Naomi. We shouldn't go that way."

"So, you don't know if the antenna complex has power?" she asked him pointedly.

Livingston shook his head stubbornly. "It doesn't matter. We should open the blast locks and stay safe in the silo complexes. We'd at least have power from the batteries, with fresh air and food until—"

"Until what?" Naomi interrupted him, tired of the man's refusal to give in to the obvious. Pointing to the door to the lab dome, she said, "We're going to lose power. Soon. And when that happens, anybody on the far side of the blast locks will be trapped. The batteries in the silo arks are there to manage the liquid nitrogen cooling system for short periods if main power goes out. Those circuits don't activate the hydraulics in any of the doors. Only the power from the lab dome does, and we're going to lose that soon when the diesel fuel ignites. And if the heat from the resulting fire is intense enough, the junction and the tunnels might collapse. You'd be buried alive."

"Fuck that," someone muttered quietly.

"But they just lit off an atomic bomb out there!" someone else cried. "We'll die of radiation poisoning!"

"That's definitely going to happen if we stay in here," Renee said tiredly as she stood up from some equipment she'd been working on with the help of a few others holding flashlights for her. "But it won't happen any time soon if we're smart. See that lovely smoke we've been breathing in? I thought at first it was just something inside that was burning. But it's from outside, folks. Those FBI cuckoos – no offense," she added sarcastically to Special Agent Franzman, whose expression hardened slightly, "– with the explosives damaged the blast valves in the intake complex. The NBC filters aren't working very well, and all the smoke that came in through the intake is contaminated." She nodded to the small pile of gear on the floor at her feet. "I finally got one of the goddamn Geiger counters working, and we've gotten the radiation equivalent to a few dental X-rays so far. Jack got more when he went after the harvester in the intake complex, but it still shouldn't be too bad." She looked around at the others, then at Livingston. "Staying in here isn't much better than being topside. At least out there the wind is working to disperse the fallout. Down here it's just going to keep concentrating and getting worse." As Livingston opened his mouth to argue, she added, "And the air in the complex behind the blast locks isn't clean, Wade. It's just as contaminated as it is in here. So shut up and give it a rest."

"What about the heat on the surface?" Jack asked. "If we were at ground zero, things topside are likely to be a bit toasty."

"No doubt about it," Renee said. "There'll probably be some local fires still burning, and the ground's going to be hot as hell. Maybe we can rig something up to pump out some fresh water to cool the ground off a bit around the antenna complex. But out there we might have a chance. Once the inferno in the lab dome kicks off when the fuel leaks into an active electrical circuit, if we're not burned to death or die of smoke inhalation, we'll definitely be asphyxiated as the fire eats up all the oxygen. Or we can choose the Wade Option and die of asphyxiation and radiation poisoning behind the blast locks. I don't know about you, Romeo, but none of those are on my Top Ten List of Ways To Die."

"I say we vote," Livingston protested, refusing to give up.

"I say," Richards growled, drawing his pistol and pointing it at Livingston's forehead, "that if another word comes out of your pie hole, I'm going to blow your head off. As I understand it, this lady," he gave a quick nod in Naomi's direction, "is in charge here. You said your piece and you were overruled. So just...shut...up."

Livingston glared at Richards. "There aren't enough respirators for everyone to make it through the tunnel," he persisted, ignoring the pistol aimed between his eyes.

"Yes, there are," Naomi grated. "If you remember our discussion from before you went to check the lines to the antenna complex, there are plenty of respirators and even environmental hazard suits in the hazardous storage silo where the elevator is. There's plenty for everybody, along with survival gear."

"We just have to do a little buddy breathing with the ones we have here so we can make it down the tunnel," Jack added.

Grudgingly, Livingston nodded, but there was something in his eyes that told Jack he hadn't conceded the point.

Richards lowered the pistol and put it back in his holster. "Idiot," he said.

With everyone's attention focused on the drama between Richards and Livingston, no one saw Renee's frown. Stepping close to Jack, she stood up on her toes and whispered in his ear, "He must really be wigged out. It's not like Wade to argue with Naomi. He worships her."

"Christ, Renee," Jack whispered back, "can you blame him? No matter what Naomi says, locking ourselves back with the silos sounds a heck of a lot better than heading up into a nuclear wasteland."

"Maybe," Renee said, but the frown refused to leave her face.

"So that's it," Naomi said. "We're getting out of here. Right now. Everyone break into your apartment teams. We've got eighteen respirators, so you've got to take a couple of quick, deep breaths as we move along, then hand it on to the next person on your team, and keep doing it until we get to the antenna complex. We'll all be coughing up a storm by the time we get there, but we'll make it. Keep one hand on the conduit line along the tunnel wall at all times when the smoke gets thick to help keep you from becoming disoriented." She paused, her gaze quickly passing over every frightened face turned toward her. "This is going to be tough, but we'll do okay. And when we get to the antenna complex, remember to go right at the junction there and into the storage silo. You don't want to go to the left."

That, thought Jack, *was the real reason no one wanted to go out through the auxiliary entrance.* The harvester's prison was in the silo to the left, and they hadn't heard from the guards there. Worse, all the cats had disappeared. Even Alexander and Koshka had run off, and Jack couldn't help but be worried for them. On the other hand, he knew they had better sense than to stand around in a growing lake of diesel fuel like Jack and the others were doing.

"All right," Naomi finished, "let's go." She turned and headed down the tunnel that, almost six hundred feet away, would hopefully lead them to the dubious safety of ground zero on the surface above.

Jack and the others followed behind her, leaving the dim light of the junction for the enveloping darkness of the tunnel.

***

The line of a hundred and twenty-three people moved quickly through the smoke-filled darkness, trying to cover the distance of nearly two football fields before they were overcome by smoke inhalation.

In the lead now, Jack crouched down as he walked to get under as much of the smoke as he could, holding one of the few precious flashlights on the floor ahead to look for debris or obstructions. He had passed the respirator to Naomi, who followed right behind him.

"This is as far as we got," coughed one of the men who'd accompanied Livingston earlier, walking close behind Naomi. "This part of the tunnel still has power. Some of the lights are still working, but most were broken by the shock of the blast."

As if on cue, Jack passed under a surviving ceiling light that cast its rays into the swirling murk.

"What's that?" he asked as he heard what sounded like the rush of air passing through a vent, somewhere still far ahead.

"It must be the antenna terminal ventilator," Naomi explained, excited. "It was designed to keep humidity from building up in the terminal. Just like the other ventilation systems, it had a blast valve to protect it against the detonation of a nuclear weapon. It must have come back on automatically after the blast pressure wave passed."

"If it's still working," Renee wheezed excitedly, "that means the terminal still has power!"

"And the smoke is starting to clear off a bit," Jack said.

He heard Naomi behind him taking a few quick breaths on the respirator as it was handed back up through their team. Jack turned to take it from her when she held it out for him, tapping it against his right arm.

His foot caught on something just as he took hold of the respirator. Off-balance and carried by the momentum of the fast pace he'd been setting, he fell flat on the floor.

"Shit!" he cursed as he slammed into the concrete, dropping the respirator.

"Stop!" Naomi shouted. "Stop for just a minute!" She didn't want Jack to be trampled. With only a few bumps and shoves, everyone behind them stopped in place. "Come on, Jack," she said. "Now's not a good time for a nap."

"Naomi, look at this," he said, his voice thick with dread.

She got down on her hands and knees to get under the smoke, and gasped at what Jack had stumbled over.

It was the body of one of the cats.

"It must have died from the smoke," she said quietly.

"Look a little closer," Jack whispered. "This cat wasn't killed by smoke."

She did, and her skin crawled. The cat's body, contorted in feline agony with its eyes still open wide and staring, lay in a small pool of blood. There was a perfectly round hole about the same diameter as her thumb in its chest. "Oh, God," she whispered, pointing a bit further along the tunnel with her flashlight, "there's another one!"

In all, Jack could see five cats. Two of them had puncture wounds, while the other three had been brutally mutilated. He silently thanked

God that Alexander and Koshka weren't among them, although he had no idea where they might be.

"It got out," he told her. "The harvester we captured at Spitsbergen got free somehow."

"What happ...ened," Renee asked as she duck-walked forward, coming to a sudden stop when she saw the remains of the cats. "Oh, Jesus."

Then she saw something else in the gloom further down the tunnel just as the smoke lifted slightly. "*Wade!*" she gasped.

Turning to look, Jack and Naomi could just barely see the outline of the barrel-chested engineer's naked body where it lay against the far wall of the tunnel. He'd been eviscerated.

Standing up and turning toward the others behind them, Naomi screamed, "*Wade Livingston is a harvest–*"

A needle-like stinger lanced out of the smoke just as Jack shoved Naomi aside. The lance struck him in the right shoulder, sinking deep into the muscle. Gasping in agony, he gripped the stinger with both hands and with a scream of pain yanked it free before collapsing to the floor.

People screamed in confusion and fear, and suddenly there was a stampede as they ran past him toward the antenna terminal. Only Naomi kept him from being trampled by brutally shoving away anyone who came too close.

As the tendril slithered back into the gloom, Richards was suddenly there, firing at it with his magnum.

The thing screeched at him before turning and fleeing down the tunnel toward the junction, disappearing into the smoke.

"*Jack!*" Naomi cried as she knelt to cradle him in her arms.

"Oh...God...that hurts," he gasped as the harvester's venom went to work. His shoulder was on fire, and already paralyzed: he couldn't lift his arm.

"The antivenin," Renee said as she knelt next to Jack. "It's back in the lab, in the refrigerator by the animal storage area!"

"I know," Naomi interjected. "I'm going back for it," Naomi said. "Jack, I'll be right–"

"No," he told her as he sat up, cradling his right arm. "You've got to make sure everyone gets out."

"Jack, you'll die!" she said. "I'll just be a minute!"

"No!" he told her fiercely, turning to look at her. "The antivenin isn't important. It may not even work." He hissed as a fresh wave of pain washed over him, and he could feel the progression of the fire in his shoulder, spreading down his arm and into his chest. "We've got to make sure the harvester doesn't get to the silos. It can still open the blast locks and find a way to destroy the seed vaults."

"Oh, God," Renee whispered. "He's right. It can open the blast locks to the rest of the complex while the power's still on back there, then light off the diesel as it closes itself off. We'd all be dead before we could get out, and it could do whatever it wanted to the seed vaults.

"But Jack," she went on, "you can't go shooting off your gun back there or this place'll go up in flames like the Hindenburg."

"That's why you have to get everyone out right now," he said as he got to his feet. "Because that's exactly what I plan to do."

"Jack..." Naomi began, but he hushed her protest with a kiss, drawing her close with his good arm.

Richards opened his mouth to say something, but Renee elbowed him into silence.

"Get everyone out," Jack told Naomi softly after their lips parted. There was a moment, just a breath of time, when he almost said something more.

Then the moment was gone. Donning one of the respirators, Jack turned and ran down the tunnel toward the junction.

Naomi watched until he had completely disappeared into the swirling smoke. Then, with Richards and Renee, she turned and followed the others toward the antenna complex.

***

Jack knew he might be running right into an ambush in the tunnel, but there was no time for caution, and he moved as fast as he could. It was a grueling effort, panting through the respirator as the agonizing pain from his shoulder continued to spread through his body. His right arm hung limply now, and he clutched his Desert Eagle in his left hand.

He expected with every step that the thing he was hunting would lash out at him, but at last his feet splashed into the sea of diesel fuel that was spreading away from the junction. Jack was amazed that it still hadn't found an open electric circuit somewhere in the power room that would ignite it, but he gave fervent thanks that it hadn't.

The door to the lab dome was still open, swung wide after Renee had made her second fix of the electrical system. The lights inside still glowed dimly, the upper level of the dome still shrouded in smoke.

Moving forward with more caution now, fighting to keep from groaning with every step from the pain, he waded through the wreckage of the lab area. It would have been easy to simply fire his pistol and light off the thousands of gallons of diesel that had poured out, but he had to make sure the harvester was here. He wanted to watch it die. He had to make sure.

In the back, near the animal storage area, he saw the refrigerator that Renee had mentioned, the one that contained the antivenin. It was on its side, open, the contents spilled over the fuel-covered floor.

I won't be needing any miracle cures, he thought grimly.

He was just turning around to scan the mezzanine level when a searing pain shot through his left hand. He screamed and dropped the gun. Looking down, he saw that the harvester's lance had passed right through the middle of his palm, and venom oozed out the tip to fall to the floor as a new burning sensation shot up his left forearm.

The lance suddenly whipped away from him, and Jack spun around to face the harvester.

"I knew you'd come."

There, her nude body glistening in the flickering light, stood Naomi. Or a biological image of Naomi.

"Jesus," Jack whispered as he fell to his knees, his right leg finally giving out on him completely. He was helpless without the gun: he had nothing else he could use to ignite the fuel around him. His only hope was to keep the thing talking until the diesel came in contact with one of the electrical circuits. It couldn't take too much longer.

"It's over," Jack told it, trying not to look at it, unable not to. "You and your other cockroach friends, however many might be left, are finished. You lost."

"So you think, Jack," it/she said. "Soon, in days, weeks, at the most, there will be thousands of us. Then millions. We'll sweep your kind from this world and make it our own. If your species survives at all, it will be as food."

Jack forced a laugh through the increasing waves of pain sweeping over him. Between the agony and the overpowering diesel fumes, he wanted to vomit. *Just keep talking*, Jack, he ordered himself. "What, are you talking about all those trucks filled with seed and your little retrovirus?" he rasped. "We got them. We got them all."

"Lies," the Naomi-thing hissed at him.

"Believe what you want. But there's no way you're getting out of here."

"Getting free isn't my intention, Jack," she reassured him, stepping closer. "You know of our vulnerability to open flame. Our kind also suffers greatly from ionizing radiation. What would make you sick would kill me." It came closer yet, only a few paces away now. "I know you must be in incredible pain," the creature said. "I could help you, Jack. I could cure you."

Something about what the harvester was doing didn't make any sense to Jack. *Why was it hanging around?* he wondered. It could just as easily have killed him, then gone through the first blast lock to hide in the missile silo part of the complex and figure out how to destroy the seeds.

Because it couldn't, his mind sang out.

"You don't know the security codes to the blast locks, do you?" he asked. The door to the lab dome had been left open, but Wade Livingston had closed and sealed the blast doors to the rest of the complex after he had brought everyone out, before his fateful journey to the antenna complex.

"No, I don't," it said. "Give them to me, Jack, and I'll let you go. And I'll also let you have this." It held forth a yellow case. "The antivenin."

"Bullshit," Jack wheezed, suddenly doubling over as the flames raging through his body entered his abdomen. "It's just a box you grabbed. Oh, God…"

"It's the antivenin, Jack," it said, stepping beside him as he writhed on the floor. "The guards talked about it while I was your captive. I knew what to look for. It didn't take me long to find it." After a pause, it added, "I must live, Jack. I'm the last of my kind now. We can sense others of our species, and there are no more. You'll have me trapped in the missile complex. I won't be able to cause anyone any harm."

Jack coughed, then said, "I don't think so. Sorry, but you're going to join the dinosaurs."

"Salvation is right here, Jack," it said softly, standing over him and holding out the box. "All I need is the code to the doors. And you will live."

"You're right about that, you bitch!"

The creature whirled around to find Naomi standing only a few paces behind it, a Taser in her hands, pointed at her doppelganger's chest.

The harvester tried to leap to the side, but Naomi was ready: she fired, and the Taser probes hit the creature in the left breast. The harvester convulsed and stiffened in mid-air, then splashed to the floor. The mask of Naomi's face quickly dissolved into a mottled blob of flesh.

The yellow box fell from its hand and Naomi dove after it, snatching it out of the deepening pool of fuel. Then she pulled a large syringe from her vest and stabbed the harvester with it. Formaldehyde to paralyze it, Jack knew.

"Naomi," he gasped as the venom's fire entered his chest. He tried to say something more, but the paralysis had reached his throat. All he could do now was twitch his left arm and leg. The pain was unbearable, as if he'd been cast into an open fire.

"Hang on, Jack," Naomi told him. "Don't you leave me, damn you!"

"Come on!" Jack saw Richards kneeling down on his other side. "We've got to get out of here! Then you can stick him with that!"

"But–"

"Now!" Without another word, Richards picked up Jack in a fireman's carry and began to pound down the long tunnel toward the antenna complex, with Naomi running alongside.

After what seemed like an eternity, Richards stumbled into the storage silo, gasping for breath as he roughly set Jack down on the floor.

Behind them, Renee closed the blast door. No matter what happened now, at least the harvester wouldn't be able to escape.

"Jesus," Naomi whispered. "Jack."

He stared upward, unblinking. His body was totally paralyzed now, and Naomi would have thought he was dead except for the rapid but shallow rise and fall of his chest as he fought to breathe. Peaceful as he appeared, she knew that he was still experiencing excruciating pain.

Her only relief was that Alexander and Koshka had finally turned up: like the other cats, they had been drawn to the harvester as soon as it had escaped. Unlike the others, however, they had survived the battle with the creature with nothing more than a few lacerations. After the survivors had reached the storage silo, someone had crammed them into a survival suit. They were complaining unhappily, but were alive and would be kept safe on the surface.

Naomi opened the yellow case and withdrew the antivenin injector. "Please, God," she whispered, "let this work." Her face set with grim determination, she plunged the short needle into Jack's jugular vein and triggered it.

The result was instantaneous. Jack went into frenzied convulsions. Naomi and Renee, then Richards, fought to hold him down as his muscles rebelled.

Without warning, he began to scream. Naomi's soul turned to ash at the sound until she understood that they were screams of pain. *He must be coming out of the paralysis*, she prayed, wanting to burst into tears at the agony he must have been in.

The convulsions suddenly began to taper off, as did the screams. Naomi looked at Jack's face and was rewarded with the sight of him looking back.

"Naomi..." he finally managed, shakily raising a hand toward her face.

She took hold of it and kissed it, crying with relief.

"Come on," Richards said, "we've got to get out of here before the fuel lights off." He looked at the closed blast door behind them. It was one of the lighter doors, only a few inches thick. "I don't know if this door will take the stress. If it can't, we sure don't want to be in here when it blows."

He handed them some environmental suits. Naomi and Renee managed to get Jack into one, then got into their own.

Naomi kissed Jack, then told him, "You're going to be okay." Then she closed the mask, sealing Jack in his suit.

After sealing her own, she told Richards, "Let's go see what hell looks like."

Richards grunted as he shepherded the FBI agents aboard the big elevator. They were going up first to check on the conditions before bringing up the EDS personnel. "I think we've already been there and done that," he muttered.

The surface, not surprisingly, was a charred wasteland. There was still a tremendous amount of smoke and steam drifting up from the ground that had been melted into glass. Everything, as far as they could see, was scorched and black.

It was still hot, but not nearly as bad as Naomi had expected: the fireball had created its own weather system, and cooler air had rushed into the void as the mushroom cloud had risen higher. The roiling maelstrom had taken in moisture from a storm front moving in from seaward, and a warm rain had begun to fall, the black rain that Naomi had remembered reading about after the nuclear attacks on Hiroshima and Nagasaki. The ground was still hot enough to be uncomfortable through the thick soles of the environmental suits, and the first drops of rain sizzled when they hit the smoldering ground. But soon there was a light but steady drizzle that partly cooled the earth beneath their feet.

It was a sobering emergence from one surreal universe into another, but Naomi didn't care. She was alive. And so was Jack. She had no idea what their future might be, or if they had one together, but now they at least had a chance to find out. As did the rest of the human race.

She looked down at Jack, whose hand clung weakly to hers as two FBI agents bore him out on a stretcher they had pulled from the survival stores. She smiled behind her mask, and could tell from the look in his eyes that he was smiling back.

"Naomi," Richards called. "Look." He pointed to a group of black specks on the horizon that quickly resolved into helicopters.

"Two Apache gunships and thirteen Blackhawks," he said. "I guess the gig's finally up."

***

The harvester awoke to find that it was alone. The last of its kind that lived, it did not cry in rage or fear as it arose from the sea of stinking diesel fuel.

It stood there, contemplating its long life and the failure of the great plan as the fuel finally reached one of the open relays in the power switches and ignited.

***

Naomi and the others flinched when a sudden rumble made the earth shiver beneath their feet.

"The fuel must've finally gone off," Renee noted blandly.

The Blackhawks settled all around them while the Apaches orbited overhead, their guns aimed at the group of survivors gathered around the antenna silo doors.

A soldier, dressed in full protective gear, hopped out of the nearest Blackhawk. He was quickly joined by three more men who took up positions on either side and behind him.

Naomi stepped forward to meet the soldier in the center, whom she assumed would be the senior officer.

"I'm Naomi Perrault," she said, her voice muffled through the mask. "We're unarmed."

"That's smart," the other man said simply. "I don't want the President kicking my ass because we had to shoot any of you." Surprising Naomi, he held out his hand, and she took it. "I'm General Ryan Macaulay from Beale Air Force Base. I've got direct orders from the President of the United States to get you and your people to safety and to secure this area."

"Orders from President Curtis?" she blurted.

"That's right," Macaulay said. "You all are heroes, he told me. Now, if you don't mind, I'd like to get you and your folks out of here."

Naomi nodded numbly, having a hard time coming to grips with this unexpected turn of events.

She watched as Macaulay turned and gave some orders to one of his escorts, who she noticed was carrying a radio. The man relayed the general's instructions, and a moment later troops spilled from the other Blackhawks. Most moved quickly to form a cordon around the base's scorched perimeter, while others, including a dozen medics, began to help her people into the now-empty helicopters.

"We'll take you back to Beale and get you cleaned up," Macaulay told her as a pair of corpsmen gently carried Jack and put him in one of the Blackhawks. Someone handed her what looked like an empty environment suit, but in fact contained a pair of extremely unhappy cats. Unable to keep from smiling, she put them aboard the Blackhawk with Jack.

"Let go of me, Godzilla!" she heard Renee cry as she broke away from a soldier who had been trying to get her aboard one of the other Blackhawks. She trotted over to their helicopter, with Richards right behind her.

"I'm riding first class with you guys," she announced as she climbed into the passenger compartment, sitting down next to Jack and taking one of his hands.

"I have to keep an eye on her," Richards grated as he climbed aboard, too.

Naomi shook her head and smiled. "Thanks, general," she said, shaking the man's hand again.

"I'll see you back at Beale," Macaulay told her.

With that, Naomi climbed into the waiting helicopter. Collapsing into her seat, exhausted, she took Jack's other hand in hers, and held onto the suit containing the squirming cats with her free hand as the Blackhawk lifted off.

Epilogue

Jack's eyes snapped open at the sound of someone knocking at the door. He'd fallen asleep on the couch next to Naomi, who had been reading.

They were in the Gold Country Inn, which served as the visitor quarters and temporary living facility for Beale Air Force Base. The inn had been cleared out prior to their arrival, and all the EDS base survivors had been quartered there after going through a thorough decontamination procedure. The entire building was cordoned off by a small army of military police, and Jack had been happy to note that the guns were pointed out, not in. Macaulay had made it clear that they weren't prisoners, but wanted them to stay put for their own safety until "things got sorted out."

"I'll get it," Jack said. He was still feeling the effects of the harvester's venom, but the antivenin had worked wonders. The medics had been forced to give him morphine for a while to deal with the pain, which diminished more slowly than the paralysis. But the pain was gone now, and aside from a persistent tingling in his right side and left hand, plus the pain from the two stab wounds from the stinger, he felt more or less back to normal.

Crossing the room in a few strides, followed by Alexander and Koshka, who were always curious about visitors, Jack opened the door.

"Special Agent Jack Dawson, I presume," President Norman Curtis said.

Jack froze, unable to speak. He felt Naomi come up beside him, her hand on his arm. The last harvester they'd killed had claimed that there were no more, but Jack wasn't taking any chances. Not now. And even if the man standing in front of them wasn't a harvester, he was a known collaborator.

Naomi looked down at the cats, who showed no more than their usual feline curiosity at anything from a human being to an empty cardboard box.

"It's just me," Curtis said, glancing curiously at the cats. "The protective detail is outside...and there aren't any of *them*, those things, the harvesters, with me. Not anymore."

Jack peered down the hallway both ways. It was deserted.

"I made the protective detail wait outside," Curtis said. "Can we talk?"

Still unsure, Jack nodded and gestured for the President to come in. The three of them took seats around the suite's small dinette table.

Neither Jack, nor Naomi said anything. They stared at the President in silence.

"Very few people know this," Curtis began, turning from his silent hosts to stare out the window, "but my daughter had inoperable brain cancer some years ago. It came as an utter and completely bitter surprise. It's one thing to lose someone you truly love. A wife or husband, sister or father. It's something else entirely to lose a child, especially the only one we could ever have. I prayed for a miracle, and would have gladly sold my soul to save her." He turned to look at them. "That's when Dr. Rachel Kempf came to me, offering my daughter a chance to live using an experimental gene therapy program."

"And you bought into it," Naomi accused, not bothering to mask her disgust.

"You're damn right I did," he told her bluntly. "For all I knew back then, which was before you were hired by New Horizons, Kempf was legitimate. And even if she'd been a carnival fraud I would've given her a chance to save my daughter's life." His voice lowered slightly. "It was only after the treatment succeeded, wiping out my daughter's cancer and asking nothing in return, that Kempf showed me that she wasn't any ordinary geneticist. But the form she revealed wasn't her true one, I know now. Nor did she tell us the truth about 'The Secret,' as we called their plan, or at least the version they revealed to us. As you well know, they lied, and those of us who were in on The Secret were taken for a ride. Used."

"If you're looking for sympathy," Naomi told him, "you've come to the wrong place."

Curtis shook his head. "I'm not looking for anything of the sort," he told her. "I know there's a special place in Hell reserved for me for what I've done, and that's that. I can't wave a magic wand and make it all better. I simply want you to understand that Kempf offered hope for my daughter, and then later offered what I thought was hope for humanity. Had I known..."

Jack could see that Naomi would never accept his words, but he could understand where Curtis was coming from. He wasn't an evil man. He had been a desperate father, and then a world leader who'd seen an opportunity to do some good. A dupe, and a fool who hadn't asked more pointed questions, perhaps, but Jack couldn't fault him for being human. And it was as close as Curtis was going to come to an apology.

"So," Jack asked, "what's to become of us?"

"We can arrange for the rest of your people to drop back into society pretty much as they were," Curtis told him. "They'll all need to have a cover story of where they were since they went underground, but that can be sorted out. Special Agent Richards is a bit more difficult, but he'll have a cover story that he was undercover, investigating EDS, and helped bring in the team that took them down. Director Ridley approved it."

Jack and Naomi both frowned at her name.

"She's another one who 'didn't know,'" Naomi said.

Curtis glared at her. "It may interest you to know that the harvesters, as you call them, cured her of Lou Gehrig's disease when she was in her twenties," he said slowly. "That's how they recruited her. But she found out that it wasn't a gift when she refused to back my decision to drop the nuke on you, and one of the harvesters...reversed the disease." He paused. "Director Ridley is currently in Johns Hopkins Hospital in Baltimore, dying. If you want to think ill of me, go ahead. But Ridley's courage in standing up to the harvester played a large role in your being alive today, and she's paid a terrible price for it."

Naomi's face flushed, and she looked away. "I'm sorry," she whispered. "I..."

"Don't apologize," Curtis said more gently. "I feel like such a fool for the government hounding you, thinking you were the bad guys when in fact it was I and the others who were manipulated like marionettes.

"But that brings me back to you two." He looked at Jack. "There's no way we can undo the whole most-wanted thing, Jack. It would completely discredit the FBI, which as you know has suffered terribly in this whole mess, and your name would never be truly cleared."

Jack nodded. He could shout his innocence from the rooftops, but no one would ever truly believe him.

"And you, Naomi, are in much the same boat," Curtis went on. "After being painted as the leader of a notorious band of terrorists, we could try to clear your name, but I don't think it would ever wash with the public."

"So what's the alternative?" Naomi demanded.

"To put it simply," Curtis told her, "I'm offering you the chance to start over, although you're probably not going to like the cover story." After a pause, he continued, "You two died in the assault on the EDS base. You had a nuke. It went off. You and lots of other people died and the good guys – a lot of them dead – won in the end."

"So we're the bad guys?" Naomi asked angrily.

"Naomi," he told her, "I'd be happy to say EDS was right. I'd even throw myself to the lions to make things better. But how do we explain all of this to the public? To the world? We...I killed over a thousand American citizens with a nuclear bomb," he said bitterly. "I can only thank God that so few people lived in that area, or the butcher's bill would have been far, far worse." His face blanched at the thought of what the same bomb would have done to a major city, certain that he would have still given the order to drop it.

"Then there's the destruction of the genebank facilities around the world," Curtis went on, "and the deaths that went along with them, including more of our own people in Colorado. EDS was framed for all those things. I know that now. But the truth isn't something the world, or our own people, are going to easily accept."

He looked out the window for a moment, the crushing weight of responsibility clearly written in the lines on his face. "Then there's the little issue of a...non-human sentient species that wants to use us as food, or as hosts, and which had extensive influence over a number of governments in the world." He had read the preliminary report from Naomi of what the New Horizons seed was really for, and what it did, and it still gave him shivers. "I don't think you realize just how close to the brink the world is right now in the wake of those attacks and the nuke. Plus the viral outbreak that, as you suggested, is probably the work of New Horizons to drive up demand for the seed. People are already terrified, and the truth of what's happened would only fan the flames of that fear. The government would collapse, and God only knows what would happen overseas. The Russians and NATO are on alert, and the Indians and the Chinese are at one another's throats." He looked at Jack, then Naomi. "Blaming the whole thing on EDS isn't fair, but people will believe it. I can get the other countries to stop rattling their sabers and work on calming the people here at home. It will buy us time to get everyone back onto saner ground."

"What if I wanted to walk out that door," Naomi said, "and hold a press conference? What if I told the world everything?"

Curtis shrugged. "I wouldn't stop you. I'll even go one better: I swear on my daughter's life, that if you want me to go before the public right now and tell them everything, I will. Right now. But you have to live with the consequences."

"He's right," Jack said quietly. Naomi turned to stare at him, a disbelieving look on her face. "Naomi, we have to think of what's more important. Neither of us is ever going to regain our credibility: you'll be known at best as a UFO crackpot, and at worst as a terrorist, and I'll always be known as a traitor to the FBI. We'll never get our old lives back. And if the President gets up and tells the world that all of this was set up by a race of things that want to wipe us off the planet, and that you could be turned into one of them just by eating corn on the cob..." He shook his head. "There'd be a panic."

After a moment, Naomi looked away. "You're right," she admitted finally. "I don't like it, but you're right."

Curtis nodded, relieved.

"So what do we do now?" Jack asked the President.

"You enter the Witness Protection Program," Curtis told him. "You start life with new identities, a new home, the whole works. With one extra twist. Think of it as a personal favor from someone who doesn't deserve to ask."

"What's that?" Naomi said.

Curtis leaned forward. "Once your backgrounds have been reconstructed, I want you two to lead a new agency," he explained. "Call it whatever you like, but I want you to track down any more of these damn creatures and kill them, investigate where they came from, and learn how we can better protect ourselves. We've spent millions of dollars and untold talent looking for other sentient life. You found them. You've seen the beast, you know the reality, and I want people like you in charge of helping to keep our planet safe. I've already drafted an executive order and I have it on good authority that Congress will roll the necessary funding into the intelligence budget under the cover of a classified think-tank. It's a done deal. All you have to do is say 'yes.'"

Jack and Naomi looked at one another. After a moment, they nodded.

"Count us in," Jack told him.

***

Carl Richards strode down the hallway at Johns Hopkins Hospital, ignoring those he passed. This time it wasn't because he was being rude, but because he was singularly focused on his duty. He had always done his duty for the Bureau. It had been the cornerstone of his life. But this was the first time that performing that duty had torn his guts out. Outwardly he was his normal calm, arrogant self. Inside, he felt like crying like a baby. It was an unfamiliar sensation, one that he hadn't felt since his wholly unpleasant childhood. Any other time he would have banished the feeling with a surge of anger at himself for being weak.

But not today. Not today.

He finally arrived at a particular door. It was guarded by four Bureau special agents, all men he had hand-picked. As acting Deputy Director, he had the authority to do that now. He also had the tremendous, crushing responsibility that went with it. Director Ridley's decision to promote him above many other more senior agents had come as a shock to many, including Richards. But with the battering the Bureau had taken since Sheldon Crane's death, Richards was the logical choice. He was senior enough, and had received something he had never sought and never wanted in the aftermath of the EDS affair: the title of hero. He had received the Presidential Medal of Freedom, the nation's highest award for civilians, and been paraded around like the first astronauts who returned from the moon. His had become a household name virtually overnight as the man who'd led the charge against home-grown terrorists who'd set off a nuke in central California. The story that the spin doctors had come up with had expertly woven fact with lies, and a Hollywood producer had already contacted him about movie rights. The public had swallowed it all, hook, line, and sinker. Richards had parroted every word the spin doctors had fed to him, had gotten everything right. And he had hated every minute of it.

This visit brought him back to the true reality, and he welcomed it, despite the uncomfortable emotions it had raised.

Duty. That was something he understood.

He opened the door to the room of one of the true heroes, and his heart ached as he stepped inside.

"Madam Director," he said softly. "I brought a little something for you."

Monica Ridley lay in the hospital bed, her once strong and proud body reduced to wasted flesh stretched over bone. The artificially accelerated attack of Lou Gehrig's disease had done in the course of days what it normally would have taken years to do. She was totally paralyzed now, except for her eyes: she could still move and focus them, and blink to communicate yes-or-no responses, but that was all.

Her systems were rapidly shutting down as the disease destroyed her body, and she had steadfastly refused any sort of artificial support beyond an IV to keep her hydrated. Richards had gotten the call from her primary physician this morning: "I don't have a crystal ball," he had said sadly, "but I think today is probably the day." The day Monica Ridley would pass from this life.

Richards had cleared his schedule, putting off his regular duties for a far higher one. He had retrieved something from Ridley's office – she remained the director, and no one had touched anything – before making the drive up to Baltimore. He hadn't taken a car with a driver, as he easily could have. Instead, he drove his black Impala, alone with his thoughts.

Looking at her now, he knew that she wouldn't acknowledge his presence with a smile or a wave, a word of greeting. She couldn't, and the knowledge was like a white-hot knife driven into his gut.

He walked to the side of the bed and pulled over a chair, seating himself so she could see him. Someone else might have thought she looked pitiful, but Richards spared pity for no one. And certainly not for a woman who'd had the courage to face this particular fate.

He began to speak and found he couldn't. He had to pause a moment to regain his voice. Pity wasn't in his vocabulary, but pride was. And at this moment, he was overcome with it.

"I brought something for you," he finally managed to repeat after clearing his throat. He held up what he'd retrieved from her office: a battered book that was a fixture on her desk, a collection of poems by Robert Frost that he knew was one of her most treasured possessions and that she read from every day. "I take it you kind of like this Frost guy?"

She blinked slowly, twice. *Yes.* The heart rate monitor beeped in the background, seemingly in time with her reply.

"Well, I'm not exactly into poetry," Richards said, forcing a smile. "It would be bad for my image."

Yes.

Richards tried to imagine the words that might have gone with that tiny reply. He suspected she would have had a few choice phrases for him. That warmed his smile.

"Okay," he went on, "you'll just have to bear with me then as I stumble through this. They don't normally put poetry in the sports section of the paper."

Yes.

He imagined her laughing at that.

"Well, let's do this," he told her, turning to a page that had the biggest and most-worn dog ear. "The Road Not Taken," Richards said, more softly now, trying to keep his voice steady. "Two roads diverged in a yellow wood, and sorry I could not travel both..."

As he read, Monica Ridley's eyes closed, and Richards liked to think that she was imagining the places and images conjured by Frost's words, that they were taking her far away from this reality to a better place.

He didn't know how long he'd been reading to her when her pulse rate monitor stuttered, then went to a flat line as her heart finally gave out.

Wiping away a tear that threatened to fall from his eyes, Richards closed the book. He wanted to stay here for a while, to try and sort through his own feelings, but that wasn't his way.

Leaning over the bed, he kissed Ridley on the forehead and placed the book in her hands. Then he quietly left the room.

Duty called.

***

Major Elaine Harris stood in front of the mirror in her quarters at Minot Air Force Base. Wearing her Class A dress uniform, she gave herself a critical appraisal, making sure everything was perfect.

Her life had been a surreal nightmare since the day she had dropped the bomb over California. When the blast wave shook the plane, she had circled around Sutter Buttes and, in violation of her own rules, peeled back the blast curtain to look outside. Her heart had nearly stopped at the sight of the black and orange mushroom cloud that rose from where the bomb, *her* bomb, had detonated.

She had spent the next few hours, for as long as the plane's load of fuel would give her, orbiting the buttes, staring at the mushroom cloud while her crew tried to help clear air traffic from the area over the radio. She finally descended into a state of near-catatonia, and her copilot had been forced to fly the plane back to Minot by himself.

The court of inquiry that inevitably followed had cleared her and her crew of any wrongdoing, and presented her with the surprising scenario that terrorists had somehow been responsible, and that she and her crew simply happened to be in the wrong place at the wrong time.

But she knew better. She had looked at the radiological data, the fallout dispersal patterns and, most tellingly, at imagery of the site after the blast. Had a bomb gone off at or below ground, there would have been a crater. A big one. But there wasn't. It had clearly been an air burst, and there was no way the terrorists could have somehow flung a nuclear weapon high enough into the air.

The subsequent investigation into security breaches that had allowed nuclear weapons to be loaded aboard aircraft without proper authorization only confirmed her suspicions. It was a practice that, to everyone's shock and dismay, had been going on for years.

No. The bomb had been dropped from her plane. It didn't matter how it had gotten aboard. She had been the pilot in command. It had been her responsibility. And thousands of innocent people had died.

She had been exonerated, although she'd been taken off flight status until the flight surgeons were confident that she was psychologically prepared to fly again.

She already knew when that would be: never. She had dreams every night, and they were filled with nightmares of the one thousand three hundred and seventy-five souls who had died from the bomb. Her bomb. The court had cleared her, but her conscience hadn't, and never would.

Looking in the mirror now, she saw what she wanted to see, what had once been: a distinguished young officer who had a bright future in the Air Force, and in life.

Before the image could fade from her mind, she put her service Baretta 9mm pistol under her chin and pulled the trigger.

***

Renee turned from her laptop to watch the news. She was a fledgling FBI agent now, of a sort. Richards had asked her to fill in as a consultant to follow up on what EDS had been doing unilaterally, but that was now a government responsibility. Pending the official stand-up of the new agency that Jack and Naomi would lead, once their personalities had been sanitized, the FBI had the bulk of the responsibility for tying up as many loose ends as possible. As for Richards, she liked him, even though he was an ass, and had a sneaking suspicion that he might feel the same way toward her. *It could make for an interesting combination*, she thought idly.

Suddenly, she spilled the coffee she'd been holding into her lap as the news commentator relayed some breaking news.

"The Justice Department announced today that the CEO, Mr. Aaron Steinbecke, and the board of directors of New Horizons Corporation have been arrested by the FBI and the company's assets and records seized in a series of massive raids across the country this morning." The video switched from the commentator's talking head to a series of clips showing FBI agents and local police SWAT teams battering down doors and entering labs and company offices, and of Steinbecke being hauled away in cuffs. "The Justice Department announcement that was released only thirty minutes ago charges that Steinbecke and the others were responsible for developing genetically modified agricultural seeds that were intended as weapons of mass destruction, and that they were working in concert with the terrorist group known as the Earth Defense Society, which was responsible for the nuclear explosion in central California last week that claimed over a thousand lives."

"Fuck you," Renee said under her breath. She had to stick with the story that she had been at the beach that day, and had never heard of EDS, New Horizons, or any of the others. It was a supreme injustice, but something she and the others couldn't argue about.

"In what is believed to be a related action," the commentator went on, the video now shifting to a view of President Curtis in the Oval Office with his cabinet, "President Curtis has ordered a full investigation of all members of the government who formerly worked for New Horizons. As of this morning, the head of the Food and Drug Administration and several other senior civilians and military officers handed in their resignations. In addition, the President has penned an executive order for the Food and Drug Administration, mandating that all products containing genetically modified organisms be banned until or unless the product has been fully evaluated for health concerns by an independent review group..."

"Looks like the President's got a new broom and isn't afraid to use it," she heard a familiar voice say from behind her.

She turned to look at Richards, who sauntered up to her workstation. She was about to make a wise-ass remark until she saw the chat message that had popped up on her screen while she'd been watching the news broadcast on the larger monitor hanging from the ceiling. It was Marion Henderson, the team leader at one of the disposal sites they'd diverted the New Horizons trucks to. The good news had been that, with Curtis seeing the light, the "terrorists" of the EDS no longer had to take care of disposing of all the seeds they had redirected: they were now working with teams of military and civilian specialists to safely and completely destroy them.

But there was a problem.

"Oh, shit," Renee whispered as she looked at what Marion had sent her.

One bag is missing from 378.

"What is it?" Richards said, leaning over her shoulder.

"We accounted for all the trucks that left the plant," Renee told him as she called up Marion over the Internet. "Every single one of them. And each one had a shipping invoice listing the number of bags of seed that had been loaded. Every truck's inventory has been accounted for. This one, truck 378, is the last to be counted, and we're missing a damn bag."

The number only rang once before Marion answered it. "Renee?"

"It's me," Renee confirmed.

"We've counted four times," Marion told her, "and every time we've come up one bag short of what's on the manifest."

"This is Deputy Director Richards," Richards interjected, ignoring Renee's frown. "Did the driver make any stops?"

"No, sir," Marion answered. "He says he didn't, and the tracking information on the truck that we pulled from the central monitoring center confirms that. The truck didn't stop for anything longer than a traffic light before it arrived here."

"And the trailer was sealed?" Richards asked tensely, exchanging a worried look with Renee. One bag, they were both thinking. How many seeds were in a bag? Thousands? Tens of thousands? And every one of them could produce a plant that could in turn produce...them.

"Yes, sir," came the answer. "With a heavy duty padlock. The drivers weren't given the keys, because the trailers were to stay sealed until they arrived at their distribution points. It was still intact when the truck got here. We had to get a torch to cut it off so we could open the trailer. It must be an error on the manifest. Or the bag was never loaded and is...somewhere else. We may never know."

"Hell," Richards growled.

A sliver of ice ran down Renee's spine. *Hell indeed.*

***

Six months later, Bryce Moore sat in a rocking chair on the back porch of his home just outside of San Antonio, Texas. The sun was just going down, and the sky was every fiery shade of red and orange. Behind him, two cats, a big Siberian male with a tuxedo coat and a white Turkish Angora with a long scar down her flank, watched him from the big window of the living room. The Siberian lived with him, while the Angora was a frequent visitor.

"Here," the woman sitting in a rocker right next to his said, taking his wine glass and refilling it. Her name was Angelina Matheson. They were coworkers, joint heads of a government think-tank that had been established here to study the long-term effects of soil erosion on agricultural productivity. Or so their friends and neighbors outside of work were led to believe. It was a topic that was important, but that most people wouldn't want to pursue for more than thirty seconds in the course of casual conversation before switching to the far more interesting details of the news or the mundane events of everyday life. It was a good cover for their real work, which was to quietly keep humanity safe, to protect the world from monsters. Parents told their children that monsters were only the stuff of nightmares, that they weren't real; Bryce and Angelina knew better.

"God, that's beautiful," Angelina sighed at nature's display before taking a sip of wine.

Turning to look at her, Bryce suddenly knew what his next painting would be. Fixing that image of her in his mind for later, he smiled and reached out to take her hand. "Not nearly as beautiful as you," he said. They had become more than friends over the months since they had begun their new lives, and he thought there was a good chance that someday she might become Mrs. Angelina Moore. Someday.

She smiled and squeezed his hand, her blue and brown eyes gleaming in the sunlight before she turned back to the blazing horizon.

They sat in companionable silence, waiting for the glow of sunset to give way to the stars of night.

Afterword

My inspiration for this story was drawn from the research my wife, Jan, and I did on that most mundane of every day topics: food. In the process of conquering some health issues a couple years ago, we became much more conscious of what we ate and, more importantly, what we fed to our kids.

Genetically modified (or engineered) organisms, GMOs, of course came up in the course of our self-education on what was going into our bodies. I'm not going to stand here and jump up and down (well, or try and throw words from the page at your eyeballs), shouting "GMOs are evil!"

But you do have to wonder. GMO products, particularly in the United States, are a big-ticket item, with companies making profits in the billions of dollars and big chunks of market share. Take soy, for example. Today, it's very difficult in the United States to get soy products that aren't GMO-based. Corn, wheat, and other basic sustenance foods used for both human and animal consumption are also very high on the GMO production scale.

I also learned a new term during my digging around: substantial equivalence. What that means is that GMO-based food should be considered the same as – and as safe as – its non-GMO cousins if it has the same basic characteristics. For example, if a GMO strain of corn looks and tastes like "natural" corn, it's *substantially equivalent*, even if its DNA has genes that were tailored from bacteria (don't laugh: bacteria, including some rather nasty varieties, are a frequent source of genetic material for the GMO food we eat).

The tight connections between federal agencies such as the Food and Drug Administration and some of the large agribusinesses that produce GMO crops came as a bit of a shock. There has been a great deal of discussion on the web about the "revolving door" for officials moving between government positions and these companies that, were I a cynic, I might consider a potential conflict of interest.

With the government's blessing, the GMO companies have been working tirelessly to ensure that you don't know if you're eating a GMO product. Despite the long and loud protestations of numerous consumer groups, there's no requirement for labels on food products to say if the product contains GMOs. In fact, at one point, there was a strong push to allow GMO foods to carry the "organic" label, again based on the concept of substantial equivalence. And in what I have to confess has been a rather shameful act for the Home of the Free and the Land of the Brave, the United States has been trying to browbeat the European countries into changing their food labeling, which currently requires GMO products to be labeled as such, to be more in line with U.S. labeling standards.

It was also interesting to discover who really determines if these GMO products are safe: the companies that produce them. There isn't a third-party "honest broker" testing the products, and there's a substantial body of evidence on the web indicating that scientists who try to perform independent testing often have sudden "career issues," or worse.

The companies do, however, put their products through an expensive testing process. While this looks great on paper, the net result is that they provide "proof" that their GMOs are safe, and the government rubber stamps it. The only real effect of requiring these expensive tests is that it's extremely difficult for new companies to join in the fun unless they have very deep pockets. It's like a high-stakes game in the back room of a shady night club. If you want to play, you'd better be ready to pay.

Even more interesting was the discovery that GMOs are patented products, and the companies that make them have a ferocious reputation for going after anyone who may be infringing on their patent rights. Even if GMO seeds were to accidentally spill out of a passing truck into a farmer's field (where non-GMO crops were being raised, in our hypothetical case), if the seeds took root and were "discovered" by a company representative who just happened to later wander through that farmer's field, the company could sue the hapless farmer for infringing on the company's patent rights. From what I learned during my research, this wasn't a rare occurrence: it happened (and still happens) a lot.

The economic effects are also interesting. Perhaps the most spectacular example is GMO cotton seed that India imported from the United States. These cotton varieties have led to a series of devastating crop failures, and instead of being the miracle plants for which India had hoped, they have left many Indian farmers deep in debt after spending a fortune for the seed. Suicides among these farmers has become a commonplace occurrence, the soil where the GMO cotton is being planted is suffering nutrient depletion (here in the U.S. we get around that simply by dumping more fertilizer into the soil, which has its own negative effects), and there have even been reports of livestock dying after eating the plants.

Last of all (well, not really: entire books have been written on this topic!) is the issue of what impact GMOs have on our health. This has probably been argued about almost as much as Global Warming (a.k.a. Climate Change), but if you look around on the web, there are more than just a few documented reports of serious health issues, including fatal reactions, pointing back to the consumption of GMO products. I also have to wonder at the seemingly ever-rising trend of cancer and other major illnesses: where is all that coming from?

And while you may think the metamorphosis of the rhesus monkey in the story into a nasty harvester was pure fiction, there is evidence indicating that chunks of DNA large enough to contain a complete gene can survive the digestive process. Not only that, but those genes can be absorbed into your body's cells. It doesn't mean you're going to turn into a bug-eyed monster overnight (hopefully), but it brings new meaning to the old adage that you are what you eat.

At the end of the day, it's tempting to just write all this up to corporate greed. After all, with some of the GMO companies making annual profits in the billions, not far behind the pharmaceutical companies (with which some of the GMO companies are very closely related, by the way), there's certainly a lot of motivation to make sure GMOs are everywhere and eaten by everyone.

But as my wife and I were talking about it one day, I suddenly blurted, mostly tongue-in-cheek, "You know, this is all so loony that only aliens could be behind it." On reflection, however, it didn't seem so strange at all.

And that, dear friend, is how this story began…

About the Author

Born in 1963, Michael Hicks grew up in the age of the Apollo program and spent his youth glued to the television watching the original Star Trek series and other science fiction movies, which continues to be a source of entertainment and inspiration. Having spent the majority of his life as a voracious reader, he has been heavily influenced by writers ranging from Robert Heinlein to Jerry Pournelle and Larry Niven, and David Weber to S.M. Stirling. Living in Maryland with his beautiful wife, two wonderful stepsons and two mischievous Siberian cats, he continues to work full-time while dreaming and writing.

Discover Other Titles by Michael R. Hicks

In Her Name (Omnibus)
In Her Name: Empire
In Her Name: Confederation
In Her Name: Final Battle
In Her Name: First Contact
In Her Name: Legend Of The Sword